Love's Choice

"There is gold, and a multitude of rubies:
but the lips of knowledge are a precious jewel."
(Proverbs 20:15)

© 2011
PREPARE NOW RESOURCES
Christian Womanhood § *Hyles Publications*
507 State Street
Hammond, Indiana 46320
(219) 932-0711
www.christianwomanhood.org

ISBN: 978-0-9845961-4-0

CREDITS:

COVER DESIGN:
Brandon McCurdy

PAGE LAYOUT
Linda Stubblefield

PROOFREADING
Karissa Carlson, Rena Fish,
Jane Grafton, and Janice Wolfe

AUTHOR'S PHOTO
Picture People

Scriptures used in this volume
are taken from the King James Bible.

Printed and Bound in the United States of America

VOLUME TWO
CROSSROADS
SERIES

Love's Choice

YVONNE COATS

Other Books by Yvonne Coats

THE CROSSROADS SERIES

A Time to Choose
(Book One)

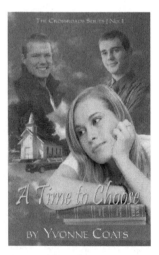

Reared in a loving Christian home in Washington state, Bethany Prescott accepts employment as a nanny in the aristocratic home of the Davenport family after graduating from high school. Bethany soon realizes how difficult her job will be when she meets Michael, her young charge.

Seeking solace in the Davenports' church, Grace Baptist Church, Bethany joins the youth group. Her sweet loveliness and unguarded naivete quickly capture the attention of handsome Scott Lancaster. Will he be the man of her dreams?

Bethany cannot possibly foresee the impact her choices will make on the lives of those she is growing to love. An unexpected meeting with John Holman further complicates the decisions Bethany must make.

Dedication

$\mathcal{I}$ dedicate this book:

- To the loving memory of my parents, Donald R. and Esther (Yadon)Walworth. My father loved words, whether it was working crossword puzzles, writing poetry, or reading a book. He passed on the love of reading to his three children. My mother was the one who could help her children with their grammar problems. She wrote for her children a cherished history of our parents' romance and early years of marriage.

- To my identical twin sister, Dawn (Walworth) Benck. We can still finish each other's sentences when we are together! She is actively involved in community affairs in Woodburn, Oregon, and in the nearby smaller town of Hubbard, Oregon, where she resides.

- To my brother, Clark Walworth, who has worked in the newspaper industry since 1978 and was recently appointed publisher of the *Coos Bay, Oregon World*, a daily newspaper.

I love you all.

Acknowledgments

I want to thank my loving, patient husband Gary who not only puts up with the time I spend writing, but encourages me to continue.

I have many loving friends and family members who have prayed for me during the writing of this second book. I owe them all a big debt of gratitude.

I owe special thanks to my dear friend and exercise buddy, Debbie Whittington, and her two precious daughters, April and Sabrina, who did not mind if she shared with me the exciting events of their courtships. They have given me inspiration and ideas for this book and the upcoming third volume of *The Crossroads Series*.

I am very grateful to Prepare Now Resources and their team of workers for publishing this book. I did not want to send it to a publishing house where it would have been "watered down."

About the Author

Yvonne Coats was born during World War II in Portland, Oregon, two minutes after the birth of her identical twin sister, Dawn. When they were 14, a brother, Clark, was born. Their father served in the Marine Corps and then worked as a salesman. They moved to Milwaukie, Oregon, where they attended a small church; and Yvonne met her future husband at the age of seven.

She did not date Gary Coats until they were both students at Portland State College. When he had obtained his master's degree from the University of New Mexico and she had graduated from Portland State, they married in 1965. The couple moved to Tacoma, Washington, in 1968, where they reared two daughters who now both have three children.

Yvonne and Gary were both saved as adults while their daughters were still young. They attend Bethel Baptist Church of Spanaway, Washington, where Gary serves on the deacon board and teaches an adult Sunday school class. Yvonne leads a ladies' Bible Study and teaches the church class for kindergarten bus children. Their youngest daughter, Christine (Coats) Wolfe, her husband, Deren, and their three daughters are actively involved in the ministries of Bethel Baptist Church.

Their eldest daughter, Debbie is the wife of Kerry Brown, who now pastors Bible Baptist Church of Marysville, California.

Table of Contents

— CHAPTER ONE —

Starting Down a New Road

"Let thine hand help me; for I have chosen thy precepts."
(Psalm 119:173)

*B*ethany Prescott woke and stretched in her bed. She did not feel like opening her eyes yet. Why were they burning? Struggling to come fully awake, she wondered if Michael was awake yet in the next room. What activity had she planned for today to keep him occupied?

Suddenly Bethany remembered—she was not at the Davenports' working as a nanny. This was her college dorm room! Full wakefulness came, and her eyes flew open as she sat up in bed. Across the room her friend, Donna Cornell, was still sleeping. Now Bethany recalled why her eyes were burning. She had cried over her goodbyes to Michael and his grandparents yesterday, and then she and Donna had laughed at each other and cried some more.

Bethany had graduated from high school and had left home soon afterward to work in Detroit, Michigan, as a nanny. After more than a year away from home, Bethany had learned to live with homesickness, but she was not totally rid of it. She was praying to be able to go home for a visit over the Christmas break, but that was more than three months away. Her college life began today.

Slipping to her knees, Bethany remembered the struggles she had gone through the previous year. When she started her job caring for Michael in his grandparents' home, she had tried to begin with good habits in her personal devotions. She had been severely tested in that area, especially after meeting Scott Lancaster.

Now Bethany was determined to walk close to God and discover His will for her life. She had almost made some wrong decisions when she thought Scott was the man of her dreams. Bethany had told her sister Betsy in a letter recently, "I am trying to get over Scott."

Bethany prayed, "Lord, please direct me into Your will for my life. I would like to get married and have a family, but only if it's Your will and You choose the man. I don't want to make a mistake and then pay the consequences for the rest of my life. If I have children, I want them to have a good, Godly father and a happy home where everyone is in agreement about serving You. Right now I want to concentrate on learning from my classes and the experiences here. Please be with me this day and in the days to follow."

Bethany went on to pray for her family, the Davenports, and many others. Then she prayed for Donna and the two unknown girls who would be arriving that day to join them as roommates. Bethany had grown up sharing a room with Betsy and knew it would take Christian love to get along with three other girls. Still, she expected it to be a lot of fun and was eagerly looking forward to meeting them.

After her prayer time, Bethany propped herself up in her bed with her Bible. It was her habit to read a chapter in the Old Testament and the New Testament. She also read a Psalm and a chapter in Proverbs. Today was September 3, so she read the corresponding chapter. Verses 13 through 15 were especially significant to her as she read that wisdom is more precious than rubies. She glanced at the ruby ring she wore on her right hand. It had been a graduation gift from her parents to remind her of Proverbs 20:15: "There is gold, and a multitude of rubies: but the lips of knowledge are a precious jewel."

Bethany looked up other verses that spoke of knowledge or wisdom, using the concordance in her Bible. She liked Job 28:18 which says the price of wisdom is above rubies and verse 28 which defines wisdom as "the fear of the Lord." In the New Testament, Colossians 2:3 says wisdom and knowledge are considered treasures. She prayed again, thanking God for the way He made the Bible fit together beautifully, and asked Him to give her of His knowledge and wisdom.

Donna woke but, seeing what Bethany was doing, waited to greet her and instead reached for her own Bible. Bethany finished first and left to take her shower. When she returned to the room, she and Donna hugged each other and jumped up and down. "Can you believe we are really at college?" questioned Bethany.

Donna answered, "I almost had to pinch myself when I woke up. A year ago I never would have believed I'd be at Bible college. I thought I'd be married to Greg and we'd be partying together."

"Greg's the one you were engaged to before you got saved, right?"

"Yes. That was so hard—breaking up, I mean. But he just wasn't interested in the Christian life. He thought I was crazy!"

"Knowing what you went through really helped me break up with Scott."

"I'm still praying for you about that."

Bethany hugged Donna again. "Thanks, Donna. You are such a great friend."

Donna was an attractive young woman with strawberry blonde hair and green eyes. Bethany had met her at an independent, fundamental Baptist church in Detroit. Donna was an enthusiastic new Christian who had befriended and encouraged Bethany when she was beginning to backslide.

The girls had been thrilled when their plans to go to Bible college meshed and they were able to be roommates. Now they hurried to finish organizing and putting away their things so the room would look good when the other two girls arrived.

Midmorning a tall, somewhat reticent girl arrived with her parents and a younger brother. After a quick greeting, she concentrated on stacking her bags and boxes neatly against one wall, out of the way. Then she hesitantly introduced herself and her family. Bethany and Donna greeted her warmly, which helped her relax.

Sarah Weeks was tall and willowy with long, straight brown hair and hazel eyes. She was six inches taller than Bethany, who was a petite five feet two inches tall with blue eyes. After Sarah had said goodbye to her family, Donna and Bethany showed her the two empty beds and dressers. They both offered to move if she wanted what they had already chosen, but she was content with one of the remaining choices.

Shortly after returning to their room after lunch, they were startled by loud banging on the door. Donna hurried to open it. A cute, full-figured girl with naturally curly blonde hair stumbled in and dumped her load in the middle of the floor. Then she exuberantly whirled around taking in the whole room and its occupants.

"Isn't this just marvelous!" she crooned in a strong Southern accent.

"Hi! I'm Cindy Burgess. What are your names? I guess we're going to be roomies." Before they could answer, she rushed on, "I'm simply thrilled to be at college. I didn't think this day would ever get here. Are you as excited as I am? Oh, I'm sorry. What are your names?" she asked, laughing at herself. The three girls laughed with her and introduced themselves.

Soon Cindy's mother and sister trudged in loaded down with bags and boxes. "Mama, Wendy, here are my gorgeous roommates. This is Sarah, and Donna, and Bethany. Isn't that the sweetest name, and look at that gorgeous blonde hair," she gushed. "I just know I'm going to love ya'll!" she exclaimed with her Georgia drawl.

After Cindy's family left, all the girls worked at getting her things organized. Cindy loved clothes, jewelry, and "everything girlish" (as she expressed it) and had brought a lot with her. Luckily she had a bedspread that hung to the floor because so many things were pushed under her bed for storage. Finally the room was organized and neat.

They had worked up an appetite and were ready to go to dinner. It had been a busy, emotional day, and they were all ready to go to bed early. However, sleep did not come soon because Cindy was a chatterbox even when the lights were off.

The first few weeks were difficult for all of them as they tried to learn the rules, find their way around campus, schedule their time, and adjust to the different teachers. They found they couldn't spend as much time in bed as they were used to, so their bodies were suffering as they adapted to less sleep.

Added to all of the newness was homesickness and acclimating themselves to a different climate. Cindy was always complaining of the cold and made frequent emotional phone calls home to her mama. Sarah showed her feelings less, but Bethany knew she sometimes cried with loneliness for home and family. Bethany had already weathered the "first-time-away-from-home" blues. However, she had many adjustments to make after a year of living in a luxurious three-room suite of her own and spending days with a preschooler. For Donna, getting away to college was a relief. Her family did not share, understand, or encourage her new faith.

The girls were quite different in personality and habits. Bethany realized right away that there would be some conflicts to work through. Even though Sarah was quiet, ladylike, and a little shy, once she was comfortable with her surroundings and acquainted with the people around her, she proved to be a very warm and thoughtful person. She often left encouraging notes on the other girls' pillows if she knew they had an exam or other difficulty to face. When she saw someone who looked sad or defeated, she would give her a beautiful handmade card, a supply of which she had brought with her. Sarah always had a cheerful, warm smile to share with others. Bethany nicknamed her "Miss Sunshine."

Sarah's schedule was as hectic as Bethany's and Donna's—all three of them had jobs to help with college expenses. Only Cindy was privileged enough to have parents who could pay all her expenses. But of the four, Sarah managed to be the most organized with her time. She was precise and very tidy. She had a place for everything and always put things in their place immediately when she entered the room.

As Bethany observed her roommates, it seemed Sarah never had to rush at the last minute to get an assignment done. Her laundry was always kept up, and she managed to have her hair, make-up, and clothes looking perfectly in order at all times. Bethany wrote home that even when she awoke in the mornings, Sarah looked all put together! The other girls all struggled to keep everything balanced.

Cindy was even more vivacious than Bethany. Just a few days after arriving, she informed her roommates that she was working hard on being more ladylike and having a quieter spirit. She was impulsive in speech and actions, unorganized, and a little careless in the housekeeping department. Cindy soon learned the hard way that the dorm monitors had high standards and expectations. After several warnings, Cindy tried harder to have her bed made neatly and her clothes and other belongings put away in the appropriate places.

Donna kept her things in order but was a "scatterbrain." To keep herself organized, she would set out things at night that she was going to need the next day so she would not forget them in the morning rush. One day she got to class and realized she did not have her paper that was due. She had set it out where she would be sure to see it! Now her grade would be lower because she would be turning it in late. That afternoon when they were all in the room getting ready to go to dinner, she complained about it, demanding to know who had moved it.

Sarah immediately confessed in a contrite voice. "Oh, no! I'm sorry,

Donna. I put that on Cindy's dresser this morning when I was picking up. I thought it was hers."

Now Cindy reacted with, "See, you always assume everything's mine. Besides, you need to leave other people's things alone. Anyway, I think I've been doing better. I've really been trying."

"I said I was sorry. I just can't stand things lying around. It just gets to me."

"Well, you don't have to be a fanatic about it," said Cindy. "Now poor Donna's grade will be lower."

Bethany spoke up quickly to try to prevent tempers from flaring out of control. "I guess we need to have a talk about this. We've all been getting along well, and we don't want to mess that up. Is everyone free tonight right after dinner?" They all answered in the affirmative and agreed to hurry back so they could discuss the problem.

As they left, Sarah apologized again to Donna who answered, "I know you didn't do it on purpose."

Sarah turned to Cindy and said, "You're right. You have been doing better. Not perfect, but better," she added with a grin. Cindy answered with a laugh, and Bethany breathed a sigh of relief.

By the time they sat down to talk, the tension was gone. Cindy frankly admitted that she had problems in the area of neatness and was trying to learn from Sarah's example. "But I'll never be as picky as you are!" she said, laughing. Sarah promised to control her desire to be constantly cleaning. They settled on a spot designated for Donna's things to be set out where she would see them. Bethany apologized for having to borrow from the others too often because she did not get her laundry done on time. She impulsively started singing, "He's still working on me, to make me what I ought to be." The others laughed and joined in.

Then they noticed that it was time to go to the devotion room. There was a mad scramble to grab Bibles, check out their appearance, and hurry down the hall to join the other young ladies from their floor. They enjoyed this time of fellowship and Bible study, even though it was mandatory. A few girls had excused absences because of their jobs—cleaning offices and classrooms in the evenings.

Cindy's gregarious and generous spirit soon made her the center of a crowd of friends and admirers of both genders. She had more time to socialize than did her three roommates who had to fit in time for their jobs. She always had a male companion to walk with between classes and to sit with in services.

Sarah's quieter personality did not attract as much attention as quickly. She had come from a church where the pastor had encouraged the young people to wait on dating until after high school graduation, as Bethany's pastor had also done. So she had not experienced dating yet. She confided in Bethany that she was looking forward to it but was also very nervous about the prospect.

Donna was already interested in Peter, the young man who had been the chauffeur for the Davenports, Bethany's employers the previous year. He and Donna were trying to keep their relationship from escalating too fast and had agreed to date others. So Donna accepted some invitations but tried to keep the relationships casual.

The college encouraged dating and asked the girls to be kind and accept at least one date when they were asked. Many of the men had never dated and sometimes found it hard to approach a young woman to ask for a date. Bethany had decided to wait on accepting any dates—her heart was still bruised over her decision to break up with Scott Lancaster only a few months before, and she did not feel ready to deal with guys or dates. She was a very attractive and vivacious young woman, however, so the young college men noticed her and tried to strike up an acquaintance. When they spoke to her, she tried to briefly talk only about class material and move away as soon as possible, discouraging anything more than friendly contact.

When any young man did ask her for a date, she used a standard reply: "I'm sorry. It has nothing to do with you, but I am just not dating anyone at this time."

Sarah noticed Bethany's polite but cool responses and asked, "Bethany, you have lots of guys wanting to date you. Aren't you interested?"

Bethany only answered, "Right now I'm not interested in guys, Sarah."

Donna had heard this exchange and sighed with relief. She had secret hopes for Bethany's future. She knew that John Holman, a man in their Detroit church, loved Bethany. He had made Donna promise not to tell Bethany how he felt. John did not want Bethany to turn to him on the rebound from her breakup with Scott Lancaster. Also, even though he was six years older and ready to marry and settle down, he realized Bethany needed time to reach her full maturity. John was waiting, but he was fully convinced that it was God's will for Bethany and him to marry eventually.

Bethany thought of John as a very good friend and was fond of him in a "sisterly" way. He had been a big help to her when she was going through the emotional turmoil of breaking up with Scott. She knew John was a wonderful Christian man, but had not entertained romantic thoughts toward him. She knew nothing of the discussion between John and Donna.

A few weeks after this conversation, Donna, Bethany, and Cindy were in their room together. Donna was telling Bethany, "I'm homesick. Even though here I'm surrounded by other Christians and at home there wasn't much understanding, I miss Pastor Butler and our friends at Faith Baptist too."

"I understand your feelings, believe me. I went through all that last year."

"Oh, I'm ashamed, Bethany. I shouldn't even complain compared to you. You haven't been home for over a year."

"Really?" interjected Cindy. "I would just die!"

"But I knew it would be like this, and that I wouldn't get to go home. So at least I was prepared. I still miss my family, but it does get easier with time."

"Believe it or not, I miss Michael and the Davenports. A year ago I wouldn't have believed I would ever say that!" laughed Bethany. "I still wake up thinking about what I will do to keep Michael occupied. Which reminds me, his birthday is coming up. Last time we went to Wal-Mart I bought a book and a birthday card. I have to get them mailed."

"It is really nice of you to remember his birthday and get him something," commented Cindy.

"I grew very fond of him. Once I was able to use a little discipline, I found out he was actually a sweet kid. He really changed after he got saved. I sure hope things are going well with his Mom and that she'll get saved."

"I know. I've been praying about that," responded Donna.

"Thanks, Donna. By the way, have you seen much of Peter?"

"Some. We've eaten together in the dining hall a few times."

"Well, that should help your loneliness," teased Bethany.

"How about you, Bethany? Seen anyone interesting?" asked Cindy.

"Not really."

"There's a guy in our English class who's real interested in you."

Bethany's head jerked up, and she looked at Cindy with alarm. "How do you know that?"

"He asked me to introduce him to you."

"Oh, no."

"What's wrong?"

"Please just discourage him, Cindy."

"Discourage him! Are you crazy?"

"I don't want to even think about guys for a while. I just broke up with one. Is the guy you're talking about tall?"

"Yes."

"Why don't you introduce him to Sarah? He'd probably like a tall, pretty brunette."

"What? You don't like them tall?" asked Cindy.

"I didn't say that. In fact, that's one of the things that attracted me to Scott. Tall, dark and handsome—that's what I thought I was looking for."

"And he was all of those?"

"Oh, yes."

"So what was the problem?"

"My grandmother always says, 'Handsome is as handsome does.' He was just too worldly. God finally got through to my backslidden heart and convinced me he wasn't the one He wanted for me."

"How did you make yourself break it off, Bethany? I don't know if I could," mused Cindy.

"My dad gave me some guidelines to think about, and I also realized I really wasn't happy. I was a miserable, emotional wreck! Hey, I've got to get back to my homework. Just spare me the intros for a while, okay?"

"If you say so, but I think you're making a big mistake. Don't you want to find a husband?"

"Sure, but I'm not in a rush. I've got lots of time. Right now I'm concentrating on my music. I enjoy choir and my piano lessons. I want to be good enough to get picked to play or sing in one of the college tour groups. My schedule is full without dating. I can barely squeeze in enough practice time as it is."

The conversation made a definite shift to the busyness of college life—much to Bethany's relief.

∾

"Do you really think you'll have a chance, Bethany?" asked Donna. "There will be lots of competition."

"Competition for what?" asked Sarah as she entered the room and wearily sank down on her bed. The college bus had just brought her back from her off-campus telemarketing job.

"For getting in a tour group as the piano accompanist or to sing."

"This summer?"

"No, you have to wait until after your sophomore year, but they'll do the auditions this year."

"Oh, I hope you make it. I'll pray for you."

"Me, too," Donna agreed. "That would be really neat."

"Especially if I could be in the group that goes to the Pacific Northwest. They visit my home church every year."

"Wow, Bethany, your family would be ecstatic!" exclaimed Sarah.

"So would I! Donna and I were just talking about being homesick. Right now I've been away for over a year."

"Are you going to get to go home for Thanksgiving and Christmas?" asked Cindy.

"Probably not Thanksgiving, and I'm not even sure about Christmas. My parents have mentioned they'd like me to, but that doesn't mean we'll be able to swing it."

"I guess we better pray about that too," put in Donna. "I'm so lucky. I don't live that far away. I guess I forget sometimes and take it for granted."

"Let's quit talking about the holidays," groaned Cindy. "They seem so far away."

"At least you can look forward to going home for both holidays. I can't afford to go home for Thanksgiving—just Christmas," replied Sarah.

"What are you two going to do during the break?" asked Cindy.

"I don't know," said Bethany.

"I haven't a clue," added Sarah.

∾

Keeping busy helped the girls keep their spirits up in spite of homesickness. They chose to do their soul winning on church bus routes, which they visited every Saturday. It was a thrill to introduce children, and sometimes their parents, to the Lord Jesus and to see many get saved. Some had never heard the Lord's name used in any way but as a curse word. Bethany remembered the change wrought in Michael's life after he was saved. She hoped she could have a similar influence on more children by working on a bus route.

Bethany and Donna worked on the same route. The first Saturday they were knocking on doors in an apartment complex. At one apartment a little brown-haired boy answered the door. His resemblance to Michael was so strong that Bethany gasped, and that startled him. He almost shut the door, but his mother called from the bedroom, "Billy, who is it?"

"I don't know. A couple of ladies."

"What ladies? What do they want?"

"How should I know?" answered Billy in a belligerent tone that showed no respect.

Bethany had to restrain herself from correcting him. Instead she called to the mother, introducing herself and Donna and mentioning the church bus.

Mrs. Logan, Billy's mother, answered that she would be there in a minute. While they were waiting, they tried to interest Billy in riding the church bus the next day. At first he just sneered at the idea and was very rude to the girls. Then they mentioned another boy a few doors back who had agreed to come. Bethany and Donna were not aware that Billy and Trevor Saunders hung around together. About the time they had convinced Billy, his mother showed up. At first she was not very receptive to the idea. After they had explained the program and mentioned Trevor, she thawed out. But she warned them, "You get those two together, you don't know what to expect! Are you sure you want the two of them to go to your church?"

"Oh, yes, Ma'am. I'm sure everything will be fine. I have had experience with little boys like Billy. In fact, he reminds me of the boy I cared for last year."

"Well, more power to you. Good luck is all I can say."

∽

The next day Trevor was up, ready, and eager to get on the bus. But when they got to Billy's apartment building, they were disappointed. Donna and Bethany knocked on the door of his apartment but got no response. They knocked louder and waited. Still there was no answer. Then they banged on the door with their fists as loudly as they could. Finally Billy came to the door and called, "Who's there?"

Donna answered, "Bethany and Donna from Crossroads Baptist Church. We talked to you yesterday about riding the bus to Sunday school."

Billy opened the door. He was in ragged, dirty pajamas. His face and hands were dirty, and his hair was uncombed.

"Billy, aren't you going to Sunday school on the bus with us today?" asked Bethany.

"Do I look like it?" he answered sarcastically.

Bethany flinched. He obviously had learned such disrespectful language from someone older. She used the same tactic she had used with Michael a year ago. She did not take the bait. Instead, she answered calmly and politely, "No, you don't look ready. What happened?"

"My mom didn't wake me up."

"But I thought she wanted you to go?" responded Donna.

"Well, she's snoring on the couch."

Bethany could see past Billy and noted that Mrs. Logan was still in evening clothes. She had only kicked off her high-heeled shoes. Donna was closest to the door and could smell alcohol. Apparently, she had been out partying quite late.

Concerned, Bethany asked, "Who did you stay with while your Mom was out last night?"

"My auntie."

"Oh, does she live close by?"

"Nah. She's staying with us. My grandma threw her out of her house because her baby cried too much."

As if on cue, a baby began wailing in one of the two bedrooms. "Now look what you did. Auntie is going to be so mad!"

"Please tell her we are sorry, Billy. We just wanted you to come to church."

"Well, I don't have my clothes on."

"Can you get dressed really fast?"

"I don't have any clean clothes, and I don't know where my shoes are."

At this point, a young woman about the age of Bethany and Donna came out of the bedroom, carrying the crying baby. "Billy, what are you doing? You shouldn't be opening the door and talking to strangers."

"They ain't strangers. Mom and me talked to 'em yesterday."

Donna spoke up. "We are from Crossroads Baptist Church, and we invited Billy to go on the bus to Sunday school. Mrs. Logan said it was okay."

"Well, she didn't tell me anything about it; besides, like he said, there's no clean clothes, and he can't find his shoes."

Donna answered, "We'll come by next Saturday to see if Billy can come. By the way, what is your name?"

"Angie."

"Hi. I'm Donna, and this is Bethany. We would love to have you ride on the bus to church also."

"Oh, that's just for little kids."

"No, it's not. We pick up teenagers and even grownups. Will you think about it? We have a nursery for the baby. It would give you a break."

"I'll think about it."

"Great."

Bethany looked at Billy and said, "Trevor is on the bus. He is going to be so disappointed. We are too."

"Why? What do you care if a kid like me comes?"

"We just like kids, and so does Jesus."

"Who is that?"

"He is God's Son. Please come to church to find out all about Him."

"Why?"

"So you can believe in Him and go to Heaven some day when you die."

"Oh, I'm not going there. Mom already told me that I'll end up in Hell. I'm too bad to go to Heaven."

"Billy, if you come to church, we'll explain all of it to you. I promise you—you don't have to go to Hell," responded Donna.

"Well, Billy," Bethany said, "we have to get on the bus and pick up some more kids. We'll come by next Saturday. Okay?"

"I guess so."

When they were back on the bus, Bethany whispered to Donna, "He reminds me so much of Michael—not just his looks—his personality and attitude. That little boy needs lots of love and discipline. I doubt he gets much of either."

Donna responded, "I think you are right. I almost cried when he asked who Jesus is."

They soon had a bus full of children from several apartment complexes. Billy's friend Trevor proved to be a handful even without Billy's influence. When they finally reached the church and had unloaded the bus, Donna commented to Bethany, "I don't see how it could be any worse even if Billy comes."

"I know," agreed Bethany. "I'm worn out from trying to keep Trevor seated and hold his attention and everyone else's too."

Every day of the following week they prayed for the children who had come and that Angie and Billy would come. The next Sunday Billy was ready, but they did not even glimpse Angie—either on Saturday or Sunday. Trevor came back also, and they soon figured out that Donna's optimistic statement was wrong—Trevor did act worse with Billy there.

As the weeks went by, both boys responded to the loving attention from the girls, as well as from the bus captain and his wife. The weeks when they did not wake up on time or could not find their clothes, the boys were heartbroken about not getting to go. Slowly, their behavior improved.

One day in early October, their prayers for Angie were answered; she finally rode the bus. Bethany sat down next to her and started a conversation.

"Angie, we are so glad you came. Have you ever been to a church before?"

"My grandma took me a few times when I was a little kid."

"Did you like it?"

"It was okay, I guess."

"Well, I hope you enjoy our church. Do you know why we bring a bus to pick up these others and you?"

"No, not really. I don't know why anyone in their right minds would pick up Billy and Trevor. They are so bad. Oh my goodness, you wouldn't believe some of the things they have done."

"Well, we want them to know about Jesus and accept Him as their personal Saviour so they can go to Heaven someday. We care about people. We have been praying for you, that you would come and get saved."

"What does that mean?"

"Here, let me explain it to you." Bethany took out her New Testament, turned to Romans 3:23, and read *'For all have sinned, and come short of the glory of God.'* That verse is telling us that we all do bad sometimes. The Bible is God's Word, and in it He calls our wrongdoing sin." She turned to Romans 5:12. "This verse tells where sin came from: *'Wherefore, as by one man sin entered into the world, and death by sin; and so death passed upon all men, for that all have sinned.'* Here God is talking about Adam and Eve and how they disobeyed God in the Garden of Eden. Have you heard that story?"

"Yes."

"Good. Now we need to see the price God puts on sin. Roman 6:23 says, *'For the wages of sin is death; but the gift of God is eternal life through Jesus Christ our Lord.'* "

Bethany explained, "Wages are something we earn, so we have earned or deserve to go to Hell—death that never ends. But God wants to give us the gift of eternal life—that means living forever with God in Heaven. I would rather go there than Hell, which is described as a lake of fire, wouldn't you?"

"Yes."

"The next thing you need to know is that Christ died for you. It says in Romans 5:8, *'But God commendeth his love toward us, in that, while we were yet sinners, Christ died for us.'* Even though it happened 2,000 years ago, when He let them kill Him on the Cross, He did it for us too. God could see into the future and knew all about us way back then!

"God gives us a promise in Romans 10:13: *'For whosoever shall call upon the name of the Lord shall be saved.'* We can put your name in there. 'If Angie will call upon the name of the Lord, Angie will be saved.' Do you believe that what I have told you is true?"

"Yes."

"Would you like to get it settled right now that you will go to Heaven someday when you die?"

"Yes. I don't want to go to Hell!"

"Good. Then all you have to do is tell God you know you are a sinner and you want to receive Christ as your personal Saviour."

Angie shyly said, "I'm not much good at praying."

"Okay. I'll say the words, and you repeat them. But you must really mean it with all your heart."

"I do. Please help me," answered Angie with tears starting to shimmer in her eyes.

After she had prayed, Bethany rejoiced with her. She explained that God wants us to publicly confess that we have accepted Christ. Bethany called Donna, who came from the front of the bus. "Now, tell Donna what you just did."

"I told God I was a sinner and wanted Jesus to be my Saviour."

"That's great, Angie," responded Donna enthusiastically and then gave Angie a hug.

Donna went back to the front of the bus to lead singing, while Bethany explained baptism to Angie. She readily agreed to be baptized that morning.

Later when they had a chance to talk, Donna and Bethany agreed that Angie's salvation made it all worthwhile—the loneliness, the homesickness, the hectic schedule, and the exhaustion when the weekend was over. Back in the dorm room that night, Sarah and Cindy shared the good results their buses had enjoyed. Cindy said, "Even though I miss home, my family, and my horse, right now I wouldn't want to be anywhere else but right here at Bible college where I am learning and experiencing so much!" All the girls agreed.

∽

Monday Bethany was called to the phone. She heard a familiar voice. "Hey, Beth, this is Scott. They won't let me in to see you! Would you leave this jail and come out here and talk to me? I'm right outside the entrance."

"You're here?"

"Of course. Now come out…"

"No, Scott, I can't do that," Bethany interrupted. "Why on earth did you come here? Did you make a big scene?"

"I just told them I think this situation stinks."

"Oh, Scott, did you have to embarrass me like this?" Bethany started choking up with emotion.

"It's no big deal. I figure you'll be out of here, so it won't matter what any of these idiots think."

"What are you talking about?"

"I'm sure you must be sick of all these rules and regulations by now. It's even worse than I thought. They won't even let me on campus to visit you. Pack up a few essentials and come with me. I'll take you back to Detroit. I have really missed you, Beth. Have you missed me?"

"Scott, I…"

"I even thought about your silly conscience and talked Melanie into coming with me so we don't have to drive back alone together."

"You dragged your sister along?"

"Yes. I'm sincere about this, and I did some serious planning. I even called the Davenports, and they said you are welcome to stay with them anytime. So you can stay there until we get married. I'll get those rings I told you about, and we can have a Christmas wedding. I'll even pay for it."

"Scott, you can't be serious," Bethany managed to choke out.

"I most certainly am. I want to get married as soon as possible."

"But Scott, I told you I'm not going to marry you. Don't you listen to anything I say? I even told you to quit calling me. And now you do this. You could get me in all kinds of trouble," exclaimed Bethany.

"Who cares? They're all weirdos anyway."

Anger drove away Bethany's tears. "Scott, just go home! I'm not going to marry you—not now or ever. That's final. You've got to accept that and leave me alone. Don't come here. Don't call. Goodbye!"

Tears stung her eyes as she turned from the phone. She wished Scott Lancaster would just go away and stay away! The phone immediately rang again, and even though the caller was persistent, Bethany ignored it and continued toward her room. Finally another girl picked it up and then called, "It's for you, Bethany."

Bethany shook her head violently. The tears were pouring down her face now, and she headed straight for her bed and collapsed face down on it. Her three roommates looked at each other in amazement. Bethany had never acted like this before. Donna rushed to her and put her arm over her heaving shoulders. Cindy and Sarah also ran to her and peppered her with questions. "What is wrong? What are you crying about?"

When she could manage a few words, Bethany whispered to Donna. "It was Scott. He tried to get on campus and then called me on his cell phone. I'm so embarrassed. I think he made a scene."

"What did she say?" demanded Cindy and Sarah.

Bethany turned over with a huge sigh and reached for a tissue. After patting her eyes and blowing her nose, she said, "Go ahead and tell them, Donna."

"It's a guy from Detroit. He came down here to see her and tried to get on campus."

"I saw him on my way in from work!" exclaimed Sarah. "He was at the front entrance. Oh, my goodness, Bethany, he is incredibly handsome. Does he like you?"

"He wants to marry her," explained Donna.

"He wants to marry you? Why are you crying about that?"

"Because she broke off with him, and he won't leave her alone."

"Isn't it hard to break up with someone that good looking who wants to marry you?" asked Sarah.

"Very hard," admitted Bethany, "and it doesn't help that he won't give up. I thought I had convinced him that it was all over between us before I left Detroit."

Sarah said, "It's too bad you couldn't work it out with him."

"Let's drop it," begged Bethany. "I really have to study."

"Okay," the other girls agreed.

But Bethany found she could not concentrate on her studies. Scott's words kept going through her mind. She reached for her Bible and opened it to Psalm 40. Verse 4 caught her attention. *"Blessed is that man that maketh the LORD his trust, and respecteth not the proud, nor such as turn aside to lies."* After meditating on the verse, Bethany prayed, "Lord, I have put my trust in You and received Your blessings. I want that relationship to continue. I can see that Scott is full of pride, and I'm thankful that You have shown me how he has turned aside to lies. He is putting his emphasis on all the wrong things, instead of Your priority of winning souls. Open his eyes and help me not to let his words get to me. I'm sorry I let him upset me so much. Now help me have peace in my heart so I can concentrate on my homework."

Later in the evening Bethany's Bible class assignment led her to Acts 13. Verse 52 said the disciples were filled with joy and the Holy Spirit after being persecuted for preaching. She felt like Scott's ridicule was a small measure of persecution that she had endured, and she determined she would let the Lord fill her with joy and the Holy Spirit instead of depression. By bedtime, when Bethany laid her head on the pillow, she was filled with peace and enjoyed sweet rest.

Persevering

"But ye, brethren, be not weary in well doing."
(II Thessalonians 3:13)

*W*hat Bethany had feared occurred—the dean of women summoned her to her office for an explanation of the incident with Scott. Bethany was able to convince her that she did not know of Scott's plans and definitely did not want him to bother her at college. She was relieved that her explanation was accepted and she was not in trouble.

Her busy schedule helped her to push the whole incident to the back of her mind in the days following Scott's attempt to see her. She did not want to dwell on Scott Lancaster. She was totally absorbed with music lessons. Studying more advanced piano was hard work but very rewarding; she was also in the choir. They were practicing to sing for chapel a few days before Thanksgiving break. Bethany was really looking forward to that. She also found the preaching in chapel services inspiring, and her classes, especially Christian Womanhood, were interesting and helpful. She was enjoying college life.

She and Donna were excited about the bus route. The attendance was growing, many children had been saved, and several had gotten baptized. Both Trevor and Billy were asking a lot of questions and seemed to be close to making a decision.

∽

A few days after Scott's attempt to get on campus, a beautiful bouquet of a dozen pink roses arrived for Bethany. In the accompanying card, Scott had written:

Dear Beth,
*   I want you to know I still love you, and I forgive you for the things you said the other day. I know you are just brainwashed—*

first by your parents and now by that ridiculous school. You are just too beautiful to waste your life like this. I will call you soon, and we can talk it all out calmly and rationally.

With all my love,

Scott

Sarah was the first one to enter the room after the flowers were delivered. She rushed to see whose name was on the envelope. She thought the arrangement would probably be for Cindy. Knowing Bethany had hung up on Scott, she was surprised that he would send such a romantic gift. She was dying to know what the card said. She was greatly disappointed when Bethany came in, read the card, and crumpled it up.

As Bethany threw the card in the wastebasket, she made an exclamation of disgust.

"What did he say?" asked Sarah.

"Oh, it was just…" Bethany struggled to express her reaction—"just stupid." Little did Bethany know that it would have been wise to let Sarah read that note.

One day a beautiful card arrived in Bethany's mail. Scott had added a note above his signature.

Dear Beth,

Don't forget I love you and want to marry you.

Scott

Bethany promptly tore up the note, letting the pieces fall in the wastebasket. Sarah was horrified. "Bethany, he spent a lot of money on that card."

"Well, I wish he wouldn't," Bethany responded.

The following week Bethany received a big box of an expensive brand of chocolates. On the card in the box, Scott had simply signed, "All my love, Scott." All four girls greatly enjoyed the treat, but Bethany expressed frustration rather than gratitude.

A few days later Bethany was told a young man was on the phone asking for her. She asked Donna to take the call.

"Hello."

"Beth?"

"No, this is her friend Donna."

"I want to speak to Beth."

"May I ask who is calling?"

"This is her fiancé, Scott Lancaster. I need to talk to her."

"I'm sorry, but Bethany can't come to the phone right now."

"You mean she won't, don't you?"

"I guess you could say that."

"Why won't she even talk to me?"

"Hold on, and I'll ask her." Donna repeated his question to Bethany.

"Tell him I have made my position very clear, and there is no need for further discussion."

Donna repeated her answer to Scott.

"She'll change her mind. A few more weeks in that prison called a college, and she'll jump at the chance to marry me."

"Click," went the phone in Donna's ear.

"How rude! He didn't even say goodbye. Just hung up."

"I'm sure he was pretty frustrated. Let's not be too hard on him. It's my fault for not breaking things off sooner. But I sure do wish he'd give up!"

"He called himself your fiancé," said Donna, rolling her eyes in disgust.

"He is one very stubborn guy," groaned Bethany.

∾

A welcome diversion from the problems with Scott came in the form of a letter from the Davenports. They not only invited Bethany to spend Thanksgiving break at their home in Detroit, but also included two train tickets with the instructions to bring along someone else who couldn't make it home. After Bethany read it to Sarah, they were hugging and jumping up and down with joy.

"Wait till you see their house, Sarah. It is gorgeous. Oh, I am anxious to see Michael! The food will be scrumptious. They'll take us to Faith Baptist, and I can see my friends there. This will be the greatest, next to being with our own families."

After calming down and thinking about it, Sarah hesitantly asked, "Are you sure they really want a stranger in their home? I feel a little uneasy about it. I mean…well, you know how shy I am when I first meet people."

Bethany hugged her again. "You'll be fine. I promise you, they will make you feel right at home and welcome. We'll have a great time. We will need to get permission from the college administration to go there, and we can both work on that."

Mr. Prescott assured the college that he did not have any reservations about his daughter's traveling to Detroit to visit the Davenports, and Sarah's parents also agreed to their daughter's accompanying Bethany. Permission was granted by the college, and the two girls eagerly awaited their Thanksgiving holiday.

A few days later Bethany received another letter. This one was from John Holman, asking if they could plan to visit Mrs. Carpenter the Friday evening after Thanksgiving. She was anxious for a visit with Bethany and her friend. The Davenports had told her about inviting Bethany and a friend for Thanksgiving.

After again reassuring Sarah that she would live through that experience, Bethany eagerly wrote back. She explained to John that in order for her and Sarah to be at Mrs. Carpenter's home with John, they would need to include the Davenports as chaperones. She asked John if he felt that would be too many people for Mrs. Carpenter to entertain.

Bethany soon received a letter from John assuring her that Mrs. Carpenter understood the situation and had already invited the Davenports to join the gathering at her home the day after Thanksgiving. The Davenports had been happy to accept. Now that they had this opportunity to look forward to, time actually sped by for the girls, helped by their busy schedules. Sarah even had a few dates, but she despaired of ever having a second one with the same guy because she was so shy and tongue-tied.

Bethany's birthday arrived, and she received cards from her family and the Davenports. Her family also sent her a beautifully wrapped gift—a sweater and skirt set. Bethany was delighted. It would be nice to have something new to wear for Thanksgiving. Even better, she received a cellular phone. Both sets of grandparents had gone in on it with her parents. Now she would feel safer on the bus route, and it would be easier to call home.

Another small package arrived for her birthday. This one was from

Scott, and when she opened it, Bethany gasped with astonishment and disbelief. He had sent a very expensive-looking necklace; Bethany suspected the stone in it was a diamond. She let the other girls admire it, then rewrapped it, and mailed it back to him.

Donna was not around when Bethany received another phone call. Bethany asked Sarah to help her out. They went to the phone together, and Bethany asked Sarah to answer it for her. When Sarah said "Hello," she heard, "Hello? Beth, is that you?"

"No, I'm one of her roommates."

"Well, is Beth there? I wanted to speak with her, please."

"Just a minute." She put her hand over the receiver. "It's a guy. He sounds very nice—he's being very polite."

"Did he say who he was?"

"No, he just said, Is that you, Beth?" and then he asked where you were and said he wanted to speak to you."

"Scott is the only person who calls me Beth. So just politely tell him I don't want to speak to him."

"Bethany, I can't..."

"Please, Sarah, I've asked him not to contact me."

"Well, what exactly should I say? I don't want to sound rude."

"Put the blame on me. Make sure it is Scott; then say, 'Bethany does not wish to come to the phone. I'm sorry. Goodbye.' "

"Okay, if you say so. Hello, is this Scott?"

"Yes, and I want to speak to Beth."

"She doesn't want to come to the phone. I'm sorry. Goodbye."

"Now hang up, Sarah."

"But I feel so rude."

"I'm sorry, Sarah, but I want Scott to get the message to leave me alone. Besides, the last time he called he hung up on Donna."

"He's that incredibly handsome guy, isn't he?"

"Yes, Scott is very good-looking," Bethany said with a sigh.

"He must be some horrible person the way you treat him when he tries to call, especially after all those nice gifts."

"No, I didn't say he was a horrible person, but there's no use encouraging him when I've made up my mind not to continue the relationship. He doesn't understand about our standards, Sarah, and he tries to get me to change. I don't want to! You can understand that, can't you?"

"I guess so."

A few weeks later Bethany received another phone call. Again only Sarah was in the room with her, so for the second time she had to ask Sarah to run interference. Sarah reluctantly agreed. In response to her "Hello," she heard a male voice say doubtfully, "Is this Bethany Prescott?"

"No, I'm Sarah, one of her roommates."

"Is Bethany around?"

She mouthed to Bethany, "It's a guy," and said into the phone, "Well…"

"Ask who it is," whispered Bethany.

"May I tell her who's calling?"

"This is John Holman."

"Hold on a minute, please."

With her hand over the receiver she whispered, "He says his name is John Holman."

"Oh, I'll take it. Hi, John, it's great to hear from you," Bethany greeted John. "Thanks," she mouthed to Sarah.

Sarah returned to their room while Bethany continued her conversation with John.

John asked, "Are you enjoying college, Bethany?"

"Oh, yes!"

"Are they keeping you busy?"

"Very! It took a lot of adjustment. I thought Michael kept me busy, but now I feel like I was really lazy last year." She laughed. "I was so tired the first few weeks, but I've gotten used to it now."

"So everything's settling into place for you?"

"Yes, except I wish I could get things settled with Scott."

"What do you mean? I thought you had made up your mind about him."

"I have, and I thought he had accepted it. But he's been contacting me."

"You mean calling you?"

"Not just that. He actually came here to try to see me and take me away from this 'prison,' as he calls it. They wouldn't let him on campus, of course, and I wouldn't go out to meet him. I have refused to take his phone calls, so he has been sending romantic cards, roses, and chocolates."

"He doesn't give up easily when he makes up his mind to go after something."

"That's for sure! But it's been a few weeks now since I last heard anything, so I hope he's given up."

"I'm sorry he is still bugging you."

"Thanks, but I'm okay. I am learning to let God be in control and give me peace."

"That is good, Bethany. Listen, I'm sorry I can't talk longer. I've got to run, but I wanted to confirm the time for Friday night next week. Would 5:30 be okay?"

"That sounds fine to me. Have you checked with the Davenports?"

"Yes, they said that was fine. Brother Davenport asked me if I would like to drive the limo, and of course I jumped at the chance. I'm really looking forward to it."

Bethany could hear the eager anticipation in his voice and laughed. "You sound like my brother when he gets a new remote-controlled car."

John laughed and answered, "I'm still a kid at heart, especially when it comes to cars."

Bethany said, "I have to go to work soon, John, but before we hang up, let me give you my new cell phone number. It will make it easier for you to reach me."

"I am glad to hear you now have one. Okay, I'm ready to take it down."

When they had ended the conversation, Bethany returned to the room. Sarah asked her about the call.

"That was my friend John from Detroit."

"Your friend? You mean another boyfriend, don't you?"

"No, he's more like a big brother. I'm not ready for another boyfriend. It's too soon. John's just a great guy and a really good Christian. He helped me through the loneliness and frustration of breaking up with Scott."

"Why did he call if he isn't your boyfriend?"

"To make plans. He is going to go with us to my friend's house, Mrs. Carpenter, the elderly lady I told you about. The Davenports will go along as chaperones. He is excited about getting to drive their limo."

"Oh. What's he like, Bethany?"

"Really nice and a serious Christian. He wants to come to school here, too. Maybe next year."

"Is he handsome?"

"He's nice-looking but totally different from Scott. He has blond hair and a football player's build."

"Sounds interesting."

"Hey, look at the time. I've got to go to work. I don't want to be late and lose my campus job. See you later."

When Bethany was gone, Sarah started thinking about what Bethany had said. Bethany sure was lucky—she had two guys calling her. No one seemed very interested in Sarah. A little spark of jealousy began to burn in her heart.

A few days later Sarah said to Bethany, "I'm not sure I'm going to go with you to Detroit, Bethany."

"Oh, Sarah, why not? I really want you to."

"I'll just be in the way—a fifth wheel. You are going to get to see that other guy that called, and you don't need me butting in."

"Sarah, that's ridiculous. I told you there's nothing romantic between us. Please, Sarah, I know you'll enjoy it, and I'll feel terrible if I leave you behind all alone. Besides, the Davenports and Mrs. Carpenter are expecting you. Please, please, pretty please…" she begged and started laughing at her own childish appeal.

"I guess it would be rude to back out now when they are all expecting me. Okay, I'll go."

"You won't be sorry, Sarah. You will have a good time. It will be lots better than staying here."

Bethany's hope that Scott had decided to give up was dashed when she received a letter the Friday before Thanksgiving. She left it unopened on her dresser, trying to decide if she should even read it.

Saturday and Sunday she was busy with the bus route. She and Donna told the children they would be gone the next weekend because of the Thanksgiving holiday. Sunday night Sarah convinced Bethany that she should read what Scott had to say. Afterward she was sorry she had not just thrown it away unopened. It distressed her to read his words:

Dear Bethany,

I hope you are proud of yourself. You have really hurt me and broken my heart. You let me think you loved me to the point that I picked out rings, and then you dumped me. Now you are rude and won't even talk to me.

I am really depressed and upset by this. I don't know if you think I'm just joking and not serious or what. I can assure you I am serious about our relationship and want you for my wife.

I thought you cared for me. You even said you did, once. I was hoping we could work out our differences with a compromise.

Anyway, your old-fashioned ideas are really over the top! I've been trying to rescue you from the fanaticism. Can't we still work something out?

I'll be waiting to hear back from you. But I'm warning you, I have just about run out of patience.

Yours with love,

Scott

Hearing from Scott no longer tugged at her heart, but this letter caused her pangs of guilt. She should have broken up with Scott much sooner. She had been so blinded with "love" that she had failed to see their relationship would not work. She had let it drag on longer than she should have. Hopefully, this letter would be his last attempt to persuade her. He was running out of patience. She was totally fed up with hearing from him. She tore up the letter without sharing it with anyone else. She fervently hoped he would not guess that she was going to Detroit for Thanksgiving. She did not want him bothering her! Worrying about that possibility took away some of her joyful anticipation.

The next day the choir was scheduled to sing for chapel. She turned her attention to that matter so as not to dwell on her worries. She would not allow Scott to spoil the special activities of her college days. Bethany thoroughly enjoyed the experience of singing with the choir for chapel. She was happy when her roommates all assured her that the choir special was well done and an inspiration to the listeners.

Tuesday afternoon Bethany, Donna, and Sarah rode with other equally excited young people on a bus that took them from the college to the train station. Cindy was on another church bus that was taking people to the airport. Cindy had been in a highly excited state for days, making it more difficult for Bethany and Sarah. At least Bethany would be with people she had grown close to during the previous year. Sarah continued to have mixed feelings about the trip to Detroit. She told Bethany it would be better than staying in the lonely dorm room by herself, but her natural shyness made the trip difficult for her.

Donna knew Sarah and Bethany had not had much time to talk and that Sarah was nervous about the upcoming stay at the Davenports. She would have lots of questions for Bethany, so Donna sat across the aisle on the train and let them sit together. Donna had a book to read and had been eagerly anticipating the chance to relax and enjoy it.

When they were settled in for the journey, Sarah turned to Bethany and asked, "Can you tell me a little about the people I'll be meeting? The Davenports and Mrs.—what's the elderly lady's name?"

"Mrs. Carpenter. You will really enjoy her, Sarah. She is an old-fashioned grandma type. Be sure you ask to see her beautiful handwork—crocheting and embroidery."

"What about the Davenports?"

"Mr. Davenport is a really nice, fatherly type. He was always very kind and understanding with me. During my stay, he rededicated himself to the Lord, changed churches, and got more involved.

"You can feel lucky that Mrs. Davenport has recently done a complete turnaround. She made my life miserable when I first got there. She didn't act like she even wanted a nanny, and yet I'm sure she wanted relief from dealing with Michael. She had almost managed to turn him into a little monster," added Bethany with a laugh. "She really made my job harder. But she has become much more mellow, actually a sweet lady. I'm anxious to see how she's progressing in her Christian growth.

"The cook's name is Mrs. Spencer. She also got saved last year and is an enthusiastic new Christian. Even before she was saved, she was sweet and thoughtful and such an encouragement to me.

"Your guess is as good as mine about Elaine, Michael's mother. All I know is that she got pregnant at a young age. I assume she was really spoiled and undisciplined like Michael. Mrs. Davenport did not believe in spanking children."

"Where was she last year?"

"On a trip to Europe."

"Wow! She does sound spoiled."

"I'm a little nervous about meeting her. I don't know how she'll respond to me—or you for that matter. I'm sure she is very worldly."

Sarah sighed, "I had hoped this would be a relaxing time."

"Me too," agreed Bethany. "I've been praying that her heart will be softened and we'll have a chance to witness."

"Hopefully," agreed Sarah.

"Anyway, I'm anxious to see Michael. I really love that little kid. And I'm looking forward to going to Faith Baptist Church. That church helped me so much! The people there are just great."

The girls lapsed into silence and were lulled by the rhythm of the train; both were soon napping.

When they arrived in Detroit, the three girls gathered up their things and disembarked. Donna's parents were waiting for her, and the girls quickly hugged before she hurried to greet her parents. Bethany spotted the Davenports' chauffeur, and he took their bags and led the way to the gleaming limousine. Sarah sank back in the luxurious seat and grinned with pleasure at Bethany.

"At least this part is relaxing," whispered Bethany.

Sarah nodded in agreement.

— C H A P T E R   T H R E E —

Thanksgiving

"It is a good thing to give thanks unto the LORD...."
(Psalm 92:1)

$\mathcal{A}$s the car pulled up in front of the house, Bethany saw the front door open wide as Michael burst out the door, ran across the porch, and jumped down the steps. Bethany did not wait for the chauffeur—she pushed open the car door and stepped out. Michael threw himself at her yelling, "Bethany, Bethany!" After sharing a big hug, Bethany looked up to see the Davenports coming out to greet her, followed by their daughter Elaine, Michael's mother.

The chauffeur had opened the other door for Sarah. They went up the steps, Sarah following Bethany and Michael, who still clutched Bethany by the hand. Introductions were quickly made, and Bethany was relieved to see that Elaine was friendly, albeit a little cautious. Michael's exuberant welcome did not seem to bother his mother.

Martha Davenport welcomed Bethany with a motherly hug and greeted Sarah warmly. Bethany secretly marveled at the change in Mrs. Davenport from the cold, domineering woman she had been a year and a half before. At that time she not only made Bethany feel unwelcome, but objected to and interfered with Bethany's efforts to improve Michael's behavior and temperament. Her salvation experience had certainly brought about a great change.

The girls were shown to guest rooms on the second floor. Michael's room, adjoining his mother's suite, was at the other end of the hallway. Bethany had used the suite during her stay as Michael's nanny.

The girls had enough time to unpack and settle into their beautiful guest rooms before dinner. After she had changed clothes and freshened up her hair and makeup, Sarah knocked on Bethany's door. Bethany invited her in. Sarah inspected the room. "This is so nice, just as pretty as the room

I'm in. And the bathroom is just gorgeous with that nice big tub and separate shower."

"You should see the one in the suite I used last year," commented Bethany. "It has a Roman tub."

"Mrs. Davenport really has a flair for decorating," added Sarah. "This is better than any hotel, and they even put candy and fruit in our rooms."

"I told you we'd get the royal treatment," said Bethany.

"It's really nice of them, especially to include me. If I can't be at home, this is certainly a great alternative."

"This year I'll get to eat Thanksgiving dinner in the formal dining room. It will be a big improvement over last Thanksgiving," said Bethany, laughing.

"What do you mean?"

Bethany explained about the miserable time she and Michael had had in the morning room because he was upset about being excluded from the adults and because she was homesick.

"You must have had some really rough times," Sarah commiserated.

"Some, but there were a lot of great rewards too. You saw how much Michael grew to like me."

"I'd call that love," responded Sarah.

At that moment that same little person knocked on their door to tell them dinner was ready. Elaine joined them as they descended the beautiful staircase to the ground floor. When they were all seated in the dining room, Mr. Davenport prayed, thanking the Lord for the privilege of having their visitors. Tonight's meal was one of Michael's favorites—spaghetti and meatballs. Mrs. Spencer, the cook, had prepared the meal with her usual flair. At one point Michael asked, "Elaine, please pass the spaghetti."

Without thinking, Bethany blurted out, "Michael, you shouldn't call your mother by her first name."

Suddenly, there was silence all around the table. Bethany blushed, looked at Elaine, and said, "Oh, I'm sorry. It just came out by habit. I mean, I got used to correcting Michael. I'm sorry; it isn't my business…" Her sentence faded away.

Elaine looked at her appraisingly, and answered, "I'm not angry. But why did you say that?"

Bethany answered, "Maybe we could talk about it later, er…privately?" with a significant glance at Michael.

Elaine shrugged her shoulders and said, "Sure. I've got lots of questions for you. Things are a lot different around here, and I hear you had a lot to do with the changes."

Bethany was glad to hear her tone was curious rather than hostile. She had been afraid Elaine might be bitter or angry. After dinner Michael asked if he could take Bethany upstairs to play with him. Before Bethany could respond, George said, "No, not tonight, Michael. You will have plenty of time with Bethany tomorrow. You can entertain yourself or sit with us while we visit and get acquainted with Sarah."

"May I sit by Bethany?"

"Yes, of course," answered George. He rose from the table and led them all into the living room. Elaine was an attractive young woman with shiny auburn hair cut in a short style. She was taller than Bethany, but not as tall as Sarah. She participated in the conversation to a limited extent, but mostly listened and observed. Bethany felt a little like a bird in a cage, but still tried to concentrate on the conversation and act natural.

After about an hour, Elaine told Michael it was his bedtime. He started to protest, but a look from his grandfather silenced him. Bethany gave him a hug and a kiss along with a promise to play with him in the morning. Shortly thereafter, George and Martha said they were ready to head for bed, and the girls responded that they were also tired. They all went upstairs to their respective rooms.

Bethany and Sarah enjoyed a good night's rest on comfortable beds, and in the morning they took turns luxuriating in the tub with rich, lovely scented bubbles. It was so enjoyable after hurried showers in the dorm bathroom. Mrs. Davenport had told them to sleep in and take their time. There would not be any specified breakfast hour. Bethany had gotten up first and had her morning devotions before her bath. When she was ready, she went down and invaded the kitchen. After receiving a motherly hug from Mrs. Spencer, she begged to be allowed to stay and eat some breakfast there while they had a chat.

Mrs. Spencer, who was one of Bethany's converts from the previous year, was happy to tell Bethany about how Faith Baptist was growing and adding new ministries. The Davenports allowed her some time off on Saturdays to go calling for the new bus route that had just been started. Bethany noted that a certain middle-aged man in the church, who had never been married and who also worked on the bus route, was mentioned often in Mrs. Spencer's conversation. Bethany was happy that her friend, who was a widow, apparently had a new "interest."

Bethany excused herself to go check on Sarah. On her way upstairs, an exuberant little boy accosted her with another big hug. He instantly started chattering and followed her back up. He waited while she poked her head into the bedroom Sarah was using. Sarah put the finishing touches to her makeup, and then they went downstairs to get breakfast for her and Michael.

Soon the Davenports joined them. After about a half hour filled with animated conversation, Elaine came in with a cup of coffee. She wasn't a breakfast person. "What are you talking about?" she asked as she entered the room.

Her father answered, "We're catching up on what's been going on in our lives since Bethany left. I was just telling the girls about your plans to start a course in interior decorating."

"That sounds like it would be interesting, and I'll bet you've inherited a natural knack from your mom."

"Why, thank you, Bethany," responded Martha.

"I hope so," said Elaine. "I think I will enjoy it. Besides, it's time for me to make my own way and let Mother and Father be rid of me."

"You know we don't feel like that, Elaine," said Martha.

"You have been very patient, Mother. But it is definitely time I learned to support myself and move out of your house."

"I am proud of you for it," said George.

"They took us in after the divorce and then gave me that wonderful trip to Europe. I've been very spoiled," she admitted to the girls.

A brief silence followed, and then a soft, tremulous voice asked, "But what about me? Where will I go?"

All eyes turned to see Michael's forlorn face with unshed tears shimmering in his eyes. Bethany, who was closest, put an arm around him, squeezed him tight, and said, "Oh, Michael. Don't you worry."

Mrs. Davenport hastily put in, "Michael, your grandfather and I love you. We aren't going to push you out of our house."

To everyone's happy surprise, Elaine rushed to him, knelt down beside him, and grabbed his hands. Looking earnestly in his face, she said,

"Michael, you and I are going to be a team. We are going to have a new start and be a family together. We'll get our own apartment, but close by so we can still spend time here with your grandparents. Does that sound okay?"

"I guess so," he answered hesitantly. Elaine got up and ruffled his hair. "You'll see. Everything will work out."

Michael brushed away the tears, and his countenance brightened. He hurried to finish his breakfast and then asked if Bethany would play with him. Bethany hesitated, looking questioningly at Sarah. Elaine said, "Go ahead, Bethany. I'll entertain Sarah for a while."

Michael led Bethany upstairs to his room. When they entered, she exclaimed, "Oh, Michael. Your room is so cute! You have new curtains and a matching comforter in a sports theme. I love the matching wallpaper border, and the walls have been painted. Who did all this?"

"Elaine."

Bethany cringed but did not reprimand him. She looked around and saw other decorations carrying out the theme. "She did a really good job. Do you like it?"

"Sure. Can we play now?"

"Of course. What shall we do first?"

Michael decided on building with his giant LEGO® set.

Meanwhile, Sarah and Elaine had gone into the living room and sat down on the luxuriously soft couch. Sarah asked Elaine if she had photos from her trip abroad.

"Are you sure I won't bore you to death?"

"Oh, no! I want to see them. I've never been out of the United States, and I want to hear all about what you saw and did."

"Well, I don't know about that. We'll stick to the pictures I took of tourist attractions. Okay?"

"Yes, that's what I meant," answered Sarah with some hesitancy and a frown. She wasn't sure what Elaine was talking about.

At noon the three young women and Michael gathered for lunch. Mr. Davenport was at work, and Mrs. Davenport had gone to a luncheon meeting. Elaine suggested they all bundle up and go for a short walk after lunch. Everyone was agreeable. Michael stayed close to Bethany, clutching her hand and chattering. When they turned around to head back, Elaine reminded Michael that he would need to take a nap since it was Wednesday and he would be going to church. He answered, "Okay. I go to big church now, Bethany. May I sit next to you?"

"Of course!"

Since Mrs. Spencer and the Davenports regularly attended midweek services, they had simpler meals requiring less clean up. This Wednesday night Mrs. Spencer served a casserole and a salad. After dinner there was a rush to get ready for church. Bethany was looking forward to seeing her friends at Faith Baptist Church. Elaine helped Michael get ready but did not join them herself.

When they arrived, Donna was waiting for them. Bethany took one look at her face and pulled her aside to speak privately, excusing herself from the Davenports and Sarah. "Donna, what's wrong? You look like you've been crying."

"I'll be okay, Bethany. It's the same old thing. My parents just don't understand, and they got very upset that I was going to church when I have just a few days to be with them. I hope it doesn't spoil the whole weekend."

"Oh, me too, Donna," said Bethany giving her friend a quick hug. "I've been praying for you."

"Thanks," said Donna and quickly turned to Sarah. "Come on, Sarah. I'll introduce you to some of the young people, and we'll find seats." Donna had seen John Holman approaching, so she hurried away with Sarah, leaving Bethany with the Davenports.

John Holman drew near, smiling broadly. He greeted Bethany with a handshake and said, "It is so good to see you, Bethany." He shook hands with the Davenports, including Michael. He spoke to Michael man to man. "Are you enjoying having Bethany back for a few days?"

"Yes, sir." Michael's sparkling eyes and huge grin matched his words.

"She's a pretty special lady to have around, isn't she?"

"Yes, sir. I miss her a lot."

"Me, too," said John in a low voice only Michael could hear.

By now other church members had come to greet Bethany warmly. The group moved on into the auditorium to find seats. John maneuvered to end up on Bethany's right with Michael on her left and Martha and George Davenport next to him on the pew. Sarah sat in another section with Donna and some other young adults.

The church the college students attended in Indiana was huge. Bethany found it exciting to see so many people working, serving, and worshiping the Lord together. Still, she enjoyed the smaller Faith Baptist Church in other ways. Here it felt like she had an extended family. Bethany was happy to be back where she had experienced a revival in her Christian life the year before.

After the service she was able to briefly greet a few more acquaintances, but she didn't want to keep the Davenports waiting. It was already past Michael's usual bedtime.

When they arrived back at the Davenports, George and Martha invited the girls to sit and visit in the living room while Elaine took Michael upstairs to get ready for bed. He was tired enough not to resist, especially after Bethany promised to play with him the next day. Martha offered the girls a snack, but they assured her they were still full from dinner.

Thursday morning was another relaxed morning. Knowing Michael would claim her time again, Bethany made sure she did her devotions before leaving her room. Before going down to breakfast, she again took a luxurious bubble bath.

At noon Mrs. Spencer put out vegetables, chips, and dip along with hot apple cider. The girls had to watch themselves, and Michael, on the quantities they ate so they could save room for the delicious dinner they knew was coming. Wonderful smells were beginning to fill the house. They sat down to a traditional Thanksgiving meal about 3:00 p.m. Michael joined the adults in the dining room and was overjoyed to sit next to Bethany.

During dinner Elaine invited the girls to go shopping with her in the morning. "We will have to get up very early to be there when the doors open. It will be wild. Are you two up for it?"

"Oh, I would love to go. My mom and I did that in Tacoma lots of times on the Friday after Thanksgiving. In fact, she and my sister Betsy are planning on doing it tomorrow." Bethany started to choke up and get teary-eyed and was glad Sarah spoke up.

"I've never gone early in the morning, but I'm game to give it a whirl. Sounds like fun."

"But I want Bethany to play with me some more," whined Michael.

"Michael," said his grandfather in a voice that George used when he was correcting Michael. "Bethany won't be gone all day. We have to let her do some grownup things too. I'll have tomorrow off. We'll do something together in the morning. I'm sure Bethany will give you some of her time in the afternoon."

"Of course," agreed Bethany. "We'll get home in time for that. I'll be going out again at dinnertime, don't forget, to see my friend, Mrs. Carpenter. But in between I'll have several hours for you."

"You're going to be gone a lot," said Michael dejectedly.

"But we still have Saturday and part of Sunday," Bethany reminded him.

That evening after Michael was in bed, Elaine invited the girls to join her in the morning room for cocoa and snacks. Mrs. Spencer had set out some of the leftovers and replenished the relish tray. There was bread and leftover turkey for sandwiches and leftover pie.

Bethany had been spending so much time with Michael that it was her first chance for an intimate conversation with Elaine.

Elaine began by telling Bethany, "You are not at all what I expected. I thought you'd be boring, homely, and out of style. But you have a cool personality, and I love your adorable laugh. You seem to be happy and to enjoy yourself. Both of you are absolutely smashing in your own ways," she added, glancing at Sarah.

"Me?" questioned Sarah.

"Thank you," responded Bethany.

"Except for being dressed a little differently, you look like my bunch. I mean your hair and makeup look great. Mother had told me you never wear trousers and you keep your necklines high. That was a shock. I didn't know there were girls nowadays who were like that. My mother has changed what she wears too. I couldn't believe it. She has gone through her closet and thrown away stuff."

"Mother told me how you had never before dated and you fell in love and then broke up with the guy because he didn't agree with your beliefs. That amazed me too."

"How about you, Sarah? Did you grow up like Bethany?"

"Yes. I never dated till I got to college. Now I've had a few dates, but I'm pretty shy, and I get tongue-tied; so I don't think any of the guys will ask me again."

"You probably wouldn't call them dates, Elaine. We have to keep our distance. No touching, and we usually stay on campus. Sometimes there is a dating bus for an off-campus activity. Often a date is just sitting in chapel together."

"Are you serious?"

"Yes."

"Man! That is weird. Oh, I'm sorry. I don't mean you are..."

"We understand. It's all a new idea for you," said Bethany. "The guy I fell for, Scott, had the same reaction."

"And neither one of you rebelled at all those strict rules when you were growing up?"

"No, it seemed natural to us. We didn't know anything else. Oh, we knew other people did things differently. We weren't totally sheltered. We saw how other people lived from working on church bus routes."

"Bus routes?"

"We helped sign up children to ride a church bus to Sunday school. We would knock on doors to find new riders and visit the regular riders on Saturday so we'd know where to stop on Sunday. And we'd ride the bus and help with crowd control on Sunday. We're doing it at college now."

"Oh, yes. I've seen children getting off a bus at Faith Baptist."

"You've gone to church there?"

"Mother and Father convinced me to go with them a few times."

"It's just like the churches we grew up in."

"Did you like it?" asked Sarah.

"Well, it did have more life than that stuffy Grace Baptist that I grew up in. But I'm not used to that talk about being sinners, and getting saved, and having invitations after every service. It makes me feel uncomfortable. I don't know," she paused. "I'm confused. It's like a war is going on in me."

"That's God's Spirit drawing you like it says in the Bible. Lots of people are praying for you, Elaine," said Bethany softly.

Elaine got up and moved restlessly around the room. Bethany and Sarah just sat quietly, praying silently.

Finally Elaine turned to them and said, "I guess you girls are really shocked that I had Michael when I was so young."

"Well, we know it happens sometimes," answered Sarah.

"We aren't judging you," added Bethany. "We're not perfect. We're sinners too."

"I sure wouldn't call you that!"

"Remember the Bible says we all sin."

"Well, God sure didn't have as much to forgive you for."

"But God doesn't look at it like that. He doesn't rate sin like we think."

"He doesn't?"

"No. Sin is sin in His eyes. We all fall short. We all need to be saved."

"And we all can be," added Sarah.

"That's what Mother and Father have been telling me. I went forward to get baptized and join the church once, but I didn't understand about being a sinner. And then I really became a sinner—I mean I got pretty wild."

"I think it may have been easier for us—we were protected from a lot of stuff like drugs and drinking. Most of our friends went to the Christian school, and most of us tried to do right and follow the teachings and rules."

"I don't know if I would have. I'm pretty stubborn. I probably still would have rebelled—especially if Mark had been around."

"Is that Michael's dad?"

"Yes. I thought he was really cool. He was pretty wild. He got me drinking and smoking pot."

"Really?" questioned Sarah.

"Yes, and he convinced me he loved me so I...well, you know. But when I told him I was pregnant, things changed fast. At first he wanted me not to tell anyone and just get an abortion."

"Oh!" both girls gasped before they could stop themselves.

"But I had heard enough at church to know that wasn't right. I just couldn't do it. It was really hard going through with having Michael though. My parents were so upset, angry, embarrassed, and sad."

"Mark reluctantly married me before Michael was born, but as you know, that didn't work out. We finally divorced. Poor little Michael. I haven't been much of a mom. I guess he would have been better off if we'd given him up for adoption."

She brightened as she added, "But I must admit, Bethany, you have really worked a miracle."

"God worked the miracle," said Bethany.

"But you had a lot to do with it. He is so different. I'm actually beginning to enjoy him. He is so much easier to be around. When he does try to throw a tantrum, my parents don't put up with it. That really surprised me. Mother used to let me and then Michael get away with anything, and she stopped Father from punishing us. They've even been trying to talk me into spanking him!"

"What a change," said Bethany with a chuckle. "I almost lost my job here because your mother thought I was spanking Michael."

"Really? I haven't heard about that."

"Tell us about it, Bethany," begged Sarah.

Bethany described how she was pretending with Michael because he had asked her how her father had spanked her, when Mrs. Davenport walked in and got the wrong impression. "What a night! Everyone was upset."

"Were you spanked, Sarah?" asked Elaine.

"Oh, yes."

"For what?"

"Things like disrespect, sassing, lying, and throwing tantrums."

"And do you agree with Bethany that Michael shouldn't call me by my first name?"

"Well…"

"It's okay. Be honest. I won't be offended. I really want to know what you think, both of you." She glanced at Bethany.

"I think it would be better for him to call you 'Mommy' or 'Mother.' I used 'Mommy' till I got older, and then I switched to 'Mom.' It's a little more personal, less formal than 'Mother,' " Sarah stated.

"I still use Mommy and Daddy most of the time," interjected Bethany.

"Really?" asked Elaine.

"We're a really affectionate family," explained Bethany.

Sarah continued, "I think letting him call you 'Elaine' makes it harder for him to respect you. It puts you down on his level instead of his looking up to you as an authority figure."

"That is a problem," admitted Elaine. "When he was born, I was still a child myself—a child having a child. I wish I'd done things differently."

Bethany said, "It isn't too late to change some things, Elaine. God will forgive you if you ask Him, and He will help you get a new start."

"I guess that is what Mother has done. It's good she told me some of this in letters and on the phone before I got home. Otherwise, I would have died of shock. I would have thought I was in the wrong house," said Elaine laughing. She glanced at her watch. "I guess we better get to bed if we are going to get up early to shop."

"Yes," agreed Bethany. "Goodnight. Thanks for the snack."

"You're welcome. Set your alarms for 4:00 a.m."

"Okay," agreed Bethany with a groan.

"Thanks for everything, Elaine," said Sarah. "It is really nice of your folks to have me."

"It's our pleasure. I'll see you in the morning—bright and early."

"Yes," agreed Sarah with a laugh as she followed Bethany out of the room and headed for the stairs.

In the morning, after cups of cocoa and Danish rolls, they all got into Elaine's convertible, a recent birthday gift from her parents, and drove to the mall. They had to leave the top up, of course. It was cold and looked like it might snow.

When they arrived at the mall, they joined the line forming to wait for the doors to open at 5:00 a.m.

The three girls returned to the Davenports' around noon, tired but triumphant over their bargains. They had all done Christmas shopping and found some things for themselves. At lunch Bethany told Michael she just had to have a little nap, but then she would spend the rest of the afternoon with him until time to leave for Mrs. Carpenter's.

Mr. Davenport quickly said, "That sounds fine, doesn't it, Michael?" Michael rather grudgingly agreed.

Later in the afternoon when Bethany was in Michael's room with him, they looked out the window and saw the first snowflakes falling. He started jumping up and down with excitement and wanted to run right outside. Bethany convinced him to wait until the next morning; she didn't have time to play in the snow and get cleaned up again for the dinner date with Mrs. Carpenter. Bethany was delighted that he agreed, as this would give them something new to do; and they would both enjoy the fresh air.

When John arrived, both Bethany and Michael went downstairs. Bethany told Michael, "In the morning we'll make a snowman. I'll tell you goodnight now because you will be asleep by the time I get home."

Michael gave her a big hug and enthusiastically exclaimed, "I can hardly wait for morning!"

John greeted Michael with a man-to-man handshake. "Hey, big guy, did you hear I get to drive the limousine tonight? I think that's cool!"

"You do? I'm kinda bored with that big ol' car. I like sports cars and convertibles."

"Me too, but remember, I didn't grow up riding in a limo, so for me that is exciting, too."

Elaine called from the head of the stairs. "Come up to your room, Michael. I'll help you build something with your LEGOS®."

"Will you really?"

"Sure, now hurry up."

∽

When she heard the car, Mrs. Carpenter came out on the porch to greet her guests. John teased her, "You weren't anxiously waiting for us to get here, were you?"

"You know I was, and I'm not ashamed to admit it. It is so good to have Bethany here again," she said as she gave her a big hug. She turned to Sarah and greeted her. "I am anxious to get acquainted with you, Sarah. Thank you for joining us."

"Thank you for having me," responded Sarah.

Turning to the Davenports, Mrs. Carpenter said, "Thank you so much for coming and bringing the girls. I am pleased to have you for dinner, also. Come right in. Let me take your coats. Just make yourselves comfortable. Dinner is ready; I just have to set out the food."

"Let me help," offered Bethany.

"Oh, let me, Bethany. You sit down and keep John company." Sarah followed Mrs. Carpenter into the kitchen.

"She is such a sweet girl," Bethany commented to John. "Always doing something for others. I've really been blessed with good roommates. They've all understood about the situation with Scott. They run interference for me when I get phone calls, as you found out."

"It really bothers you to have to talk to him?"

Before she could answer, Mrs. Carpenter called them to the table. "I'll tell you about it later," Bethany promised.

Mrs. Carpenter had used Thanksgiving leftovers to make a delicious casserole which she served with a green salad. She had kept the menu light, knowing they all had enjoyed big meals the day before. Mrs. Carpenter, John, and the Davenports enjoyed hearing the girls tell about their college experiences.

After dinner the two girls helped clear the dishes and fill the dishwasher; then John and Bethany sat down to continue their conversation. Mrs. Carpenter took Sarah to her craft and sewing room. Martha and George Davenport were looking at Mrs. Carpenter's photo albums.

John said, "You were going to tell me why it bothers you so much to talk to Scott."

"It's because he makes me feel so guilty."

"About what, for goodness sake?"

"He says I led him on and hurt him terribly. And I guess he's right."

"What do you mean, Bethany? I can't believe you intentionally did that."

"No, but it ended up that way because I wasn't honest with him right up front about my standards; I honestly thought I could change him."

"Now wait a minute, Bethany. There is no reason for you to beat yourself up. I happen to know Scott knew from the start that you weren't like the other girls he dated, and he wanted to change you."

"How do you know?"

"I overheard him say it to some guys at the office right after the dinner party at the Schaefer's home. It made me so angry!"

"It did?"

"Yes, I wanted to defend you."

"But we hadn't even been introduced yet, had we?"

"No, but somehow I just knew from the moment I saw you that you were…" he paused while he groped for a word, "special." I thought about you a lot after that evening—even before we met at the library."

John continued with his former topic. "Another time at the office Scott confronted me in the hallway and told me to leave his girl alone."

"When was that?"

"After we went to the concert that time with Peter and Donna. I wasn't about to listen to him because I knew he just wasn't right for you and he wasn't being honest with you. Bethany, while he was acting like he was serious about you, he was dating other women."

"You know that for sure?"

"Yes."

"That's weird, especially since he's telling me now that I led him on and how I'm breaking his heart."

John laughed derisively. "Breaking his heart? He doesn't look like a man with a broken heart. When did he say that?"

"In a letter he sent me."

"Just recently?"

"Yes. That's why I don't take his calls. It's hard enough to read it without hearing him say it."

John got up and paced around the room, slamming a fist in his other palm. "Scott irritates me. No, he makes me angry with the way he treats you. What a liar! Bethany, he's still dating other women."

"What? How do you know?"

"One of the women at work almost lost her job for going out with him. They don't allow employees to date each other. He dropped her in a hurry and apologized all over himself—he's working hard at climbing the corporate ladder. Don't worry about poor little Scott's feelings. I think his problem is pride because you broke it off."

"He says I dumped him, hurt him, and caused him to be depressed."

"I'm telling you, Bethany, he's not hurting, and he's not depressed. He might even go so far as to get you to drop out of school and get engaged, and then he would break it off so his ego would feel better. Don't let him put a load of guilt on you. He's a real ladies' man who plays the field constantly and brags about it."

Bethany at first felt angry and then suddenly broke into laughter. She realized she was free of guilt and concern for Scott's feelings at last. "Thanks, John. Once again you came to the rescue. My knight in shining armor." She laughed again, then fell silent with embarrassment. That sounded too romantic.

Bethany quickly switched to a safer topic. "You mentioned you thought Scott's problem was pride. God showed me a verse one day that helped me understand why Scott doesn't see things our way. Let's see, there should be a Bible here somewhere." Spotting one, Bethany went to a side table and picked it up.

"The Lord showed me this passage the day Scott embarrassed me by trying to get on campus." She opened the Bible to Psalm 40 and began to read. *"I waited patiently for the LORD; and he inclined unto me, and heard my cry. 2He brought me up also out of an horrible pit, out of the miry clay, and set my feet upon a rock, and established my goings. 3And he hath put a new song in my mouth, even praise unto our God: many shall see it, and fear, and shall trust in the* LORD. *[4]Blessed is that man that maketh the Lord his trust, and respecteth not the proud, nor such as turn aside to lies."* (Psalm 40:1-4)

"See how the last part of verse four describes Scott?"

John read the passage. "I really like verse one. It's a good reminder. It is so hard to wait patiently sometimes."

He kept his eyes on the Bible. He did not dare look at Bethany, as he wanted so much to be able to tell her how he felt about her. But he was sure the time was not yet right. "Oh, look at verse three. That applies to both of us, doesn't it? I'm hoping the Lord will let me use my singing in whatever He leads me to do."

"Me too. And also the piano. I want to start by going on tour. Auditions will be coming up in a few months for the groups that will be formed for a year from now."

"You mean the summer after your sophomore year?"

"Yes. I'm praying I'll get in the group that goes to the Pacific Northwest. They always visit my home church. They are there for our youth conference. That would be so awesome!"

"I'll remember to pray for that."

"Thanks."

~

Sarah and Mrs. Carpenter returned to the room to see Bethany and John sitting side by side on the couch sharing the open Bible. Mrs. Carpenter smiled with delight, and her eyes sparkled; but she concealed her hopeful feelings.

Sarah sighed inaudibly. He was so cute, but she might as well be a ghost. John had no eyes for anyone but Bethany. What was even more irritating was that either Bethany didn't know John was interested, or she did not care. Maybe she liked to keep guys dangling and hurt them. She was certainly callous toward that other handsome hunk who was chasing her.

Mrs. Carpenter pulled a table to the center of the room. As John went to bring chairs, she explained to Sarah and the Davenports, "This is our tradition. We almost always work on a puzzle together. I hope you don't mind."

"Oh, no. I enjoy jigsaws," Sarah answered.

"We are enjoying your photo albums, so you four just go right ahead and work on the puzzle," Mr. Davenport replied.

Sarah joined Mrs. Carpenter, Bethany and John, leaving the Davenports to enjoy the photos alone. While they worked on the puzzle, they chatted. John said, "It looks like things are going better with Elaine and Michael. I've seen her at church several times with the Davenports. Brother Davenport has asked the whole church to be praying for her. He's not sure she's saved."

"She seems to realize that. We haven't had a real opportunity to try to lead her to the Lord, but we did have a good talk Thursday night and a fun time with her this morning."

"Oh, what did you do?"

Bethany said, "Now, John, can't you guess?"

At first he frowned with concentration; then he smiled. "Ah, the light finally came on. It's the day after Thanksgiving, the biggest shopping day of the year. Did you spend a fortune?"

He listened with indulgent patience as Bethany told him about the cute skirt and blouse set she had found, and Sarah described the costume jewelry that was exactly what she needed to accessorize one of her outfits.

"Well, I'm glad you are having a good time. I'm sure you were ready for some relaxation."

"That's for sure," agreed Bethany.

John then turned the conversation toward Sarah, asking her about her family and home church. "Do you like college life so far?"

"Yes, even more than I had expected. Seeing all those other young people that are excited about serving God is an inspiration."

"How about you, Bethany?"

"It's wonderful."

"Well, I have some news for you, Bethany."

"What's that?"

"I'm definitely going to start there next fall. I have been accepted and sent in my registration fee. I'm all set."

"That's great, John."

Sarah asked, "Do you plan to go into full-time Christian service?"

"Yes."

"As a pastor?"

"That part I'm not clear on yet. I'm praying for the Lord's direction. Will you both pray for me about that?"

"Of course," answered Bethany.

"I will too," responded Sarah.

After about an hour of conversation mixed with John's teasing, Mrs. Carpenter served dessert and coffee. Then the three young people bid her goodbye and stepped out on the porch while the Davenports were thanking Mrs. Carpenter for the enjoyable evening. She, in turn, thanked them for coming.

When they arrived at the Davenports, John stopped at the front entrance. Before the girls got out, he commented, "I hate to see this evening end. I have enjoyed it so much."

"Me too," answered Sarah. "Mrs. Carpenter is so nice; she really put me at ease."

"Didn't I tell you so?" responded Bethany. "Thanks so much for making the arrangements, John. Mrs. Carpenter has been just like another grandmother to me, and I really wanted to see her."

"You are welcome. But it was self-preservation. I would have been in real trouble with her if I had not gotten you there." He laughed, and the girls joined in. "But it wasn't just that; I have really missed our Friday evenings."

"Don't you still spend time with her?"

"Of course. But it isn't the same without you, Bethany."

"Well, it is nice to know I am missed. Goodnight, John."

When he had left to put away the car, Sarah said, "See what I mean?"

"What?"

"You said he wasn't interested in you."

"Not in a romantic way."

"Oh, right."

"I mean it. We are just good friends."

"Do you really expect me to believe that, Bethany?" asked Sarah, as she turned away and hurried up the steps. She entered the house, said goodnight to the Davenports, and immediately went upstairs.

Bethany looked after her and shrugged her shoulders. Then she went into the living room and greeted Elaine.

"Where's Sarah?" asked Elaine.

"I guess she's tired. She headed upstairs."

"Is anything wrong? You look disturbed," inquired Mrs. Davenport.

"I don't know. Sarah seemed upset. Maybe it was just my imagination."

"Do you want anything, Bethany? I'm making myself some hot cocoa," said Elaine.

"Thank you. That does sound good. Shall I run up and ask Sarah if she wants to join us?"

"Please do."

But Sarah turned down the treat, telling Bethany she was going to get ready for bed.

Bethany went thoughtfully back down, thinking about what Sarah had said earlier. She had been sure Sarah was wrong, but now she was remembering some of the things John had said. Could he be interested in her? But even if that were true—and Bethany insisted to herself that it could not be—why did Sarah appear unhappy? Suddenly Bethany snapped her fingers together as the thought, "Sarah must like John." Then she wondered why that thought bothered her.

She was glad to join Elaine for a steaming mug of cocoa and push aside all her troublesome thoughts.

Elaine asked, "Sarah isn't coming?"

"No. She's getting ready for bed."

"What did you girls do tonight at your friend's?"

"After a delicious dinner, Mrs. Carpenter showed Sarah her handwork while John and I visited; then we all worked on a jigsaw puzzle. I love doing them, and of course there's no time for anything like that at college."

"What did she fix for dinner? It would be hard to have company for dinner the day after Thanksgiving."

"She kept it light for that reason. She made a casserole from leftover turkey and a salad."

"I'll have to file that away for the future."

"Are you interested in homemaking? I thought you wanted to be a career woman."

"Since I already have a family started, I'll have to do both. I find I am getting more and more interested in the homemaking part. I'm looking forward to that apartment with just Michael and me."

"Well, good. It won't be easy trying to juggle both."

"It's going to be quite a change for me after all the traveling and partying. Like I said before, I have been thoroughly spoiled."

"Well, you seem to be wanting to make a change."

"Yes, I really do."

"Don't forget the place to start is with Jesus."

"If He'll have me."

"Of course He will have you. He doesn't turn away anyone who comes to Him with a sincere heart."

"Bethany, you don't know all the things I've done."

"Jesus will forgive anyone for anything. Think of the Bible stories. Look how He used Moses even though he had killed a man. He forgave David for adultery and murder. Peter denied Him, but he turned out to be the leader of the other apostles. And the list goes on."

"I hadn't thought about all that. Every time I talk to you, you leave me with lots to think about. I'm not getting any sleep with you here," laughed Elaine. "I'll see you in the morning. Are you ready for snowball fights and building snowmen?"

"Yes, but I may have to borrow a few things from you, if you don't mind. I didn't really come prepared for playing in the snow. It should be deep enough to have lots of fun; it was coming down pretty heavy when we came home."

"Good. That will make Michael very happy."

"Yes. Are you going to join us outside?"

"Sure. I have to learn to keep Michael occupied. Maybe I'll get some ideas from you."

"I'm no expert. I just try to play with him at his level and do the things he enjoys."

"Well, he sure likes having you around. He has really missed you."

"I miss him, too. Goodnight, Elaine."

"Goodnight. See you in the morning. I'll dig out some extra gloves and things."

"Thanks."

～

In the morning Sarah also decided to go out and enjoy the fresh snowfall. Fortunately, she and Bethany had both brought their culottes and warm socks. They borrowed gloves and scarves from Elaine. The four of them built forts and had snowball fights, made "angels" in the snow, and built a giant snowman. Michael was thoroughly entertained, basked in all the attention, and was delighted with the snowman. They took one break for a quick sandwich and mugs of steaming cocoa and then played for two more hours. Finally, even Michael was tired, cold, and ready to go inside.

They took turns resting and taking warm soaking baths, and finally all were ready for the rest of the afternoon and evening. Elaine and Sarah came downstairs first and sat by the fire in the living room talking quietly. Elaine had grown comfortable with the girls and began to open up more with Sarah. She told her that for years she had been smoking marijuana at parties. She had traveled to Europe with some of her "party friends," and they had no problem finding places to hang out, dance, and smoke in each city they had visited. She told Sarah that she didn't really see or remember much of the first cities they visited. She didn't have many photos of those places either. Now she was sorry she had not taken advantage of the great opportunity to learn about the other cultures.

When Bethany came downstairs, she remembered that Mr. Davenport had requested that she meet with him when she was done playing outside. So she went to his study door and knocked. He invited her in and arranged two chairs facing each other. When they were both seated, he asked, "Bethany, are you aware that I received a phone call recently from Scott Lancaster?"

"Yes, he told me about it. I am so sorry he bothered you."

"Don't worry about that. I'm just concerned about his, or should I say, your plans?"

"They aren't my plans, Mr. Davenport. I have been firm and direct with him that I am not marrying him. I have even refused to take his calls. It's very annoying. He came to the college to take me away and caused me a lot of embarrassment. I am hoping he has gotten the message and will just leave me alone."

"Well, that is a load off my mind and a great relief. It really confused me when he asked if you could stay with us until the wedding. I thought you had broken off with him and had started dating John Holman. John is such a fine young man."

"I'm not really dating John, Mr. Davenport. He is just a very good friend who was helping me through a difficult time. I'm not ready for another relationship."

"Well, that's probably very wise. You are still young. There's plenty of time for serious relationships later. Thanks for clearing up this matter."

"Thank you for your concern," said Bethany as she rose to leave. She turned back at the door. "Oh, Mr. Davenport, I want you to know, I have kept my parents informed of everything that has been happening."

"Good, good. I'm glad to hear it. You are a fine young woman, Bethany."

"Thank you, sir."

Bethany went to the living room to join the other girls. Martha Davenport and Michael had also wandered in to enjoy the fire. Michael was telling his grandmother all about their fun in the snow. Soon it was time to go in for a delicious dinner of homemade turkey soup, French bread, and a salad.

After dinner Michael begged Bethany to spend her last evening with him in his room, and she readily agreed. The other two girls again settled together by the fire. They talked of other things for a while, and then Elaine seemed compelled to continue unburdening herself to Sarah. She told her how she had started tiring of the drinking and partying. She found herself waking each day with a hangover and feeling sick—physically and emotionally. She skipped a few parties and instead did some sightseeing. She discovered she actually could have fun apart from the excesses of socializing.

While they were talking, Bethany played with Michael until it was close to his normal bedtime. She encouraged him to get ready for bed. After he had brushed his teeth and was in his pajamas, she took him to say goodnight to his grandparents. When she and Michael stood at the entrance to the living room, Bethany could tell that Sarah and Elaine were in earnest conversation, but Elaine stopped and gave Michael a hug and kiss. "I hadn't noticed the time, Bethany. Thanks for being a nanny for the night. I didn't mean for you to have to do that."

"I enjoyed it, Elaine. I'll take Michael up and tuck him in if you want to continue your conversation with Sarah."

"That would be great, if you don't mind. Is that okay with you, Michael?"

"Sure."

"Goodnight then."

As Bethany and Michael left, Elaine turned back to Sarah and finished telling her about her trip. "I found a new set of friends—some others around my age who were also more interested in some sightseeing. I enjoyed the beautiful architecture of the old cathedrals, and we went through some of the old family castles that have been opened to the public. You saw the pictures I took. I think my traveling is what rekindled the interest in interior decorating that's been lying dormant.

"But I'll be honest with you, Sarah. I didn't completely stop partying. I was more cautious, drank less, and quit using pot. Some of the others were experimenting with the heavier stuff, but I left that alone. I'm too much of a chicken for that."

"That's a good thing to be a chicken about," interjected Sarah, smiling.

"I discovered it felt good to wake up without a hangover and feel like enjoying another day. What's strange is, I felt like something outside of myself was pulling me away from all that."

"That was because your dad and Bethany were praying for you."

"Oh! I hadn't put that together," said Elaine thoughtfully. After a few minutes of comfortable silence (which Sarah spent praying silently), Elaine continued. "I really think I want to go in a different direction, try to be a better mother to Michael, get training, and support both of us."

"What about letting God help you with all that? How about getting saved? You said you aren't sure you really were born again as a child."

"Sarah, there are things I have to change in my life, things I'll have to stop doing—drinking, partying, and smoking pot, although I haven't had a joint for several weeks and don't miss it much."

"You've got it a little mixed up, Elaine. You're trying to do it backward."

"What do you mean?"

"You don't clean yourself up first. You come to Jesus; then let Him do the cleaning up."

"But from what I've heard, He doesn't approve of those things."

"That's true, and those are just the outward things that show. There are many other things, like your thoughts and motives in your heart, that He will work on. You come to Him with trust and a sincere, willing heart, and then His Holy Spirit will be inside you helping you with all those issues. If you are sincerely sorry for your past sins and want God to change you, you can be saved. You do believe the Bible is God's Word?"

"Yes."

"And that Jesus is God's Son, God in a human body?"

"Yes."

"And do you believe that He died, was buried, and rose again?"

"I believe all of that."

"So the only question is your willingness to give your life over to Him. You have given the impression you aren't thrilled with the results of doing things your way. Are you ready to accept Him as your Saviour and receive a new life?"

Elaine rose to her feet. "It's getting late, Sarah. We're both tired, and I need a little time. I thank you very much for your concern. I'll see you in the morning. Goodnight."

Sarah was disappointed and afraid she had pushed too hard. On her way to bed, she stopped at the room where Bethany was staying. She told her about the conversation; then they prayed together for Elaine's salvation.

When the girls awoke Sunday morning, they both immediately thought about Elaine and started praying. They were excited and hopeful when they saw her come downstairs dressed for church. Michael responded the same way, but openly.

"Elaine, are you going to church with us today?"

"Yes, I am. But Michael, do you think you could start calling me Mom?"

"Sure."

"I know it will be hard to remember at first. You'll have to break the habit of calling me by my name and train yourself to use Mom."

"I'll try real hard if that's what you want, Elaine—I mean Mom."

As everyone burst into laughter, Michael ducked his head with embarrassment. Elaine put her arms around him in a hug. When he looked up and saw her smiling lovingly at him, he looked around and joined in the laughter.

"That was pretty funny, huh?"

"Yes, Michael, that was pretty funny. I'm sorry I laughed, but…"

"It's okay, Bethany," answered Michael.

The Davenports entered the room. "What was so funny?"

Michael said with a hint of pride, "Mom asked me to call her Mom, and I said, 'Okay, if that's what you want, Elaine.' "

George and Martha laughed.

"It just slipped out, but I want to call her Mom."

"That sounds like a great idea," said George Davenport. "Is everyone ready? It's time to leave for church."

When they arrived at Faith Baptist Church, the three girls went to the young adults' class. Donna had arrived early and had saved an empty pew. There was just enough room for all three of them to join her. John came in just before starting time; he had been picking people up with the van.

∽

Sarah watched John, and she was sure she saw disappointment register on his face when he had to sit in the row behind them. She pushed down the feelings this aroused—she wanted to concentrate on Elaine. She had kept up a running, silent prayer that Elaine would accept the Lord.

After class John walked with the four young women to the auditorium. He led them to an empty pew and managed to station himself next to Bethany. Elaine was on the other side, then Sarah and Donna.

The pastor preached on being thankful for all Christ did for mankind on the Cross. Elaine was so moved by his description of the Crucifixion that she had to pull out a handkerchief. At the invitation she whispered to Sarah, "Will you go up with me?"

Sarah was ecstatic as she nodded her head in the affirmative and led the way out of the pew. When they got to the altar, Elaine told Sarah she wanted to be saved and asked her to pray with her. Bethany stole a peek, and when she saw them leave, she surmised Elaine had gotten saved and was going to be baptized. Bethany asked John to get Michael from his class, which he was happy to do.

Michael had experienced this with his grandmother, and this time he knew not to speak out. But he added his hearty "Amen" to the men's when Elaine came up out of the water.

After the service Michael rushed to Elaine and wrapped his arms around her. "Oh, E…Mom, you got saved!"

"Yes, and it was partly because of the change I saw in you."

"Wow!" was all he could manage in response.

Elaine reached for Sarah with tears in her eyes, murmuring, "Thank you, thank you. And you, too, Bethany," as she turned to her and gave her a hug also. The Davenports joined in the celebration, and each gave their daughter a hug, with tears in their eyes. "Now I really can have a fresh start!" exclaimed Elaine. She drew Michael to her, put her arm around him, and they walked out of the church together.

CHAPTER FOUR

The Green-Eyed Monster

"Let us walk honestly...not in strife and envying."
(Romans 13:13)

Sarah sat with Donna during the train ride back to college from Detroit. She spoke to Donna in a low tone that Bethany could not overhear, telling her about her conversations with Elaine. It had been a positive boost to Sarah's self-confidence that she had been used by God to help Elaine to make a decision for Christ.

Then Sarah described their outdoor activities of Saturday morning with enthusiasm. But her countenance changed when Donna asked, "How did you like Mrs. Carpenter? Did you have a nice visit with her Friday night?"

"Oh, Mrs. Carpenter was sweet, and John's a really nice guy, but being there kind of ruined the whole weekend for me."

"Why?"

"Because it upsets me to see the way Bethany treats John."

"What do you mean?"

Sarah ignored the question and changed the subject. "Mr. Davenport had a private talk with Bethany on Saturday. She told me that it had something to do with that guy who wants to marry her. I bet Mr. Davenport is shocked that she's stringing two guys along at the same time."

"Sarah!" exclaimed Donna with surprise.

"What?"

"It's nothing like that."

"Oh no? They're both madly in love with her."

"Shush. She might hear you."

"So? I'm sure she knows that."

"That's just the point. She doesn't," whispered Donna.

"Oh, right," answered Sarah sarcastically and then ended the conversation by opening a book and beginning to read.

Bethany was oblivious to the conversation between Donna and Sarah. She spent the time on the train writing thank-you notes to the Davenports, Mrs. Carpenter, and John. She had brought note cards with her, knowing that once she got back on campus the hectic schedule would begin.

When they were back on campus and in their dorm room, Donna finally found a few minutes alone with Bethany. "What happened while you and Sarah were in Detroit? She seems upset with you. It's not like her to be critical and negative."

"I don't know. She seemed to have a lot on her mind after we visited Mrs. Carpenter Friday night. She just seemed to get distant and cool. Maybe she was disappointed that John didn't show some interest. John and I talked a lot while she and Mrs. Carpenter were looking at craft stuff. I thought she was enjoying herself. I hope she didn't feel like we were excluding her. Oh, I just can't stand it when someone's upset with me. I'll try to talk to her as soon as possible."

This proved difficult, as Sarah was avoiding being alone with Bethany. When Bethany did finally manage a few private moments, Sarah refused to open up about what was troubling her. Bethany tried to apologize for possibly hurting her feelings, but Sarah brushed it off with, "There's nothing to apologize for." She then hurried from the room, leaving Bethany disturbed and confused.

Bethany shared her disappointment with Donna. "I can't get Sarah to open up. I just don't know what's going on. She said there wasn't anything for me to apologize about. Has she said anything to you?"

"Not much, but I think you're right that it has something to do with John."

Bethany reacted to this thought with anxiousness, which she didn't understand. She asked herself why she should care if Sarah might be interested in John. After all, he and Bethany were just good friends. And hadn't she decided to leave guys out of her life for a while? Pushing aside her thoughts, she asked Donna, "Will you try to talk to Sarah again?"

"Okay."

The next day Donna found an opportunity to talk to Sarah privately. "Sarah, what is wrong between you and Bethany? She is really upset about your attitude toward her, and she doesn't know what she did to you."

"She didn't do anything to me."

"Then why are you so cool to her?"

"Donna, I used to think Bethany was this sweet, sincere Christian; now I'm not so sure."

"What do you mean?"

"I don't like it when girls string guys along, seeing how many trophies they can accumulate."

"Trophies?"

"Yes. You know, the guys fall at her feet, and she just pushes them away and ignores them. I think she likes breaking their hearts."

"Oh, Sarah, that's just not true. You don't know all the facts."

"I've seen enough to think I do."

"What guys are you talking about?"

"There's lots of guys around here that look at her longingly and try to get her attention, and she's just cool to them. But I especially meant that tall, dark, handsome dude who came here to see her. And John has eyes for no one but Bethany. I thought he was cute and a really nice guy, but he hardly knew I existed. He treats Bethany tenderly, hangs on her every word, and looks at her lovingly. And how does Bethany respond? Oh, she's polite, but she treats him like a friend or a big brother. I don't think that's what he wants! And she just throws away the expensive cards that other guy sends her."

"Scott," interjected Donna.

"She just tramples all over both of their hearts."

"Sarah, that's not fair. It really isn't like that."

"Isn't it? You're just prejudiced in her favor. You think she's Miss Perfection."

"Sarah, what has happened to you? Let me explain some things."

"No, no. Just forget it, Donna," answered Sarah as she walked away. "You can't explain away what I can see with my own eyes."

Donna reported back to Bethany. "I tried, but Sarah won't listen. I wanted to explain to her about Scott."

"Scott?"

"Yes, she thinks you're breaking his poor little heart," answered Donna with sarcasm.

"But why should that make her this upset? She avoids me as much as possible and hardly speaks to me."

"I know. It's getting uncomfortable for everyone in our room."

"It just doesn't make any sense to me."

"Bethany, I think she's jealous, and maybe she doesn't even realize it."

"Jealous of me? Why? I've told her John is just a friend and that it is all over between Scott and me."

"I guess she's not convinced," answered Donna cautiously. It was all she could do to keep from blurting out, "Can't you see that John loves you?" But she had promised John she would keep his secret until he felt Bethany's heart was healed. Donna hoped Scott would leave Bethany alone. Then maybe Bethany could think about someone else—like John, hopefully.

∽

Sarah's mood improved somewhat when she was asked for a lunch date. The young man named Paul was tall and nice-looking. He laughed and joked a lot but also had his serious moments. He was the same man Cindy had spoken to Bethany about, and she had followed Bethany's advice and introduced him to Sarah. Previously they had eaten dinner together and sat in chapel next to each other, but weeks went by between these "dates." Unfortunately, just before Sarah left to meet Paul for a third date, Bethany had opened and read a note out loud that came from John. He was responding to the one from Bethany thanking him for taking them to see Mrs. Carpenter. He had ended his note with: "It was great seeing you, Bethany. Things just aren't the same around here without you."

Sarah had said, "See what I mean, Bethany?"

She had been irritated when Bethany answered, "He is just talking about Mrs. Carpenter's missing me, or he misses my singing duets with him at church."

Sarah had not been able to shake off her irritation and was not in a happy mood during the date with Paul. She did not realize how much it showed in her countenance.

The next time Paul saw Bethany, he asked her, "What has happened to Sarah? She was so sweet and cheerful—like sunshine everywhere she went. And now it's like a cloud came over."

"I don't know. Pray for her. I think she's struggling with something, but I don't know what it is. I feel like it has something to do with me, but I can't think of anything I did to offend her."

One afternoon Cindy burst into the room and instructed her three roommates to get ready to go to Wal-Mart. She had made friends with a junior girl named Julie, who was considered an "approved girl." This meant the freshmen girls could go off campus with her. Julie had her own car and was willing to take all of them. Immediately there was a flurry of activity as the girls got ready to take advantage of Julie's offer. It was an opportune time, as none of them were scheduled to work and it was after classes. However, Sarah did not join in the preparations.

Cindy asked her, "Aren't you coming?"

"No, I don't want to."

Cindy took her aside. "What's wrong, Sarah? Why don't you want to take this chance to escape the dorms for a while?"

"I have to be around Bethany enough as it is. I don't need an hour in the car with her. This will be a nice break from her."

"Sarah! What brought this on?"

Sarah simply shrugged her shoulders and gave no answer.

When the girls were ready to leave, Bethany noticed Sarah was not joining them. "Sarah, aren't you coming? I thought you needed some stuff and wanted to go shopping."

"I don't want to go today," answered Sarah.

Bethany surmised that Sarah's unwillingness to accompany them was probably because of her, and much of her enthusiasm about shopping and spending time with friends seeped away. The other two girls felt bad about the situation, and all of them were perplexed as to what had caused the change in the normally sweet Sarah. They were all a little droopy when they got in the car. Julie asked, "Where's Sarah?"

All three answered simultaneously, "She didn't want to come."

"What's wrong?" asked Julie.

Cindy answered, "We don't know. She seems to be upset with Bethany."

"Didn't you two spend Thanksgiving together at your friends' house?"

"Yes, my former employers'. I just don't know what happened, and she won't talk to me."

"Goodness. I hope you can work things out."

"Me too," said Bethany, almost in tears.

"Yes, it's affecting all of us," Cindy added. "Sarah's miserable, and she's making all of us miserable. It is so unlike her."

Julie said, "Why don't we pray about this right now? Who wants to start off? I promise I'll keep my eyes open while I pray along," she said laughing.

Bethany prayed first, followed by the others. Then they talked of other things until they reached Wal-Mart.

One day Donna returned to the dorm room and found Sarah there alone. Donna felt impressed that this was a good time to try once again to talk to Sarah. She began, "Sarah, I know you don't want to talk about it, but I really think we have to clear up the problem between you and Bethany."

Sarah put up her hand to stop her, but Donna ignored it.

"Sarah, you are naturally a sweet-spirited girl. It's not like you to treat anyone like you've been treating Bethany. I'm not sure what the problem is, but from things you have said, I think it has to do with John and Scott. I don't know Scott personally, but Bethany has told me about the situation. A girl has a right to change her mind, doesn't she? They were never officially engaged. She broke it off before that happened. He had pulled her down spiritually—she had backslidden. When she got back into a good church, she realized it and knew she had to break up. But Scott is very prideful and didn't want to accept that."

"How do you know? You just said you don't know him."

"I recently called John to verify everything Bethany told me. He and Scott work in the same office. He told me Scott was dating other women the whole time he dated Bethany, and he still is. He isn't acting like a man with a broken heart."

"But what about John? I could tell he really cares for Bethany."

"He is trying to hide that from her."

"Why?"

"Because he doesn't want her to turn to him on the rebound. He wants to be sure she is totally free of feelings for Scott before he lets her know how he feels."

"How can she not know?" asked Sarah skeptically.

"Because she was so preoccupied with getting over her feelings for Scott and getting ready for college. And she met John while she still cared for Scott. John reminds her of her dad, so she thinks of him as a brother."

"I don't know, Donna. Are you sure she hasn't fooled both you and John?"

"I'm sure. If you will just look at her and the situation with an open mind and pray about it, I think you'll see I'm right. Will you at least do that?"

"Sure, Donna. Now let's drop it for now, okay?"

"I'll be praying," answered Donna.

The very next day in chapel services, the preacher just "happened" to preach from Romans 13:13: *"Let us walk honestly, as in the day; not in rioting and drunkenness, not in chambering and wantonness, not in strife and envying."*

After reading the verse, he said, "Today I am taking the first phrase and the last phrase of this verse to concentrate on. So it would read, *'Let us walk honestly…not in strife and envying.'* The Apostle Paul, under the inspiration of the Holy Spirit, wrote this passage as an admonition, a warning, and a commandment. We Christians, brothers and sisters in the Lord, fellow church members, workers together in the same ministry, friends, maybe roommates, whatever the relationship, we are all still just forgiven sinners. We all have the sin nature. We are not always going to feel harmonious. We are not going to agree, so therein is the potential for strife.

"We aren't all going to have the same successes in our lives—whether it be in our secular jobs or church work. Or maybe it's in your love life—I know you are all looking for mates while you are here." There was some laughter, and then he continued. "Now you cannot deny it—just look around in this room. How many couples are sitting together?"

After a ripple of laughter, he went on, "We are all weak, sinful humans, and we will be tempted to engage in strife and envy. Often the two go together. In Galatians 5:16-22, strife and envy are both listed in the works of the flesh. Should we desire those traits in our lives? No! Paul is telling us these are works of the flesh, and the flesh lusts against the Spirit. He tells us to walk in the Spirit, and then we won't fulfill the lust of the flesh. Too often we yield to the flesh instead of the Spirit.

"Let's look at verse 26 of Galatians 5, which says, *'Let us not be desirous of vain glory, provoking one another, envying one another.'* Provoking would cause strife, and again we are told, in the same verse, not to envy. The Lord also covered this subject while He met with Moses on the mountain. Let's look together at Exodus 20:17 and read one of the Ten Commandments which says, '*Thou shalt not covet thy neighbour's house, thou shalt not covet thy neighbour's wife, nor his manservant, nor his maidservant, nor his ox, nor his ass, nor any thing that is thy neighbour's.*' Coveting and envying are the same. According to this verse, envy is serious business in the Lord's eyes.

"Young ladies, are you coveting someone else's wardrobe, thereby being envious of another because she can buy nicer clothes than you? What about envying another's hair or good looks? Are you coveting another one's boyfriend, or are you jealous because she has a boyfriend and you don't?"

"Young men…" Sarah did not hear the rest of the sermon. She had seen herself in the speaker's words. She had been telling herself that she was just reacting to Bethany's actions. Now she was forced to admit that she was envious and jealous because Bethany had two handsome men interested in her. To tell the truth, she was also envious of Bethany's poise, good looks, and outgoing personality. Sarah thought about how she had treated Bethany and remembered what Donna had told her the night before. Feeling more and more convicted, she rushed forward when the altar call was given. As she tried to pray, tears began falling, and finally she got up and hastily left, knowing she was barely holding back racking sobs. She found a restroom, went into a stall, and let them come. When she could finally stop, she quietly prayed for God's forgiveness and the courage to apologize to Bethany.

Finally, Sarah left the restroom and rushed to the dorm room to repair the damage to her eyes and makeup. She hoped she wouldn't see Bethany yet. She wanted to talk to Donna some more first. She prayed the Lord would work that out for her.

She had her back to the door but could see it in her mirror. She was relieved when she saw Donna come in. She rushed to her. "Donna, please finish what you have been trying to tell me. I've been too stubborn to listen. I feel so awful." The tears started again.

Donna grabbed a tissue and thrust it at her. "I'm glad to see you are letting the Lord speak to you, Sarah. Everything will be okay."

"I don't know if Bethany will ever forgive me," sobbed Sarah.

"I know she will, Sarah. Relax. Come on, quit crying. She is not angry, just very concerned. The Lord will forgive you, too. You did ask Him at the altar, right?"

"Oh, yes. That sermon really showed me what a horrible person I have been. I let the green-eyed monster take over."

"The green-eyed monster?"

"That's what my grandmother called jealousy. I thought I was too good of a Christian to ever let that happen. I guess that means I had pride too. I really have been rotten." She cried even harder.

"Sarah, Sarah, it's okay." Donna hugged her stricken roommate. "Hush. Let me tell you what you wanted to know, and then you can calm down before you talk to Bethany."

"Oh, I dread that so much," wailed Sarah.

"Now don't start again," Donna hastily answered. "Dry your eyes and listen." Sarah quieted and Donna began, "Scott was trying to get Bethany to be a modern woman. He wanted her to be a career woman. And he tried to get her to kiss him."

"Are you serious? How could he do that? Did they date alone?"

"Unfortunately, yes. One time he took her to a Christmas party in his car. She thought it would be okay because it wasn't far. Another time he tricked her by taking the other couple home first, and once it was in a garden at a wedding reception.

"She also realized he wouldn't be a spiritual leader—he didn't go soul winning or even attend church faithfully. So she had good reasons for breaking up with him, and I already told you how he was playing the field the whole time."

"And you really think that she doesn't know that John likes her?"

"I really believe that. I have a terrible time keeping my promise to John, keeping my mouth shut about it," answered Donna.

"I have been unfair to her, and really, the Lord showed me I was just jealous. It seems like Bethany has everything, you know? Beauty, talent, personality, and two guys wanting her. But it is wrong of me to envy her, and I've caused all kinds of strife. I feel awful, but I try to remember that the Lord promises to forgive me. I hope she will, too."

"I know she will. Sarah, shall we pray together now? We have about ten minutes before Bethany's due to be back here."

"Oh, yes, please. Let's pray that I'll make things right and I'll have the right words and courage to do it!"

When Bethany entered the room, Donna slipped out, leaving the two girls alone. Sarah hesitantly approached Bethany. "I need to apologize to you, Bethany. I have treated you awful and made everyone in this room uncomfortable. I made myself believe I was justified in being critical of how you treated Scott and John. I wanted to believe you were stringing them along and being distant to guys here just to get a bunch of men as trophies. Yesterday Donna explained some things to me; and today, after I got right with the Lord, she told me more about why you had to break up with Scott. In chapel the Lord showed me I was jealous of you."

"But why, Sarah? I'm nothing great."

"You are beautiful, self-confident, and talented. You had two handsome men calling you. I was envious. It was sinful, and I'm sorry. Will you still be my friend, Bethany, even though I was jealous and unkind to you?"

Bethany responded with a question of her own. "Donna told you about Scott and me, right?"

"Yes."

"Can you still be my friend, knowing how backslidden I was last year?"

Sarah looked at Bethany with a question in her expression. She saw Bethany's friendly smile and burst out laughing. "Of course. But will you forgive me?"

Bethany reached for Sarah and gave her a hug. "You are forgiven. I want us to be good friends. You are one of the sweetest girls I've ever known, and you have talents and abilities I am trying to copy."

"Like what?" asked Sarah, astonished.

"Organization, time management, the gift of caring, your talent for decorating and making those beautiful cards, always looking so put together. I could go on and on. I have to be careful not to envy you! That was a really good message today in chapel."

"It certainly was," agreed Sarah. She was pensive for a few minutes. "You know, Bethany, I started having negative thoughts, and I let them remain and fester. They finally became actions and hurtful words."

"My mom told me once that she uses a Bible verse she memorized to keep from doing that. She made me memorize it, too. It's II Corinthians 10:5, *'Casting down imaginations, and every high thing that exalteth itself against the knowledge of God, and bringing into captivity every thought to the obedience of Christ.'* "

"Oh, that is good. I'll have to memorize that, too. Thanks, Bethany."

The two girls hugged again. Sarah said, "I am glad to have that behind me. Now I need to apologize to Donna and Cindy. Then the atmosphere in this room can get back to normal."

Sarah apologized to both girls at the first opportunity. Everyone was relieved. Having the spirit of love and acceptance dominating instead of envy and strife made life so much easier.

They could concentrate on their studies and other responsibilities and start thinking about Christmas with real anticipation and happy hearts. Bethany had received a ticket for her trip home from her parents. She could hardly wait—there was now only one more week of classes before Christmas break.

That Sunday on the bus, Bethany and Donna once again announced that they would be gone, and this time for two weekends. They assured the children that they would be attending church in their hometowns and encouraged them to be faithful to church if they possibly could. Bethany said, "We want to be with our families for Christmas, but we will miss all of you." Donna nodded her head in agreement.

Christmas at Home

"...Come home...and refresh thyself...."
(I Kings 13:7)

On the way to the airport, Bethany was seated next to a girl named Kathleen Durham. Her family attended Bethany's home church in Tacoma, Washington, and they often fellowshipped with Bethany's family. Bethany was one year older than Kathleen, and Kathleen had a brother the same age as Bethany's brother Brian. She had also started Bible college in the fall.

The girls discovered that not only had their parents purchased tickets for the same flight, but they were also seatmates. Bethany told Kathleen, "Having you to talk to will help the time go more quickly. After a year and a half away from home, I can't wait to get to Sea-Tac and see my family."

Kathleen said, "Bethany, I don't know how you did it! I don't think I could have."

"The Lord helps you do what you have to do. I cried a few times, especially at Thanksgiving and Christmas. But I was determined to stick it out."

"It must have been awful. Did the time just drag by for you?"

"Oh, no! Not with Michael around—the little boy I cared for. There was never a dull moment."

"Only a bratty little kid for company? I would have gone crazy."

"I had evenings off, and I went to church with the family. I met a guy at church who captured my attention."

"What is he like?"

Before Bethany could answer, they arrived at the airport. When they had completed check-in and were seated next to each other in the waiting area, Kathleen pursued the subject.

"You said you met a guy. That sounds interesting."

"That's what I thought at first, but I ended up having to break it off."

"Why?"

"He didn't have our standards. He wanted to date without chaperones, hold hands, and kiss. I had a hard time getting him to leave me alone even after I got to college."

"Oh, he's the one who tried to get on campus?"

"You heard about that," murmured Bethany, embarrassed.

"I'm sorry, Bethany. I shouldn't have blurted that out. You know how that kind of thing gets around. It's not like it happens every day."

"I know. Anyway, I guess he finally got convinced that I was serious about breaking up. Now I'm trying to forget all about him."

"That must be hard. I heard he is really handsome."

"He is. But other things are more important in a guy; and he definitely doesn't fit with what I want in a boyfriend or someday a husband. Realizing that makes it a whole lot easier. When he wanted to get engaged, I asked him a bunch of questions. He isn't like our dads—not a strong, serious Christian. He doesn't go soul winning, and I don't think he tithes or reads his Bible on a regular basis. He wanted me to be a career woman and was not interested in having a family. We really did not have much in common."

It was time to board their plane. Bethany was happy to get off the subject of Scott. When they were settled and the plane was in the air, Kathleen asked Bethany what it was like to work as a nanny. Bethany told her about the beautiful house and grounds and the lovely suite of rooms she had used. She also shared some of the frustrations and problems with which she had had to deal.

"How did you manage to stick it out? I think I would have been on a plane home after the first week."

"I don't know. I guess I'm just stubborn about giving up. And in the end some really great things happened in the family for whom I worked. The grandfather re-dedicated himself to Christ; his wife, the cook, and the chauffeur were saved. Little Michael also got saved, and it really made a difference in him."

"Wow! Was that all because of you?"

"More like in spite of me. I was backslidden for a while."

"What do you mean?"

"I spent too much time thinking about Scott and talking to him on the phone. My personal devotions suffered. He got me to questioning the standards with which I have been reared, but thank God I went to a revival meeting and got things right. But the Lord is so gracious and forgiving—He did let me lead them to salvation.

"When Sarah and I went there for Thanksgiving, she got to witness to Michael's mother, and she accepted the Lord. That was really exciting."

"I'm confused. If Michael has a mother around, why were you caring for him?"

"Her folks had given her a trip to Europe."

"Oh, my! It must be nice."

"Really, we are much better off. She and Michael were spoiled and undisciplined, and now she has issues to overcome with which we will never have to struggle."

"I hadn't thought of that."

"Being with the Davenports has really made me appreciate my family and our church. Oh, I am so happy to be going home for two weeks."

"I know. There will be so many fun things to do. This year we can go to Mrs. Painter's party for the graduates."

"Yes, and I'm looking forward to working on the bus route and seeing how the kids have grown; and I want to help my mom in her children's church class. There's so much, and I'm ready for all of it. Then we'll go back to school and rest up from our break!"

Kathleen clamped her hand over her mouth to muffle her laughter. "You're probably right about that!"

Both girls took a nap until the stewardess came by to offer a snack. After eating, they read books each had brought.

When the plane arrived at Sea-Tac Airport, located between Seattle and Tacoma, it seemed like it took an eternity to disembark, walk into the terminal, and finally make their way to the baggage claim area.

Bethany looked around and immediately spotted her brother and sister holding a banner between them that read WELCOME HOME, BETHANY. They were enthusiastically jumping up and down, waving and yelling her name. Bethany ran toward them but found herself in her mother's embrace before she reached them. "Mommy, Mommy," choked out Bethany as she burst into tears. When her mother released her, Mr. Prescott enveloped her in his strong arms. "Oh, Daddy, it is so good to be hugging you again," Bethany whispered as tears streamed down her face. He gave her a tighter squeeze and passed her to her eager siblings.

Betsy and Brian each gave her a hug. Brian was dry-eyed, but he cleared his throat suspiciously. Betsy was weeping and croaked, "I missed you so much!"

"Me, too," said Bethany as they pulled apart and wiped away their tears.

Mr. Prescott took charge. "Let's get your luggage and get you home. Even though we can all sleep in tomorrow, we don't want to stay up too late. We are going to need energy for all the things we have planned for the next two weeks."

Brian and Mr. Prescott divided her luggage between them, and they all headed for the car. Betsy grabbed Bethany's arm and chattered non-stop as they followed their dad through the airport. "Tonight we're going to decorate the tree—we've been waiting so you could help us."

"Thank you. It's usually up right after Thanksgiving. How could you stand it?" asked Bethany with a giggle.

"It was my idea to wait."

"Oh, Betsy, you are so sweet."

"We put out the rest of the decorations. I hope you don't mind."

"Not at all. I was looking forward to coming home to a decorated house. It's a perfect plan."

"Did you decorate your dorm room with the things we sent?"

"Of course, and it looked as nice as a dorm room can."

"Next week Daddy is taking time off, and we're taking inner tubes to Paradise."

Bethany squealed with delight. It had been three years since she had been to the popular winter play area on Mt. Rainier. "This is going to be a great vacation!"

When they finally got to the car and everyone was settled in, Mrs. Prescott peppered Bethany with questions all the way home. Bethany filled her mother in on the Davenport family and everything that had occurred over the Thanksgiving holiday she had spent with them. Betsy was biding her time until she could have Bethany's undivided attention to ask all her questions about every aspect of college life.

When they arrived at their house, Bethany got out of the van and walked outside instead of entering the house from the garage. The rest of the family started taking in her luggage, but Bethany was totally oblivious to this fact. She was walking around in the rain looking at the decorated house and yard. Her family had left the lights on when they left, knowing that Bethany would enjoy seeing them when she arrived.

Done with her perusing of the outside decorations, she tried the front door. It was still locked. Playfully she rang the doorbell repeatedly until Brian arrived on the run and flung it open. "All right, all right," he greeted her with a grin. "We heard you already."

"Thanks," answered Bethany as she rushed in and looked all around. Bethany hurried from room to room, seeing all the familiar objects in their usual places. In the living room a beautiful undecorated evergreen tree stood in front of the bay window.

Bethany exclaimed, "Oh, you already have it up, all ready for decorating. Has it been there like that since Thanksgiving?"

"No," said Betsy. "We did all the other decorating right after Thanksgiving, but we just put up the tree yesterday."

"Did you and Mom go shopping on Black Friday?"

"Yes, I'll have to show you the pretty dress I found."

"I had so much fun that day with Elaine Davenport and Sarah," responded Bethany.

"You'll have to tell me all about Elaine, and college, and well, everything," said Betsy and ended with a laugh.

Suddenly Bethany remembered her luggage. "Oh, I need to go get my luggage from the car."

Betsy stopped her. "We already took care of it. It's all up in our room."

"I'm sorry. I was just so anxious to see the house all lit up."

"It's okay. Now come see the rest of the house before we start on the tree. We have a few minutes while Dad brings in the box of ornaments." Betsy grabbed Bethany's hand and dragged her toward the stairs.

"Ooh, you guys have it all looking so great," enthused Bethany.

"You better appreciate it," growled Brian as he met them on the stairs with a frown that looked forced. "I had to help a lot since you weren't here. 'Brian hold this, Brian help me, Brian go get—whatever.' "

"You poor baby," said Bethany, laughing as she patted his shoulder in passing. "I'm so sorry."

"You somehow don't sound sincere," he shot back.

Betsy and Bethany went on up the stairs, laughing. After a thorough inspection of the decorations in every room, the girls went back down and entered the kitchen, drawn by the smell of fresh popcorn. Mrs. Prescott thrust a sandwich in Bethany's hand, knowing she had missed dinner. Between bites Bethany helped Betsy get out bowls and cups for hot-spiced cider, which was simmering on the stove.

Brian and Mr. Prescott came in, and they all grabbed a bowl of popcorn and a mug of cider. They put on a CD of instrumental Christmas music and let it play quietly in the background as the family worked together to decorate the tree. James and Brian put on the lights with good-humored complaints about all the directions they received from the three female family members. Brian questioned, as he did every year, "Do you have to be so particular?"

The three ladies answered in unison, "Yes, we do," and everyone laughed.

By the time they had it decorated to their satisfaction, Bethany was drooping with fatigue. As much as she wanted to squeeze the most possible out of every minute of her time at home, she had to give up and go to bed.

She barely had enough energy left to brush her teeth and cleanse her face. She skipped brushing her long, golden hair, pulled on her nightgown, and collapsed into bed. She was asleep almost instantly and did not awaken when Betsy came into the bedroom an hour later. The younger girl was enjoying the opportunity to stay up later than her usual bedtime during the school break.

Awaking refreshed in the morning, Bethany quickly showered and dressed, picked up her Bible, and went down to the living room. She found her mother there, sitting with her Bible opened on her lap. She had finished reading it, however, and was gazing at the tree. When she heard her daughter's footsteps, she turned to greet Bethany with a smile. As Bethany sat down beside her on the couch, Margaret said, "I was thinking of all that the tree can symbolize. The manger and the Cross were built of wood. It's an evergreen tree, and Jesus gives us everlasting life. We decorate it with lights—Jesus is the light of the world. It was cut down and will die, as Jesus gave Himself for us in death. The star at the top, of course, reminds us of the special star the wise men saw. They brought gifts, and we have gifts under the tree. The gifts also remind us that Jesus was the greatest gift ever given. We hung our ornaments on the tree. In I Peter women are told to put on "*...the ornament of a meek and quiet spirit....*" The gold garland reminds me of the streets of gold in Heaven, and all the red decorations remind me of the blood of Jesus."

"Oh, that is all so beautiful. Thanks for sharing it with me, Mom."

"I'm glad we had this time together. I'll let you have your devotions now while I start breakfast."

"Do you need my help?" asked Bethany, starting to rise from the couch.

"No, no. Just enjoy the quiet time while you can," answered her mother with a smile.

At breakfast Bethany's heart overflowed with emotion when her father prayed and gave thanks for Bethany's being there with them. It took her a few minutes before she could begin eating. Mrs. Prescott was having the same problem. They sneaked glances at each other and burst out laughing. After finishing her breakfast, Bethany asked, "What do you have planned for today?"

Margaret answered, "Daddy wants to take his girls out for a day of shopping and lunch." Both girls squealed with delight. Mrs. Prescott continued, "Brian and I have our own plans," and she winked at Brian. The girls and her husband looked at her inquisitively, but because it was the Christmas season they refrained from prying.

As she helped her mother clean up, Bethany commented, "I am really looking forward to our day with Daddy, but I would love a day of shopping with you too—or at least a few hours."

"Of course! That is scheduled for tomorrow, after you and Betsy finish visiting the bus route."

Mr. Prescott came into the kitchen. "Well, is my beautiful 'five-foot-two, eyes-of-blue' date ready to go?"

"Oh, Daddy," protested Bethany, laughing and blushing as she gave him a big hug before hurrying away to get her coat and purse.

On the way to the mall, Mr. Prescott asked, "Who wants to pray for our shopping trip?"

"I will," volunteered Bethany. "Don't forget to keep your eyes open, Dad," she teased.

"Okay, I'll try to remember. But it is a habit to close them when I'm praying," he teased back.

Knowing she would probably be shopping with Betsy in Tacoma, Bethany had bought a gift for her while shopping in Detroit with Elaine and

Sarah. Today she wanted to find something extra special for her mother. She asked Betsy for ideas.

After a morning of shopping, Mr. Prescott took the girls for lunch at a Mexican restaurant. Then they shopped for a few more hours. Finally, Mr. Prescott asked, "Are you two done with your shopping now? I hope so because my feet are killing me."

Bethany answered, "Oh, no. I have several more things to buy." When Mr. Prescott groaned, Bethany laughed and said, "I was just kidding you. I'm ready to go. How about you, Betsy?"

"Anytime is fine with me."

"Then let's get out of this madhouse," said Mr. Prescott.

On the way home, Mr. Prescott took the girls to a Starbucks for a special treat. As they returned to the car, Bethany enthused, "This has been a wonderful day! Thanks for everything, Daddy!"

"My pleasure," answered her dad.

∾

When they got home, Brian was anxious to tell them about "the great day" he had spent with Mrs. Prescott. They had also done Christmas shopping and then stopped at a fast-food restaurant.

Mrs. Prescott had picked up some Chinese food "to-go" on the way home, so no one had to spend much time in the kitchen. After they had enjoyed the meal and done the little bit of clean up, they gladly sank into comfortable chairs in the family room to watch a video. Father and son went to bed at 9:00 p.m. as they were planning to get up at 4:00 a.m. for their hunting trip. Mrs. Prescott and the girls stayed up talking for another hour and then went up to bed.

Saturday morning Bethany and Betsy enjoyed a pancake breakfast before heading for the church for the bus meeting. Bethany met up with Kathleen at the church, and they were warmly greeted by their many friends and were both happy to be back on familiar ground. Bethany drove to Betsy's bus route area to do some door knocking with her sister. By the time they quit at noon, they had signed up several new riders and had led two people to the Lord. Thrilled with how the Lord had used them, they drove home to have a quick lunch and then go to the mall with their mom. It only took about a couple of hours to finish their shopping. On the way home they picked up a broasted chicken for dinner.

∽

Sunday was an enjoyable day for Bethany—her first time in the college and career Sunday school class in her home church and then working with her mother in her children's church class.

After dinner and naps in the afternoon, they returned for the evening service. It was a thrill for Bethany to be back in the church in which she had been reared and to hear her own pastor again.

∽

On Monday they stayed home to make preparations for their trip to Mt. Rainier the next day. The three young people were excited about the prospect of a day of playing in the snow, and Brian added to the commotion with teasing and pulling tricks on his sisters. They went to bed early so they could get an early start on Tuesday.

On the way to the mountain, they visited and sang along with CDs. Then Brian and Betsy each played with their Nintendo DS, and Bethany took a nap. At Paradise, they enjoyed sliding on inner tubes and throwing snowballs at each other. After a hike, they went back to tubing, except for Mrs. Prescott who retired to the lodge to sit by the warm fire. On the way home, they sang again for a little while until all three young people fell asleep. At home they enjoyed a snack and hot cocoa and then headed for bed.

On Wednesday morning when Bethany was working alongside her mother in the kitchen cleaning up after breakfast, Mrs. Prescott suddenly asked, "Bethany, where did my little girl disappear to?"

"You mean Betsy? I don't know."

Margaret laughed. "No, darling, I'm talking about you. You have changed into a young woman. You are so much more mature than when you left for your job at the Davenports."

"Do you really think so?"

"Oh, yes. I suppose you can't help but change when you go through things like the trials with the Davenports and then your experiences with dating, falling in love, and breaking up with Scott."

"I'm not sure I really was in love with Scott. I think it was more falling in love with love and with what I wanted him to be, rather than who he really is. Oh, Mommy, I came so close to making some drastic mistakes. I shouldn't say mistakes. The truth is, I was tempted to sin several times and almost gave in. I feel so bad about that."

"But Bethany, you didn't give in to the temptations, right? You resisted committing the sins?"

"Yes."

"Then don't burden yourself with guilt. Even Jesus was tempted to sin, remember. It's only sinful when you act on the temptation. You can rejoice that God helped you not to sin. I was praying for you, and He answered my prayers. You have a lot of mature insight now."

"I hope it keeps me from making foolish mistakes in the future."

"I hope so too, but none of us ever get mature enough to never make mistakes."

"You seem like that to me, Mom."

"Well, I am glad I hide my faults that well," said Mrs. Prescott, chuckling. I can assure you, I haven't reached perfection. I still struggle in several areas of my life."

"Like what, Mom?"

"Oh, like controlling my tongue."

"What do you mean?"

"Avoiding gossip is one area. Our natural man wants to repeat everything we hear. Another is watching what I say when I get frustrated, especially with your dad."

Shocked, Bethany said, "I thought you and Daddy had a great marriage."

"We do," Mrs. Prescott hastened to reassure her. "But it is true that opposites attract. I remember a statement I read in a *Christian Womanhood* magazine, 'The goal in marriage is not to think alike, but to think together.' Men and women just don't think alike, and in the best of marriages, there will be areas of disagreement. I guess God designed it that way to help us grow by learning to give up our way. Marriage mirrors our relationship to God. Ephesians 5:22 says, '*Wives submit yourselves unto your own husbands, as unto the Lord.*' In I Peter the scriptures remind us that Christ submitted to go to the Cross, right before the Scripture speaks again about wives being in subjection to their husbands. Our carnal natures and the teachings of the women's movement fight against that principle, but Jesus gave us an example to follow.

"We must keep dying to ourselves, surrendering to God, and working on our relationships all of our lives. It is a lot easier when you are married to a strong Christian man who leads his wife and family with love. I feel so sorry for the ladies who have husbands that don't serve the Lord or aren't even saved."

"I know. I'm so glad I found out that Scott wasn't like that before it was too late."

"The Lord is good!"

"Yes," agreed Bethany.

∽

That afternoon Mrs. Prescott brought in the mail and commented, "It looks like we received several more Christmas cards. Bethany, this one is addressed to you."

"Me? Let me see." Her mother handed her the envelope. "There's no name with the return address. Maybe it's from Donna, but it doesn't look like her handwriting. May I have the letter opener?" She slit the envelope and pulled out a beautiful Hallmark card. The inside of the envelope was gold and the front of the card had a gold-embossed manger scene with the message, "Wishing you a joyful Christmas!"

"Oh, it is beautiful!" she exclaimed, and quickly opened the card to see who had sent it. It was simply signed, "John." Enclosed was a note. Bethany passed the card to her mother and Betsy so they could enjoy it while she read:

Dear Bethany,

I hope you do not mind that I got your address from the Davenports. I hope you are enjoying your time home. I am looking forward to a few days with my family in California. Have a blessed Christmas. Savor every minute and every activity with your family and friends there.

Sincerely,

John

"John. Is that the other young man that you met last year who attended the more fundamental church?" asked her mom.

"Yes. That was so thoughtful of him. I didn't think to send him one."

"It probably would not have been appropriate, Bethany."

"But we are just friends, Mom."

"Still it is best for you to wait for the man to write first. Now you can send a note to him to thank him for the beautiful card."

"I will," promised Bethany.

After they had looked at the rest of the mail, Bethany took her card to the girls' bedroom and stood it up on her dresser.

Betsy came in and commented, "That adds a festive touch to our room. John seems like a really special guy," she added, with a questioning tone and a knowing look at her sister.

"You heard me, Betsy. We're just friends. I don't need another boyfriend right now."

"I'm wondering if he feels the same way," commented Betsy.

"Here, read the note."

Betsy took it and read the short letter from John.

"See, nothing romantic."

With disappointment Betsy had to agree. "Yes, but still, he bought you a special, expensive card."

"Oh, Betsy," answered Bethany dismissively.

"Have you dated anyone at college?" asked Betsy.

"No."

"Why not? Surely someone has asked you. You are too beautiful and sweet for them not to notice."

"I've discouraged anyone who acted interested, if you must know."

"Are you serious?"

"I told you I am not interested or ready for another boyfriend or even casual dates. It hasn't been that long since I broke up with Scott. That was really hard."

"I know. I'm sorry."

"It's okay, but let's not talk about guys anymore, all right?"

"Sure," agreed Betsy. "Why don't you tell me about Elaine and everything that happened at Thanksgiving. And I want to hear all about college, too."

Bethany shared about how Elaine had gotten saved and answered all of Betsy's questions about college life until their mother came to the bedroom door and invited them to go out for a walk with her.

The three of them took a brisk walk. The air was cool and crisp and had a refreshing scent after the recent rain. When they got back to the house, the girls stayed outside a few minutes to join Brian at the basketball hoop. Then they went in to get ready for the mid-week church service. As she went upstairs to change clothes, Bethany hummed a Christmas carol. She was definitely ready for tomorrow to arrive!

On the way to church, Bethany commented, "I am so glad Christmas fell on Thursday this year. I love going to church on Christmas Eve. It really keeps our minds centered on the real reason for Christmas."

After enjoying several Christmas hymns, announcements, and prayer requests, the pastor began his sermon with a startling remark. "The reason for the season is not Jesus. The real reason for the Christmas celebration is all of us sinners. We are the reason Jesus came to earth, so He could redeem us with His blood. We will be celebrating the greatest gift of all—our salvation." Bethany listened attentively to the interesting sermon and never once thought about opening gifts the next morning.

At five o'clock Christmas morning Bethany awoke. She was surprised that all was quiet—she thought Brian would have roused them all by now. She lay in bed for a few minutes savoring the pleasure of being home on this special day. She thanked God for working it out for her to be home and also for His great gift of His only Son. There still was no sound from anyone else, so she got up, put on her robe, and crept silently down the stairs.

Wanting to surprise everyone, she worked quickly but quietly in the kitchen, putting on the coffee and making cocoa for Brian and Betsy. She warmed the croissants, which they traditionally enjoyed on Christmas morning, browned the pre-cooked sausage links, and poured orange juice. Soon the aromas brought the rest of the family to the kitchen. After enjoying the simple breakfast, they trooped into the living room to find the surprises in their stockings. Besides the small gifts, Mrs. Prescott had put fruit, nuts, and chocolate in each stocking.

After getting ready for the day, the family again assembled in the living room to open the packages under the tree. The room was warm and welcoming because of the fire Mr. Prescott had started in the fireplace.

Bethany was happy with every gift she received, but she was ecstatic when she opened a box and found a lap top computer from her parents and grandparents. What a help it would be! Bethany was anxious to see how her gifts were received. She was rewarded by everyone's expression of appreciation and pleasure for the gifts she had given them.

After all the gifts had been opened, the girls cleaned up the mess while Mrs. Prescott went to the kitchen to start dinner. The girls joined her when the living room was back in order. Soon wonderful aromas were filling the house. When the family was called to the table, they all agreed everything tasted as good as it smelled.

When the dishes were cleaned up, they played games, watched videos, and had a snack before finally calling it a day. In their bedroom before falling asleep, Bethany murmured, "What a wonderful day!"

❧

The next Sunday after the evening service Betsy, Bethany, and some other young people went out to a coffee shop.

Monday morning Bethany was delightfully surprised to see several inches of snow on the ground when she looked out in the morning. She woke Betsy with her squeal of delight. They banged on Brian's door to rouse him, and all were soon downstairs eating a hurried breakfast before donning their warmest clothes and going out to build a snowman and have snowball fights.

The snowman wasn't very big—rarely is there enough snow in Washington to build a tall snowman with two snowballs for the body and a smaller one for the head. When Mrs. Prescott joined her children outside and inspected their snowman, she commented, "It's too bad we can't have a bigger, traditional one. I heard a lady give a devotional message once about the things a snowman represents for her.

"She mentioned snowmen are made with smiling faces to reflect the joy we Christians share. 'I guess that's why I like real ones,' she mused, 'but my collection of snowmen figurines make me smile and feel happy just looking at them. The three snowballs remind me of the Trinity; and the stick arms can represent Jesus on the Cross with His arms open to everyone who will come to Him.' "

"I never thought of snowmen like that," commented Betsy.

"Me neither. I like that," added Bethany.

The Prescotts had invited Kathleen's family to spend New Year's Day with them. Mrs. Prescott fixed a delicious dinner, followed by dessert that the girls had made. After dinner the adults settled in the living room for a visit. Brian and Kathleen's brother, John, spent the afternoon in the family room where they played with Brian's X-Box. Bethany and Betsy took Kathleen to their room and showed her what they had received for Christmas. Then they looked at school albums and listened to Christian music CDs. At Betsy's urging, the two older girls shared their experiences at college. Kathleen had already had several dates with a young man and needed no urging to share her impressions of him.

Kathleen's family left at 6:00 p.m. Both families wanted some time alone with their college student on the last night before they returned to Indiana.

Friday morning they had time to pack Bethany's belongings before heading for the airport for her flight back to Indiana. She had to take an extra suitcase with her for the things she had purchased as well as the gifts she had received.

∾

Once again Bethany and Kathleen had seats on the plane next to each other, and they enjoyed comparing notes about their activities while at home. Then Bethany took out paper and a pen and jotted a note to John, thanking him for his thoughtfulness in sending the beautiful card and sharing with him about her Christmas break activities. She ended the letter by asking him about his Christmas holiday. When that was done, she took a nap until the stewardess brought a snack and drink.

At the airport in Chicago, they saw many familiar faces and soon joined many others on a college bus sent to bring them back to campus. The holiday was over. Tomorrow they would be back to their busy schedule, and Bethany found herself happily anticipating it.

CHAPTER SIX

Cupid at Work

"...and he loved the damsel...."
(Genesis 34:3)

After Christmas break the girls were excited to be back together in their dorm room. They were anxious to share about their holiday activities. Sarah was showing pictures of her family's skiing trip. Cindy uttered a startled exclamation and asked, "Are those culottes you're wearing?"

"Yes."

"In the snow? I'd be wearing my jeans or snow pants."

"We don't wear pants. We always use culottes for sports activities. For playing in the snow, my mom makes special culottes from the same material used in ski pants. We wear long underwear under them with socks pulled over the underwear."

"Wow! You really take the dress standard seriously."

"Yes, we do. We believe Deuteronomy 22:5 means we shouldn't wear men's clothing. God wants men and women to look different."

"I just can't see it. I don't believe it matters to God. I mean, I wear jeans to ride horses and things, but they're made for women. I don't feel I am wearing men's clothing."

Sarah answered, "I don't want us to argue, but I'll give you a few things to think about. First, sometimes from a distance you cannot tell if a person is a woman if she is wearing pants, especially since some guys wear their hair really long. I think God wants people to be able to tell the difference, and He wants to see women looking feminine.

"Second, in I Timothy women are commanded to wear modest apparel. Unless a skirt is too tight, pants outline your figure more."

"Well," said Cindy, "I've known some real good Christians who wear pants."

"I do too. I'm not saying that automatically makes you a bad Christian."

"Another thing," Cindy added, "it's a real inconvenience in some situations."

"That can be true, but my mom has overcome some of that with her sewing abilities. But even if we do have to give up some activities, did God say the Christian life would always be easy or that we wouldn't have to sacrifice sometimes? It seems a small thing to do in comparison to what Jesus did for us or even what Paul and others went through."

"Maybe when you get to Heaven you'll find out God really didn't care."

"Even if that were to happen, what have I lost? God will know I was willing to try to please Him the best I knew how. I am not saying I am a better Christian than others or that I've arrived at perfection or something. You know I'm not perfect. You saw how I struggled with jealousy. God works on all of us at different times, in different ways."

Cindy turned to Donna. "How about you? You did not get saved until recently. You grew up wearing pants, I'm sure. When you're around home, do you still wear them?"

"No, I'm convinced that Sarah's stand is right. I threw away all my pants the same time I got rid of my immodest blouses and my music tapes."

"How does your family feel about that?"

"They think I'm nuts. They call me a fanatic."

"But they let you come to school here?"

"They aren't happy about it. They don't give me any financial help or encouragement."

"Wow! I have to hand it to you. You must have really been convinced by your pastor."

"I did hear it from my pastor. But I read the Scriptures and prayed about it and developed my own convictions."

"What about you, Bethany?"

"I was reared like Sarah. In high school I had a friend who felt like you, and she tried to get me to change. I thought about it because you are right about it being inconvenient at times. Plus there is the desire in us to be like other people and not stand out as different. So I decided to study it out for myself and pray about it. Like Donna, I decided it was right for me. I wanted to live as separated and as pleasing to God as possible. I don't condemn people who don't agree, but I've made up my mind for myself.

"I also felt that if I changed on one point, it might lead to me letting down in some other areas. One step can lead to more and more, and I might find myself doing things I never would have thought possible. I'm not going to start down that road. I came too close to doing that last year."

"Well, enough on that subject," Cindy said with a grin. "Tell us what you did over Christmas, Bethany."

Bethany was relieved that the discussion had ended without tension or hurt feelings. "We went to the mountain to play. Mt. Rainier is quite close to where we live. But we just went sliding with inner tubes. Here, I have pictures, too. I also went to a dinner for the alumni of our Christian school. It was busy, and it was great to be home."

Donna shared that her time at home had been better than she expected. Her parents were convinced that she was really sincere and serious about the Christian life and going to Bible college. They had not harassed her about her decisions while she was home. "I'm hoping their hearts are softening a little. Maybe one day they'll let me really share the Gospel with them, and they will listen with open minds."

The other three girls whispered encouraging words and promised to keep praying for Donna's family.

Saturday on the bus route, the children, and even some of the adults, were enthusiastic about the girls' being back. Many of the children ran to get their favorite (and sometimes only) Christmas gift to show to Bethany and Donna. Sunday on the bus, Bethany sat down next to Billy. Trevor was on Billy's other side. Bethany asked about their Christmas activities. They had already shown her the gifts they had received. Billy had spent a few nights at his grandmother's house, which he definitely enjoyed. Angie, sitting in the seat behind Billy, leaned forward and whispered to Bethany that her sister Cathy (Billy's mother) wanted to be free to go out or have her boyfriend spend the night. Angie had gone to her mother's with Billy.

Bethany changed the subject by asking Billy if he knew why they celebrated Christmas? He answered, "My Sunday school teacher said it is Jesus' birthday."

"That's right, Billy. I am glad you listened and learned that from your teacher. Jesus was the greatest gift ever given to us by God."

Billy was trying to process her words and was quiet for a few minutes. Trevor had also been listening, and he asked, "Why did God give Him, and why was He a gift? He was just a little baby."

"Yes, but remember that when He grew up, He started telling people about God and healing people and doing miracles, like when He walked on the water and quieted the storm. And then He died on the Cross for us so we can go to Heaven."

Billy asked the next question. "Why did Jesus die on the Cross? And how does that help us go to Heaven?"

"Well, we all do bad things sometimes, right?"

"Yeah. Especially me and Trevor," he said with a grin and poked Trevor.

"But that isn't funny. Remember, God calls it sin, and He hates sin."

"Yeah, I know," Billy admitted, getting serious again.

"How about you, Trevor? Do you know that the stuff you two do sometimes is sin?"

"Yeah. But we stopped stealing from the store a while back."

"Shush," admonished Billy, putting his hand over Trevor's mouth.

"Well," continued Bethany, pretending she didn't hear Trevor's confession, God wants you to be sorry for your sin, and He wants to help you so you won't want to do bad things."

"How can He do that?" asked Trevor.

"Well, if you ask Jesus to forgive you for your sin and be your Saviour, He will come in to live in your heart. His Spirit I mean. Having His Spirit living inside you will make you feel bad when you do something wrong. Soon you will start doing more good things than bad. And He will stay with you forever, and when you die someday, your spirit will go to live with God in Heaven."

"But what if we do something bad again? Won't He go away?"

"No. That is what is so wonderful about Jesus. He comes in and never goes away."

Angie spoke up. "Like me, Billy. You know sometimes I get angry and yell at you. But Jesus is still in my heart. I know, because He makes me feel sorry when I do that. And He answers my prayers, like giving me a job and fixing it so I can go to the junior college to take classes so I can get my G.E.D. There is also the daycare for little Annie and everything."

"Yeah, you are nicer than you used to be," admitted Billy.

"Thanks," said Angie, her voice betraying her astonishment by this admission from Billy.

"So, do you want to do what Angie did and what Donna and I have done? Do you want to ask Jesus to forgive you and come to live inside of you?" asked Bethany.

"Yeah," answered Billy without hesitation.

"Me, too," added Trevor.

"Now you must both really mean it. You understand everything I told you?"

They both nodded their head. "And you are sorry for the bad things you do?"

"Yeah. It's not really much fun. Lately, I feel bad when I do stuff," answered Trevor. Billy nodded his head in agreement.

"Doing bad includes being sassy and not obeying your moms, you know," added Bethany.

"Our Sunday school teacher has been telling us that. We have been learning Ephesians 6:1: '*Children, obey your parents....*' That's all I know so far," responded Billy.

"Well, that's a good start. So, do you want to ask Jesus to be your Saviour?" asked Bethany. Both boys nodded in the affirmative. "Okay. I'll help you with the words. You can both say them out loud so Angie and I can hear you. You just have to mean it in your heart."

"I do," they both answered in unison. Bethany led them in a simple prayer and then asked them, "Now where is Jesus?"

"In my heart," they both answered.

"Will He ever leave you?"

They thought for a few seconds. Their features brightened as they remembered what she had said earlier, and they both answered with a resounding, "No!"

"That's right!" exclaimed Bethany, giving both of them a hug. You seem to really understand. Now let me explain about baptism."

"We seen Angie get baptized," said Billy.

"Yes, I know you did. When you stand in the water, you are a picture of Jesus on the Cross. When the pastor puts you under the water for a few seconds, that is a picture of Jesus' body being buried. When you come up, it is like when He came back to life—the resurrection. You are leaving your old life and coming up to be like a new person with Jesus in your heart. Jesus wants us to be baptized right away after we are saved. Both of your moms already signed a permission slip. So do you want to be baptized today?"

"Sure," answered Billy.

"Okay," said Trevor.

"That's great, guys!" exclaimed Bethany. "Jesus also wants you to tell others about what you did. I'll get Donna to come back here, and you can tell her, okay?"

The boys were happy to do that, and later at church they were both baptized.

Bethany and Donna hugged each other when the second boy came up out of the water. "What a great day!" exclaimed Donna.

⁓

A few weeks later Cindy burst into the dorm room and spun around and around, finally collapsing on her bed.

Bethany questioned, "What was that about?"

"Randy asked me to go to the Valentine banquet with him."

Bethany squealed with delight for her friend. "That's great. Did you bring a dress you can use?"

"Yes. Look, I'll show you."

The girls were admiring it when Donna came in. "Is that for the Valentine banquet?"

"Yes. Randy asked me. Are you going?"

"Yes, Peter and I decided to let ourselves enjoy a special date night."

"Ooh," squealed Cindy. "Maybe we can sit together. That is, if Peter doesn't mind."

"I don't think he'll care."

Cindy then thought about Bethany and asked, "Are you going?"

When Bethany said, "No," Cindy offered, "Maybe someone will ask you."

"I hope not. I really don't want to go, Cindy."

"Aren't you ever going to stop moping over that Scott?"

"I'm not moping, but I'm also not in the mood for dating yet. Anyway, I wouldn't want to go to something that special if I hadn't already had several dates with the guy."

"Bethany, you are missing all the fun."

"Don't worry about me, Cindy. You just have fun. I'm really not sad or feeling left out."

A few days later Sarah (in her quiet, sedate manner) told the girls that Paul had asked her.

"Aren't you excited?" questioned Cindy.

"Of course."

"You sure don't show it," answered Cindy, shaking her head in perplexity.

Sarah grinned as she said, "This room can only contain one like you, Cindy." All the girls laughed together.

∽

On February 12 Bethany found a card in her mail. This time she recognized the handwriting and remembered the return address—it was from John. When she opened the envelope, she found another beautiful Hallmark card. This one was a Valentine wish to a "Special Friend." John had added a note:

Dear Bethany,

I hope you are well and enjoying college. I am doing well, but getting anxious to start Bible college. I am still taking courses at the Bible institute, so I will be a junior when I get to Bible college. I miss you at church and on Friday evenings at Mrs. Carpenter's. We did have some wonderful times at her house, didn't we?

Thank you for your note after Christmas.

Have a happy Valentine's Day.

Sincerely,

John

After reading his note, Bethany mused that it was going to be nice to have John around to talk to next year. Somehow he always managed to lift her spirits, give her a good laugh, or just be pleasant company even if they weren't talking. They enjoyed many things in common, like classical music, working jigsaw puzzles, and singing. He also was a spiritual leader without being preachy or putting someone else down. Yes, she was definitely looking forward to John's presence on campus.

∽

The night of the banquet, Bethany kept busy helping the other three girls with their hair, jewelry, and makeup. They were all so pumped up with excitement that she was glad for some peace and quiet when they finally left. She collapsed on her bed and enjoyed reading a book she had received for Christmas. After a while she noticed the unusual quietness. She put her book down and thought about the others at the banquet. She hoped they were enjoying themselves, and she had a moment of wistfulness, remembering that she had turned down several invitations. Rather than be gloomy, she talked to the Lord about her feelings. She concluded, again, that it was best for her not to go this year and reminded herself there would be other opportunities. Then she decisively picked up her book and was soon engrossed again.

Bethany intentionally stayed up reading until the other girls returned, knowing they would just awaken her anyway. She helped them out of their dresses and listened to all their animated chatter. Finally fatigue claimed all of them, and the room grew quiet.

The next day Sarah came into the dorm room waving an envelope at Bethany. "We got a letter from Elaine."

"Ooh, let me see!" exclaimed Bethany.

Sarah ripped open the envelope, and the girls put their heads together to read the letter.

Dear Sarah and Bethany,

How are you two wonderful friends and sisters in the Lord? I cannot thank either of you enough for the influence you have had in Michael's life and mine. We have settled into our own apartment now. Michael has accepted the change amazingly well. (My parents and I prayed a lot about that move beforehand.) There have been some necessary attitude adjustments. Michael had to test me to see if I would really stick to the new regimen. I had prepared myself for that with lots of prayer, counseling with pastor, and observing my father with Michael. It's like a crash course in child rearing.

Everything is so different than the way I was reared. I have been reading How to Rear Children by Dr. Jack Hyles. It is a really helpful book.

I think Michael almost died of shock the first time I spanked him! He learned quickly that I wouldn't tolerate kicking, screaming, or throwing things. He goes to his room until we are both calm, and then I remind him what the punishment is for, administer it, and afterward we cuddle and play. Most of the time he is a happy, contented little boy. We have grown so much closer.

There is something else I thought you would like to know. When I was cleaning out my closet at home and packing things for the apartment, I threw away every low cut blouse and all my pants. When my parents found out, Father told Mother to take me shopping (which was a good thing since I didn't have a lot left!).

It has been easier to make the change than I thought it would be. It helped a lot when pastor said, "If you want your children to grow up and follow the dating standards and stay in church once they are on their own, then you parents need to be living according to what you hear me preach. If they see you ignoring Bible standards in your everyday lives away from church, how can you expect them to incorporate them into their lives?" That statement really made me think!

I found a job in a department store in the home decorating department, and I love it. I started the interior decorating course at the community college, and I am helping on a bus route on Saturdays, so I am very busy. But that is good, as I don't have time to even think about the old lifestyle. My former friends have pretty much given up on me and rarely even call, which is a relief.

By the way, Father asked me to invite you both to come for a visit during your spring break, unless of course you are going home for the week? Isn't it the week after the pastors' conference at the church there? I hope so because it would be the same week as my break from the vocational college.

I have to run. Thanks again. Hope all is well for both of you.

Love,

Elaine

"Oh, wow!" exclaimed Sarah. "She is really growing and changing. That is so exciting."

Cindy had entered the room while the girls were reading the letter. "Who are you talking about, and what is so exciting?"

"Elaine, Michael's mother. Remember we told you Sarah got to lead her to the Lord when we visited over Thanksgiving break? She is really serious about the Christian life. Here, read it. It's a real blessing to hear her enthusiasm."

While Cindy read the letter, Sarah asked Bethany, "Do you want to take them up on the invitation? I can't afford to go home during spring break."

"I would love to go there again. How about you?" asked Bethany.

"Oh, yes!"

"As soon as I get done with my homework, I'll write back and tell her we would both love to come. I thought we would have to spend spring break here."

They both pulled out their books, but before they could begin studying, Cindy gave the letter back to Bethany and said, "She makes me feel like the world's worst Christian!"

"Why? What do you mean?"

"She's a brand-new Christian, and she is giving up pants."

"But didn't you tell us your pastor doesn't preach or teach about it, that even his wife wears pants sometimes?"

"Yes, but my mom takes the *Christian Womanhood* magazine, so we knew that some people believed that way, but it was easier just to ignore it. But here at college I've heard teaching on it several times, and we had that discussion after Christmas break. God keeps putting it in front of my face—do you suppose He might be trying to tell me something?" she asked with a grin. "I am going to pray about it and talk it over with my mom when I go home for spring break."

Bethany hugged her and said, "See, I told you that you aren't a 'bad' Christian. You are open to change."

A few weeks later Cindy made another twirling entrance into the room. "What's happened now?" asked Sarah with a laugh. Donna and Bethany were also wondering what big announcement Cindy's behavior heralded.

"Randy asked me to be his girlfriend. Look, he gave me his high school ring. He is so cute, so nice, and so much fun."

"Well, he should be a good choice," mused Donna. "Didn't you say he grew up in a good church?"

"Yes, and his father is the pastor. I really like him." She grew more sober. "I think I'm falling in love."

Bethany gave her a hug. "I'm happy for you. But give it a little time. Don't rush things."

"I'll try not to," laughed Cindy.

"That's really neat," added Sarah.

For several weeks Cindy appeared to be floating on clouds. Occasionally, the other girls had to bring her feet back to earth and remind her of the studying she needed to do.

Bethany and Sarah received another letter from Elaine.

Dear Friends,

My parents, Michael, and I are all excited that you accepted our invitation. I should have waited to tell Michael. He is driving me crazy with his anticipation.

Here is the plan. Pastor, John Holman, my parents, and some others from the church will be attending the conference. They will drive so they can bring you back with them.

I am looking forward to showing you my apartment, and we can shop and maybe go bowling. Michael and I will move back to my parents' home for the week so we can have more time together.

So long for now. See you soon.

Love,

Elaine

P.S. Please tell Donna that my parents would be happy to give her a ride also. Her parents could meet her at our house if that is convenient.

Donna was happy to hear of the invitation and promptly wrote a note to the Davenports accepting their offer and thanking them for their consideration. She called her parents and gave them the Davenports' address. Her parents were very pleased with the thoughtful offer.

One Friday night Bethany and Donna went together to the campus bowling alley. Cindy was there with Randy. They were obviously having a good time until some other young men came in and briefly pulled Randy aside to talk for a few minutes. Randy grinned and nodded his head in agreement, then went back to his bowling game. Bethany noticed that Cindy was talking to him earnestly and looked upset.

After that, Bethany began to detect a change in Cindy. She appeared troubled and anxious about something. Bethany finally found a time when they were alone in the dorm room and asked her about it. "Is something wrong, Cindy? You don't look as happy or bouncy."

"I'm just tired."

"Why? Things haven't gotten any busier."

"I don't know—I guess I'm just not sleeping really well."

"Is there a reason for that? Are you worrying about something—one of your classes?"

Hesitantly Cindy asked, "If I tell you something, will you keep it a secret?"

"Yes, I'll do my best."

"Well, it's Randy."

"What's the problem?"

"He's hanging around the wrong crowd."

"Here at school?"

"Yes. A few think it is funny and cool to break the rules. I'm not sure what they do. I think they sneak out after curfew or something. Randy thinks it is funny and just laughs when I express concern. When I asked him why he is hanging around with those guys, he said, 'Just for the fun of getting away with something.' I was shocked. I said, 'You are a pastor's son. What would your dad think?' He just laughed and said, 'He'll never know. What he doesn't know won't hurt him or me.' " Cindy began to cry. "Bethany, what should I do?"

"You might think about breaking up with him."

"Oh, no, I don't want to do that—not yet. Couldn't you think of something I could say that might stop him?"

"Well, what about the book of Proverbs?"

"Oh, that's a good idea. Help me find a good verse."

Both girls got out their Bibles and started searching through Proverbs. "Here, Cindy. Copy this one so you can remember it. Proverbs 10:23 says, 'It is as sport to a fool to do mischief: but a man of understanding hath wisdom.' Oh, there are so many that would apply to his situation. Copy this one, too. Proverbs 2:11-14, 'Discretion shall preserve thee, understanding shall keep thee: To deliver thee from the way of the evil man, from the man that speaketh froward things; Who leave the paths of uprightness, to walk in *the ways of darkness; Who rejoice to do evil, and delight in the forwardness of the wicked.' "*

The next day Bethany found time alone with Cindy. "What did Randy say, Cindy?"

"He just laughed it all off."

"What are you going to do now?"

"Keep trying. I don't want to give up on him."

"Guard your heart, Cindy. Don't let yourself grow any fonder of him. I know by experience that it just makes things worse if you ignore the problem and put off making a hard decision."

"What do you mean?"

Gently, Bethany said, "I'm only saying this for your sake, Cindy. I don't want to see you get pulled down. Maybe you should give him back his graduation ring. It might shake him up."

Cindy answered a little sharply. "No! I don't want to do that."

"But he's just making you miserable."

"Never mind," interrupted Cindy, and she hurried from the room.

∽

Bethany prayed often for Randy and Cindy. She did not want Cindy to repeat the mistakes she had made. Bethany could understand Randy's effect on Cindy. He was physically attractive, courteous, and witty. There was always laughter when he was around. Bethany fervently hoped he would not stray any further and would return to the path his parents had started him on.

∽

At Faith Baptist Church in Detroit a few Sundays before the pastors' conference in Indiana, Mrs. Carpenter spoke to Elaine. "I hear Bethany and Sarah are coming here for their spring break. That is so nice of your parents."

"Yes, and I'm so glad. I'm looking forward to the visit so much. Fortunately, I am having my break from vocational school the same week. So Michael and I are going to move back home for the week."

"Oh? I didn't know you were not living with your parents."

"We moved out in January to an apartment. I've enjoyed decorating and furnishing it, mostly with hand-me-downs from my parents, but I think it looks okay. I have been extremely busy since I also started the interior decorating course at the vocational school."

"Are you enjoying it?"

"Very much so."

"Back to the subject of Bethany and Sarah. Do you think I could borrow them Tuesday night?" asked Mrs. Carpenter with a twinkle.

"Sure."

"I need to talk to your parents."

"Mother is over there," said Elaine, pointing across the auditorium.

"Excuse me, dear, while I go ask her about it."

A few minutes later, Mrs. Carpenter found Elaine again. "Your mother said she was quite sure that will work out. If you are going to be staying there, why don't you come over on Tuesday too?"

"Oh, I wouldn't want to intrude."

"You wouldn't be intruding. I have been wanting to get to know you better."

"Well, if you don't think the girls will mind."

"I'm sure they will be delighted. Don't eat at home. I'll have dinner."

"Won't that be too much for you?"

"No. I have a woman who helps me with cleaning and cooking. It will only be one more than I had the Friday after Thanksgiving. Please say you will join us."

"All right. I'd be happy to. Thank you so much."

"That's settled then. Excuse me. I better catch John and make sure he is free that night."

John was glad to hear Mrs. Carpenter's plan. The weeks of the pastors' conference and spring break were going to seem like Heaven to him!

George Davenport called Bethany to inform her of Mrs. Carpenter's invitation and to make sure Tuesday night was all right with her. He told her that Elaine and John were also invited, as well as he and his wife. Bethany assured him she would be looking forward to it.

Bethany received a brief note from John a few weeks before the pastors' conference.

Dear Bethany,

I'll be coming to the pastors' conference in a few weeks. I would like to sit with you during the sessions if that is possible and you don't mind. Pastor said he is pretty sure you will have to get permission ahead of time. It would make me extremely happy if you would do that. Please let me know.

Sincerely,

John

Bethany made inquiries and then spoke to the proper authorities. She obtained permission to sit with John in the sessions and to spend time with him on campus. Then she sent a note back to him.

Dear John,

I have received permission to sit with you, and we can also walk around campus together. I got your note just in time before I signed up to help one of the speakers sell his books.

I am looking forward to the preaching and the change from the usual schedule. I am excited to get to see my friends from Faith Baptist.

It is so nice of Mrs. Carpenter to have all of us for dinner on Tuesday night. This time Elaine is going with us. It sounds like she is really growing spiritually. That is so exciting!

See you in a few weeks.

Bethany

In a few days Bethany received a reply.

Dear Bethany,

Grandma Carpenter is also inviting Donna and Peter for the Tuesday night dinner. I was concerned that having that many for dinner would be too much for her, but she insists it won't be. Her housekeeper will help her. I made her promise to fix something simple.

I am going to meet Peter at Donna's home and ride with him to Mrs. Carpenter's. He wants a chance to meet Donna's parents. The Davenports have also agreed to go by there to pick up Donna. They are so helpful and understanding. See you next week.

John

⁓

The Sunday before the conference, Bethany and Donna told their bus riders that they would be gone the following weekend. They were greeted with expressions of disappointment. One of the adults who came faithfully expressed everyone's feelings, "We miss you when you are gone."

"Well, that is nice to hear," answered Donna.

"We will miss all of you too," added Bethany.

Monday Bethany awoke in an excited state of mind. The hours seemed to drag by until the time came for her, Donna, and Sarah to meet the delegation from Faith Baptist Church at a designated spot. The men all greeted them warmly, and Mrs. Davenport embraced Bethany with a motherly hug. They had obtained permission to take the girls with them to dinner at a nice restaurant off-campus, which they thoroughly enjoyed. Then the three girls sat with the visitors during the service that night. The entire week was an enjoyable time of hearing inspiring preaching and sharing fellowship with good friends.

Several times John and Bethany broke away from the rest of the group to eat lunch together or to stroll around the campus so Bethany could show him various places. Much of the time there was playful teasing between them, but at other times they discussed the sermons they were hearing.

John was secretly watching to see what kinds of activities dating couples were enjoying. He was thinking ahead to the following fall when he and Bethany would both be on campus. He noticed couples using the bowling lanes and the miniature golf course and recognized that many spots on campus would be perfect for frisbees and whiffle ball in the spring. He would come prepared.

One day while they had lunch, he observed, "Several couples seem to be eating together. Is this where some of the dating takes place?"

"Yes, and there is the snack shop. Remember? I showed it to you."

"Oh, yes. Have you had any dates?" he asked casually, fearing he might not like the answer, but forcing himself to ask the question that had been haunting him.

"No, I decided just to wait until next year. I have been plenty busy without that, and there was a lot of adjusting to do just getting used to college life."

"That was probably a very wise decision," agreed John, struggling to hide his relief.

When the conference was over and the girls' luggage had been stowed in the trunk of the Davenports' limousine, the three girls were happy to relax in the luxurious seats. John had ridden with the Davenports, and as usual, he entertained everyone with his lively banter. Part of the time they had serious discussions about what they had heard and learned at the conference. The big car purred along silently and smoothly, and after the busy week with services lasting late in the evenings, soon most of the party were dozing.

They reached Detroit in the late afternoon. Donna's parents were waiting at the Davenports' home as planned. Donna introduced her parents to everyone. They expressed their gratitude to the Davenports, who responded that they were happy to have the opportunity to be a blessing.

The Davenports insisted that John stay for dinner, which was ready and waiting for them. Elaine and Michael also joined them; they had moved enough of their clothes for a week's stay and were settled into the nursery suite. Elaine had heard how tiring the conference would be, so she had not planned any activity for Saturday. But she had several things planned for the following week—if the girls were agreeable. During dinner she asked if they liked bowling. Bethany responded, "I like trying." After the laughter died out, she added, "You will really laugh when you see me trying it. The first time I went with Scott and his sister and her fiancé, I got up for my turn, swung my arm back, and bowled backwards. The ball simply flew behind me, right off my hand!" This brought on harder laughter, and Bethany joined in and laughed at herself.

Sarah finally was able to gasp out, "You poor thing. How embarrassing! I would have died on the spot!"

"I did the only thing possible," responded Bethany. "I laughed along. This time I will be more careful about the size of the finger holes."

John said, "You have such small fingers, it must be tough to find a ball to fit." He remembered looking at her graduation ring and noticing how small it was. He recalled Bethany's telling him it was a size four.

"They do make them small enough for children, you know. It just takes some time to find them."

"Children's size!" said Mrs. Davenport with a smile. "You certainly are dainty, Bethany."

"When do you plan to go bowling?" asked John.

"I'm not sure," answered Elaine. "Would you like to join us?"

"Sure. But it would have to be in the evening. My vacation from work is over," he said with an exaggerated sad face that sent Michael into giggles.

"That would be okay, wouldn't it, girls?" asked Elaine.

"Oh, yes," answered Bethany and Sarah simultaneously, "if your parents can accompany us. We don't want to ask too much of them."

Martha Davenport spoke up, "I can't remember the last time I went bowling! Let's go along and try our hand at it, George."

Looking doubtful and then grinning, George answered, "Of course we will go along. As for the bowling, trying is the key word. Bethany will not have to worry about being the worst bowler there; that's for sure!"

Bethany added, "Why don't we ask Donna and Peter to join us for that, also?"

"Good idea. We can talk to them at church," suggested Elaine.

John left shortly after dinner as they were all tired and ready to get to bed early. He thanked the Davenports for their hospitality as well as transportation to the conference. At the door he said, "I'll see you all at church Sunday." Just before going out the door, he stopped to give Michael a high-five. Michael was all smiles. John made him feel important and was his hero.

On Sunday they talked to Donna and Peter. They were delighted with the idea. Donna suggested Monday night, as her parents had a regularly scheduled club meeting and would not miss her or be upset that she was going out during her few days at home. She had already told them of her plans for Tuesday night, and they knew she would be going to church on Wednesday. They were grudgingly accepting her new lifestyle.

Monday the three young women stayed home, and Bethany gave Michael several hours of her undivided attention. That night John and Peter met the four young women and the Davenports at the bowling alley. The Davenports had brought Michael along. He thought it was great fun to watch Bethany throw her ball in the gutter several times. Before the evening was over, with coaching from John, she managed to actually knock down a few pins! Tuesday Mrs. Davenport babysat so the three girls could go shopping. Mr. Davenport slipped money to Elaine so she could treat the girls to lunch.

Tuesday night Michael stayed home with a babysitter. Mrs. Davenport had instructed Mrs. Spencer to fix things for dinner that Michael especially liked and to make a very special treat for dessert. His menu included homemade pizza and a chocolate cake with thick chocolate frosting!

They drove to Donna's house and were invited in for a short visit with her parents, whom they had all met briefly a few days earlier. Bethany was glad to see they were warm and hospitable, and Peter seemed comfortable. He had been there visiting and getting acquainted for about a half hour. After the introductions Peter walked with them to the limousine. He heaved a comical sigh of relief and jokingly wiped his brow. But he was seriously pleased with how his first meeting with Donna's parents had gone. He had prayed for them so much that he had almost felt like he knew them. Donna's eyes were sparkling with joy because he had been manly and courageous enough to go to her home even though he knew how difficult her parents had been about her Christian life.

John drove up, and Peter joined him for the ride to Mrs. Carpenter's home. The others got back into the limousine.

When they arrived, Mrs. Carpenter's home was filled with the delicious aroma of lasagna, toasted garlic bread, and salad. A delicious peach cobbler had been prepared for dessert. They were all acquainted with Mrs. Carpenter from the church in Detroit. Peter had attended there the previous year while chauffeuring for the Davenports. Over dinner they laughed together about some of the bowling scores and shared with Mrs. Carpenter some of the truths that had been especially meaningful from the pastors' conference.

The girls helped with cleanup while John and Peter visited with the Davenports. Then Peter and Donna played a board game while John and Bethany worked on a puzzle. Elaine and Sarah settled down with an album of Mrs. Carpenter's photos of her life with her husband. She had not had children of her own but had enjoyed and helped many young people through teaching Sunday school and being a foster parent for many years. She shared some of her experiences with the girls and the Davenports, and when they left, they were full of admiration for her, although she had a humble spirit and did not feel she had done anything extraordinary.

Wednesday the weather was nice, so they took Michael to the zoo. By the time they got home, all three young women collapsed for a nap before dinner so they would not have a problem staying awake in church. Michael was persuaded to do the same, and even though he was reluctant and insisted he didn't need a "baby nap," he too slept for about an hour.

Thursday morning Elaine took them to see her apartment. Michael proudly showed them his room. Elaine had used a sports theme with matching bedding, curtains, and removable wall decorations. Bethany and Sarah were impressed at how Elaine had achieved a beautiful, yet cozy effect in all the rooms.

Thursday afternoon the three young women and Peter rode the train back to Indiana to return to college. Sarah mentioned how anxious she was to get back, since she was missing Paul. The other girls had noticed they seemed to be getting very serious about their relationship.

Bethany shared the thought that their first year was almost done! They all agreed it had gone quickly but had definitely been a life-enriching experience. Sarah took this opportunity to tell the others that she did not plan to return the following year. Donna and Bethany were surprised and disappointed. "Oh, Sarah, We'll miss you so much!" exclaimed Bethany. "Are you sure about this?"

Donna asked, "Why aren't you coming back, Sarah? I thought you enjoyed college."

"I have, but I never did plan to get a degree. I want to get a job and save up money for my wedding."

"Wedding!" exclaimed Bethany and Donna together. "Are you and Paul engaged?"

"Not formally," explained Sarah. "We have talked about marriage, but we are waiting to see how we feel in another year. He is coming for a visit this summer, and we will correspond. He is going to continue studying here for his degree in pastoral theology. If things work out, we will probably get married before he finishes. He has a good-paying job. I'll take more courses in the marriage and motherhood department then."

Donna responded, "Oh, Sarah, you will make a wonderful pastor's wife."

As usual, Sarah responded with modesty and humility. "I don't know about that."

"Oh, yes, you will," Bethany supported Donna's remark. "You will be perfect!"

"Well, I just hope it works out. I would love the chance to try to do my best, with God's help and as Paul's wife."

"This is so exciting!" added Bethany.

"Yes, but you have to keep it to yourselves. Please, promise me."

"Of course, if you want. But what about Cindy?"

"It would just bubble right out of her! I want to wait to tell her when school is over, just before she leaves campus," said Sarah not unkindly. "We don't want to announce it yet."

"That is probably a very good idea," agreed Bethany. Donna nodded, with a smile. "Does Paul know you are telling us?" asked Bethany.

"Of course I cleared it with him. He knows I just couldn't hold it in any longer," answered Sarah laughing.

"Just think, you are the shy one who didn't think you would get a date, and here you are the first one with marriage plans," added Bethany.

"Possible marriage plans," corrected Sarah.

"I sure hope I can find a better-paying job," interposed Peter who had been listening to the excited girls. "This waiting is hard," he said with a significant look at Donna, who blushed crimson.

"I guess we all better pray about that," answered Sarah. "Hey, Bethany, jump in and join us; the water is great," she teased.

Bethany just smiled and said, "Right now, I have my mind on making the tour group."

Donna responded, "That's right. Auditions are coming up. Is it this week?"

"Yes, and I am starting to feel nervous."

Sarah said, "I have heard you sing. You won't have any problem."

"But that isn't the only thing that affects their decision. Christian character is considered as important as singing ability."

"You shouldn't have any problem in that area, either," responded Donna.

"I hope not. I keep thinking they might disqualify me because of Scott's coming here."

"Well, you couldn't control that."

"I know, but…"

"We have all been praying. Quit worrying and just do your best. It's in the Lord's hands," Donna said, interrupting Bethany.

"I'm trying," Bethany assured her.

Crossroads and Decisions

"It is as sport to a fool to do mischief...."
(Proverbs 10:23)

The first day back at college, Cindy told her roommates that while she was home she had told her parents that she was under conviction about wearing pants. She had showed them Deuteronomy 22:5 and asked them if she could replace her pants with a split riding skirt or pleated culottes. They had agreed, and she had found a seamstress who took her measurements and would have several made for her by summer. The other girls were pleased to hear of her decision.

The next day Bethany had the audition and interview for the touring group. Now came the really hard part—waiting to find out if she had been selected. She had tried out for either singing or accompanying one of the groups on the piano. The experience had been stressful, but all the nervousness over it would be worth it if she were chosen.

With the audition behind her, Bethany could concentrate on other things. She and Sarah sat down together to write thank-you letters to Elaine, the Davenports, Mrs. Carpenter, and John. They used some of the beautiful cards that Sarah had made by stamping and cutting decorative edges. In the envelope to Elaine, Bethany added a short note to Michael, which Sarah decorated with a whimsical animal figure. Bethany complimented her friend. "Sarah, you are so talented in so many ways! That is so cute. Michael will love it."

Sarah replied, "God is good. He gives us all abilities in different areas."

"Well, you certainly put yours to good use!"

Saturday on the bus route Angie, Billy, Trevor, and several others were excited to see Bethany and Donna. They had all missed them the previous weekend. The little boys wanted hugs and promises that the girls would be on the bus the next day. It endeared them to the girls' hearts even more.

They would not let themselves dwell on the future—long summer breaks and eventually leaving the area when they finished college. How would they ever be able to leave these children?

Cindy had come back from spring break more excited about Randy than ever. He had called her every day during that week. But one day Bethany found Cindy face down on her bed, her shoulders shaking as she tried to muffle her sobs with a pillow. Bethany hurried to her and softly asked, "What is wrong, Cindy? Do you want to talk about it?"

"Oh, Bethany, I was half hoping you'd come and half hoping you wouldn't."

"Well, one half of you got your wish," said Bethany, trying to get Cindy to relax a little.

Cindy straightened up, and Bethany handed her a tissue. She didn't laugh, but Bethany did get a crooked grin out of her. "I guess you are right. I really need to talk to someone."

"Maybe you should go to a faculty member?"

"Oh, no," Cindy answered and put out her hand imploringly.

"Okay, but don't tell me anything I'll be bound to report. Is it Randy again?"

"Yes," sighed Cindy. "He grabbed my hand, and I had to pull it away. When I asked him what he was doing, he said, 'I missed you during spring break. I kept thinking how nice it would be to hold hands with you. Don't tell me you don't want to. I can see the longing in your eyes. Come on, Cindy. I love you, and you love me, don't you?' "

"I told him I thought I was beginning to. He laughed that funny laugh that made me like him in the beginning and said, 'I knew it, and if we love each other, what's wrong with holding hands?' I didn't know how to answer him, so I just left him; and he was calling after me and saying, 'Don't be a stick-in-the-mud. I know you want to as much as I do; you're just afraid of getting caught.' What he said is true, Bethany. I don't want to get kicked out."

"You've got to keep thinking about how your folks would feel and how embarrassed you'd be back home. Everyone would figure out you got expelled."

"But what can I say to him? I don't want to lose him."

"You sound just like me—last year," sighed Bethany. "Just tell him, it's the rule here and that should be enough. But there's also a verse. Let me see. Oh, yes, I Corinthians 7:1 says, *"Now concerning the things whereof ye wrote unto me: It is good for a man not to touch a woman."*

"Oh, that's good. A Bible verse to back me up. Let me write it down."

"Okay, but don't be surprised if it doesn't work on Randy."

"Bethany, don't be such a pessimist."

"I'm sorry, Cindy, but what you are going through is much like what I went through with Scott."

The next day Cindy dejectedly reported back to Bethany that Randy had paid no attention to the verse. In fact, he got angry and asked her who was giving her all her ideas. When she admitted talking to Bethany, he became more irate. He had calmed down some when Cindy stated, "I don't know about any specific rules you've broken, and I want it to stay that way." He laughingly asked, "Are you sure you don't want to hear about the fun I'm having?"

Cindy sadly replied, "No."

Randy went on. "How about we have some fun and break a rule together? How about letting me kiss you? We're adults now. We don't need these baby rules."

"What did you do, Cindy?" asked Bethany breathlessly.

"I backed away and said, 'Don't you ever listen to anything I tell you? You need to start reading Proverbs again and stop hanging around those other guys.' "

"He just said he had read it many times, why did he need to read it again? Then he added, 'I've been a good boy all my life. I just want a little taste of adventure. It's not like I'm breaking a law or something.' I'm afraid he is sneaking out with those other guys, and they're drinking or something."

"Oh, Cindy, I hope not."

"I know. I told him I hoped he wasn't, and he just said, 'Don't worry about me. I'm just having a little fun.' "

"Then I told him he was rebelling, and he didn't like that. He said, 'Stop preaching and give me a little kiss. No one's looking!' He tried to grab my hand again. So I left. And he laughed." By now, Cindy was sobbing dejectedly. She gulped back her tears and went on. "I turned around and said, 'Proverbs talks about people who act foolish and don't want to listen to parents or God. There are always consequences.' He just laughed and said, 'Don't worry.' "

"What are you going to do now, Cindy?"

"I'm going to be careful but keep trying to convince him. I'll make sure there are lots of people around when I talk to him."

"Cindy, don't let your heart get too involved. I know what I'm talking about. Already he is talking about kissing, after he started out just wanting to hold hands. It's always like that when a person rebels. They progress from one thing to something more serious."

"I can't believe Randy will go very far. He's a pastor's son."

"I know, but he still has to decide for himself whether or not he is going to live a separated life."

The next day Sarah found a letter in her mail, which was addressed to both Bethany and her. The return address showed it was from Elaine.

Dear Friends,

Michael wanted me to write and share our good news. He is so excited! This will be his last year at public school. After the meetings at the church, Pastor Butler felt led to start a Christian school for the children. It will start up this fall. My father insists he wants Michael to go and knows I could not afford it right now while I am taking the interior decorating course. I really wanted Michael to be able to go after Pastor announced it, but I couldn't see how. I prayed about it without saying anything to my parents, and God took care of the rest. He is so good to us! (And so are my parents!)

I am so relieved that he will be in a Christian atmosphere. Hopefully, he won't end up like his dad and me.

I have been thinking about Mark a lot. I even contacted his mother to see if she knew where he was. She would not even talk to me. She thinks I caused the divorce and that was the reason why he left the area. I'm afraid he has gotten into some serious trouble that she won't talk about. I have heard rumors through the years. Please join me in praying for him—I'm sure he needs to be saved.

I hope all is going well for both of you. I'll be praying for you during these last few weeks of school and your finals. Bethany, have you heard anything about the results of your auditions for the tour groups? I am praying for the outcome of that, too. Michael is also. He is very faithful and sincere in praying for you every night at bedtime. I call him my little preacher boy since he told me he thinks that's what he'll be when he grows up. He admires Pastor Butler and John so much!

That's about all the news for now. I hope both of you will keep in touch with me during the summer. What are your plans?

Goodbye for now,

Elaine

A few days later when Cindy entered the dorm room, Bethany could see she looked upset. She went to her and quietly asked, "Do you want to go somewhere private and talk?" Cindy gloomily nodded her head in the affirmative and followed Bethany out of the room. When they had found a secluded area and were settled, Bethany asked Cindy what had happened.

"You won't believe what Randy said today. He thinks tattoos are cool! Not only does he want to get one, but he wants me to do it too!"

"You'd get expelled for sure!"

"I know, and my mama would kill me. I wouldn't do it, but I don't know how to answer him. He says there's nothing in the Bible against tattoos."

"I know some verses, Cindy. I'll find them for you when we get back to the room; but I warn you, it won't make a difference to Randy. He has his mind set on rebelling, and he won't obey it even if you show him from the Bible."

"Oh, Bethany, don't be so hard on him. He might listen."

"I'm sorry, Cindy, I shouldn't be so negative. I hope Randy will listen, but I just don't want you to be hurt anymore.

"Cindy, you need to pray about yourself and decide what you are going to do. Why not let this be the final test as to whether you need to break up with him? Show him the verse and see how he reacts. If he doesn't accept God's Word again, I hope that will convince you."

"Okay, Bethany. That sounds like a good idea. You find that verse, and we'll pray about Randy's accepting it. If he doesn't, I'll break off the relationship. I don't want to run with the rebellious crowd or be tempted to do wrong and get kicked out of school. I have been thinking about going for a teaching degree."

"That's great, Cindy. Let's go back to our room now, and I'll find that verse. But remember, if he won't listen, what are you going to do?"

"Break it off."

"For sure?"

"For sure."

When they got to the dorm room, Bethany pulled out her Bible and found where she had written the references on a flyleaf. She turned to them and copied them down for Cindy.

Leviticus 19:28, *"Ye shall not make any cuttings in your flesh for the dead, nor print any marks upon you: I am the LORD."*

Deuteronomy 14:1, *"Ye are the children of the LORD your God: ye shall not cut yourselves...."*

Two days later Cindy stopped Bethany in the hallway to make arrangements to meet where they could talk privately. She was not smiling, and she looked very sad and exhausted. Bethany's heart went out to her, and she prayed fervently for her friend and also asked God to give her wisdom to be a help to Cindy. When they met at the appointed place, Cindy blurted out, "Oh, Bethany, he wouldn't listen. I had to break it off like we agreed. I gave his ring back. But it's so hard!" she wailed. "I just didn't think he would be so stubborn and rebellious or that it would be so hard to make this decision. I was trying to guard my heart, but he is so cute and so much fun. Why won't he listen?" Cindy broke down crying so hard she could not say any more. Bethany did not try to say anything. She just put her arms around Cindy and let her cry.

That same day candidates for the tour groups were told who had been chosen. Bethany had been so keyed up waiting for this news that she had been having trouble sleeping soundly or concentrating fully in her classes. She went to the bulletin board where the names were posted for the various groups. Hers was on none of them!

It was a crushing disappointment. Tears swam in her eyes, and she just barely managed to blink them away instead of letting them stream down her face. She went back to the dorm room as quickly as possible, threw herself on her bed, and let the tears and sobs come. Donna came in and found her like that and was immediately concerned. Bethany managed to convey the problem, and Donna started crying with her, knowing how much Bethany had wanted to be selected. Donna managed to regain her composure, gently pulled Bethany to a sitting position, and put an arm around her while reaching for tissues with the other. She thrust one at Bethany and used the other herself. Bethany said, "Thanks, Donna. I'll be okay. I should not have gotten my hopes up so much."

"You shouldn't feel bad about wanting it; at least it is something good, an opportunity to serve the Lord. And it is natural to be upset. I'm upset for you."

Bethany gave Donna a hug. "You are a true friend, Donna. I'm glad God gave me such a wonderful friend."

Bethany managed to pull herself together, fix her makeup, and go to her on-campus job with Mrs. Morgan, a faculty member in the music department. Mrs. Morgan could not miss the telltale signs of crying.

"Bethany, is something wrong?" she asked with concern.

Bethany, barely managing not to break down again, admitted that she was very disappointed about not having been chosen for a tour group.

"Oh, yes, how many times have I seen girls in tears over that? There just aren't enough openings to go around for all the people who want to do that."

"But I have some news that I think you'll like. Maybe it will help take away some of the pain. Each year we choose a few of the voice students to be in an ensemble that sings for church, not just chapel. You were chosen."

This news did cause Bethany to brighten. "Oh, that will be great. Thank you so much, Mrs. Morgan."

"Well, it wasn't entirely my doing, but you are welcome. And Bethany…"

"Yes?"

"Don't give up on the tour groups. I want you to try again next year."

"Yes, Mrs. Morgan. I was planning to."

"Good. Now we better get to work. I have a big project for you to do."

"Oh, good! That will keep my mind off things."

"That's the spirit!"

In spite of this cheering conversation, Bethany continued to struggle with her feelings. Coupled with her concern for Cindy, her emotions caused life to seem bleak. For several days she spent much time alone, praying and crying and going over and over in her mind what might have been the reason she was not chosen. Cindy found her looking sad, with red-rimmed eyes, in the dorm room and expressed her sympathy. Bethany pushed aside her brooding to ask Cindy how things were going for her.

Cindy responded, "English class is the hardest. Randy is always trying to sit next to me, or if I glance in his direction, he winks at me. After class he tries to walk with me."

"Oh, Cindy, I am sorry. I have been wrapped up in myself. I could have helped you with that. Why don't you wait outside the door for me, and we can go in together, sit together, and leave class together?"

"Oh, thank you, Bethany. That would be a big help."

That afternoon, thinking she had herself under control, Bethany called her mom. But hearing her mom's voice broke down her defenses, and she started sobbing.

"What's wrong, Bethany?" asked Margaret Prescott with concern. "Are you sick? Were you in an accident? Has something terrible happened?"

Bethany managed to stifle her sobs long enough to tell her mother what was upsetting her. Margaret was instantly relieved but did not say so to Bethany, knowing this was a great disappointment for her daughter. She said, "Go ahead and let it all out. A good cry can be very therapeutic. I'll call you back this evening when you can talk. I love you, and God loves you, Bethany."

"I know," Bethany managed to respond. She hung up the phone.

When they talked later, Bethany said, "I worked so hard for that goal, and I am so disappointed."

"I know, Sweetheart. Life can be full of bumps in the road. You just have to climb over them and keep going. Eventually, the road gets smoother. If it were smooth all the time, we would never grow. We would stop depending on God."

"Sometimes I wonder if growth is worth all the pain."

"I know it seems like that now. But believe me, it is. God is doing a work in you to prepare you to work for Him. There is always another chance, at another time. You can try out again next year."

"But the summer after my junior year seems so far away!"

"I know, dear, but you will be surprised how fast the time passes. My, I can't believe it's almost two years since you graduated, and your freshman year of college is almost over!"

"I just can't figure out why I didn't get picked. Do you think it was because Scott came here and made that fuss?"

"I don't have any idea, but I doubt that. Don't dwell on it and get bitter. Maybe it was just simply too many good candidates, and quite possibly many of them were older than you, and this was their last chance. I'm sure it also depends on how the voices blend and whether they need sopranos or altos. Just hang in there, honey. You made it through breaking up with Scott; you can make it through this."

"Mommy, I did get some good news that helps a little."

"What was that, Sweetie?"

"I was chosen for an ensemble that will sing for church services instead of just singing for college chapel."

"Why, that's wonderful, Bethany! Your dad will be so proud of you."

"Yes, like Mrs. Morgan said, it takes away some of the sting."

"Well, we better go for now, Bethany. You will be home in a few weeks. I am so eager to have you here for a few months!"

"I'm looking forward to it, too, Mommy. Except for the job hunting part."

"We are praying with you about that. I'm sure something will work out. Goodbye, Bethany."

"Goodbye, Mommy."

∾

A few days later John called Bethany to find out if she had been chosen for a singing group.

"Unfortunately, no," answered Bethany.

John could hear the disappointment in her voice. "Did they tell you why?"

"No, they just post the names."

"I am sorry, Bethany. I know tour was important to you, but you will have other chances. You have three more years of school, so you can try again. In the meantime, let God help you learn how to deal with disappointments. That will help you all through life. Believe me, I know what I am talking about when I say we all have to learn to wait for things that are dear to our hearts. I believe that God uses disappointment to force us to draw closer to Him."

"You sound like my mom," said Bethany with a sigh.

"Oh, no! I certainly don't want to sound like a mother," responded John teasingly.

In spite of herself, Bethany had to laugh. "There you go again, rescuing me from my blues."

"Being your knight in shining armor?"

Bethany was glad he could not see her blush as she stammered, "Yes, I guess…something like that."

John laughed and said, "Well, I better run. I hope I helped raise your spirits a little."

"You did. Thanks for calling. That was very thoughtful."

"You are welcome. Your finals should be coming up soon. I'll be praying for you."

"Thanks. I need it."

"I'm sure you'll do great. Goodbye, Bethany."

"Goodbye."

John's call helped Bethany for a few days. Then she fell back into speculating, which eventually led to moping and resentful feelings directed at Scott. A week after her previous call, Margaret called Bethany again to see how she was doing.

"Not very well, Mommy. I can't quit thinking it might have been because of Scott. Cindy and I are both pretty depressed." Mrs. Prescott knew what Bethany was referring to because, after obtaining Cindy's permission, Bethany had asked her mother to pray for Cindy.

"You are both at a crossroads, Bethany. You can stay down in the dumps and get bitter, or you can decide to put on a smile and keep on doing what's right. It really won't be the end of the world if you never get chosen. I honestly think you will have a good chance next year, but not if you let a bad spirit take over.

"Concentrate on helping Cindy. Try to raise her spirits, and you will be amazed how much it helps you. Write her notes or give her hand a squeeze. Be there for her if she wants to talk. Doing for others is wonderful medicine for your own discouragement."

"Thanks, Mommy. I'll try," promised Bethany.

∽

The next time she had time to talk to Cindy, Bethany said, "Cindy, do you remember that one chapel speaker who was here recently and talked about being accountable to someone?"

"Yes."

"Well, I think we both need that. Let's make a point of asking each other about how we are handling our problems. If I'm not careful, I will blame Scott and get bitter, so you have to ask me if I am harboring bad feelings and speculating about the reason why I wasn't chosen. I need to accept it and go on."

"And you need to be sure I am staying away from Randy and not thinking about him all the time," said Cindy.

During the next few weeks in addition to their daily "checkups," Bethany wrote encouraging notes to Cindy and squeezed her hand when she passed her. Gradually, she noticed that Cindy looked more peaceful, and she felt better also. One day they found time to go for a walk together across the campus. Cindy told her it was still hard but she had peace, knowing she had done the right thing. She had begun to pray for Randy whenever she found herself worrying about him and what he might be doing. She tried not to dwell on the good times they had during the few months when she had been his girlfriend.

Bethany responded, "Believe me, Cindy, I know exactly what you are going through, but you are doing the right thing. There are other guys. God has someone special for you, someone who wants to do right. And there is always the possibility that Randy will straighten up."

"Did you have trouble sticking to your resolve, Bethany?"

"Of course I did. It was a real struggle, and I just had phone calls. But remember that Philippians 4:13 says, *"I can do all things through Christ which strengtheneth me."*

Cindy sighed. "I know. I just wish he wasn't so cute."

"Quit thinking about that. Remember, it's what kind of character a man has that is important."

"You know, Bethany, I still can't believe he's rebelling and backsliding like this. He was reared in a pastor's home."

"Hopefully it won't last long."

"Do you think I should wait for him?"

"No. I think you should date other guys if they ask you, which I'm sure they will."

"What about you, Bethany?"

"I don't know. I'm not ready to date again yet. Remember, I liked Scott for a whole year. But I really would like to be a wife and mother some day."

"I guess we both have plenty of time."

Bethany laughed. "We don't have to worry about being old maids yet. And right now we better go to our room and do some studying. Finals are next week!"

The next day both girls noticed Randy's absence in English class. They looked at each other with meaningful, questioning looks. After class Cindy excused herself and followed a young man who lived in the same dormitory as Randy. "Excuse me."

"Oh, hi. It's Cindy, correct?"

"Yes. I was just wondering if you knew anything about Randy. He was not in class today."

"You haven't heard?"

"What?"

"He and several others got expelled yesterday. The ones in my dorm cleaned all their stuff out of their rooms and left before curfew last night."

"Oh, no! I was afraid that would happen," murmured Cindy. She managed to choke out, "Thank you," and hurried back to Bethany, with tears in her eyes.

Bethany whispered, "What happened, Cindy?"

"Just what I was afraid of. He got expelled."

"I'm sorry, Cindy."

They hurried back to their dorm room, where Cindy cried quietly for a few minutes and then wiped away the tears with a huge sigh.

"Are you okay?" inquired Bethany.

"Yes. I was halfway expecting it, so it's not much of a shock. They were bound to get caught at whatever they were doing. I'm sure they were breaking some rules. It is probably for the best before they dragged other guys into it. I kept hoping Randy would stop before it was too late. I don't know what he'll do now."

"I feel sorry for his parents."

"Me, too. What a disappointment for them and an embarrassment!"

Bethany hugged Cindy. "I'm just glad you didn't let him pull you down with him."

"Yes. The whole situation taught me a lot! Sometimes life's lessons are pretty painful."

"Don't I know!" agreed Bethany.

Later in the day they heard even more details and were sorry to learn that Randy's attitude had not been good. He had cursed, ranted, and raved against the college administrators for not letting him finish the year since he was so close and complained how he had lost credit for everything he had done. He had shown no repentance and was so loud that security had to be called. Cindy was embarrassed. "I hope nobody remembers that I was wearing his ring."

"Hopefully everyone will forget by next fall. Anyway, I think most people who knew you were his girlfriend also knew you broke up with him a while back."

"I'm afraid people will ask me if I knew what was going on and if that's why I broke up."

"You can truthfully say there were issues between you that caused the breakup. Just leave it at that."

"Thank you, Bethany. I'm too upset to think clearly. That will be a good answer. You have been such a good friend and so much help."

"It worked both ways, Cindy. Now let's go to our room and try to study for our finals."

"Good idea. I just hope I can concentrate."

"We have to get things ready for leaving, too."

"Oh," groaned Cindy. "That is something else I learned the hard way. Next year I'm not bringing nearly as much stuff."

Bethany laughed. "I'll be anxious to see if you can stick to that resolve."

∾

Bethany had barely gotten settled with her books when her phone rang. Her mother greeted her, "Bethany, I have some good news for you."

"Great! What is it?"

"I think I have found a summer job for you."

"Doing what?"

"It's a nanny's job right here in Tacoma."

"How many children?"

"Twin girls."

"That should be interesting!"

"They are the cutest little girls, and they seem to be well-behaved."

"You've met them?"

"Yes, the family—the Porters—just joined the church. They just got stationed here. Both parents are in the Army. He just left for a six-month deployment."

"Do they realize I can only work a few months?"

"Yes. It will work out quite well. Mrs. Porter is getting out of the Army in September. Her mother will come for the few weeks between your leaving and her daughter's getting out."

"How old are the twins?"

"They recently had a birthday and turned seven."

"What are their names?"

"Hope and Joy."

"How cute!"

"So, shall I tell her you want the job?"

"Did she tell you what the salary would be?"

"Yes, it's not quite as good as you were getting with the Davenports. I still think it's fair, and you could start right away." Margaret told Bethany the dollar amount, and Bethany agreed it was acceptable.

"Tell them I will take the position. It will be great to have a job ready and waiting for me! I was dreading job hunting. Will I be living with them?"

"Not on a regular basis. She said there might be times when she would need you overnight."

"That should be fine. This is perfect! I can be home with my family in the evenings. What about weekends?"

"She said you would be free most weekends."

"The Lord is so good! I really was hoping I could live at home for the summer. I've missed you all so much!"

"You know, we were hoping for the same thing, for the same reason, Honey. I'll tell Mrs. Porter you want the job. Now I better let you get back to your studies."

"Yes, I definitely need to do that. But one more thing before we hang up. Keep praying for Cindy. Randy and some others got expelled. She is taking it quite well, but of course, it is upsetting."

"I have been praying for both of them. I better add his parents to my list. Give Cindy a hug for me, okay?"

"I will. Thanks, Mommy. Goodbye. See you soon."

"Goodbye, Bethany. I'll be praying for your final exams."

With her mother's good news to buoy her spirits, Bethany returned to her studies with new enthusiasm. Later when all the girls were in bed, the friends talked quietly for a few minutes. Bethany had not wanted to disturb the other girls earlier, so she shared her good news with them now. Cindy did not have to get an outside job, but she knew she would be helping with chores like cleaning out the horse barn. That was a small price to pay for the hours of enjoyable horseback riding she was looking forward to. Donna would have to go job hunting. Sarah was going to look for a more permanent job but was not ready to tell Cindy about her plans. She would wait till the following Friday. They would be attending the commencement exercises that night and then leave for home on Saturday. For now she merely indicated that she too would be job hunting.

Donna confided to the other three that she was disappointed that she wouldn't get to see Peter much. "He is staying in Indiana so he can keep his job. We are praying that he can get a raise soon. He is coming to Detroit for at least one weekend to see me and to have another counseling session with Pastor Butler." In the past Pastor Butler had told them not to rush into a serious relationship since they were both new Christians and they both wanted to complete Bible college. Now they wanted to seek his advice about dating each other exclusively. They had tried dating others during this past school year, but neither one was attracted to anyone else of the opposite gender. Their hearts were definitely fixed on each other.

The usually exuberant Cindy grew quiet after that. Donna felt bad, knowing Cindy was thinking about her own disappointment in the romance department. Conversation ceased, and soon they were all sleeping.

∾

The weekend was emotionally draining as they visited for the bus route on Saturday and rode the bus on Sunday for the last time. Tears flowed as they said goodbye to the children they had learned to love.

The next week was exhausting as they took their final exams, packed, cleaned their room, and worried over their grades. Friday afternoon Sarah asked Cindy to go for a walk across campus with her, and she told her about the hopes and dreams she shared with Paul.

As expected, Cindy squealed with delight for her friend. Other people walking nearby turned to look in their direction. "Shush," implored Sarah. "We aren't telling many people because nothing is for sure yet."

Cindy clapped her hand over her mouth, "I'm sorry. I'll keep it to myself. Do Bethany and Donna know?"

"Yes, I've told them."

"Oh, good. At least I can talk to them about it," said Cindy with a mischievous grin.

Sarah playfully hit her on the arm. "You are so bad!"

"Hey, I just thought about something."

"What?"

"You won't be here next year," lamented Cindy. "I will miss you so much!"

The girls hugged. "That is sweet of you, Cindy. I will miss all of you, too, and college. But Paul and I really want to start our life together. I still have to convince my parents though, so who knows what will happen."

"I'll be praying for you to know and follow God's will."

"Thanks, Cindy. Paul and I definitely want that!"

They went back to the dorm room together. Donna was helping Bethany pin up her hair. Bethany had one more exciting but nerve-wracking event to get through—the choir was singing for commencement. As soon as Cindy and Sarah were in the room with the door shut, Cindy burst out, "Isn't Sarah's news exciting? I am so happy for her!" The other girls could tell Cindy was very sincere in spite of her own heartache.

The girls soon left their room to find seats for the commencement exercises. Bethany reported to the choir room. There was a lot of nervous giggling, but they controlled it when the director arrived and started giving instructions about entering and leaving and then put them through some warm-up scales. After they had sung their number and returned to the choir room, the director expressed his appreciation for all their hard work, which had paid off that night. He was pleased with their performance. Bethany felt that his praise was a beautiful way to end her first year of college.

Back at the dorm room the girls changed for bed. Cindy suggested that they all keep in touch over the summer. They decided to exchange addresses and phone numbers in the morning before leaving for home. Home! How good that word sounded to Bethany! Three months to enjoy her family, sleep in her own room, and attend her home church, Trinity Baptist in Tacoma, Washington! With these happy thoughts, she drifted off to sleep.

The next morning was hectic and chaotic as all the girls tried to get ready, say goodbyes through tears, and pack last minute items in their suitcases. Cindy had already shipped many of her extras home. All the girls except Sarah had put some belongings in storage so they would not have to lug them home and then bring everything back in the fall. Each girl wrote down her phone number and address for the other three, with the promise that they would keep in touch.

Bethany managed to squeeze in a short prayer time before the bus taking them to the airport arrived. She asked God to protect her (remembering how she had barely missed being on a flight that crashed when she left home to be a nanny at the Davenports).

When she arrived at the airport and was boarding the plane for home, she tried not to think about her near escape two years earlier. Instead she concentrated on other things. She thought about Joyce, the woman she had led to the Lord on her flight out to Detroit. She hoped Joyce had taken her advice about getting in a good church.

∽

On this flight Bethany did not have Kathleen as a seatmate. When Bethany was settled in her seat, she silently prayed that this trip would be without incident and that she might have an opportunity to be a witness.

Sitting next to her was a middle-aged man. As soon as they were off the ground, he began reading a newspaper. Bethany had not had a chance to do her devotions that morning, so she pulled her New Testament from her purse. After reading from her Bible, she read a book until the snacks and drinks were served.

While they drank their soft drinks, the man struck up a conversation. "Are you going home from college?"

"Yes, sir."

"I have a daughter about your age. She attends the University of Washington in Seattle. Where do you go?"

"I have been attending a Bible college in Indiana."

"I thought that was a Bible I saw you reading. What are you studying at Bible college? Do you just have Bible classes?"

"Oh, no. We also have the regular courses like English. I'm also taking music classes."

"Are you studying to be a minister?"

Bethany was startled by this question but quickly regained her composure and explained, "No, we are Independent Baptists, and we don't believe in women being pastors."

"Oh? Then what are you majoring in?"

"My major is music education."

"You said you were an Independent Baptist? I haven't heard of that denomination."

"It isn't a denomination. Each church cares for its own affairs, but we go to conferences and meetings at other churches that believe the same."

"I go to a non-denominational church. How is yours different?"

"I don't know what your church is like—I've never been to any except Baptist. So I'll tell you about my church, and you can compare. Basically, we believe the whole Bible, literally, and try to follow its teachings as closely as possible. We do things like the first churches. When a person understands that he is a sinner (we all are) and he repents and calls on the Lord for forgiveness, he is born again or saved. The book of John speaks of Jesus' telling a very religious man that he needed to be 'born again.' It is a spiritual birth that each individual must accept for himself; it has nothing to do with joining the church or going to classes or taking communion. After a person is saved, he is baptized as a testimony to others—like a married person wears a ring to show he is married. We don't baptize babies because they don't know they are sinners and can't get saved. Also, when we baptize people we put them under the water in a tank in the church. After that they can join the church. At your church, do they tell you that you are a sinner and that you need to trust in Jesus as your Saviour?"

"No, not exactly."

"In John 14:6 Jesus said, '...*I am the way, the truth, and the life: no man cometh unto the Father, but by me.*' God the Father is in Heaven, so to go to Heaven, you must go through Jesus. He also said in John 3:18, '*He that believeth on him is not condemned: but he that believeth not is condemned already....*' So everyone is condemned to punishment in Hell until he believes on Him."

"Well, I believe in Jesus."

"But the verse says believe on Him; that is, trusting Him for forgiveness, knowing you aren't good enough to go to Heaven on your own. Once you believe that, it is simple—you just pray and ask for the gift of salvation."

"Wow! This is all new to me. I've called myself a Christian for years, but now I wonder if I really am."

"We believe there should be a definite time in your life that you can look back on and know that you were saved. That's why Jesus called it being 'born again.' We know a date, time, and place of our physical birth, and the same should be true for the spiritual."

"Could I show you some verses from my Bible that outline God's plan?"

The man glanced around nervously. "I'd rather you didn't right now. But I am going to check into all this."

"Here, take this little tract. It has Bible verses that outline what I've been saying and even shows how to pray. Also, when you get home, get out your Bible and read the book of John. If you have questions, you can call my church. The number is in the tract. Or come visit one of the services—the days and times are in there also."

"Well, thank you very much. Maybe I will. Your church isn't that far from my house. I have driven by it several times."

"We'd love to have you and your whole family."

"We just might do that."

While her seat companion thought over all she had said, Bethany relaxed and soon fell asleep. She did not awaken until the plane started its descent to land at Sea-Tac Airport.

Since it was Saturday afternoon when Bethany arrived, the entire family was waiting for her at the baggage claim. Brian and Betsy had made another sign to welcome her home. The greetings were not quite as emotional this time, as it had been only six months since Bethany was last home. With the help of a rented luggage cart, they headed for the car with all of Bethany's belongings. She was glad she had left some in the college storage.

Bethany enjoyed the ride home, catching up on the news from her home church. She was sorry to hear about some families who had been reassigned elsewhere by the Army. But she was not surprised; reassignment happened all the time at Trinity Baptist Church. It seemed that the Lord always brought new families to replace the ones they lost, and more—the church was having steady growth. She was anxious to get acquainted with the new families, especially the Porters, her new employers.

CHAPTER EIGHT

A Crossroad for Sarah

"…in the multitude of counsellers there is safety."
(Proverbs 11:14)

The next day at church Bethany met the twins, Hope and Joy Porter, and their mother. The twins looked exactly alike, and their outfits were the same—same dress, same ribbons and hair clips. Bethany could see it was going to be a challenge to distinguish one from the other. They were shy but politely acknowledged Bethany's greeting.

Sunday afternoon Bethany went to choir practice with her dad. Betsy rode along since she and another teen girl watched the choir members' children during the practice. Mrs. Prescott would bring Brian later for the evening service.

After the practice Bethany went to the restroom to check on her hair and makeup before church. One of the Porter twins was also there. Bethany made a stab in the dark. "Hi, Joy."

The little girl responded with a shy smile and said, "Hi, Bethany."

Bethany thought, "Good, I guessed correctly." She said, "I must have guessed right?"

"No, ma'am, I'm Hope."

"I'm sorry I called you by the wrong name."

"It's okay. I'm used to it."

"I'm sure you are," answered Bethany with a smile. "I'll see you tomorrow, Hope. We will have to find a way for me to tell you apart. I'm sure some people can."

"Our mother can and daddy sometimes. It is hard for him at first when he comes home from being at the war."

"I can understand that," responded Bethany while glancing at her wristwatch. "We better get to the auditorium. It's almost time for the service to begin."

"Ooh, I don't want to get in trouble for coming in late!"

"Don't worry, Hope. You have a couple of minutes," Bethany reassured her as they both hurried toward the auditorium.

After the service several people stopped to tell her they were happy to see her. Several asked her if she would be returning to college in the fall, and some asked her if she had dated anyone particularly interesting. She responded with a simple "Yes" and "No." Many asked her the usual questions about what her major was and what classes she liked best. It was heartwarming that so many people were interested in her. When her dad was ready to go, she excused herself. At home she had a small snack and then laid out clothes for the next day.

When she and Betsy were both in bed, Betsy asked, "Are guys still an off-limits subject?"

"No. I'm looking forward to dating in the fall."

"Did you see anyone there that you are interested in?"

As Bethany thought about her sister's question, to her own surprise she realized the answer was no. She had met some young men who were nice, serious Christians. Some were also very good-looking, but she did not feel attracted to any of them. "You know, Betsy, I'd have to say no."

"No? Then how are you going to start dating?"

"I don't know," mused Bethany. "Well, for one thing, they ask us to give a guy a chance by accepting at least one date. Some of them find it hard to get up the nerve to ask. Who knows? Maybe I'll change my mind once I get to know some of them better."

"I hope so. I can't imagine you as an old maid."

Bethany had a good laugh at that comment. "Betsy, I'm only 20. Let's not worry about that yet. Anyway, we better go to sleep. Tomorrow I have to get up early to start my new job."

"Okay. Good night. Try to be quiet in the morning so I can sleep in."

Laughing, Bethany answered, "You better read Proverbs where it talks about the sluggard."

Betsy playfully threw a pillow at her.

Bethany thought about the conversation in the morning while she drove to the Porters' home. Was there something wrong with her? Did she not enjoy the company of men? Unexpectedly, John's face flashed across her mind. "I was always comfortable and content in his presence," she thought.

He could entertain, console, give wise counsel, or challenge her—it seemed that he could read her mood and respond to her need.

She found herself comparing the men she had met at college with John. It was hard for them to compete. He was older and much more mature—both spiritually and socially. She and John could talk seriously one moment and the next be teasing and laughing together.

Again she realized she was looking forward to his being on campus in the fall. Arriving at her destination cut off her musing.

This first day the twins greeted her shyly. Their mother told her which was which, but Bethany knew she would have a problem identifying them the second they moved.

Mrs. Porter handed Bethany two typed instruction sheets and went over them with her. "This tells you what the girls are allowed to do and what is off-limits. If something else comes up that they want to do and you feel it is questionable, just say no until you have a chance to discuss it with me. I also listed several different items you can fix for lunch. At the bottom is my cell phone number should you need to reach me in case of an emergency. The other sheet is divided into days and lists the chores they must do before playing every morning. I didn't write this down, but they are not allowed to fight—no hitting or kicking. If they start squabbling and can't get along, put them in separate rooms for a while with a library book. I want them to spend some time each day reading anyway. If they don't obey you immediately, give them a time-out. When I get home, you will give me a report, and they will get something stronger. Do you have any questions?"

"Do the girls have hay fever or other allergies?"

"No, they are quite healthy and have no special problems."

"One other thing—I guess my mom explained that sometimes I would have her car and other days she would drop me off. On the days like today when I have it, do you mind if I take them to a park or something?"

"Not at all. Once in a while you could take them to play miniature golf. I'll pay you for gas and the admission fee."

"Do they have any special friends at church who might invite them over? If so, what should I do?"

"I doubt anyone will call since we haven't been in the church very long. I prefer that things like that be planned in advance, not spur of the moment. So in that case, the other party should call back in the evening when I am home. But that gives me an idea. Maybe I should invite some girls their age to come over to play. Would you mind having extras for a few hours?"

"Not at all. Shall I make you a list of families with girls their age who know me and might be willing to let their children come over to play?"

"That would be very helpful, Bethany. Would you girls like that?"

"Yes!" they answered in unison.

"Well, I think that covers everything. I better get going. You girls obey just like you would if I were here."

"Yes, ma'am."

Mrs. Porter gave both girls a kiss and a hug. "Goodbye. I love you."

"We love you, too."

The girls ran to the window to wave until their mother was out of sight. Then Bethany asked, "Have you done today's chores yet?"

"No, ma'am," they answered together.

"How do you two do that?"

"What?"

"Say things together in perfect unison."

One twin answered, "We don't know. It just happens."

"Well, it's awesome. Now let's look at your chore list." When the girls groaned, she added, "Get it done as fast as you can, and then you will have the rest of the day for fun things."

"Will you take us somewhere?"

"No, not today. I want us to get used to each other, and I want to get used to your house and your routine. I also want to try to tell you apart." The girls just grinned at her. "Are you planning to make it hard for me?"

"That's part of the fun of being twins."

"Okay, but if I say it is important for me to know which one you are, you have to tell me. It is part of obeying me."

"Yes, ma'am."

"Now go make your beds. Then, Hope…for now raise your hand, you have to empty the wastepaper baskets. Joy, you are to fill the dog's dishes. Oh, you have a dog?"

"Yes, come on, We'll show you."

"Whoa!" The girls skidded to a stop—they had been heading for the back door. "Go make your beds first, please. Then Hope can collect some of the baskets, and we'll all go out in the yard together."

Their faces registered their disappointment, but they said, "Yes, ma'am" and obeyed.

Silently Bethany was praising the Lord for this job—it was so much easier with children who had been taught to obey right away than it had been when she started caring for Michael.

After the chores were done and Bethany had "met" Trixie, the dog, the girls got out their bicycles and rode on their own street. Bethany ran up and down the street with them several times to their delight, then retired to the porch with a cool drink.

The girls changed to scooters then went to the back yard and threw a ball for Trixie to fetch. Soon they went back to bike riding. Shortly before noon Bethany called them in to play in the house while she prepared lunch. She had not had much opportunity to study them to find any difference that would help her know them apart. After a few minutes at the table, she asked them to tell her their names. She thought Joy's face was just a little rounder than Hope's and thought maybe she could use that. She announced, "I think I might be able to tell you apart. We will see after lunch."

When the table was cleared and the dishes put in the dishwasher, Bethany said, "Now go out of the room and then come back in. I will try to guess your names. You have to tell me if I am right or wrong, okay?"

"Yes, ma'am," they replied with big grins as they headed out of the kitchen. They liked this game.

"Come back in," Bethany called.

The girls came back in, their grins still in place. Joy said, "Now don't tell her your name, Hope." Instantly she put her hand over her mouth as Bethany burst out laughing.

Hope playfully hit her sister on the arm. "You messed it up."

"I know, but you did it last time with Pastor Noble." Turning to Bethany she said, "One of us is always doing that!"

"Well, go out again, and this time don't say anything."

The girls came in again, and Bethany pointed to one and said, "I think you are Joy."

The girls grinned and shouted, "You're wrong!"

"Are you serious?"

"Yes," they gleefully replied in unison.

"Okay, stand still for a minute." After studying them for a few minutes, Bethany said, "Let's try it again."

The girls left and re-entered. Again Bethany was wrong. Finally, on the seventh try she got it right. "Now you can go play."

"Could you take us for a walk around the block? We aren't allowed to go by ourselves."

"Sure. I could use some more exercise. Shall we take Trixie along? Do you have a leash?"

"Yes," the girls answered together again. "I'll go get her ready." Again they answered simultaneously. "I said it first," Joy said. "I get to do it."

"No, you didn't," said Hope, her voice rising. "Let me do it." She tried to push past Joy to run for the back door.

"No! I want to," challenged Joy and stood her ground, blocking Hope's way.

"Girls, girls, if you don't stop arguing, we won't take Trixie. You said it together, so I will decide. One will put the leash on her and bring her around to the front yard, and the other will put her back when we return. Choose a number between one and ten. The one closest to the number I'm thinking will get her ready. Okay?"

"Okay," both girls grudgingly answered.

"No grumbling if you lose. Hope, you give me a number. Now Joy. Okay, Joy was closest. Go get the dog ready. We will meet you in the front yard."

After the walk, Hope put the dog in the back yard and hung up the leash in its proper place. Joy was asking Bethany if they could watch a video as Hope came in. Bethany consulted the instruction paper and saw they were allowed one hour, so she agreed. While they watched a children's video, she went into the kitchen, poured herself a cup of coffee, and read a novel.

In the afternoon, shortly before Mrs. Porter was due home, Bethany helped the girls check the whole house and pick up and straighten anything out of place. When she arrived home, Mrs. Porter was pleased with the way the house looked and also noted the girls were neat and tidy. She was reassured about her choice of a nanny by their enthusiasm about their day.

The girls had twin beds in a shared bedroom, and that night after their mother had tucked them in and prayed with them, they started plotting where they would ask Bethany to take them the next day. They watched eagerly for her arrival the next morning from the front window but turned away in disappointment when they saw Mrs. Prescott drop off Bethany.

Bethany noted their woebegone looks and soon ascertained the cause. "We can still make it a fun-filled day if you will try to get over your disappointment and put on happy faces. Now hurry and do your chores, and then I will play with you. Do you have any board games we could play?"

"You mean it? For real? You will play with us?"

"Of course."

Both girls gave her a big hug. "You are the best nanny ever!" exclaimed Joy.

Hope added, "Our last nanny wouldn't do anything with us. She was so boring."

"Well, get going now. I think we will have to find lots of things to do indoors today. The weatherman said it would rain."

This day was more of a challenge for Bethany, but she managed to keep the girls entertained with board games, hide-and-seek, and acting out Bible stories. The girls also had plenty of toys for indoor use—dolls and a play kitchen among other things.

Wednesday morning the girls were delighted to see Bethany driving the car. The minute she came in the door, they rushed to her, both talking at once. "I heard the weatherman—it's going to be nice today. Can we go to the park, please?"

The other one was saying, "We want to go to a park with slides and swings. Please, Bethany?"

Mrs. Porter interrupted and admonished them. "Bethany is in charge. If she says you are staying home and just playing quietly by yourselves, that's what you'll do. She doesn't have to take you places or entertain you the whole time. Understand?"

The twins' eager faces fell; their smiles faded. "Yes, ma'am."

"Now run along to your room. I'll be there to say goodbye in a minute. I want to talk to Bethany privately."

"Yes, ma'am."

When they were out of earshot, Mrs. Porter told Bethany, "It is up to you what you want to do. They have plenty to occupy them here, but like I said before, I don't mind your taking them somewhere occasionally. Just don't let them persuade you too often. I don't want them to always get their way or get what they want."

"I understand perfectly. It is how I was reared."

"Good. Well, have a good day. I'll go tell the girls goodbye."

When their mother was gone, they started begging again. "If you do your chores quickly without whining, I'll take you to a park. So you better hurry. While you are doing your work, I will make us a picnic lunch. Hope, do you know if there is a picnic basket?"

"Yes, I'll show you where it is."

"Joy, is there an old tablecloth we can use?"

"Mom has a plastic one we can use."

"Good. Find them for me and then do your chores, please."

A picnic in a park with play equipment was a strong motivator, and soon they were ready to go. Bethany enjoyed the day as much as the girls did. They went back to the house in time for a nap, to be ready for the mid-week service that night.

At the Prescotts', Margaret received a phone call Wednesday morning from George Davenport. He wanted to speak to James, so she gave him his work number. When he reached James, George explained that John Holman had asked him to call and get permission to give him the Prescotts' phone number as he wanted to speak with Mr. Prescott.

"What do you know about him?" James asked.

"He is a fine young Christian man. He is planning to go into the ministry."

"Do you have any idea what he wants to talk to me about?"

"I am sure it has something to do with Bethany."

"Go ahead and give him the number."

"John was wondering if it would be okay for him to call you at work?"

"Yes, it would be okay, but why doesn't he want to call me at home?"

George answered, "John said something about not wanting Bethany to know about the call." Puzzled, James said he would be looking forward to the call.

At church that night Bethany stopped the twins and tried to tell them apart. Again she failed. The twins grinned with delight. "I'll get it yet," promised Bethany. By Friday Bethany was guessing correctly a little more often than not. Now she was smiling, and the little girls were disappointed.

❧

Thursday morning James received a phone call from John. "Thank you for allowing me to call you, sir," he began.

"No problem," answered James. "But I am wondering about the secrecy."

"I will explain about that. I wanted to ask for your permission to date Bethany. I will be starting in the fall at the Bible college where Bethany attends. I have been taking courses through my church's Bible institute in the evenings and have two years' worth of credits. I feel called into full-time Christian service, but I'm not sure in what capacity as yet. I already have a business degree and have worked several years. I realize I am five years older than Bethany, but I honestly don't think that will be a problem. She seems quite mature. She and I have spent much time together, double-dating when some friends needed chaperoning. We also went to an elderly lady's house many times to keep her company. I always had Mrs. Carpenter in my car when I picked up Bethany. As far as Bethany was concerned, I was helping her get over the disappointment of having to break up with Scott Lancaster. For me, it was like a date, but I didn't call it that, as I knew Bethany needed time to heal. I wanted to speak to you privately about this so I can gradually work toward a real date when I feel she is ready to accept it."

John paused to give James an opportunity to respond. "Thank you for your consideration. I appreciate your asking me for permission to date. Now please tell me why you want to date my daughter."

"Frankly, sir, I already love her. In fact, I could not get her out of my mind from the first time I saw her. Not only is she attractive, but also I immediately suspected she was a separated Christian by her demeanor. It seems the Lord orchestrated our first meeting, and I honestly feel He has chosen her for me. Of course, I have not shared this with Bethany. That is why I called you privately. I don't want her to know how seriously I take dating her until I feel she shares my feelings even a little bit."

"And how do you know George Davenport?"

"He and I and Mrs. Carpenter all attend Faith Baptist Church in Detroit. Bethany first attended there when I told her about a revival we were having—that was when we first met. She got the Davenports coming, and they switched their membership."

"How did you first meet?"

"We were both heading for the library at the same time. It was icy, and she was trying to balance a stack of books and keep her footing. Michael ran away from her. I caught him for her, and we struck up a conversation. I soon realized she was the young woman I had seen with Scott Lancaster at a Christmas party we all attended."

"Well, young man, I don't have any reservations about your dating Bethany. Her mother and I were hoping she would start dating this year. You do realize that she will probably have dates with other young men? I have heard that they encourage the young ladies to accept at least one date from any man that invites her."

"I know, but I am thinking it might be for the best for her to experience dating with more than just Scott and me. That said, I'll be praying that she doesn't fall for any of them," he added and then laughed.

James laughed with him. "I guess you will just have to trust God to bring it all about if it is His will for you two to be together."

"Yes, sir. I have been growing in the trust department this last year and a half."

"I will be praying for both of you to know His will."

"Thank you, sir. There is one other thing before I let you get back to work. May I have your permission to call Bethany a few times this summer?"

"Yes, but she will wonder where you got the number."

"If she asks, I can tell her about my call to Brother Davenport, his call to you, and then this call. I will just leave out the part about dating until later."

"That should work." James gave John the Prescotts' home number.

"Well, thank you very much, sir."

"Thank you for calling. I am looking forward to meeting you in person sometime."

"I feel the same way. Goodbye."

Saturday evening when Mrs. Prescott answered the phone, she called to Bethany, "It's for you."

"Thanks, Mom. Hello?"

She heard, "Hi, Bethany."

"John! It's nice to hear from you, but how did you get my number?"

"I contacted Mr. Davenport and asked him to call your dad to see if it was okay for him to give me your parents' number. Your dad gave Mr. Davenport his work number to pass on to me. I talked to him and asked if he would allow me to call you. He said yes and then gave me the home number."

"That was complicated."

"Yes, but I wanted to be sure your parents didn't mind my calling you."

"That was very considerate of you."

"Are you enjoying being home, Bethany?"

"Yes, it's great. How are things with you?"

"Time seems to be dragging. I am so anxious for it to be time for school to begin."

"I guess you are excited about going to Bible college."

"Very much so. What have you been doing?"

"Well, I'm working as a nanny again. I don't think I've talked to you since my mom got this job lined up for me."

"You're right. I wondered if you had a job for the summer."

"It is perfect. I come home at night and have the weekends off."

"For whom are you working?"

"The Porter family—they are new in our church. Both parents are in the Army. He is deployed right now. The mother is getting out in the fall but needed someone to care for her twin daughters until then."

"Twins! That should be interesting. Are they identical?"

"Yes! It has been a week of guessing games. They love it when they fool me, but they are very well-behaved and respectful. When I really need to know which is which, they tell me the truth. I am beginning to get it right more often than being wrong."

"It sounds like you enjoy your job."

"Yes, very much. What a difference from caring for Michael when I first started at the Davenports! These girls have been taught to obey and know what discipline is."

"That's good. What else are you doing to keep busy?"

"I am visiting on a bus route Saturdays and riding the bus Sundays. I also joined the choir."

"That should make the director happy. You have a beautiful voice."

"Thanks. I'm not sure the choir director could be objective about me."

"Why is that?"

"My dad's the director."

Bethany heard John's hearty laugh and joined in. She enjoyed making him laugh. It did not take much—John was usually in an upbeat mood. Rarely had she seen him looking pensive, and he definitely was not a melancholy person. The only time she could recall seeing him angry was when they discussed how Scott had deceived her. That was when she had called John her "knight in shining armor." She still blushed when she thought about it. And he had remembered and teased her about it later. Abruptly she brought her mind back to the phone conversation. She had missed something he said. "Excuse me, what was that?" asked Bethany.

"I asked if you are having nice weather."

"Oh, sorry, I let my mind wander for a few seconds. The weather is not too bad. It is too early for really hot weather, but it isn't raining a lot. The twins have been able to ride their bikes and scooters most days."

John asked, "Where did your mind wander to Bethany? What were you thinking about?"

"Well…" she hesitated, embarrassed, but went on, "…I was thinking about your laugh and how I enjoy hearing it."

"I like your laugh, too. It is soft and tinkly, very feminine."

There was a short silence. Bethany was tongue-tied, an unusual occurrence for her.

John rescued her by asking, "Are you looking forward to going back to college in the fall?"

"Yes, but I am going to thoroughly enjoy being here in the meantime."

"Good. Well, I guess I better get off. I need to review for the class I'm teaching tomorrow."

"Oh, you have a class now?"

"Yes, for the last month I have had the fifth and sixth grade boys' class. They keep me on my toes. I will miss them when I leave for college."

"Well, thanks for calling."

"I'll talk to you later. Goodbye."

When she put down the phone, Betsy pounced. "Who was that?"

"My friend, John. He's the one I told you about in a letter."

"A friend, huh?"

"Yes, that's all it is."

"Right," responded Betsy with a smirk.

Bethany playfully slugged her on the arm. "Oh, just go away."

When they rejoined the family, her parents looked up with curiosity showing on their faces. "That was John Holman, my friend from the church in Detroit. We sang together, and I played for some of his solos. We went over to Mrs. Carpenter's house to keep her company several times. He helped me a lot when I was upset about breaking up with Scott."

Betsy asked, "How did you get to that lady's house, Bethany?"

"John would pick her up and then come and get me, and the same when I went home. You don't have to worry about him—he has very strict standards for himself when he is with a girl."

"Well, that is good to hear," said Mrs. Prescott. "What did he call about?"

"Just to see how I'm doing, whether I had found a job and stuff. I guess you knew he was going to call, Dad. Why didn't you tell me?"

"He wanted to surprise you."

"I see," mused Bethany. "Well, I've got to go up and check on my clothes for tomorrow. I might have to iron something." Bethany headed for the stairs, humming "People Need the Lord," a song she and John had sung together.

James had shared his conversation with John with his wife. Now Mrs. Prescott looked at her husband and raised her eyebrows in a questioning way. He smiled and shrugged his shoulders.

∞

In Georgia that Saturday afternoon, Cindy also received a phone call. In response to her hello, Randy said, "It is so good to hear your voice, Cindy. I miss you. Did you hear what they did to me at that college? I had to leave campus without even saying goodbye."

"That was your own fault, Randy. You know the Bible says, '...*be sure your sin will find you out.*' "

"What makes you think I was committing a sin?"

"You were breaking rules. You were out past curfew or something, weren't you?"

"So? That wasn't a big deal."

"You weren't obeying authority. You were purposely rebelling. You even told me you were enjoying breaking the rules."

"You sound like my parents—nag, nag, nag."

"I am sure they are heartbroken and concerned about you."

"They are just worrying about how the people of the church will take it. My dad is worried about his precious work because he started this church from scratch."

"You should be proud of him."

"Well, I'm not. I think he cares more about all those other people than his own kids. He never had time for me and my brother."

"I'm sure as a pastor he has been busy and on call, but I think you are exaggerating. I'm sure he spent time with you and cares very much. Didn't he go to all the sporting events you were in?"

Reluctantly Randy admitted, "Yes, I guess so. But all we had in our small school was a basketball team. Besides, he would have watched the games whether or not I was playing because he is the pastor.

"My folks wouldn't let me play on little league teams or anything like that because they had games on Sundays. I wanted to be more involved in sports."

"We all have to make some sacrifices to serve God, but look what He sacrificed for us."

"You have an answer for everything, don't you?"

"No, but the Bible does."

"Well, you don't know my dad, and you don't know what it's like to be a P.K."

"My best friend here is the pastor's daughter. She doesn't feel that way."

"Give her time. Her eyes will open, and she will feel just like I do."

"You didn't feel like this when we first started dating. Someone else gave you these ideas, and you have fallen for Satan's lies and tricks. I am going to pray for my friend—that it never happens to her."

"Pray all you want. You can't stop the inevitable."

"Randy, it isn't inevitable. I know other P.K.s who have grown up and gone into the ministry themselves, and prayer does work."

"Oh, yeah? My mom keeps saying over and over, 'I don't know what's happened to you. I've prayed and prayed for you and taught you about the right ways all your life. How can you have this attitude and do these things?' What I did was not that serious anyway. We just stayed out late cruisin' in a guy's car."

"That's all?"

"Pretty much."

"Oh, so there was more. Did you start drinking, Randy?" choked out Cindy. The thought had brought the tears she had been holding back.

"Maybe I did, and maybe I didn't. It's not a big deal."

"Oh, come on! You know as well as I do that Proverbs 23:31 says, '*Look not thou upon the wine....*' A person never knows if he might have a weakness in that area that will lead to his being an alcoholic. If you never take the first drink, it can't happen to you. Verse 20 says, '*Be not among winebibbers...*' and verse 21, '*For the drunkard and the glutton shall come to poverty....*'

"Why don't you give up all this rebellion and get right with God? You are breaking His heart too. You are almost 20. It is time to grow up and act like a man."

"I know. I wish people would treat me like that."

"You haven't earned that privilege or their respect."

He snorted derisively in answer.

"What are you going to do this summer?"

"I'm thinking about going into the Army."

"The Army?! Do you think you won't have people telling you what to do there? Why do that? Why not just stay home and get a job?"

"Because if I am living in my folks' home, I have to follow their rules, including going to every service. I've heard it all many times. I don't need to hear it again."

"I'd say that's exactly what you need," retorted Cindy.

"Oh, quit nagging and listen to what I really called about."

"What did you really call about?"

"I want to come and see you."

"What?!"

"Just listen. Don't tell anyone. When I get in town, I'll phone you and set up a place to meet. We'll go out on the town. I'll show you places in your city you never even knew about. I've got some money in the bank. I'll draw it all out, hop on a bus, and be there in a few days. I miss you. I've just got to see you."

"Don't bother getting on that bus, Randy. I won't meet you. I won't go out with you. I thought you got the message when I gave your class ring back."

"What's the matter, Cindy? Are you too good for the likes of me? I'm just a P.K. I don't live on a big spread with horses."

"It has nothing to do with that."

"Oh, no?"

"No. I just don't want to do the things you are doing."

"I'm not doing anything now. My folks practically have me on a leash!"

"Well, that's good."

"No, it isn't, and I'm not going to stand for it any longer. I told you. I'm going to split."

"Well, don't come here."

"Come on, Cindy. Give me a break. I love you."

"Right now you don't love anyone but yourself, Randy."

"Can't you say something that isn't critical?"

"Randy, I enjoyed going out with you. You had good manners. You could make people laugh and have a good time—you were a lot of fun. But that was before you got this rotten attitude. I refuse to let you influence me in the wrong way."

"This isn't getting us anywhere. I'll call again in a few weeks. Maybe you will miss me enough to let me come visit you. Goodbye for now, Beautiful."

Cindy cried for a while; then she called Bethany. She had to share with someone, and her parents were not home. Bethany listened to her recital of the conversation, then prayed with Cindy and assured her she was praying daily for Randy. Cindy then asked Bethany if she had gone on any dates. Bethany told her no, but that John had called.

"That's interesting," said Cindy.

"You are as bad as Betsy," answered Bethany with a laugh.

"Aren't you looking forward to seeing John on campus?" asked Cindy.

"Well…"

"Be honest," prodded Cindy.

"Okay, I admit I am. He is a good friend."

"Sure, sure, just a good friend. Let me know if there are any more developments."

"Yes, Cupid. I'll talk to you later."

❧

The next day at church when choir practice was over, the Porter twins came in from playing on the church playground equipment. They were perspiring, and some of their hair had come loose from ponytails and was straggling around their faces and down their backs. "Oh dear, look at you two!" their mother exclaimed. "And I need to talk to some ladies before church."

Bethany overheard and spoke up, "I would be happy to help them if you would like me to."

"That would be a big help, but I hate to impose."

"I really don't mind."

"All right then. Here's a brush. Please take them to the restroom."

"Do we have to go to the restroom? She's just going to fix our ponytails. We want to see our friends before church starts, and that will make us miss them," whined Joy.

Hope added, "We're too tired to walk clear to the restroom."

"I hope you aren't arguing with me. That's what it sounds like."

"No, ma'am," both girls replied instantly.

"That's better. When you are done, you find Mrs. Nelson." This friend did not sing in the choir, so she sat with the girls and saved Mrs. Porter a place to sit when the choir members went down from the platform.

On the way to the restroom, Joy was still whining. "Why does Mom make us go to the stupid restroom?"

"I am sure she has explained it to you. What did she say?"

"That it isn't good manners to fix our hair in public," began Joy.

Hope interrupted, "And it isn't proper."

Joy retorted, "I was going to say that if you would give me a chance."

"Hush girls, don't start fighting. So if you know what your mom said, why are you asking me?"

"Because we see other people doing it. So why can't we? Our friend's mom fixes her kids' hair in the auditorium."

"Just because someone else does something doesn't make it right."

"Well, Mom makes a big deal out of it—like it's a sin or something," pouted Joy.

"I am sure she did not say it was a sin, did she?"

"No," both girls admitted reluctantly.

"She is trying to teach you to have good manners. It is better not to do your hair or makeup or file your nails in front of everyone. They are personal things you don't need to do in front of men. A girl or a woman brushing her hair and flipping it around gets guys to look at her. She is calling attention to herself."

"But we are just little girls. We don't even like boys."

"If your mom did it now in the auditorium, you would get the habit and start thinking it was okay. Then when you got older, you would keep doing it. You aren't the only ones, by the way. I was taught the same thing."

"Oh," said both girls, thinking over what Bethany had said as they entered the restroom with her and submitted to getting their faces and hands washed with a paper towel and their hair brushed and put back into neat ponytails. When Bethany was finished, they waited while she checked her makeup and hair. Knowing someone else was taught the same things as they were helped put them in a less petulant mood. Bethany walked back to the auditorium with them and found Mrs. Nelson, and then she went to line up with the choir.

Bethany was glad to have a mostly stress-free job. It was an opportunity to rest from her busy college life. The twins were usually easy to handle with only an occasional "off day" when nothing made them happy. The twins did not like long separations, so sending them to separate rooms was always a quick fix for bad attitudes.

Arrangements had been made with several of their church friends for playmates to spend part of a day or for Bethany to take the twins to the others' houses. She also took them to parks and miniature golf courses several times.

In the evenings she enjoyed being with her family and occasionally had phone calls from Kathleen or other local friends. She heard from Sarah, who was frustrated because her parents did not agree with the plans she and Paul had made. She had agreed to have a meeting with her pastor to get his opinion. Paul was also going to counsel with his pastor in the near future. His parents were also advising a more cautious courtship.

When Donna called, she had more exciting news. "Peter got the raise, so we should be able to afford to get married before he finishes college. He came down last weekend, and we counseled with pastor again. We told him that we had both dated others and didn't date each other very much during the school year. But we are both still serious about each other and didn't find anyone else who we are interested in. So pastor suggested we date exclusively for a year, and if our parents agree and finances permit, he will marry us next summer. If it happens that way, of course I will want you to be my maid of honor."

Bethany squealed with delight. "Thank you, Donna. I'd love that!"

Donna continued. "We could have the wedding a few weeks before school starts. You could come stay out here with the Davenports. I am sure they would not mind, and then you wouldn't have two airfares."

"That does sound like a good plan. Would you go back to college or work after you're married?"

"I will probably work part-time and take some courses. I don't know for sure if I will finish the secretarial program. It takes three years."

"Well, I hope it works out for you two."

"Thanks, Bethany."

∾

A letter came from Elaine:

Dear Bethany:

The Lord is so good! I found a Christian daycare for Michael. He is enjoying it. They have crafts, Bible verse memory, as well as play-time. All the children are from Christian families who are active in their churches—that is a prerequisite for enrolling your children.

Everyone in our family is growing in the Lord. I can't believe my mother! She is going soul winning with a ladies' group! I never would have believed it a year ago. (I would not have believed any of the things going on in my life, either!)

Do you have as much of a problem finding modest clothing as I do? I am seriously considering taking a sewing class so I can make my own. Everything in the stores has plunging necklines and short skirts!

I haven't heard anything from or about Mark. I am praying for him. The Lord knows where he is and what he needs in his life. The more I pray for him, the less angry I feel toward him, and the more the Lord shows me my own faults in our relationship. I hope we can make some kind of connection again in the future. Michael needs his dad. It is strange, but without my saying anything, Michael has been asking about his dad. On his own he started praying for him! Isn't that awesome?

How are things with you? What have you been doing this summer? I am sure you are enjoying being with your family. Write back if you have a minute to spare.

Love,

Elaine

Bethany sat down and wrote a short letter in reply, telling Elaine about her job, Sarah's struggles, and her phone calls from John. She assured Elaine that she also was praying for Mark.

A few weeks after his first call, John called again. He asked Bethany how her job was going as well as her summer vacation. Bethany shared with John about some of the times the twins had fooled her, filled him in on Donna's plans, and shared Sarah's frustrations. Bethany also mentioned that the tour group from the college would be at her church the following week for their annual youth conference. "I am really hoping it will be a blessing for my sister Betsy and our other young people."

"Let's pray to that end, Bethany, and also for guidance and direction for Donna and Sarah. By the way, how are things with Cindy? Didn't you tell me at spring break that she was interested in one particular young man?"

"Yes, we need to pray about that also." Bethany told John a little about that situation, and then he prayed for all their concerns before hanging up.

A few days later Bethany heard from Sarah again. "Well, I will see you back at college after all."

"Why? What happened?" Bethany hated to even ask for fear that Sarah and Paul had broken up. She was relieved to hear Sarah's explanation.

"We had four sets of counselors who all said the same thing without having consulted each other. We can't ignore that, but that doesn't mean I'm happy about it." Sarah began to cry.

"At least both of you are willing to listen to your counselors. And you still have each other. I know it's hard to wait to be together."

Sarah gulped back her tears. "I'm sorry, Bethany. You are right—at least we aren't breaking up like you and Cindy had to do. I'm sorry I was being such a big baby."

"Don't be sorry. I'm sure I'd cry in your situation. But time will go fast. Remember how quickly it went by last year?"

"Yes, but I wasn't wanting it to hurry by either."

"Are you going to be girlfriend/boyfriend or date others?"

"Everyone is in agreement that we can at least do that. Basically we already had that relationship without making it official. We both just stopped dating anyone else. Paul said he will have a surprise for me when I get back there."

"Maybe a promise ring?"

"I don't know. He won't say what it will be."

"Surprises are nice."

"Yes, but it makes me even more anxious for summer to be over! It is a good thing I am so busy with my job. And Mom and I are doing some window shopping to get ideas for a wedding in case we do end up getting engaged."

"That sounds exciting!"

"Yes, Mom and I are having a good time now that I have accepted the change of plans and quit fighting for what I wanted."

"It is hard to give up our way, isn't it?"

"Yes, but I can see the Lord using it to help me mature and grow spiritually."

"That's great, Sarah! Well, I'll see you in Indiana then. September will be here before we know it."

"I hope the time goes by fast," said Sarah. "Goodbye for now."

Summer Activities

"Can two walk together, except they be agreed?"
(Amos 3:3)

One evening Bethany received a phone call from a young man named Bob. He was calling to ask Bethany out for coffee. He had struck up conversations with her several times at church recently. He had graduated from the church school one year before Bethany and was now attending the University of Washington. He asked if she would like to go to a local coffee shop on Friday night. "I know we need chaperones, so if you are interested, I would like to ask your father if your parents would help us out."

"That sounds like fun, Bob. Would you like me to give the phone to my dad?"

"Yes, please."

After Mr. Prescott had greeted him, Bob asked if he and Mrs. Prescott would be willing to accompany Bethany and him to the coffee house on Friday night. Bob offered to treat them. Mr. Prescott asked him to hold while he spoke to his wife. Then he returned to the phone.

"We would be happy to go with you two Friday night. It would be something different for us—we haven't had a date there for quite a while. But you don't need to treat us. I will make it a date for us and buy for my wife and me. I quite often take my wife out on Friday nights anyway."

"I really appreciate it, Brother Prescott."

∽

Friday night Bob came to the Prescotts' home to pick up Bethany and her parents. When they arrived at the coffee house, Mr. Prescott told the young people that he and his wife would take a separate table. Bethany enjoyed the date and appreciated Bob's buying her a latte. They talked about college life and compared their quite different experiences. Bob told her he was taking a pre-med course and that he wanted to be a pediatrician. Bob asked her to sit with him at church Sunday, and she agreed. They left after about an hour, and Bob drove them home.

After they sat together at the morning service, Bob asked her if she would sit with him again in the evening. She politely turned him down, explaining that she wanted to sit with her family. During the morning service, she could not sit with her mother as Margaret taught a church hour class.

The next Wednesday night was the beginning of their church's youth conference. A tour group from the Bible college was there to participate in the conference, which lasted until noon on Friday. She knew some of the young ladies slightly and enjoyed visiting with them and hearing about their experiences on tour. It gave her pangs of regret that she had not been selected for the following year, but she hid those feelings from everyone.

Thursday night when Betsy got home from the youth conference, she was eager to share with her family that she had gone to the altar and made a vow to keep herself pure and save her first kiss for the altar. Bethany and her parents were overjoyed that their prayers had been answered. Many others among the young people had also made decisions.

Bob sat with Bethany in the young adult Sunday school class and walked with her to the auditorium. He asked if he could save a place for her to sit when the choir came down, and she agreed. She enjoyed his company but was concerned that he might already be getting too serious. That afternoon she spoke with her mother about her concerns. "Mom, when you date, isn't it basically determining whether you could consider marriage with the person?"

"Well, I think it can be just casual friendship and companionship even if you know you could never be serious about the other person."

"How can you let the other person know that is all it is?"

"Are you thinking about Bob?"

"Yes. He is very nice, but I feel strongly that God wants me to marry a man going into full-time Christian service."

"If he asks you out again, you could say something like, 'I enjoy your company on a friendship basis, Bob. I hope that you are not wanting it to be more than that.'"

"Thanks, Mom. I think that would work."

The following Thursday Bob called Bethany again. "I was wondering if you would enjoy going miniature golfing tomorrow night?"

"That sounds like fun."

"Do you think your parents would be willing to come along again?"

"I think so. Let me check with them to be sure they don't have a family activity planned."

Mr. Prescott told Bethany that he did not want to leave Betsy and Brian alone on Friday again so soon, and if Bob did not mind, the family would go. "You two can split off and go on one of the other courses," he added.

Bethany returned to the phone and gave Bob the answer.

"Good. I'll come by about seven o'clock, if that's okay? Then we will figure out the transportation."

"That will be fine. Thanks, Bob. Goodbye."

"Goodbye until tomorrow, then."

Friday evening the Prescotts allowed Bethany to ride with Bob, with Betsy along as their chaperone. The rest of the family followed in their car. The three young people enjoyed visiting in the car on the way to the miniature golf course; then Betsy joined her parents and Brian. After enjoying that activity, they stopped at an ice cream parlor on the way home. Again Betsy was riding in Bob's car, so he insisted on paying for her treat, even after Betsy assured him she had brought some cash. He kiddingly told her it was her wages for acting as chaperone. When they reached her home Bethany invited him to stay and visit for a while. She had clued her family in earlier that she needed to talk to Bob privately, so Betsy went on into the house. Bethany and Bob sat down on comfortable porch chairs. Margaret, James, and Brian also went into the house.

"Bob, I have enjoyed our times together. It is very nice of you to take me places and buy me treats. You were very considerate of Betsy tonight, and I appreciate it very much. But I wanted to be sure you were not expecting anything more than just a friendly companionship."

"Thanks for being honest and open with me about that, Bethany. I can assure you, that is all I have in mind, also. I have many years of schooling ahead of me. I am not looking for a serious relationship with anyone at this time."

"Good. Then we can just relax and have a good time. But don't you think you should date some other girls, also?"

"I suppose, but frankly, you are the most attractive and the most intriguing; you are just so alive!"

Bethany laughed. "Thanks for the compliment."

"What about you? Have you had dates with anyone else?"

"Actually, it has been almost a year. But I do have a friend who has been calling me. But think about it, there aren't a lot of young people our age around church."

"That's true. Guess you are just stuck with me," he said and laughed. "Well, I better run. We both have to get up for bus meeting tomorrow. See you there."

"Okay. Goodnight," responded Bethany as Bob rose to leave.

When Bethany went into the house, her dad remarked, "Bob seems to be hanging around you a lot. Is he seriously interested in you?"

"No, we talked about that. We both just want to enjoy each other's company on a casual basis. He has lots of schooling ahead of him—he wants to be a doctor."

"I think he will make a good one," her dad responded. "Well, good night, Bethany."

"Goodnight, Daddy."

Cindy received a second phone call from Randy. She asked, "Where are you?"

"In my apartment."

"Are you still in your home town?"

"No. I wanted to really be on my own, so I moved across the state. I got a job and found some guys to share an apartment."

"I thought you were going to enlist."

"What you said made sense, so I decided not to."

"So, do you like your job?"

"It's okay."

"What are you doing? Is it something that can become a career?"

"It could, but I'm not sure I want it to. I'm working with a roofing company."

"Oh! Be careful, Randy."

"See! You do still care."

"I never said I didn't. What do you do with your free time?"

"My roommates know how to throw a party. We've had some good times."

"You mean you are drinking. Randy, I've been reading up on alcoholism. If you ever black out, you know, wake up in the morning and don't remember what you did the night before—take that for a warning that you are heading toward being an alcoholic. I wish you wouldn't drink at all or do drugs. Please, Randy. You will destroy your mind and your body like it says in Proverbs 5:11, *"And thou mourn at the last, when thy flesh and thy body are consumed...."*

"You really do still care, don't you? I think if I called you and told you I was in town, you would break down and meet me."

"Do you know what I would do? I would take my dad with me and meet you."

"Why would you do something stupid like that?"

"So he could try to get your thinking straightened out and get you back on track."

"You wouldn't really do that."

"Yes I would."

"Why, Cindy? I know you like me. You even agreed to be my girlfriend."

"If things had stayed the same, I would have loved to have you come for a visit and meet my parents." Cindy was crying now, and she barely managed to talk between sobs. "You ruined everything." Crying too hard to say more, Cindy hung up the phone.

❧

Summer break was going by quickly for Bethany. She and Kathleen went shopping together and visited in each other's homes some evenings. Kathleen's family had the Prescotts over for a barbecue. Bob spent several Friday nights at the Prescotts' and took Bethany out to dinner one night with the pastor and his wife as chaperones.

John called again. "Are you having a good summer, Bethany?" he asked.

"Yes. I have been so busy, I am going to have to settle down soon and get serious about shopping and packing for school. Time is going by so quickly."

"I wish it were true for me."

"Don't you ever go out?" asked Bethany.

"You mean on a date?"

"Yes. I have been having lots of fun dating a guy from our church. It's just as friends, which is all I want right now."

Hiding his own longings and reactions to her comments, John answered, "No, I don't seem to find anyone I wish to ask out. But I'm sure I will when I get to college."

"No wonder this summer is dragging by for you," answered Bethany sympathetically.

Wishing to change the subject, John asked about her roommates for whom he had been consistently praying.

"I think Cindy still cares a lot for Randy. It is hard on her. She won't give in and let him lead her astray, but she prays for him constantly. Sarah and Paul are both going back to college. I am so proud of them for listening to their parents and their pastors. I haven't heard anything more from Donna since I last talked to you.

"I have exciting news about my sister Betsy. She made a vow at the Youth Conference to stay pure and to save her first kiss for the altar."

"That's great, Bethany. An answer to our prayers!"

"Yes. Thanks for joining me and my parents in praying for that."

"Let's thank the Lord for that answer and for Sarah and Paul's decision."

After leading in prayer, John asked, "What else do you have planned before school starts?"

"Next week we have Vacation Bible School. Since the twins will be going, I will help with that and then drive them home when it is over at noon. The following week my dad is taking a week's vacation. We are going to drive down to the Oregon coast and stay at Cannon Beach. Besides walking and playing on the beach, we will go to some of the tourist attractions. When we get back, I will have a week to get ready before leaving for college."

"The trip sounds like fun. You will have to tell me all about it when we get to school."

"Sure. What are you doing these last few weeks?"

"I am flying to California to visit with my family this coming week."

"Oh, that is wonderful! I am sure you are excited about that."

"Yes. I am looking forward to seeing them all. Then I will head for Indiana to try to get a job lined up. I have some appointments for interviews."

"I will be praying for you about that."

"Thanks, Bethany. What about you? Do you have a job for next year?"

"I have been very fortunate. I am going to continue working for Mrs. Morgan in the music department."

"That's great. Well, I better get off. I probably won't talk to you again until I see you at college. I am looking forward to that."

"Yes, we will have lots to catch up on. These next few weeks will be very eventful. Goodbye then, until September 4 in Indiana."

∽

The twins were excited about Vacation Bible School when Bethany arrived at their house Monday morning. She helped them finish getting ready and drove them to church. She found the area in the auditorium marked for their age group, and then she joined the teacher whom she was assisting with the kindergarten class. After enjoying the opening session, each class moved to its designated classroom. There was so much to squeeze in to the allotted time that the morning flew by for Bethany. When she joined the girls at the car for the ride home, it was obvious that they had enjoyed the experience. She listened to their excited chatter all the way to their home, and it continued while she prepared lunch. She finally had to tell them to stop talking so they could eat! It was like that every day, and the twins were sorry when Friday arrived.

Bethany reminded them that she would be going on vacation with her family the following week and then spend the rest of the time shopping and packing before flying back to Indiana. But the great news for them was that their grandmother was arriving Saturday afternoon! Even though they were happy and excited about that, they clung to Bethany and cried when it was time for her to leave for the last time as their nanny. Their sadness brought back painful memories for Bethany of the previous summer when she had left her job as Michael's nanny. Bethany hated goodbyes! She had grown very fond of the little girls, and she cried with them. Mrs. Porter rescued the situation by saying, "Give Bethany one last hug. She needs to get home for her dinner, and we need to go bake the pizza I brought home."

"Pizza!" they exclaimed in unison. "Thank you, Mommy." Bethany gave each girl a last hug and hurried out the door. In the car she found a tissue and wiped her eyes and blew her nose before starting the car and driving home.

Of course when she got home, her brother Brian noticed she had been crying and began teasing her. When he saw it was really bothering her, he said, "I'm sorry you are sad, Sis, and sorry I teased you."

"It's okay. It's just that the twins cried, and it made me cry. They are so sweet and so much fun. I will miss them. Let's just think about next week. I am excited about our trip, aren't you?"

"I can hardly wait!"

"Wait for what?" asked Betsy as she came upon them in the middle of the conversation.

"Our trip next week, what else?" answered Brian.

"Guess what I just found out, Mr. Smarty Pants?"

"What?"

"Dad has made arrangements with the motel manager to let us have the pool to ourselves before and after the normal hours."

"Oh, that's great," squealed Bethany.

"Wait till you see what Mom has made us to wear swimming!"

"You mean we don't have to swim in our culottes?"

"Right. Come on, I'll show you."

The two girls went to Mrs. Prescott's sewing room where she was finishing up Bethany's "swimsuit" before going down to finish dinner. "So this is why you took my measurements when I got home?" asked Bethany.

"Yes. I did some experimenting, and I think these will work for us."

"Let me see," asked Bethany.

"I have a little more sewing to do on yours. Here, look at Betsy's. See, I bought regular swimsuit fabric and made pantaloons with an attached overskirt and a matching short-sleeved shirt. There is elastic in the legs of the pantaloons, and they come to just below our knees."

"That is really neat, Mommy. You are so talented!"

"Well, I hope they work out okay."

"They look like they should," observed Bethany.

"I think they will be great," added Betsy.

"Could you girls make a salad and set the table for dinner so I can finish this last little bit?"

"Sure," they answered and headed for the stairs, chattering about their mom's creation as they went.

At dinner that night James was happy to hear the report that the new "swimsuits" were ready. He suggested that they all start their packing for the trip that evening since Saturday and Sunday would be busy. "I want to get an early start on Monday morning," he explained.

Everyone pitched in on clean up after dinner, and afterward James and

Brian went to the attic and retrieved suitcases. Everyone got most of the clothing they would need packed that night. Saturday Mrs. Prescott gathered and packed food items. They had reserved a motel room with a kitchenette and would fix some of their meals there. Of course, with three teenagers she also had snack items to eat in the car.

Sunday morning Hope and Joy Porter found Bethany and introduced her to their grandmother, Mrs. Carter. She could see there was much mutual love between the girls and their grandmother, and she knew they would enjoy the next few weeks.

Mrs. Carter told Bethany, "I don't know if I can possibly live up to the standard you set as a caregiver. The girls have gone on and on about what a great nanny you are."

"Well, that is nice to hear. But I know they have been anticipating your arrival, also."

"We do have a good time together," said their grandmother.

In the evening when the service was over, the Prescotts hurried home and put some of the luggage and food boxes in the car. Then they went to bed early, setting their alarms for 5:00 a.m. They wanted to spend as much time as possible at the beach. Monday morning they had a quick breakfast of dry cereal and ate snacks in the car. They sang songs and played several games to pass the time. The three teenagers had also brought books to read. Mrs. Prescott visited with her husband and occasionally pointed out something of interest in nature.

When the family finally arrived at their destination, they unpacked the car and settled into the motel room and then headed for the beach. They were happy that it was sunny with a warm breeze blowing. They had brought beach balls and plastic discs. They returned to the motel and made sandwiches for lunch. After eating, they returned to the beach with buckets and shovels, and the whole family worked together on building a sand castle.

After cleaning up in the motel room, Mr. Prescott took them out to eat in a local restaurant for dinner. They enjoyed the meal, walked around for a while, and then returned to the motel.

The Prescotts watched a video they had brought with them until bedtime. The next morning after hearing a weather forecast on the television, they decided to drive along the coast to some of the attractions they wanted to enjoy. They already knew it wasn't going to be a nice day for playing on the beach. They followed this routine all week—if it was nice, the family stayed in Cannon Beach and played; but when it was chilly, windy, or rainy, they found other things to do. It was a wonderful time of relaxation for all of them. They used the pool during off-hours several times. Mrs. Prescott and the girls found that their new "swimsuits" worked better than just wearing culottes. On Wednesday evening they attended a local Baptist church they had visited on past trips to Cannon Beach.

The family headed for home Saturday afternoon. Part of the time in the car, Bethany worked on a list of things she needed to buy before going back to school and another list of things she needed to pack. She was getting excited about going back to college. She was anxious to meet her new roommates, hoping they would get along as well as last year's group. She found her thoughts straying to John. She was looking forward to telling him all about her trip and hearing about his. She had two more Sundays at home; and then she would leave the next Tuesday so she could arrive the day the dormitories would be open. The following day would be registration and the first chapel service.

Her last Saturday at home she visited on Betsy's bus route and rode the bus on Sunday. She had gotten attached to some of the children here during the summer. At church she had to say goodbye to many people, including the Porter twins again. She wished she could just sneak quietly away! And she had this to go through on Tuesday with her family.

When all that was behind her, she gratefully sank into her seat on the plane next to Kathleen. "Do you hate goodbyes as much as I do?"

"Yes. The only thing that helps is remembering where I am going and how much I enjoyed being there last year."

"It must help—I don't see any telltale signs of crying in your face. I'll have to try that in the future, but I don't know if it will work for me. I am pretty sentimental."

"Well, tell me about your family's trip to the coast. That will help get your mind off leaving home."

"Okay. It was a great vacation. My dad called ahead and made arrangements for us to have the pool to ourselves. We went swimming four times. When we go home for Christmas, I'll have to show you what my mom designed for us to wear. It was so much better than trying to swim in culottes.

"We all worked together and made a fantastic sand castle the first afternoon. One day we started out early and drove down the coast to the Sea Lion Caves. A couple of other days we took shorter drives and stopped at scenic spots and historic landmarks. We really had a good time."

"It sounds like it. I love it when we go to the Oregon coast."

"So, what did you do since we last talked a few weeks ago?"

"I've had a few dates with Bob. I hope you don't mind?"

"Of course not. We have an understanding—we both only wanted a platonic relationship. We aren't interested in each other on a romantic basis. He is very nice and lots of fun. Where did you go?"

"We went to the miniature golf course with his parents along as chaperones. Then we went to a coffee stand before going home. One night he came to the house, and we played board games. I enjoyed my time with him very much. Why did you want to keep it to being just friends?"

"I feel God wants me to marry someone who is going into full-time Christian service."

"Great! I won't have competition from you then."

"Oh, do I detect a budding romance?"

"I don't know. We were just having fun together. He talked some about his medical studies. He has a long way to go. I hope I get to see him during school breaks, and I hope he will ask me out some more. I am afraid there is more interest on my part than his."

"I will pray with you about that. Maybe as he gets closer to finishing, Bob will let himself get more interested in you. He would be getting a real catch."

"Thanks, Bethany. I don't know about that, but I think he is definitely special."

"I agree. He is a lot of fun and a good Christian, as far as I can tell. He told me he found a good church not too far from the university and is actively involved when he is at school."

"Yes, he works in their bus ministry. Are you going to date this year at college?"

"Yes, I am looking forward to it."

"Anyone special in mind?"

"Well…my friend John called several times, and we talked about getting together to tell each other about our trips. He went to California to see his family. I used to think about him as a big brother type, but now…"

"But now, what?" pressed Kathleen.

"I don't feel that way anymore. He is a special friend, and I hope we will have some dates."

"Do you think it might become more than friendship?"

"Maybe. He called several times, but I'm not sure what that means. He kept the conversations pretty casual."

"Personally, I think he likes you."

"Why do you say that?"

"Every time you go to Detroit, he manages to spend time with you. And when he came for the pastors' conference, you two went off together quite a bit."

"He wanted to tour the campus before he came this semester."

"Well, I for one don't believe that was all he wanted. I think he wanted time alone with you."

"I kind of hope you are right, but I think you are reading too much into it."

"We will see."

"The girls grew quiet. After sitting and mulling over Kathleen's words for a while, Bethany pulled out a novel and began to read. After the stewardess brought snacks and a drink, she put the book down and took a nap. When she awoke, Bethany read her book until they arrived at O'Hare International Airport. She commented to Kathleen, "Well, here goes our second year. I wonder what changes it will bring in our lives?"

A Challenging Responsibility

"When my father and my mother forsake me,
then the LORD will take me up." (Psalm 27:10)

*W*hen Bethany reached campus to begin her sophomore year of college, she immediately started watching for familiar faces. It wasn't long before she spotted Sarah and Paul walking together. They saw her at almost the same moment and turned toward her. Sarah and Bethany hugged, and Paul greeted Bethany warmly. Bethany asked, "Are you two as excited as I am about being back here?"

Paul answered first. "Yes, very much so, and not just because Sarah is here. I just love the atmosphere here and all the opportunities to serve the Lord. I have decided to work with the sailor ministry—just to have different learning experiences. I will miss the bus kids, though."

Sarah added, "I'm happy. Once I got reconciled to the idea of putting our other plans on hold," she glanced at Paul, smiled and continued, "I regained my enthusiasm for college life. I want to learn all I can so I can be a true helpmeet for Paul in his future ministry. Do you remember that I told you Paul had promised me a surprise?"

"Yes! Did you get something already?"

"Look!" Sarah pointed to the necklace she was wearing.

Bethany saw a heart-shaped pendant with a sapphire dangling inside the heart. "It's beautiful, Sarah. It's your birthstone, isn't it? Your birthday is sometime this month, right?"

"Yes, it was for my birthday; but Paul said it is also a daily reminder that he loves me and we have plans for a future together."

"That is sweet. I am so happy for you two."

Sarah smiled at her friend and then asked, "Bethany, have you heard from Cindy lately?"

"Not for a few weeks, but I'm sure she's here, even though she is brokenhearted over Randy. He sure doesn't appreciate what he threw away. She has grown so much in her spiritual life since this time last year."

"I just hope she doesn't lose that special vibrant zest for life. She was so much fun to be around!"

"Hey, there she is!" cried out Bethany joyfully, breaking away and running to greet Cindy with a hug. "Come over here, Cindy. Paul and Sarah are anxious to say hello."

The two girls linked their arms together and hurried back to Sarah and Paul. As they were chattering, Donna, Peter, and John quietly walked up and greeted them, startling all four.

"Oh, where did you come from?" blurted out Bethany.

"Detroit," answered John with a mischievous grin.

"Oh, you…I meant I was looking around just a minute ago, and I did not spot you."

"Oh, so you were watching for me?"

Blushing and stammering, Bethany blurted out, "I mean I was watching for familiar faces."

John laughed. "I am sorry. I shouldn't tease you, but it is so much fun."

"You are so bad," responded Bethany, but then couldn't help laughing with him. She reached for Donna and gave her a big hug and then greeted Peter warmly. John had met all the girls and Paul when he had visited the campus during the conference he had attended the prior spring. He acknowledged the other two girls and shook hands with Paul.

Paul asked John, "Do you think you will enjoy college life? Most of us are younger than you by several years. We may drive you crazy."

"I am looking forward to it, even though it will be quite a change from having my own apartment. At least I won't be lonely as I have been sometimes in the past few years."

"I guarantee you won't have time on your hands," assured Paul.

"Amen to that," added Peter. "But the busyness helps the time go by quickly, and for some of us that is extremely important." He winked at Donna, who blushed but nodded her head in agreement.

"Are you girls settled into your rooms yet?" asked John.

"I'm not," admitted Bethany. "I haven't even been there yet. I probably should go get unpacked and organized. Tomorrow will be busy with registration and chapel."

"Could we meet somewhere tomorrow, Bethany, and eat lunch together?" asked John. "We were going to tell each other about our trips."

"Sure, let's meet at the mailroom at lunch time."

The group began to break up and disperse in several directions. John told Bethany, "I'll see you tomorrow then."

Peter told Donna, "Let's meet at the mailroom before chapel."

"Okay. See you then."

Donna and Bethany walked together in the direction of the girls' dormitory. "Bethany, do you know any of your roommates?"

"I know one." Bethany answered "Amy was in one of my classes last year. The other two are freshmen. How about you?"

"They are all returning students whom I know only slightly."

"I hope both of us will have roommates that get along."

"Me too."

The girls talked about their summer activities until they split up to go to their respective rooms. When Bethany entered her new dorm room, she found one of the freshmen girls sitting on a bed looking bewildered. She was a cute girl, a little taller than Bethany, with dark eyes and curly black hair. Bethany greeted her in a friendly tone. "Hi. It looks like we are going to be roommates. I'm Bethany Prescott, from Tacoma, Washington."

"I'm glad you came. I don't know what to do next. I'm Carrie Douglas from Chicago."

"You must be a member of Crossroads Baptist Church."

"Yes, for about a year. I'm a bus kid. My bus captain got some people together to sponsor me to go to college. It's nice of them, but I'm scared to death!"

"I'm a sophomore this year, but I remember what it was like last year. I'll help you all I can, but there really is no need to be scared. Everyone here is very kind. Our dorm supervisor is great—she really seems to love college girls."

"I don't feel very loveable," confessed Carrie.

"Why would you say that?"

"Because I'm just a new Christian, and I don't always do things right," she said with tears glistening in her eyes.

Bethany sat down next to her on the bed. "None of us are perfect—no matter how long we've been saved. Would a hug help?"

Carrie inched further away from Bethany. "I'm not much of a hugging person."

"That's fine. I won't do it then. How about we get started organizing and putting our things away. You can see there isn't a whole lot of room. Now let's see, you were here first so you can pick which bed you want and also choose the drawers and which part of the closet you want."

"Oh, I don't want to pick first. I'll just take the leftovers."

"That's sweet of you, but not necessary. Now do you like this bed in the back of the room or the one closer to the door?"

"This one."

"Okay. Now do you want the top bunk or the bottom?"

"Do you think the other girls will mind if I take the bottom?"

"Of course not."

"Well, I don't want to push for my own way and be selfish or anything. But I really don't like climbing up."

"That will be fine. I'm sure the others won't mind. In fact, I'll take the upper, okay?"

"If you're sure."

"Now, let's pick the closet and drawer spaces."

"Oh, Bethany, will you please decide? Just tell me where to put my things."

Bethany could see that would be the fastest and easiest thing to do, so she agreed. Before they finished, the door opened, and another girl arrived. Already realizing that Carrie was painfully shy, Bethany introduced herself and Carrie to Allison Waters, a freshman from Oregon.

Allison exclaimed, "I remember you, Bethany! I didn't know your name, but I recognize you. Our youth group has gone to your church for the youth conference for several years."

"Are you Pastor Waters' daughter?"

"Yes."

"You have grown up and changed since I saw you last. I have missed the last three conferences."

"Weren't you home this last summer?"

"I was, but I didn't help out at the conference because I was working; and at the Wednesday night service it was so crowded, I was sitting way in the back."

At this moment Amy Prentice, a sophomore from Florida, arrived. Again Bethany handled the introductions. She then told the two newcomers that she and Carrie had begun putting their things away. "Does either of you prefer the top bunk?"

Both girls responded in the affirmative. "Really? You both would like a top bunk?"

"I do," responded Allison, "but if they are taken I'll be fine with the lower."

Bethany answered, "Actually, I would prefer the bottom, so one of you can be on the top of the one in the back, and one on the top of this one closest to the door."

"You go ahead and choose, Amy, since you are older," Allison offered.

"Okay, I would like the one up front."

"Great! I was hoping you would choose it," said Allison.

"It looks like everyone got what she wanted. How easy was that? I hope that keeps up," said Bethany with a grin. "Carrie and I just have a little more unpacking and organizing to do. You two should have time to get most of yours done before time to go for dinner."

As she got out her sheets to begin making up her bed, Allison asked, "What happens tomorrow?"

Amy answered, "You have to register and sign up for your classes for the first semester. Then we will have the first chapel service for this year. Everyone has to attend chapel."

"What is chapel like?" asked Carrie.

"Pretty much the same as a church service," said Bethany. "We have one every day."

Carrie inquired, "Doesn't that get tiresome?"

"It didn't for me," Bethany assured her. "They always have exciting speakers—different ones all the time."

Amy added, "And the guys are so responsive, yelling 'Amen' and everything. It definitely does not get boring."

"Would you tell us about how to enroll for classes and how to find our way around?" requested Allison.

The two older girls gladly told the other two anything they could think of that would be helpful. The time raced by, and the girls were finishing when Bethany noticed the time and suggested they get ready to go to dinner.

In the dining hall Bethany and Amy were greeted by many students they had met the previous year. Allison was outgoing and friendly and found friends from her home church to sit with. Carrie stayed close to Bethany and watched her to know what to do. Amy also found a group of friends to sit with. Bethany and Carrie sat down at a table and were soon joined by one of the young men Bethany had met the previous year. He had asked her for a date several times until she had finally told him she did not intend to date at all during her freshman year. Anthony wasn't going to waste any time—he asked Bethany to sit with him in chapel the following day.

Bethany hesitated until she remembered there would be a break between chapel and time to meet John for lunch. Anthony was a sandy-haired, stockily built young man, not as slim as Scott and shorter than John. Bethany agreed to sit with him during the first chapel service of the year. When they had finished their dinner, Anthony excused himself, saying he had to finish unpacking.

Bethany asked Carrie if she would like to take a tour of the campus to help her learn her way around. Carrie was enthusiastic about the idea and thanked Bethany profusely, even saying it a few more times even after Bethany had assured her she would enjoy the walk and had nothing better to do. Bethany talked as they strolled, telling Carrie about her family, her summer job caring for the twins and about her experiences as Michael's nanny. She tried to draw Carrie out by asking about her family, but Carrie was immediately, obviously uncomfortable. She only managed to say she was an only child before turning the conversation in another direction. By the time they returned to the dormitory, Bethany's conversational abilities and topics were used up. It was obvious that this girl was going to need a lot of loving help, and Bethany was going to need a lot of patience!

The girls passed the dorm supervisor, Miss McGuire, in the hall. She stopped Bethany, and asked, "Do you have a few minutes? I'd like to talk to you about something."

"Yes, ma'am." Turning to Carrie, she asked, "Do you have your room key?"

"Yes, I'll go on to the room. See you later."

Miss McGuire invited Bethany into her apartment and asked her to sit down. "I see that Carrie Douglas has arrived and that you have gotten acquainted."

Bethany answered, "Yes," with a slight hesitation.

"What does that mean, Bethany?"

"It is hard to get to know her. She listens but doesn't participate in a conversation. I mean, she doesn't want to say anything about her family or offer any information about herself. She seems shy, no, not just shy; it is a lack of self-confidence, I think. In fact, she told me she is scared about being at college."

"You are very perceptive, Bethany. I can see I made the right decision when I put her in a room with you."

Bethany responded with a startled, "Oh!"

"I know you have a busy schedule, but I am hoping you can be like a big sister to Carrie and help her as much as possible. I want you to keep me informed on her progress, and if something comes up that you cannot handle, please let me know. She is," Miss McGuire hesitated, searching for an appropriate word, "a troubled young lady with much to overcome. Are you willing to take this on?"

"I will try my best, Miss McGuire. I hope I can live up to your expectations and the trust you have in me. It is more than I have for myself, I'm afraid."

"You will do fine, I am sure. She just needs a lot of love and patience. Of course, this is all just between you and me," she added as they stood.

"Oh, yes, ma'am," said Bethany as she headed for the door. Before returning to her room, Bethany found an empty lounge and spent some time in prayer about this added responsibility. She asked the Lord to help her regard it as an opportunity to serve rather than a burden.

When she returned to the room, Carrie anxiously questioned, "Are you in trouble, Bethany?"

"No, Carrie. Just because a teacher or counselor asks to speak to you, it doesn't automatically mean you are in trouble." She offered no additional explanation and was relieved that no one questioned her further.

The next day she met Anthony as planned, and they found seats together in the chapel. A few minutes later Carrie spotted Bethany and took the seat next to her. Bethany was trying to be polite and attentive to Anthony, but Carrie kept asking her questions. Finally Bethany whispered to Carrie, "I am supposed to be having a chapel date with Anthony."

"I'm sorry, Bethany." Carrie turned bright red from embarrassment and started to rise to find another seat, but the preacher stepped up to the pulpit to begin the service. Carrie was too upset to even hear the preaching.

Likewise, Bethany was feeling like she had failed before she had begun with Carrie. She was praying about it and missed much of the message. When the service was over, Carrie hurried away before Bethany could say anything to her. Anthony was commenting on the service and asked her what she thought about one of the points the preacher had covered. Bethany was embarrassed and had to admit she had not really heard that part of the sermon. Now she felt like she had gotten off on the wrong foot with both Carrie and Anthony.

∾

What a relief it was to meet John later and just relax! He had a calming effect on her. She asked him to pray about something that she was not at liberty to share with him, and he assured her that he would. In fact, he included it in his prayer for the food. As planned, they each shared about their trip and the time spent with their respective families. Bethany could tell that John also came from a close-knit family. When they finished eating, John suggested they go play table tennis. Bethany readily agreed, and they had fun playing a fast-paced game. Then John walked her back to her dormitory before leaving for his job.

When Bethany entered the room, she could tell Carrie was still upset about the incident in chapel. She was not crying but could not bring herself to look directly at Bethany as she mumbled an apology. "Carrie, it is okay. I wasn't upset with you; I was just trying to remind you that Anthony had asked me to go to chapel with him. Everything is okay; don't worry about it anymore, please."

"I'll try not to," was Carrie's mumbled response.

The next day was a free day except for everyone's attending chapel. Classes would not start until the following day. Bethany invited Carrie to go to breakfast with her. She had to coax Carrie and assure her she really wanted her to go with her before Carrie agreed. On their way, Carrie told Bethany, "You don't have to put up with me all the time. I am not pretty and popular like you, and my clothes aren't very nice. I don't want to embarrass you."

"Carrie, I am not embarrassed to be with you. You need to stop thinking like that. Relax and enjoy college life. You aren't bad looking—you are actually quite pretty. I love your curly hair."

"I don't know much about fixing it up or wearing make-up and things."

"You have a nice complexion without make-up, but if you really want to learn to use it one of us in our room can show you. I like your hair the way it is—I think your clothes look fine too."

"My clothes aren't as nice—I have to get them at thrift stores," she whispered.

"So? Where do you think some of mine come from? My family often shops at thrift stores. A lot of other families in our church do too."

"Are you serious? You aren't just saying that to make me feel better?"

"If I were doing that, I would be lying."

"Oh, I didn't mean to call you a liar. Whenever I open my mouth, the wrong things come out. See, I am always messing up."

Bethany tried to get Carrie to lighten up and get her mind off herself. She laughed and said, "Exactly what comes out of your mouth? Do you have a frog or something in your throat?"

Carrie retorted, "I am not trying to be funny!" She stomped off.

Bethany decided to let Carrie cool off a little and just followed a short distance behind her. Before they reached the dining hall, Carrie turned around to check if Bethany was still there. Seeing her, she came back and said, "I am sorry, Bethany."

"So am I, Carrie. I wasn't making fun of you. I just want you to lighten up a little. Let's forget it and go get some breakfast."

"Okay."

During the next few days Bethany tried hard to be a friend and "big sister" to Carrie. The other girl would cling to her whenever possible and tell Bethany how miserable she felt when they were apart. Bethany tried to introduce her to others in hopes she would make more friends, but Carrie did not seem to find anyone else with whom she was as comfortable. She did not seem to fit in and was always a silent onlooker, unable to join in conversations. Carrie was consumed with her own problems and feelings of inadequacy. Bethany wondered what made her so insecure, but Carrie did not share anything about her childhood or her family.

Friday Bethany went to see Miss McGuire to ask for ideas to help Carrie. She sought her opinion about Saturday. "Do you think I should take Carrie with me on my bus route? She is clinging to me and not getting acquainted with other girls. She practically runs away if a guy speaks to her or even looks her way. I can tell some are even interested in her. She really is quite pretty, but I can't convince her of that." Without intending to or realizing she did it, Bethany sighed.

Miss McGuire was perceptive and answered, "I think you need a break, and we have to push the bird out of the nest a little. Amy Prentice is also in your room, correct?"

"Yes."

"Amy and I work on the same route. I'll take Carrie with us."

"Are you sure? I didn't mean to complain or…"

"Don't worry about it, Bethany. I don't expect you to be a mother hen all the time. Carrie can't be dependent on one person. You have done more than I expected, and I appreciate what you have done."

Bethany was actually relieved but did not say so.

Friday after chapel, John waited for Bethany outside the entrance. As usual, Carrie was walking with Bethany. John asked if he could join them and then tried to have a conversation with both girls. Carrie was not responsive; she just listened as Bethany and John talked. John asked Bethany if they could have dinner together Saturday evening. Now Carrie found her tongue and blurted out, "Some other guy just asked her. What was his name, Bethany?"

Bethany concealed her irritation at Carrie's rudeness and answered, "Jim Rider. I'm sorry, John. He just asked me as we were coming out of chapel."

"I can see a man has to be quick around here," responded John with a smile. He was reminding himself that he had told Mr. Prescott it would be a good idea for Bethany to date others. He was now having second thoughts about that idea! "I'm putting in my bid for Monday lunch. How about it?"

"I'd like that," answered Bethany.

When John had left, Carrie complained, "You are too popular!"

"Carrie, there are guys who want to ask you for dates, but you practically run away if they look like they are going to talk to you!"

"I get too scared."

"Scared about what?"

"I don't know what to say or how to act."

"You can just talk about a chapel message or about a class. Just listen to the guy and respond to what he says."

Saturday Carrie was disappointed when Miss McGuire told her she would take her on her bus route. She was brave enough to speak up when things didn't work out the way she wanted. "I wanted to go with Bethany."

Miss McGuire was firm. "I think my route will be a good place for you to start."

Over the next few weeks, Carrie continued to cling to Bethany whenever possible. Bethany tried to introduce Carrie to some of the young men, but she blushed and said nothing. If they sat down beside her, she just froze, and they would give up.

Carrie would whine and feel sorry for herself but could not seem to rise above her insecurities. Bethany was learning to do a balancing act between giving Carrie extra attention in an effort to boost her morale and trying to start her own social life.

Bethany tried to accept the first invitation from each young man who asked her. After that she had to turn down some invitations in order to have time for practicing and working as well as keeping up with her classes. With some of the young men, she knew right away they would not be right for her. With others she enjoyed follow-up dates, but she found herself comparing all of them to John. She tried to be fair; she knew she felt more comfortable and at ease with John, partially because she had known him longer. She constantly prayed for God's guidance in this area of her life. She was not certain about John's feelings for her. Sometimes she was convinced he had a romantic interest, but at other times she was not so positive. He was keeping things between them casual. He was older and very mature. "Maybe he thinks of me as a little sister, just as I thought of him as an older brother for so long," she pondered. "I am not sure about my own heart—what relationship do I really want with him?"

∾

About the beginning of October, Bethany noticed that Carrie was isolating herself more, even from Bethany. She started staying in the dorm room in the mornings after the other girls left, saying she was not quite ready and that they should go on without her. Bethany was concerned that she might have anorexia because she never saw her come into the dining hall for breakfast. But then she noted Carrie made up for the skipped meal with a good-sized lunch, and she did not appear to be losing weight. However, Bethany continued to feel uneasy about Carrie's behavior. She increased her prayers for Carrie and asked John to pray for "someone she was concerned about." John too had noticed Carrie's withdrawing from others—even more than she had before. Because he was certain Carrie was the one Bethany had asked prayer for, he did so daily.

One morning while Bethany was praying, she felt impressed that she should return to the dorm room to check out what Carrie was doing in the mornings. In order to have an excuse to return, she intentionally "forgot" her sheet music she would need for her piano lesson. Bethany had not expected, nor was she prepared, for what she discovered.

When she entered, Carrie hurriedly thrust something into her drawer and started tugging at her blouse, trying to tuck it in. Bethany ran across the room, grabbed Carrie by the shoulders, and turned her around. Bethany was horrified to see blood staining the front of Carrie's blouse. She lifted the bottom of her blouse to see a bleeding cut on Carrie's stomach. Bethany couldn't help but see other places where there were scars or partially healed cuts.

Bethany lifted her eyes to Carrie's stricken face. "Oh, Carrie, what are you doing?" At that instant she remembered hearing a preacher talking about cutting being a form of self-mutilation that was becoming a nation-wide problem among young people. They cut or scraped themselves as a means of self-punishment. Bethany spun Carrie around and pulled up her blouse to look at her back and sides. They were in the same condition!

Carrie shouted, "Quit! Leave me alone."

"Carrie, you are hurting yourself. This is horrible."

"Oh, I just have some scratches. Don't worry about it."

"I am worried—those aren't scratches. What are you using to cut yourself? You have scabs and old scars. Why are you doing this?" she continued as she pulled open the drawer to find a small knife Carrie had tried to hide.

"I told you to leave me alone. It's no big deal."

"Yes it is, Carrie. You could get infection, or you could accidentally cut too deep. Cutting yourself is dangerous."

"I don't care. I'm no good anyway," Carrie sobbed. "Why can't you just leave me alone?"

"Because I care about you. You are my friend."

"Nobody really cares about me—not even you. You are too busy having dates and everything."

"Oh, Carrie, I have tried to include you in things and walk with you when I can. Look at the time; we both have to get to class. Do you have a Band-aid to put on that cut?"

"Yes, right here."

"Get it on, and I'll walk with you. We have to meet today and talk about this. How about two o'clock in the lounge down the hall?"

"I don't want to talk about it."

"I don't care. We have to. This is serious. You meet me then, or I will go to Miss McGuire."

Carrie perked up a little. "If I meet you and talk to you, will you promise not to tell anyone else? I don't want to get kicked out of college."

"I can't promise that, Carrie. We will see after we talk."

"Bethany," wailed Carrie.

Bethany interrupted, "We have to go now! Two o'clock in the lounge, Carrie. No arguments."

"Oh, all right," agreed Carrie, sulkily.

Bethany had a terrible day! She could not concentrate on anything! She forgot that she was supposed to meet Anthony for lunch. Instead she looked for John and sat down by him to ask him to pray especially hard that afternoon. Mrs. Morgan asked her if anything was wrong when she was working; she definitely was not her usual happy, efficient self.

"I am concerned about something. Please pray for me to have wisdom and courage about a serious matter."

Finally two o'clock arrived. She hurried to the lounge and was relieved to see Carrie there. No one else was around. They spoke in low tones. "Carrie, you really need to talk to someone about your cutting. Why are you punishing yourself?"

"I don't like to talk about it, Bethany."

"I know it is hard, but you must, Carrie. I could see old scars. You must have done this in the past. How did you stop, and why did you start again?"

"I got caught before, and my stepmom and my social worker made me go to counseling. I guess it helped some. Right around then, I started riding the bus to church, and I got saved. I was happier than I've ever been before, so I didn't feel like I needed it."

"It helps you feel better, somehow?" asked Bethany, trying hard to understand Carrie's feelings and motives.

"Yes, when I feel like I am real bad."

"So you are punishing yourself, like I thought. But why? What for?"

Carrie started crying, and with tears streaming down her face, she haltingly, painfully opened up to Bethany. "One of the girls told me to stop whining and thinking about myself all the time. Another girl said I was messing up your dates with guys and keeping them from talking to you. I am just stupid and bad—just like my stepdad always said."

"That isn't a very nice thing for a parent to say to a kid!" exclaimed Bethany.

"I'm sure he was right. I always mess up everything and do the wrong thing."

"What was he talking about, Carrie?"

"Oh, once I accidentally broke a lamp. I knocked it over when I was swinging my schoolbag around. That was really stupid. He said I was always sassing him. I thought I was just asking questions, but I guess I shouldn't have or something."

"What happened to your real dad, Carrie?"

"I don't know. I never knew him. My mom didn't marry him, and she wouldn't tell me much about him. I was so glad when she got married to Jim because I thought now I'd be like other kids and have a dad." Her voice dropped even lower, and Bethany had to strain to hear. "But I don't think he liked me; he was mean. My mom said it was my fault—that I was just a very bad little girl."

"Carrie, what did he do to you?"

"He used his belt—the buckle part. It cut me, and sometimes he burned me with his cigarette. He would laugh and say that I should be a good girl; then he wouldn't have to do it. I tried, Bethany. I tried so hard to be good so he would love me, but I couldn't. Sometimes he locked me in a dark room or even a closet, and he wouldn't let me go out to use the bathroom or anything. Then if I wet myself, he would whip me. Sometimes he would not let me eat dinner. If I cried because I was hungry, he'd make me go longer before he gave me any food."

"Carrie, that is awful. That is torturing a child."

"That is what the judge said when someone finally found out and he was arrested. My mom was so mad at me for telling that she screamed at me in the courtroom and said he only did it because I was so bad. She said she hated me because she was so angry when they made me tell on him. So they took me away from her. I was in different foster homes for a while, and then finally I was sent to Mr. and Mrs. Briggs. They were nice to me, but I never felt like I deserved everything they did for me."

"Carrie, there is no reason for you to deserve less than everyone else. Most children have parents who are kind and loving to them. Why would you deserve less from foster parents?"

"I told you—I am just bad and stupid."

"Carrie, that just is not true, and you need to stop thinking like that. Thinking you are bad and stupid is leading you into hurting yourself. You should be glad your stepfather isn't around to hurt you instead of making up for it by hurting yourself. Cutting yourself isn't going to solve anything. Even if no one liked you or loved you, God is still with you. He loves you."

"I don't think even He could love me," whispered Carrie.

"Carrie, have you been reading your Bible?"

"I try, but I can't seem to concentrate."

"Well, it is full of verses about God's love and protection of His children. Somehow you have to get your mind off yourself so you can think about God and others. Tell Him you are sorry; then read in Psalms every single day. Every morning ask Him to help you to trust Him, to forget about yourself, and to help you not to cut yourself. Will you try to do that?"

"Yes."

"Okay. I am going to check back with you, and you must let me see your stomach, back, and arms whenever I ask."

"But what if someone is around?"

"I won't ask unless we are alone."

"Then you won't tell anyone else?"

"I won't promise that, Carrie. I don't know if I can help you enough. We will see in a few days."

"I'll do better. I promise."

∾

The next day when Bethany saw Anthony, she apologized for missing their lunch date.

"What happened, Bethany?"

"Something came up that was really important. It made me so upset that I couldn't even think straight or remember anything. I am really sorry."

"Did it have to do with Carrie?" he asked.

His question startled Bethany and gave her away, in spite of her answer, "I can't talk about the situation, Anthony."

"I knew it was something to do with Carrie. You better be careful; she is going to spoil everything for you."

"What do you mean?"

"She is going to destroy your social life."

"Anthony, I am just trying to be her friend. She really needs one. People are more important than my social life."

"Well, I hope you don't keep missing our dates because of her."

"Anthony, I never said it was because of her. It was only one date, and I said I was sorry."

"Okay, Let's forget it. Will you meet me today to make up for it?"

"Sure."

When they met, Bethany tried to give Anthony her undivided attention. It was very hard to forget about everything Carrie had told her. Also, she was constantly worried about Carrie. That afternoon Carrie managed not to be alone with Bethany. It was obvious to Bethany that her behavior was intentional, and it made her more concerned than ever. The following day went much the same way, but in the evening she found Carrie in the dining hall, sat down by her, and stayed with her on the way back to the dorm. She whispered, "Remember our agreement. Come with me to the restroom, Carrie."

"Oh, Bethany, everything is fine. We don't have to do that."

"Yes, we do. Right now, Carrie; come with me."

"Oh, okay," responded Carrie with an irritated tone. Bethany had prayed that they would have some time alone and was relieved to see that no one else was in the facility right then. "Quick, take off your cardigan and let me see your arms." Carrie complied. "Now show me your stomach." Carrie barely lifted the bottom of her blouse. "What are you hiding? Let me see." When Carrie just stood there looking miserable, Bethany pulled up her blouse. "Again, Carrie? What did you use this time?"

"My fingernail scissors."

"Oh, Carrie. I don't think I am going to be able to help you."

"Don't give up on me, Bethany. Please. I'll do better."

"I don't know. I have to think and pray about this. When we get back to the room, I will ask you to let me borrow your fingernail scissors. And you will give them to me."

"Oh, all right," sighed Carrie.

"I am trying to help you," said Bethany, with irritation and frustration in her voice.

"I know; I know."

Bethany did not sleep well that night. She tossed and turned and prayed most of the night. The next day she watched for John to come into chapel and asked him to meet her after the service. She did not even think about what other people who saw her would think. She was turning to John, her "big brother" for desperately needed advice. She did not even notice Anthony, who was sitting close enough to hear what she said. He thought, "She forgets to meet me, but walks up to that guy and asks him to meet her! What's the deal?"

When she and John had reached a place where they could talk without being overheard, Bethany told him everything about Carrie's problem. She was fairly certain that this problem was too serious for her to handle alone. She wanted his assurance that she would be doing the right thing to go to Miss McGuire, in spite of Carrie's pleadings.

John agreed that she needed to share it with the dorm supervisor as soon as possible. "You have told her all the correct things, Bethany, but she has to be willing to put them into practice. People with these kinds of problems need to be responsible to someone, maybe several times a day. Her healing will be a long process. You don't have the time or the training to take on such a huge responsibility."

"I feel like I have failed her," sighed Bethany.

"Don't beat yourself up. You have tried to be a loving, caring friend. Carrie may be angry at you for a while, but in the long run, she will realize you had no choice."

"Do you ever wonder why God lets a person get into situations like this? I mean, He knew it was beyond my abilities."

"He could be preparing you for some future ministry. Or maybe He is teaching you how to recognize this kind of problem. You have learned a little about the difficulties of helping someone overcome this type of addiction. It will someday be of use to you to help someone else."

"This is one of the hardest things I have ever had to do."

"I know, sweet…" John caught himself before finishing the affectionate title.

Bethany looked up, startled, but John was looking off in the distance. She thought, "I must have heard wrong." Out loud she said, "Thanks for the advice, John."

He answered, "Let's pray about this before we go to our classes."

As he left her, John was mentally kicking himself for the slip of his tongue. In his mind he thought of Bethany as his sweetheart, and the word had slipped out unintentionally. He would have to be more careful until such time as she was ready for a deeper relationship.

∾

Bethany went to see Miss McGuire at the first possible moment. She reasoned that if one has to do a hard thing, it is better just to get it over with. She told her everything that had transpired and expressed her frustration at having failed to help Carrie. Miss McGuire assured her that she could not have done more. She had not expected Carrie to have such a serious problem—the college had not been informed about her cutting episodes. She prayed with Bethany, asking the Lord to help all of them through the next few days. Then she reminded Bethany that Carrie would probably be angry with her, at least at first, and to lean on the Lord for comfort and strength to get through the difficult time ahead. She suggested that Bethany not go back to her room that evening until it was time for lights out. Maybe Carrie would not blow up at her with the other girls in the room.

After dinner Bethany went to her room, picked up her jacket and books for studying, and spent the evening in the library. She spent more time praying than studying and did not return until the last possible moment.

Miss McGuire had approached Carrie as she returned from the dining hall. She invited her into her room. Carrie was instantly on the alert. "I have lots of studying to do, Miss McGuire."

"I need to see you now, Carrie."

Reluctantly Carrie followed Miss McGuire into the room and sat down when the dorm supervisor indicated the couch. "Do you know why I want to talk to you, Carrie?"

"No," she mumbled without looking at the dorm supervisor. She desperately hoped it wasn't about the cutting. "How would she know? Had Bethany told this woman?"

"I think you have a pretty good idea. Is there something you want to share with me or something I can help you with?"

"I don't think so."

"Well, I think so, Carrie. I believe you have a serious problem with self-mutilation."

"What do you mean?"

"Aren't you cutting yourself?"

"Who told you that? I just have some little scratches from a bad itch."

"Maybe you should show me these little scratches."

"No, I don't think…I mean, I'd rather not."

"Because they are cuts made from a knife or scissors, isn't that right?"

"That sneak, Bethany! What did she tell you?"

"I want to know if what she said is true. She said you feel like you need to punish yourself, and you do so by cutting."

"Some friend she is. I begged her not to tell," sobbed Carrie.

"So it is true?"

Carrie nodded her head in the affirmative. "So what did you just do, when you said you just scratched an itch?"

"I don't know. What do you mean?"

"Carrie, you added another sin by lying to me about this."

"I'm sorry. See, that is what I told Bethany. I'm always doing bad things."

"We all sin, Carrie. I just wanted you to see that this problem of yours leads you further and further into sin. Because, Carrie, it is a sin for you to cut yourself."

"Why? I don't hurt anyone else but myself. Why should anyone care if I am only hurting myself, anyway?"

Reaching for her Bible, Miss McGuire said, "Let me show you Who you are hurting, besides yourself." She turned to I Corinthians 3:16, '*Know ye not that ye are the temple of God, and that the Spirit of God dwelleth in you?*' Also, I Corinthians 6:19 and 20 says, '*What? know ye not that your body is the temple of the Holy Ghost which is in you, which ye have of God, and ye are not your own? For ye are bought with a price: therefore glorify God in your body, and in your spirit, which are God's.*' Do you understand those verses, Carrie?"

"Not really."

"When you were saved, the Lord began to live inside you. These verses talk about a temple. That is what they called a church when Jesus was alive. Now His Spirit lives in saved people instead of a building like a temple, so our body is His temple."

"Okay. I understand."

"So that means we can't do just anything we want to our bodies. Let's look at a couple more verses. These verses also teach that it is not right for believers to get tattoos. The first one is Leviticus 19:28, which says, '*Ye shall not make any cuttings in your flesh for the dead, nor print any marks upon you: I am the* LORD.' The second one from the Old Testament is Deuteronomy 14:1, '*Ye are the children of the* LORD *your God: ye shall not cut yourselves, nor make any baldness between your eyes for the dead.*' I realize that these verses are referring to people's cutting themselves to mourn for the dead. That is what the unsaved around them did. But who was leading the unsaved people to cut themselves?"

Carrie looked at her questioningly.

"They didn't believe in God, so they belonged to Satan. The Devil was leading them to do it. Who do you think is leading you to cut yourself? We know it's not God. He would not want you to mutilate yourself. So who is leading you to cut yourself, Carrie?"

"The Devil," she said with astonishment showing on her face.

"And if you are doing something that the Devil likes you to do, what do you suppose God calls it?" When Carrie did not answer and looked puzzled, Miss McGuire went on to explain. "It is sin, Carrie."

"But I only cut myself because of the bad things that happened to me. So why would God blame me and call it sin?"

"Because you make the choice to cut yourself, and you don't have to. You can have victory over this sin. For you it is a temptation to do it because somehow it makes you feel better. But I Corinthians 10:13 says: '*There hath no temptation taken you but such as is common to man: but God is faithful, who will not suffer you to be tempted above that ye are able; but will with the temptation also make a way to escape, that ye may be able to bear it.*'"

"How can I escape it?"

"You are going to need a lot of loving help. But you have to want to quit before anyone can help you."

"I do want to. It really makes me feel worse about myself, not better."

"That is good. I am glad to hear you say that. You have taken the first step. God will help you with this process if you let Him."

"I don't know if I really believe that He will."

"Why do you say that, Carrie?"

"Well, He let the bad stuff happen to me."

"God gave us the story of Cain and Abel at the beginning of His Word to show us He will not keep bad things from happening. Cain and Abel were the very first children in the world, and one viciously killed the other."

"But why, Miss McGuire? Why won't He keep it from happening? He has the power, doesn't He?"

"Yes, but if He controlled everything, we would be like puppets on a string. We would not be able to choose whether we are going to love and obey Him. He wants our love and obedience to be freely given—not controlled by Him. He also allows the bad to teach us lessons. Maybe He has something special planned for you, like helping other people and showing others that with God's help, they can overcome the bad that comes into their life."

"I don't feel like I can overcome anything. I thought I was going to be okay, and then I started—she pointed to herself and whispered—this cutting thing again. God can't use me. And that just isn't fair. Other people didn't have the things happen to them like they did to me. Like Bethany has a really neat family. They call her and send her stuff all the time."

"I know. Life isn't fair. But there are always others who have it even harder than we do. Think about people whose children die or people with cancer. Have you heard about Job in the Bible? Lots of horrible things happened to him and his family."

"Job? I guess I haven't read about him yet."

"Maybe you should. A book of the Bible is named for him. It is just before Psalms. I admit parts of it are a little hard to understand. But even if you read the first few chapters then skip to the last few, you will get an idea of what happened and how God blessed him in the end."

Miss McGuire rose. "You better go to your room now. It is almost time for lights out. We will talk some more, very soon. You need to read your Bible, pray, and try to get your mind off yourself. I want you to know, I will be discussing this with the dean of women."

"Do you have to?"

"Yes, Carrie, I do. This is a serious problem, and you need help. I want to see that you get the help you need. We do care about you very much. No matter what happens, I want you to remember that it is for your good. Let me pray with you before you leave." After praying, Miss McGuire said, "Goodnight, Carrie."

"Goodnight, Miss McGuire."

Talking with the dorm supervisor had calmed Carrie, but she was still angry with Bethany. Forgetting that Bethany had befriended her more than anyone else, she inwardly raged at her. Carrie thought, "Oh, why did she have to come back to the room right then?" Carrie was too upset and too much of a baby Christian to realize the Lord had brought it about for her good.

Carrie did not want to talk to anyone and certainly not about her problem or what had transpired with Miss McGuire. But her countenance gave away the fact that she was terribly upset. She tried to ignore her roommates when she entered the room. She quickly gathered up what she needed to get ready for bed. Before she could leave for the restroom, Amy stopped her with a question.

"Is there something wrong, Carrie? You look so upset. Can we help you with anything?"

"No. I'm fine," she answered before leaving the room.

Bethany was already in bed with her face turned to the wall. Nevertheless, Amy asked, "Bethany, do you know why Carrie is upset? I don't care what she said. It was obvious on her face."

"Let's all just pray for her," said Bethany.

The next morning Bethany left the room before Carrie but waited for her in a nearby lounge she would have to pass on her way out of the building. Bethany was relieved when Carrie came out with Allison, made eye contact with her and glared, but then walked on with Allison. Carrie's glare was easier to take than having a verbal confrontation.

That evening the girls gathered with Miss McGuire for the scheduled devotional time. When Carrie entered the room, Miss McGuire quietly asked her to stay after the others left at the end. Carrie's stomach had been in knots all day, dreading the promised second talk with Miss McGuire. Now she found a seat as far from Bethany as possible and sat with her head bowed so no one could see the fear and tears on her face. She rose slowly at the end so she could be at the back of the group of girls filing out, hoping no one would notice she was staying behind. When all the other girls had left, Miss McGuire asked Carrie to accompany her to her room again.

When they were seated, Miss McGuire said, "Carrie, I have been praying about your problem all day. I haven't talked to the dean of women yet. I have set up an appointment with her for tomorrow. Before I speak with her, I want to hear your story. Bethany told me some, but I want to hear it from you. Please go ahead and tell me about your childhood and all the difficult things that happened to you."

Carrie began but soon dissolved into tears. Miss McGuire handed her a tissue and waited patiently for her to regain her composure and go on.

When she had finished, Miss McGuire said, "I want you to memorize Psalm 27:10, Carrie."

"What does it say?"

"Here is my Bible. Please read it out loud, Carrie."

"*When my father and my mother forsake me, then the* LORD *will take me up.*"

"You don't know your real biological father, and your stepfather was cruel and unloving, but you have a Heavenly Father Who loves and cares for you. Cling to Him, Carrie." She stood up to end the meeting. "Please come to my room tomorrow night right after dinner."

"Yes, ma'am."

The next day Miss McGuire met with the dean of women about Carrie's problem. They discussed some steps to take that would help her. Carrie's cutting was a sin addiction that could be overcome, but she would need to become consumed with God and serving others rather than dwelling on herself and the addiction. Both knew it was extremely important for her to get help before the problem became worse. Somehow Carrie needed to be convinced that God truly loved her. She would need to be accountable to someone on a regular basis, possibly as often as four times a day. Her healing would be a long process.

The dean concluded, "I am sorry to have to say this, but we just don't have that much time to invest in one person. I am afraid Carrie will have to drop out of college for a while and work through this. Hopefully, she can return to school next year. Before we tell her this decision, however, I would like to line up someone to help her so hopefully she won't feel pushed out and abandoned. I have someone in the church in mind. She is a single lady, so a family would not be disturbed. She has a similar background, and at one time suffered from anorexia, which, as you know, is also a sin addiction. She overcame it and is now a healthy, happy, well-balanced young woman. She has a job, which she is able to do from home, and she is actively serving the Lord. I will contact her today, but it is only fair for her to have some time to pray about it. When are you meeting with Carrie again?"

"Tonight."

"Find out when she last cut herself. Even if it's only been one day since, praise her and encourage her to keep it up. I would like you to give her your cell phone number and tell her to call you or come to your room whenever she feels tempted. This may be very time-consuming and emotionally draining for you for a few days. Are you willing?"

"Yes, of course," answered Miss McGuire.

"Good. Feel free to contact me if you need help. Let's pray before you leave."

∾

That evening Miss McGuire told Carrie that she would have to check in with her every day. She also told her to contact her whenever she felt tempted to cut herself. "If you really want to get over this desire to do yourself harm, I am offering you help because I care about you. You have to make the decision to take the help, and I hope you will. I am sorry some of the girls were critical. There are always going to be people or events in our lives that will cause us distress. We have to learn not to let it throw us. Overcoming self-injury behavior takes staying very close to the Lord. With all the criticism you received as a child, it will take time for you to learn to change your response to such things.

"Now you better go to your room. You probably have studying to do. Will you contact me if you feel tempted?"

"I'll try," promised Carrie.

"Remember, you told me you want to stop this unhealthy behavior."

"I know. I really do, but I don't know if it's possible. I think I was just born to be a loser."

"You are wrong about that assessment, Carrie. We are all born with the ability to be choosers. You can choose to have the victory over this, or you can choose to be a loser. I hope you will make the right choice. That is what I am trying to help you do.

"Let me pray with you before you go."

A few days later Miss McGuire stopped Carrie on her way out of the dorm for breakfast. She was walking with Allison again. "Could I see you, Carrie?"

"Now?"

"Yes, please."

Carrie thought Miss McGuire wanted her to check in early instead of right after her last class, as they had been doing each day.

When they were in the room with the door shut, Miss McGuire said, "We have an appointment with the dean of women today at 10:00 a.m."

"I have a class then," protested Carrie.

"You will have to miss it, Carrie. Meet me here, and we will walk to her office together."

Reluctantly Carrie answered, "Yes, Ma'am."

At the appointed time, Carrie obediently met Miss McGuire. She was feeling very uneasy, both physically and emotionally. Her breakfast had not settled well on her stomach as she was very nervous about the upcoming meeting with the dean.

The dean of women greeted Carrie warmly. "Come in and make yourself comfortable, Miss Douglas. Miss McGuire told you she would be talking to me about your problem. I want you to know that we will not punish you in any way. But you need more help than we can give you on a long-term basis. I was glad to hear that you have been going to Miss McGuire for help these last few days. That shows you want to be an overcomer."

"A what?" questioned Carrie.

"An overcomer. It means you want to overcome your problem, to quit cutting. For some it means not drinking or not taking drugs, or any number of other things. Having a strong desire to quit is an important step."

"What did you mean about your not being able to help me?"

"You need someone to help you like Miss McGuire has been. But your recovery will be a long process. The years of abuse you suffered caused this. You won't get the victory over this issue in a few days or even a few weeks. You need to learn some new ways to handle stress.

"You will need to leave college for a while."

At this point Carrie burst into tears, and moaned, "No. No. No."

The dean waited patiently. Neither lady approached Carrie to give her a reassuring hug as they might normally have done. Carrie had rejected that show of affection with Miss McGuire, just as she had with Bethany.

When Carrie finally quieted, the dean continued. "We want you to return just as soon as you are able to cope. As I said, this is not a punishment. Eventually you will see that it is for your own good."

"Normally, when a student leaves because of misconduct, we do not refund the money she paid in advance for the semester. In your case, we are going to, except for the amount for your room and board for the time you have been here. The funds will be kept for when you are ready to return. Some of it will be spent on a cell phone to help you to stay in contact with a lady who has agreed to help you. She will be here in a few minutes to meet you, help you pack up your belongings, and take you back to your foster parents' home. Her name is Miss Linda Jordan. She has had a problem similar to yours, and she has successfully overcome it and, at the same time, effectively dealt with her past."

Carrie had been listening while the tears continued to trickle from her eyes. "You mean I have to leave right now?"

"Yes. We feel that would be the best plan."

There was a knock on the door, and Miss McGuire opened it for Miss Jordan. She was an attractive woman with red hair and green eyes that sparkled when she smiled. She greeted Carrie with a warm smile and a handshake.

She asked, "How do you feel about things, Carrie?"

"I feel like everyone is running my life."

"I don't blame you. I once felt like that too. Our goal is to get you to the point of running your own life, with God's leading, in a constructive way rather than a destructive one. We want to get you back here as soon as possible."

"I don't think I want to come back here," proclaimed Carrie and broke down sobbing again.

"That will be your decision, of course."

"Why can't I decide things for myself right now?"

"And what would you decide?" asked Linda.

"I don't know. Maybe not to let you help me or to just go somewhere on my own—away from this school and the church and everything," Carrie choked out.

"Well, I hope you don't decide to do that. For right now, I think we need to go pack up your belongings and drive you home."

"Home? I don't have a home—not a real one."

"Your foster parents sounded kind, caring, and concerned about you when I spoke with them. They want to be part of a team effort to help you become a stable, happy young woman." Miss Jordan was moving toward the door as she spoke.

The dean addressed a question to Carrie. "Do you want to see Bethany or your other roommates to say goodbye?"

"No!" Carrie angrily exclaimed as she marched out the door.

In the dorm room, Carrie flung herself on the bed and cried.

"Carrie, you might as well get up, help me, and get this over with. Tears aren't going to change anything. You told the ladies here that you wanted to change. I can't help you if you don't cooperate."

"Did I ask for your help?"

"No, but I am volunteering."

The two locked gazes until Carrie dropped her eyes and said, "Oh, okay."

She got up and listlessly took things from her drawers and threw them on the bed. Miss Jordan patiently coaxed her along until all her belongings were packed. As they carried things to the car, Carrie kept her head down so as not to make eye contact with anyone. Finally everything was in the car. She would not admit it, but Carrie was relieved to be leaving. Deep inside she knew she had not been ready to handle the stress of college life.

Carrie sneaked a look at Miss Jordan. She seemed nice—even though she was a little bossy. Would she really be able to help her?

Musings

"Trust in the LORD *with all thine heart;*
and lean not unto thine own understanding." (Proverbs 3:5)

Miss McGuire tried to watch for Bethany's return to intercept her but missed seeing her. When Bethany entered the dorm room, she was shocked to see that all of Carrie's belongings were gone. Tears stung her eyes as she hurried to the dorm supervisor's room and knocked on the door.

"Bethany, I'm glad you came. I wanted to talk to you. Actually, I wanted to warn you," she continued as she gestured for Bethany to come in. "I see I am too late for that. I can tell by your face that you have been to your room."

"Yes. What happened?"

"We have sent Carrie back to her foster home. The dean knew of a young single woman from the church who had a similar problem at one time. She has agreed to help Carrie—if Carrie will accept the help. Since her employer allows her to work from home, Carrie will be able to call her at any time—day or night. Her bus captain agreed to use some of the money contributed for her expenses here for a cell phone to make it easier for her to call for help whenever and wherever she is when the temptation to cut is overwhelming. We told her this is not a punishment, and we hope she will want to return to the college. I doubt that she will be ready before next fall."

"A whole year?" questioned Bethany.

"I am afraid so. These things take time. College is stressful, so she needs to deal with these other issues before adding classes to her plate."

"I wish I could have said goodbye to her."

"Carrie wasn't able to face you or her other roommates."

"May I write to her so she knows I still care?"

"I think that would be an excellent idea. Would you mind if I looked over your letters before you sent them?"

"Not at all. I would feel better if you did. I don't want to say anything wrong. How do I get her address?"

"I think it will be best for me to send them on to her after I approve them. If she responds to you directly, then you can write back and mail them yourself."

"Thank you, Miss McGuire. Oh, I just feel so bad for her," she sobbed, unable to hold back her tears any longer. Miss McGuire hugged Bethany until she was able to regain her composure. "Come into my bathroom and use a cold washcloth on your face before you leave, Bethany. We want the least amount of attention given to this as possible."

"What shall I say if people ask me about her?"

"Just say she dropped out for now, but she might return later."

"Okay."

"Does anyone else know about Carrie's problem, Bethany?"

"Only John Holman, my friend from the church in Detroit. He is older and very mature. I knew I could trust him. I asked him if I should come to you about it. He assured me it was the right thing to do."

"Please tell him what I told you about keeping it as quiet as possible."

"I will, but I know he would not say anything to anyone."

After washing her face, Bethany left Miss McGuire's room and hurried toward her own. On the way, she met Allison and Amy. "What's going on, Bethany?" asked Allison.

Bethany put her finger to her lips and said, "Let's go back to our room."

Once there, Bethany said, "Carrie dropped out for now."

"Why? How do you know?" inquired Amy.

"When I saw that her things were gone, I went to ask Miss McGuire about it. She said Carrie wasn't ready for college life yet."

"Will she come back?"

"Maybe. If she wants to."

"They will let her?"

"Yes."

"Come on, Bethany. You're not telling us something."

"I'm telling you what Miss McGuire told me."

Allison asked, "But what was going on? Lately, Carrie was really upset about something and kind of secretive. She was always visiting Miss McGuire. I'd see her coming out of her room."

"I'm sure Miss McGuire was trying to help Carrie with whatever was upsetting her. Miss McGuire said we shouldn't make a big deal out of it so Carrie won't be too embarrassed to come back." Bethany gathered up some books and said, "I'm going to the library to study. I'll see you later."

When she was gone, Allison said, "I could see Bethany had been crying. I know there is more to this."

Amy said, "Bethany is trying not to gossip. It's best if we just drop it and don't ask her any more questions. We are probably better off not knowing."

"I guess you are right," sighed Allison. "I've been trying to learn that lesson."

"What lesson?"

"That curiosity gets me in trouble or leads me to find out things I think I want to know. Usually I'm sorry I asked because then I have to fight the temptation to tell someone else."

The two girls tried to study until dinnertime, but like Bethany who was in the library, they had a hard time concentrating.

Back in the dorm room after dinner, a strained silence filled the room. They were all relieved when it was time for lights out.

The following day John waited for Bethany at the entrance to the chapel and asked her if they could sit together. Anthony saw them and was upset. Bethany had turned him down just that morning. She was still so upset she did not notice his watching her. John leaned down and whispered, "We need to talk after chapel. I'll walk you to your class." She just nodded in response.

Later as they walked, John asked, "What happened to Carrie? I didn't see her this morning."

"She is back with her foster parents. The college found someone to work with her. Hopefully, she will come back to college next fall."

"I am relieved to hear that. I don't think she was ready to cope with college life yet. She has to work through all that happened in her childhood first."

"Yes, that's what the dean of women decided. By the way, Miss McGuire asked me to tell you they want to keep it as quiet as possible. I told her we didn't need to be concerned about you, but of course, she doesn't know you like I do."

"Thank you for that vote of confidence, Bethany. Here's your classroom. Before I go, did you hear about the dating bus that's going to a shopping mall next Friday?"

"I didn't pay much attention."

"I think you need some diversion—especially after all this stress over Carrie. Shall we go?"

"Yes, I would like that."

∽

The next day Anthony asked, "I guess Carrie got kicked out? I haven't seen her around."

"Don't be telling people that, Anthony. She just dropped out for now. She will probably come back next year. She needs time to work out some situations in her life."

"I should say so! Such as how to quit feeling sorry for herself and following you around like a puppy dog."

"Anthony, don't be so critical! Neither of us has gone through what she has."

"Well, it is time she put it behind her and went on."

"I'm sure it is, but she hasn't been saved very long. These things take time."

"Well, I for one am happy she is gone. Maybe you can pay attention to your social life now. Do you want to go with me on the dating bus to the mall next Friday?"

Anthony was disappointed when Bethany turned him down, explaining that she had already been asked. He was not in a happy mood when he left her.

Bethany was not very happy with him either. She felt he was being overly critical and definitely not compassionate toward Carrie. She could not help comparing his reaction to John's.

Later that week Jim Rider asked her to accompany him on the dating bus trip to the mall. She said, "I am sorry. I have already been asked by someone else."

"How about having dinner with me followed by a game of Ping-Pong tomorrow night, if you are free."

"Yes, I am free. That sounds like fun."

After the evening with him, Bethany thought about how much easier it was to carry on a conversation with John. Jim was nice, but he didn't talk much or kid around like John did so easily. She was glad John had been the first to ask her for the outing to the mall. She was looking forward to it eagerly.

∾

On Saturday during bus visitation, Donna asked Bethany about Carrie. Bethany gave the standard reply she had been using, that Carrie had decided to drop out for now, but she would probably come back later. Donna replied, "I am not sure what was going on, but I think it was very demanding for you. I have a feeling you were trying to help her with some problem. I can see you are already more relaxed, like a big load has been removed."

"Please pray for Carrie, Donna. I hope she will come back to college eventually."

Donna asked, "How is your dating life going?"

"John is taking me on the dating bus trip to the mall. I am looking forward to it. Last night I had a date with Jim Rider."

"How did that go?" asked Donna.

"Okay. He isn't very easy to talk to."

"What about Anthony?"

"I am a little upset with him right now. He didn't seem to have a very compassionate response to Carrie's decision to leave. To be honest, I keep finding myself comparing other guys to John. I try not to. I don't think it is fair to make comparisons because he is older and more mature. But I can't help it. I am just more at ease, relaxed, and happy in his presence."

"So why don't you just stick to dating him?"

"Do you think I should?"

"Maybe."

"I don't know. I feel like I'd like to date several young men before I settle on one so I can compare personalities, manners, and ambitions. Besides, John doesn't act like he is ready to date me exclusively. Sometimes I think he feels like I am a little sister."

"Are you sure?"

"Well, not all of the time. I don't know." Bethany's voice trailed off.

"Well, you haven't had a lot of dates with anyone yet."

"How are things with you and Peter?"

"Just great. I am more sure than ever that he is right for me."

Their conversation was cut short by reaching Billy Logan's house. He was always happy to see them and had much to share with them every week. It seemed they ended up spending more time at his house than anywhere else on the route. His Aunt Angie and her baby, Annie, had just moved out. They got the address from Mrs. Logan and were glad it was only a few blocks away. When they had finished the rest of their route, they called on her.

Angie was glad to see them. She was excited to be on her own and happily showed them her apartment and the few pieces of furniture she had been able to obtain. She assured them she wanted to be picked up in the morning for church. The girls expressed their pride in her accomplishments. She had obtained her G.E.D. and moved on to a better-paying job. She was receiving on-the-job training, and her employers were happy with her progress.

When they left, Bethany commented to Donna, "Seeing our convert doing so well has really given my spirits a lift and encouraged me. I have been a little down because of my concern for Carrie."

"I am glad to hear it," said Donna.

The following Monday Bethany saw Cindy and Sarah at chapel and arranged to meet them for lunch. When they sat down, she teased Sarah, "I can't believe this. We actually have you to ourselves without Paul around."

"He needed some extra time to study for an upcoming test. It is really hard for the guys working in Chicago those long hours and taking a full course load too."

"I'm glad John doesn't have such a grueling schedule. He saved up enough to only have to work part-time." As soon as the words were out of her mouth, she realized it sounded like a girl speaking about a boyfriend. The other girls had noticed it also and were looking at her with strange expressions. A big grin appeared on Cindy's face, and Sarah had a questioning look.

"So," began Cindy.

"Forget it, Cindy. I don't know why I said that," begged Bethany, blushing crimson.

"Are you two dating exclusively already?" asked Sarah.

"No. I'm also dating Anthony and Jim. Although, I admit I'm beginning to have doubts about Anthony."

"Why?"

"Never mind. I'd rather not say." She tried to change the direction of the conversation by asking Cindy, "Are you dating anyone interesting?"

"Several nice guys have asked me out, but so far I just can't seem to get interested."

"Have you heard anything from or about Randy?"

"No."

Seeing this topic still upset Cindy, Bethany hastily changed the subject by asking about how the others were doing with an assignment from one of the classes they were all taking.

∽

The next day Anthony sat down next to Bethany during chapel and afterward asked her to have lunch with him. Over lunch he commented that she was looking more rested and relaxed. "I knew things would be better for you when Carrie left."

Bethany tried to give him the benefit of the doubt. She reasoned he was trying to compliment and encourage her, but she could not help thinking that he was still being negative about Carrie.

∽

The week seemed longer than normal. Bethany was actually surprised at herself because she was so eagerly anticipating her date with John. Finally, Friday night arrived, and he met her at the dorm and walked with her to the bus. They were allowed to sit together as long as they maintained the appropriate distance. The couple kept up a lively conversation all the way to the mall. Once there, they joined Peter and Donna and another couple. They all enjoyed strolling through the stores. Thinking ahead to Christmas, several of the group, including Bethany and John, found some gifts for family members. As they walked down one hallway, John stopped in front of a jewelry store. "Oh, let's go in here and do some dreaming," he said casually.

When an employee asked if they needed help, John said they were just looking. Everyone looked in all the cases and joked around about wanting the most expensive items they could spot. When they came to the section with wedding sets, John casually asked, "Which ones do you girls like best?" He noted that Bethany did not point to solitaire engagement rings. She liked sets with smaller stones beside or around the large center diamond, but still simple rather than the more elaborate styles. He filed this information away for a future day he hoped would come for them.

Next they all headed to the food court, and each man bought his date a drink and dessert.

When it was time to get back on the bus, both Bethany and John were sorry the evening was almost over, though neither one spoke the thought aloud.

∽

The following Monday both Sarah and Bethany received a letter from the Davenports, inviting them to spend the Thanksgiving break at their home again. Elaine and Michael would also be staying at the house, so the three girls could have lots of visiting time. They both were happy to write back, accepting the invitation. Paul had already told Sarah that he would be going home for Thanksgiving.

When Bethany mentioned the invitation to John, he indicated that Pastor and Mrs. Butler had invited him to stay at their house. Mrs. Carpenter was planning to have them all over on Friday as she had done the previous year.

At school Bethany had to plan carefully and schedule the use of her time. She was taking private piano lessons again, choir, and other required courses for a music education major. She managed to squeeze in time to write to Carrie on a consistent basis, at least once a week, in spite of not receiving any replies. One week she was excited about telling Carrie that a young man had asked her, "Where is the cute girl with the black curly hair that used to hang around with you? I was thinking about asking her for a date."

Several young men had asked Bethany for dates. She had had a few more dates with Anthony, but the feeling that he was not right for her increased. Finally, she turned him down so many times in a row that he got the hint and stopped asking her. Keeping busy made time fly by, and when Thanksgiving break arrived, Bethany commented to Sarah that it seemed like the school year had just begun.

∽

The girls enjoyed the change of routine, visiting with friends, playing with Michael, the delicious dinner, and the early Friday morning shopping trip with Elaine. John managed to sit with Bethany at church Wednesday

night and eagerly looked forward to Friday evening. Bethany also constantly had anticipation of the visit to Mrs. Carpenter's house in her mind while
enjoying all the other activities. She was fond of Mrs. Carpenter and
enjoyed the many wonderful memories of evenings spent at her home, but
what her mind kept dwelling on was what she would do with John. They
always had such good times working on a puzzle together. How she hoped
Mrs. Carpenter had one ready for them! They would laugh and tease each
other as they worked on the puzzle. John's favorite trick was to hide a piece
so he could put the last one in, if they got that far.

Bethany had shared with John about how her mother put out hummingbird feeders and the whole family enjoyed watching the little birds. He
had found a beautiful puzzle picturing hummingbirds and had already sent
it to "Grandma Carpenter" to have set up and ready for them to work on.
She had started it, hoping they would be able to finish it on Friday evening.

The evening was all that both John and Bethany were secretly hoping it
would be. Elaine and Sarah also had a good time, helping with the puzzle
part of the time. Elaine had brought an embroidery project she was working on with help and guidance from Mrs. Carpenter. Sarah was also interested in many types of hand-stitchery, so that kept the three occupied part
of the evening. This busyness delighted John—the more time just the two
of them were interacting, the better he liked it. George and Martha
Davenport played a board game together.

Bethany and Sarah traveled back to college on the train. Donna and
Peter were also returning and had seats close to theirs. Peter had spent the
holiday with Donna's family, and they were excited that her parents had
accepted him. Donna's parents were showing interest in the Christian life
and had asked Peter some questions. They were hopeful that her mom and
dad might soon accept Christ as Saviour. The four of them visited for a
while, but at last the many activities they had enjoyed caught up with them,
and they all took naps.

In the days following the break, Bethany thought much about her relationship with John. She enjoyed being with him, and her heart was beginning to react in funny ways whenever she caught sight of him. She actually
caught herself looking for him quite often.

She noticed he seemed to want to be with her also. He spent time with her at least once a week, usually more, in either a planned date or managing to find her and sitting with her in chapel or the dining hall. Yet, he kept the conversations general, with no hint of romance—except when he teased her about her slip of tongue when she had called him her knight in shining armor.

Dates with Jim Rider had gradually decreased until he no longer asked her. She did not care, and she did not mind seeing him or Anthony dating others. She was happy for them and actually felt relief. She almost wished the other young men would stop asking her since she had such a full schedule, and she enjoyed the time with John so much more than with any other guy she had dated.

All through the early weeks of December, she pondered the situation and even became a little anxious about it. She was totally confused as to why he asked her for dates but treated her more like a little sister? Was he only feeling protective of her? Fortunately, her busy routine kept her from having too much time to worry about it.

∽

Bethany was definitely ready for the Christmas break when the time came. She needed some time to unwind and relax, surrounded by her loving family. But the day after her arrival, when the first excitement had calmed down, the thoughts returned to bother her. Betsy noticed her older sister sitting and looking off into space, with a slight frown creasing her forehead. "What's wrong, Bethany?"

Startled, Bethany jumped up and said, "Oh, nothing! I was just thinking…about things."

"About guys or a guy?"

Bethany tried to laugh it off. "It was nothing. Nothing important. Let's go out for a walk."

Later that day her mother spoke to her about it. "Bethany, you seem to have something on your mind. Do you want to talk about it?"

"Maybe I should. Something is bothering me a little. It's about John—you know the guy who called me during the summer."

"The one who called your dad first to get permission?"

"Yes. Well, he has been asking me for dates."

"That's a problem?"

"No. The problem is, he isn't being romantic. I mean, I know we haven't dated very long, and it would be too soon to be serious or anything. But he seems casual. I feel like he is treating me like a kid sister, yet he seems to want to be with me. And I haven't seen him date anyone else. Maybe he isn't interested in getting serious, or he doesn't want to ever get married. We haven't really talked about that. Or maybe I ruined my chances with him by treating him like a big brother."

"In what way?"

"I confided in him and asked him for advice."

"So you think he is treating you like a sister because he knew that's how you felt and what you expected? Just because you asked his advice? Or did you tell him you thought of him as a big brother?"

"No, I didn't tell him that."

"Did you tell anyone else?"

Bethany's eyes widened and her hand flew to her mouth. "Oh no! I told Scott."

"Would he have repeated it?"

"Maybe, but I'm not sure why."

"Could he have been worried about your relationship with John? Was he jealous?"

There was a pause as Bethany thought back. "Yes! I told him that because he commented on all the time I was spending with John. I told him he didn't need to be jealous. Mom, I bet he repeated that." Tears sprang to her eyes. "Oh, Scott, what have you done to me? No, it's really my fault. I shouldn't blame him," sobbed Bethany.

Mrs. Prescott put her arms around Bethany and just held her weeping daughter. Then she whispered, "Bethany, it has been an emotion-packed two years. You've gone through so much, and you've learned and grown a lot. Use what you have discovered from all the experiences. Keep trusting and leaning on the Lord. He can and will work it out if John is part of His will for your life. Have you prayed about this or just worried and stewed, as my mother used to say?" she asked with a touch of humor to lighten Bethany's mood.

"You're right, or I guess Grandma's right," admitted Bethany. A small grin showed her mother's tactic had worked. "How awful. How could I have forgotten to take it to Him? Maybe I haven't learned as much as you think."

"It happens to all of us sometimes, Bethany. We need to keep relearning or at least be reminded of things in our spiritual walk. Don't beat yourself up, but do begin to put it in the Lord's hands. It sounds like you want to get serious with John."

"I think so, but I really did not realize it until I started talking to you, mom. But John probably thinks that I could never think of him like that."

"I wouldn't worry, sweetie. If he is asking you for dates, he is obviously interested. And he doesn't sound like the kind of man who would give up easily." Mrs. Prescott was being careful not to give away what John had shared with Bethany's dad earlier in the year.

Bethany went to the bedroom she shared with Betsy, closed the door, knelt by the bed, and began to pray. First, she told the Lord she was sorry for not coming to Him and for worrying instead. Then she spent some time in thanksgiving and praise before going to Him with her concerns and prayer requests. When she rose from her knees, she felt much better. Her mother's calm reassurances had also helped her.

Bethany was more encouraged later that day when she answered the phone and heard John's voice. "Hi, Bethany. This is John. How are you?"

"Great. I am enjoying the break from college and being with my family. How about you?"

"I am having a good time teasing my sisters and playing Horse with my brother."

"Who is winning?"

John laughed. "Did you have to ask me that? I'm afraid I'm out of practice."

"My dad and brother play that a lot. Sometimes I go out and try to make baskets. Not this trip though. We have had too much rain. So you are teasing your poor sisters. I feel for them. My brother does his share of that."

"Didn't you know that is what brothers are for?"

"Oh, you think so? You think that's what God made them for?"

"Certainly."

"Now why would He do that?"

"To help you girls learn patience." John answered, following it with a hearty laugh.

"Men! You have an answer for everything, especially to give yourselves excuses," retorted Bethany, trying to sound serious and put out, but not pulling it off.

"Bethany, don't be too hard on us! What would you do without us?"

"I have to admit, I wouldn't want to find out," she answered with a softer tone.

John's heart gave a leap. "So, you enjoy having us men around."

"Sometimes."

"Just sometimes?"

"Well, it depends on who the man is."

"Oh, well, I hope I fall in the group that you enjoy. Do you miss me just a little?"

Startled by his question, Bethany gasped, and there was a pause before she answered cautiously, "I have thought about you a little."

In a serious tone, John responded, "I am very glad to hear it. I think about you a lot. I miss you."

Bethany's response was a soft, "Oh."

"I have to go. Mom just called me to dinner. Can't miss that—got to keep up my strength."

Bethany laughed.

"May I call you again in a few days?"

"I would like that."

"Good. Goodbye for now."

"Goodbye. Thanks for calling."

Bethany went to the kitchen to see if her mom needed help. Hearing her hum and seeing the smile on her face, her mom asked, "Was that John?"

"Yes."

"You seem to be feeling better about things."

"Yes." Bethany looked around to be sure Brian or Betsy wasn't around and then confided quietly, "He said he misses me."

"Ah."

"What can I do to help?"

"Peel the potatoes."

Margaret was very pleased to hear Bethany humming the whole time she worked and to see her looking relaxed and happy. She had to fight back tears. Her mother's heart was both happy and sad—at the same time. Her little girl was growing up, and they would be losing her to some man, possibly this John Holman. She hoped he was as fine as he seemed from what they had learned of him. She prayed as she worked.

CHAPTER TWELVE

A Budding Romance

"And the damsel was very fair to look upon...."
(Genesis 24:16)

The next day Bethany received a beautiful Christmas card in the mail from John. The front of the card read, "To Someone Very Special." Bethany's heart gave a little leap when she read it. Enclosed in the card was a special magnetic bookmark about the size of a matchbook. It folded over the top of a page and the magnet held it in place. It was decorated on the front with a hummingbird. Bethany had wondered if he would send a card again. She had not sent him one, knowing he was planning on being in California again. She did not know his parents' address. Now she looked at the return address and saw he had mailed this one after he got to California.

She asked her mother, "Mom, would it be okay for me to get a special card for John? If I went to the store this morning and mailed it at the post office, it would at least get to him before New Year's. He mailed this from California, so now I have his parents' address."

Her mother thought a moment. "He sent you a nice one last year too, didn't he?"

"Yes. And this year he enclosed a little gift—see, a hummingbird bookmark."

"Well, isn't that unique. I haven't seen one like that before. That should stay in a book or Bible without falling out. What a great idea. We will have to look for some of those. But back to your question, I think it would be fine for you to reciprocate with a nice card. Nothing mushy, though."

"Of course not," agreed Bethany. She called Betsy and asked, "Do you want to go to the card shop and post office with me?"

"Sure. What are you getting?"

"A card for John. Mom, do you have some pretty notepaper I can use to write a thank you for the bookmark?"

"Certainly." Her mother hurried to find something for Bethany to use.

"Thanks, Mom. Come on, Betsy; Let's get our coats and go. I want to get it mailed so he will get it before New Year's. You can look at what he sent me on the way there."

At the card shop it took about 15 minutes before Bethany found a card she thought was appropriate. Since it would get to him after Christmas, she picked one that said "Happy Holidays." She asked for Betsy's opinion, and she agreed it was a good choice. Back in the car, Bethany carefully addressed it with her best, unhurried handwriting. She wrote a short note thanking him for the bookmark, also in her best handwriting. Then she headed for the post office where she bought a stamp and slipped the envelope in the outgoing mail slot.

That afternoon her mother answered the phone and then called Bethany. Before taking the phone, she whispered, "Is it John?"

Smiling, her mother whispered back, "I think so."

"Hello."

"Hello, Bethany."

"John, I am glad you called. I just got the beautiful Christmas card today. Thank you for the card and the magnetic bookmark. What a neat idea! I haven't seen them before. I am really going to enjoy using it. I get so tired of dropping bookmarks when I'm reading my Bible."

"You are welcome. I found it in a little gift shop here in town. At first I wasn't real happy that my sisters dragged me in there, but when I saw that I instantly thought of you. You had mentioned watching the hummingbirds, so I thought it was perfect."

"It is. You are very thoughtful. So you took your sisters shopping?"

"Yes, they talked me into it."

"You don't sound very enthusiastic."

"Generally, I don't get really excited about it. But I must admit, that day turned out to be fun and productive. They helped me find gifts for my parents and brother and something special I have been looking for. I already had their gifts, remember? I got them when we went on the dating bus to the mall. So I am all set for Christmas."

"That's good. I still have a few items I need to get. My mom, sister, and I are going tomorrow. I need help with gifts for my dad and brother. Sometimes you guys are hard to buy for."

"I suppose so. For you gals, a guy is usually safe with some jewelry or perfume."

"You are learning," laughed Bethany.

"Well, I have to go. I have a very important appointment."

"Really? What is that?"

"A golf date with my dad and brother."

"Real important," laughed Bethany. "Have a good time."

As was getting to be usual, Bethany left the phone conversation smiling and humming. Betsy saw her and said, "I know who was on the phone."

"Mom probably told you."

"No, she didn't. I can just tell by the way you look and the way you hum. It is always the same tune when you have been talking to John. You were, weren't you?"

"Yes. But what is the tune? I didn't know I was always doing a certain tune. Are you sure?"

"Yes, I am sure. If you don't believe me, ask Mom. It is 'People Need the Lord.' The first time you did it was when he called last summer."

"You sure have a memory for details."

"When there is romance involved, I do," Betsy answered with a big grin.

"Oh, you…" Bethany sputtered, "you are impossible."

"So why do you hum that? Does he sing it to you over the phone or something?"

"Of course not! I guess it is because it was the first song we sang as a duet. Besides, I just like that song."

"So, is there romance in the air?"

"Well…"

"Come on, Bethany. Please."

"I think there might be a little beginning."

"Is that all?"

"I'll keep you posted if there are any developments."

"Promise?"

"Up to a point. There has to be privacy if two people are going to trust each other."

"I suppose so," answered Betsy, sounding disappointed.

"Why are you so interested?"

"Because I am a female, I guess. And it is going to be a long time before

I ever reach that stage of life. It already seems like it will be forever before I even start college...."

"Yes, but the time will go quickly if you don't dwell on how long it will be. Instead, enjoy your high school years. Have fun singing in groups, playing on the volleyball team at school, and participating in other group activities. You will be surprised how fast the time goes by when you are there and look back to this conversation."

"Well, it seems long to me," insisted Betsy.

"Well, you can't live someone else's love life. You will just have to have patience. But I will confide in you some. I promise. Now that is enough talk about romance. Let's take a walk."

"Good idea. I'll ask Mom if she wants to go with us."

The girls and their mother enjoyed a brisk walk. When they turned around to head back to the house, Brian saw them and called to them to wait for him. He challenged the girls to a race up their driveway. The younger siblings beat Bethany, who arrived on the porch breathless. "I am not getting enough exercise these days."

"You are spending too much time having dates. Do you sit and look lovingly into the guys' eyes?" Brian teased.

"No! I am not at that stage with anyone. Actually, I do get some exercise on some of my dates. We play Ping-Pong or bowl."

"Oh, I am impressed! That will really keep you in shape."

"Oh, forget it. Come on, Betsy. Let's see if Mom needs us in the kitchen."

"I hope it doesn't tire you too much, Sis," Brian called after her.

"I can see he hasn't changed," Bethany commented to Betsy. "Same horrible tease."

"We wouldn't know what to do if he quit," said Betsy.

∽

The next day Brian and Mr. Prescott spent a little time finishing up Christmas shopping and then went bowling. The girls and Mrs. Prescott spent longer at the mall. Even after all the gifts were bought, they went into some interesting shops to just look.

Sunday Bethany was happy to be back in her home church, fellowshipping with friends. It was good to hear her pastor preach again.

She enjoyed Christmas Eve and Christmas Day with her family. This year they had not planned special activities. Bethany was happy to have a quiet, stay-at-home vacation. The evening of Christmas Day, Bethany received a phone call from Donna. As soon as they had greeted each other, Bethany could tell Donna was bursting with excitement. "What is it, Donna? You sound very excited about something."

"Guess what I got for Christmas."

"From Peter?"

"Yes."

"Donna! Don't tell me it's an engagement ring?"

"You're exactly right, and it is beautiful."

"I'm soooooo excited for you! Tell me all about the ring and how he gave it to you."

"It's white gold with a nice-sized solitaire diamond. He got a wrap ring for the wedding band. He doesn't want me to try it on, but we put them together so I can see the effect. It will be really striking. It fits around the solitaire so two baguette diamonds are on both sides of it."

"I can hardly wait to see it! So when did he give it to you?"

"We always open some of our gifts on Christmas Eve. He had conspired with my mom, so after dinner she kept me in the kitchen talking and helping with clean up while he hid the ring on the tree! After we had opened everything we planned to open that evening, he said, 'Now, Donna, you need to look at the tree very carefully.' So I went over and started looking at the tree, not even knowing what I was looking for. He had not even hinted that he might have a ring for me now. In fact, I thought he might not even be able to afford a diamond ring at all, and we would just get matching bands. He had to coach me some to get me to look in the right place. I couldn't believe my eyes when I finally spotted it. I asked, 'Is it real? Is it really for me?' How stupid can you be?"

Bethany laughed. "Believe me, I understand perfectly. I can say some pretty stupid things when I am taken by surprise like that. What happened next?"

"Right in front of my parents, he dropped to one knee and asked if I would accept the ring and accept him as my future husband. I never wanted to kiss someone so much in all my life, but of course I didn't! Instead I said, 'Oh, yes, Peter. I want to very much,' and then I started crying which, of course, totally confused him. When I got control, he showed me the wrap ring; and then I held out my hand, and he slipped the diamond ring on my finger. It is so beautiful, and I am so happy!"

∽

Later in the week another card came, addressed to Bethany. She saw by the handwriting and return address that this one was also from John. Curious, she quickly opened it to find a computer-generated card. It was well designed with a picture of a knight in armor on a horse. Inside were the words:

> *John Holman, knight of Christ's Kingdom, requests the honor of escorting Miss Bethany Prescott, daughter of the King of Kings, to the upcoming Valentine banquet to be held at Crossroads Baptist College. I would consider it an honor to escort you and to serve as your knight in shining armor for the evening.*
>
> *I will be waiting with hopeful anticipation for your answer.*
>
> *Sincerely,*
>
> *Sir John Holman*

Bethany was very surprised by his request. The banquet was almost two months away. She had not even thought about it yet! How amazing that John was planning that far ahead and being so romantic! He must really want her to go with him. Maybe she didn't need to be concerned about her "big-brother" remark.

On Saturday Betsy answered the phone when it rang. She heard, "Hello. Is that you, Bethany?"

"No, this is her sister, Betsy."

"Oh, hello. This is John Holman. It's nice to speak to you, Betsy. I have heard a lot about you—all good."

"Thank you. I am sure you want to speak to Bethany."

"Yes, please."

"Just a moment, please." She put her hand over the receiver and called, "Bethany. The phone is for you."

Bethany came eagerly and asked, "Is it John?"

Betsy rolled her eyes. "Who else?"

Bethany took the phone and said, "Hello."

"Hi, Bethany."

"John, thank you for the unique invitation."

He laughed and asked, "You liked it?"

"Yes, except I'm still embarrassed when you bring up that subject."

"You mean the knight?"

"Yes. I don't know what made me say that."

"Please don't be upset at yourself or me. Believe it or not, I did not use it to tease you."

"Really? That is a little hard to believe," she answered laughing.

"I know. I probably tease you too much."

"No, don't change. That's natural to you; it's part of who you are, and I'm used to teasing from my dad and brother."

"You really don't mind?"

"No."

"Well, anyway, I truly wasn't teasing in the invitation. I am glad you called me that. You started something I want to keep going. I like the image it makes. It is a picture of what I believe a man should be with a woman. I want to be your knight."

"You mean protective?"

"And helpful, watchful for anything that might harm you, and respectful of you. For instance, did your parents tell you that when I called last summer, I also asked permission to date you?"

"No, I did not know that. So, I guess that means you haven't just been wanting companionship and friendship?"

"No, I would like more than that."

"What about this protectiveness though? Is that a brotherly attitude?"

John's heart sank. "If that's still how you want it."

"No, it isn't. So you did know that I said that. I suppose Scott told you?"

"Yes."

"Can we just forget that I ever said that?"

"I would be glad to!" John responded, and she could hear the joy ringing in his voice.

"Good. Then that's settled."

John asked, "Now what is your answer to the invitation? Do you need time to think about it? I hope no one else has already asked you."

"Yes, no, and no."

"What?"

"Yes to the invitation; no, I don't need time to think about it; and no, I haven't been asked already."

John laughed and shouted, "Praise the Lord. He does love me."

"What do you mean?"

"He answered my prayer."

"You prayed about taking me to the banquet?"

"Of course. It is an important first step."

"First step?"

"In a possibly serious relationship," he answered soberly. "Or am I rushing you?"

"No, I am ready to try that road."

"Thanks, Bethany."

"Thank you!" she answered.

"I can hardly stand it till this break is over," he said in a lowered voice. "Can you hear me okay?"

"Yes, just barely."

"I don't want to hurt my mom's feelings. But I want to talk to you face to face."

"I know. I feel the same way."

"Which airport are you flying into?"

"O'Hare."

"What time do you arrive, and what is your flight number?"

"Just a minute. I have to go look at the ticket."

She found her purse and gave him the information.

"Great! I will get in just a little while before you. So I will wait at the baggage claim for you—if that is okay?"

"Of course it is okay."

"Well, I guess we better get off and use the little time we have left with our families."

"Goodbye then, Sir Knight. I'll see you in Indiana in less than a week."

With John's "goodbye" ringing in her ears, she was practically dancing when she hung up. She was not just humming "the song" but singing it joyously at the top of her lungs. Her mother came hurrying from upstairs, and Betsy rushed to Bethany also. Brian hung over the banister and looked down. Her mother asked, "Bethany, what on earth?"

"You know that invitation to the banquet that I got?"

"Yes."

"Well, John said he prayed that I would accept. And he said it would be a first step in..." She hesitated and then went on, "...a relationship." She wanted to keep some things to herself, hugging to her heart alone the words, "A serious relationship."

"That's wonderful, Sweetie," said Margaret, hugging the excited girl.

"Oooh, Bethany!" shrieked Betsy.

"Is that all? Girls!" said Brian with disgust, as he headed back to his bedroom.

After their mother went back upstairs, Betsy followed Bethany around peppering her with questions. "Did he sound really romantic? What else did he say? Why wouldn't you show me the invitation?"

Bethany tried to think what else she could tell her persistent, curious sister. "Okay. He said that when he called dad last summer to get permission to call me, he also asked for permission to date me. He did that to show respect for me."

"Is that all?" asked a slightly disappointed Betsy.

"That's all I want to share. But don't you see? I haven't been sure if he was just being friendly or really wanting to date me, because he has been keeping the conversations casual. Now I know he is...interested in me as more than a friend."

"I think that has been obvious for a long time," retorted Betsy.

"Well, I needed reassurance. Now that is all I am going to tell you."

"Oh, come on, Bethany. I know there had to be..."

Mrs. Prescott had just come back downstairs and interrupted Betsy. "That's enough, Betsy. Leave your sister alone now. These things are personal."

Betsy reluctantly subsided with an audible sigh. Bethany headed for the coat closet. "I am going out for a little walk."

"I'll go..." Betsy was cut off by a shake from her mother's head. Mrs. Prescott whispered, "Let her have some time alone, Honey. She has a lot to think and dream about."

༺༻

That night in their bedroom, Margaret shared the incident with her husband, who then held her in his arms while she cried. He understood.

His own heart was aching at the thought of losing his eldest daughter to another man, while at the same time rejoicing over her happiness.

Bethany mostly dreamed her way through the rest of the Christmas break. She was living for the day she would be back on campus and could see John.

On their trip back to college together, Kathleen could see a difference. "What happened over the break? Did you fall in love or something?"

"I wouldn't go quite that far yet, but I did have some meaningful phone conversations with John. He even sent me an invitation to the Valentine banquet."

"What? That's almost two months away!"

"I know."

"Wow! No wonder you look like you are in a daze."

"I've got to pull myself together. I have been doing stupid things. I'm not usually so scatterbrained. Let's talk about something else. How are things going for you? I saw you and Bob sitting together at church."

"Yes. We saw quite a lot of each other these last two weeks. We are trying not to get too serious, but our hearts seem to be working against our brains that are trying to caution us. He still has so much schooling ahead of him," she said with a sigh.

"Did you talk about the future?"

"Not really. I think he knows that would make it worse, so we avoided the topic."

"Well, he sounds like he is being wise and responsible."

"I know. Even my dad said that, and he really appreciates it."

"Are you two dating others?"

"Yes. I don't know about him, but I really don't enjoy it much with anyone else."

"I know what you mean."

The girls' conversation died out. Bethany found herself daydreaming and musing again. "I have to stop this. I am even making myself nervous about seeing John face-to-face. At the same time I am anticipating seeing him with such excitement. That is stupid! I have always been comfortable with him. And I have to settle down and study for that upcoming test. Okay, Bethany, you need to pray again and then think about something else." She did, and it helped some as she took out her notes and reviewed the material.

Still, when the plane started its descent, her heart was pounding and her mouth was dry. And her emotions were not due to fear of the landing.

John was at the luggage claim area waiting for her. He greeted her in a softer, more romantic tone than he usually used. That change did not help the state of her heart. She barely managed a soft "Hi, John," in return.

"Don't tell me you are going shy on me."

Bethany blushed and could not reply. Realizing the situation was different between them, he said, "Hey, it's just your same old knight in shining armor."

Bethany laughed and responded, "You did it again."

"What?"

"Rescued me. You need to add that to the list of duties for the knight. If I remember correctly, you mentioned protective, helpful, watchful, and respectful."

"Did you memorize that conversation?"

Again Bethany blushed.

"I have been replaying it over and over in my mind, too," he said softly.

"I thought only we females did that?"

"Nope. Now let's get your luggage and go to the meeting area for the college bus."

When they had claimed it all, he insisted on pulling hers, except for her small carry-on bag. He had one bag, which he carried as a backpack. As they walked, they carried on a conversation. It was easier than when they were standing and looking at each other.

After a few minutes of sharing about their Christmas activities and the gifts they had received, Bethany said hesitantly, "John, there is something I have been wondering about. I mean, I have a problem; I don't know how…"

"Are you wondering about whether or not you should continue to date other guys?"

"Are you a mind reader, too, Sir Knight?"

They laughed together before he answered. "Believe it or not, I talked with your dad about that, too, when I called him last summer. I told him I knew you would be dating other guys."

"Why did you assume that?"

"With your natural beauty and personality, it was a given. The guys at college aren't blind."

"Oh, sorry I asked. I wasn't inviting a compliment."

"I know. I have learned that you aren't stuck on yourself. Anyway, I think you need to date more than just Scott and me before you settle on…" he paused and then finished, "anyone."

"But I haven't seen you date anyone else."

"I already had that experience when I went to the state school."

Bethany's heart sank. "Oh. Did you date a lot?"

"No, because it was hard to find Christian girls, and even then they didn't always have the same standards. Most of them thought I was really weird because I wanted to have a chaperone."

Bethany laughed. "Sounds like Scott." She was relieved to know that he had kept the dating standards. "So you think I should keep on dating other guys?"

"For right now, yes."

"Okay."

"You don't sound very enthusiastic."

"I know." She left it at that because she did not know what else to add without sounding too forward.

He understood and switched subjects by asking her about how her studying was going.

They reached the meeting area and greeted other students who were also waiting. Then Bethany edged away from the group, and he followed. She asked in a low voice, "I am still wondering why you didn't date when you got here? The girls here wouldn't think you were weird." There was a long pause. "John?"

"Could I hold off on answering that, Bethany?"

"I guess so."

"I really would rather wait."

"Okay," she agreed.

The Bud Begins to Open

"...It is better that I give her to thee,
than that I should give her to another man...." (Genesis 29:19)

*B*ethany enjoyed being back at college, even though she had a full schedule. She continued to write to Carrie every week, work her job, attend her classes, and spend weekends in the bus ministry.

The first Saturday back after Christmas break, when Bethany and Donna stopped at Angie's house, Angie noticed Donna's engagement ring. "Donna! Is that an engagement ring?"

"Yes, Peter gave it to me on Christmas Eve."

"Tell me all about it, if you don't mind that is!"

"Actually, there is nothing I like talking about more," said Donna with a laugh. She described how Peter had hidden the ring on the tree and had to prompt her before she saw it."

"Did he kiss you after he put it on your finger?"

"No, Angie. We are saving our first kiss for the marriage altar."

"Are you serious? What would be wrong with kissing now that you are engaged?"

"We both want to save it for our life's partner."

"Yes, but if you are engaged, you know who that will be."

"Hopefully, yes. But what if we broke up or one of us was tragically killed before the wedding? Then if the one who was left found someone else later, they would not be able to meet that person at the altar as absolutely pure and chaste, never having experienced even a kiss with anyone else."

Bethany added, "And things like that do happen sometimes. I remember when I barely missed being on an airplane that crashed; I heard people talking in the airport who had lost loved ones. One young woman was sobbing because her fiancé was on that flight, and their wedding was supposed to be in just a few days. One never knows. I made a vow years ago that I would wait until I was at the wedding altar. I don't want to have memories of someone else's kissing me when I first kiss my husband."

"Goodness, you two really take all of this seriously. It must be hard to wait."

"Sometimes it is," admitted Donna, "but I am sure it will be worth it."

"Do either of you actually know couples who waited like that?"

"Yes," they answered simultaneously.

"I had heard some about not touching and things in Sunday school class, but I wondered if anyone took it seriously."

"Lots of couples do," Bethany assured her.

Suddenly, Angie began sobbing. "What's the matter, Angie? We didn't mean to upset you."

"I already lost my purity. A good Christian man will never want to marry me."

"Angie, God has forgiven you for that, and it is under the blood of Jesus. He can work it out that a man will also forgive you and still want you for his wife."

"Are you sure?"

"Yes," answered Bethany, "I recently read a real-life story much like yours. Eventually, the young woman did marry a wonderful Christian man."

"Just make a promise to yourself and to God that you will live right from now on. He will honor that."

"Thanks, Donna, I will do that at the altar tomorrow at church."

Both girls hugged her and encouraged her before leaving.

∽

Three young men she had not dated before asked Bethany out during January and the first week of February. She was polite and tried not to show how uninterested and bored she really was. She turned them down when they asked for a second date by saying, "It's been nice, but there is someone who is special to me. It wouldn't be fair to you for us to continue dating. Why don't you ask one of my roommates, Allison or Amy? Neither one has a serious interest yet."

The young men thanked her for her honesty, and she was happy to see that two of them took her advice. Both of her roommates were asked out.

The situation was entirely different with John. She never turned him down. If she had a schedule conflict with an activity he suggested and it was impossible for her to make a change, she would tell him honestly and suggest a different time. John was happy to see that she was comfortable with him, yet not to the point of taking him for granted, being possessive (as he had seen happen with other young women), or being too forward. They were both anticipating the Valentine banquet with impatience. One day John asked her what color dress she would be wearing.

"I have been meaning to talk to you about that. I was thinking of wearing the blue dress I got for the Christmas dinner at the Schafers'. But I want you to be honest with me—will it bother you since I was dating Scott that night?"

"Not at all, Bethany. You looked wonderful in that dress, and that is when I first saw you—even though we didn't meet one another. It actually will evoke good memories for me. Does it bother you to wear it?"

"Not enough to throw it away after only wearing it twice," she answered and laughed.

He grinned in response, and then asked, "When was the second time?"

"A Valentine date with Scott. We double-dated with his sister and her fiancé." Thoughtfully she mused aloud, "That was another disastrous night."

"What do you mean?"

"After the Christmas party we argued because I wouldn't drink or dance and had asked to leave the Schafers' early. For the Valentine date, we had a romantic dinner in a fancy restaurant, preceded by the arrival of flowers, balloon bouquets, and a corsage. Afterward, he dropped off his sister and Paul at her house and then took me home. When we arrived at the Davenports, he tried to…" her voice dropped as she recalled the painful moment, "…force me to kiss him. I stopped him with a comment about sexual harassment." Her face brightened as she went on, "But that is all behind me. I thank God I had the courage to keep my vow and later to break up with him. This upcoming evening will definitely be a whole different matter!"

∽

Finally the day arrived. This time Bethany joined in the excited preparations with her roommates, both of whom had been invited by one of the young men Bethany had had one date with in recent weeks. A corsage had arrived for Bethany—a beautiful white orchid with blue ribbon and tulle. She decided to pull the sides of her hair up and pin it with a decorative clip.

She had brushed her hair until it was shiny and smooth and hanging down her back. She had been letting it grow quite long. The three girls helped each other with zippers and pinning on corsages.

When Bethany met John in the reception area, she could see the admiration in his face. She was thinking that he looked extremely handsome in a rented tuxedo. He had a blue bow tie and cummerbund to match her dress. Bethany was touched by his romantic thoughtfulness. He always took her by surprise when he showed this side of his personality since he had purposely been casual with her for the two years they had known each other. Bethany thanked John for the beautiful corsage.

"You are welcome. Do you think the color of the ribbons is okay?"

"It's perfect, John."

"I'm glad you think so. I thought the first one the florist selected was too light. I was afraid it wouldn't show up against your dress."

"You have a fantastic memory. That was two years ago, and we didn't even meet, let alone have a conversation so you could have observed it up close."

"Like I said, I have memories of seeing you that night."

Throughout the evening Bethany felt like she was living a dream. John was attentive and entertaining and refrained from his usual teasing in order to keep the atmosphere romantic. Bethany had by now regained her composure and sereneness in his presence, the relaxed ability just to be herself that she had always felt around him until he had started showing his true feelings. She knew she did not have to worry about his physically forcing her to hold hands or kiss, as Scott had done. They weren't in an expensive restaurant like Scott had taken her to, but it felt just as romantic.

As he walked her back to the dormitory afterward, he asked, "Well, Bethany, are you enjoying dating a variety of guys?"

"To be honest with you, no. I have been accepting just one date and then turning them down. And that's only because the administration asks us to give the men a chance, as I told you."

"If you are in a boyfriend/girlfriend relationship, you aren't expected to do that, right?"

"Correct."

"Are you ready for that? With me?" John was almost breathless with anxiety that she wouldn't be ready or that she might have found someone else.

"Yes. But I do want to call my parents tomorrow and confirm that it is okay with them." After his conversation with Mr. Prescott, John was not concerned about that.

"I don't want to rush you into anything, Bethany."

"You aren't. It's not like we just met, as it is with the other guys here. We knew each other in Detroit."

"And dated."

Startled, Bethany asked, "What do you mean?"

"You don't think I was just being a good friend or big brother, trying to help you get over Scott, do you? Or helping Donna and Peter out by double-dating? In my heart I was having dates with a young woman I was very much interested in."

"Back then?"

"Yes."

"But you didn't show it. You acted casual, even after you got here."

"I know. I didn't want you on the rebound, and I wanted to be sure you no longer cared for Scott. I'll tell you more another time."

"There's more?"

"Definitely more," he said with a grin that showed his dimple.

Bethany had begun to watch for that dimple. It gave him an endearing, boyish look. She worked at getting him to grin so it would show.

John went on, "I have something for you to seal our new relationship."

"Ooh! What is it?"

"That's a secret for now. I don't have it with me, but you will receive it soon. Then you can tell those other guys to bug off. Oh, excuse me, I mean you can say, 'I'm sorry. I'm in a relationship,' and then flash the...thing."

Bethany was laughing so hard tears started. He had tried to mimic her feminine voice.

When Bethany called her parents the next day, they both got on separate extensions at her request. "I wanted to tell you about the banquet and ask you something."

Her mother asked, "How did the evening go?"

"It was very nice. John ordered a corsage for me and was very kind and attentive all night. He even managed to refrain from teasing," she added with a laugh.

"Oh, so you are dating a tease, like your father?"

"Very much like him," agreed Bethany.

"What kind of flowers were in your corsage?" asked Margaret.

"A beautiful white orchid, with blue tulle and ribbons, a shade darker than my dress. He remembered it from two years ago when he saw me with Scott at that Christmas party. And we didn't even get introduced that night!"

"I'm impressed," responded her mother.

"I was too. Afterward he asked me to be his girlfriend and to date him exclusively. I said I was ready, if you both approved."

Now Mr. Prescott spoke up. "I talked to George Davenport about him and even got Pastor Butler's phone number and talked to him. I have discussed it with your mother since he had asked for permission to date you. We have no reservations about him or about your having a more serious relationship with him."

"Oh, I am glad for that!" answered Bethany with enthusiasm.

A few days later Bethany found a letter in her mailbox with no return address or stamp. She realized it had not come through the postal service, so it must have been from John. Maybe it had to do with the secret he had mentioned. Excitedly, she tore it open. There was a simple note: Go see Cindy.

She watched for Cindy during the lunch break and found her in the dining room. She hurried to her. Cindy met her with a smile and handed her a sealed envelope. Bethany quickly tore it open, only to find another short note: Go see Sarah.

"Unbelievable!" she exclaimed.

Cindy laughed. "What does it say?"

"Go see Sarah."

Cindy laughed again. "You didn't expect John to make it easy, did you?"

"I shouldn't have, knowing what a tease he is. What do you know about this?"

"He told me you were going to date each other exclusively. I am happy for you," she added, hugging Bethany.

"Thanks, Cindy. Do you mind if I don't stay and visit?"

"Of course not. I would be excited and curious too. I just saw Sarah walk by the door."

"Which way was she going?"

Cindy pointed, and Bethany hurried away. She caught up with Sarah and grabbed her arm, too breathless to call her name.

Sarah turned, and her face lit up when she saw Bethany. "Did you need something?" she asked innocently.

"I thought you might have a message or something for me from John?"

"I do believe I might have an envelope addressed to you."

"May I please have it?"

Laughing, Sarah retrieved a sealed envelope from her purse.

Again Bethany tore it open with anticipation. Another message like the first two simply read: See Donna.

"Oh!" she exclaimed with exasperation. "I hope he doesn't know any more of my friends." Then she laughed. "John isn't making this easy."

"Be sure to let me know how it turns out."

"I will. See you later."

"You don't happen to be going to look for Donna, are you?" teased Sarah.

Bethany just waved as she hurried away. However, she couldn't find Donna until later in the day, when they both were finished working. She was waiting outside Donna's dorm room when Donna arrived. "How nice of you to come for a visit," Donna said with a big grin.

"Do you have something for me?" asked Bethany, without an answering greeting.

"Come in and sit down," answered Donna. "I do have a message for you."

As soon as she was seated, Bethany asked, "What is it?"

"Are you free tonight?"

"I have some studying I have to do."

"Can you spare about a half hour after dinner?"

"Yes."

"Okay, go to the bowling alley. You will find another envelope. You will have to search a little. You have to wait until after dinner."

"Will you go with me to dinner and then the bowling alley?"

"I'd love to. Oh, Bethany, I am so excited for you!"

"Thanks, Donna. I think you can tell I am very excited myself! I think I've been rude to all my best friends."

"Don't worry. We all understand."

"Let me freshen up a little, and I'll be back here in ten minutes. I don't think I can eat anything. My stomach is full of butterflies."

Donna laughed as Bethany dashed out the door. When Bethany was gone, she went to the phone and called John on his cell phone. "It's all set. Go hide the envelope at the bowling alley."

John thanked her and made a call to Peter before heading for the bowling alley.

While Donna and Bethany were at dinner, John and Peter were busy in several locations. Bethany could only eat a few bites, then gave up and tried to sit patiently while Donna finished a hurried meal. She was almost as excited as Bethany.

At the bowling alley, Donna helped Bethany search. It wasn't a big area, so it didn't take long to find an envelope with her name on it, hidden under the ball with the smallest finger holes on the ball rack. This note contained an enigmatic message: Hope you are having a bouncing good time. I hope you net the prize.

This statement gave Bethany a short pause before she snapped her fingers and said, "I think he's talking about the table-tennis area. The two friends hurried there. Donna spotted John, who was watching from a discreet distance and behind furniture so as not to be seen by Bethany. He was making sure no one else found the envelope. Bethany was too absorbed with her search to notice him. It didn't take her long to find an envelope taped under the Ping-Pong table. The note inside said: Go to the reception area and find a box in a planter.

There were several potted plants, so it took a few minutes to locate the box. John had moved where he could watch the box, but still Bethany did not see him. He quickly left as she read a note attached to the box: Go to the outdoor bench before you open this.

Bethany, trailed by Donna and Peter a little ways behind her, hurried to the bench. John was waiting with a grin.

"Oh, there you are," panted Bethany, more from excitement and anticipation than actual physical exertion. She sank down on the bench. "Now may I open this?"

"Yes, but when you see what is in it, remember our phone conversation during Christmas break, after I sent you the invitation for the Valentine banquet."

"Our conversation?"

"I think you'll know what I mean when you see what's in the box. This is what I told you I found when I was shopping with my sisters in December."

When Bethany opened the little box, she saw a silver pendant on a chain. Picking it up, she realized it was a knight on a horse. "It's pretty, John, and I see you were serious about keeping the knight image going."

"I think it will become a personal symbol for our relationship."

"I had no idea what I was starting with that innocent remark, but I like the idea and the necklace," she said as she clasped it around her neck. She smiled at John and said, "Thank you so much. I did not think I would ever feel this way about the knight, but it surely has become a romantic symbol. I love romantic touches. I must admit that I have been surprised at your romantic side since you can be such a tease."

"Do you think you can enjoy the company of a man with both of those characteristics?"

"Oh, yes, Sir Knight. Because that same man has some other very positive character traits, such as being serious about spiritual things and about serving the Lord. He also has very good manners, is kind to old ladies and children, and is sensitive and understanding of others. I could go on, but you get the idea."

"I am humbled by your compliments, Bethany."

"They are all true. You deserve the compliments."

"I don't believe I have told you exactly why I admire you and want to date you."

"I would love to hear it, but can we do it another time? It will be something for me to look forward to. I need to do some studying, Peter and Donna are hanging around, and my other friends are going to expect me to show them what you gave me."

John turned and saw Donna and Peter watching from a distance, both with big grins. "I see what you mean. Let's go show Donna, and then I'll walk you back to the dorm. It will be getting dark soon anyway."

Bethany rose from the bench and accompanied John over to where Donna and Peter were waiting. John thanked Donna and Peter for their help. Donna looked at the pendant. "A knight on a horse? It is pretty, but what is the significance?"

Bethany looked at John, wondering how he would explain it. "Let's start toward the girls' dorm while I tell you about it," responded John. "It is a symbol for our relationship. It started as a joke after an innocent remark Bethany made, but I began thinking about how that's the way I feel about my role. If necessary, a man should be helpful, protective, and even fight for the safety of the woman he cares about. When I found the pendant, I thought it would be perfect for a symbol that we have a boyfriend/girlfriend relationship. I wanted her to have something so the other guys would know she has agreed to date me exclusively."

"I think that is great," said Donna enthusiastically.

"Very appropriate," agreed Peter.

When they reached the dorm building, John asked Bethany to meet him for lunch the following day. She was happy to agree. When she went in, she sought out Sarah and Cindy to show them the pendant and shared an explanation similar to John's. She then went to her own room, did the same with Allison and Amy, and settled down to try to study. That was difficult to do after all the excitement. She forced herself to concentrate, promising herself a little time to relive every moment and dream a little before going to sleep about what the future would hold. The next day John found her in chapel and sat with her. Later they met for lunch, as planned.

They did not have time for a long conversation, so the things John had on his heart to share with Bethany had to wait. He was looking forward with anticipation to Friday night when they would have a little more time.

At five in the afternoon, her time, Bethany called home, knowing her mother and Betsy would be interested in knowing what John had given her. Betsy answered, and Bethany described the whole evening for her. "Ooh, that must have been fun, and so romantic," responded Betsy.

Bethany then told her what the pendant looked like, and used the simple explanation John had used. "He really is romantic, isn't he? That is really neat, Sis."

"Let me talk to Mom now, please."

"Okay, I'll call her."

Bethany could hear Betsy clamoring up the stairs to take the phone to her mother, calling her name and then chattering to her about how romantic John was and how lucky Bethany was to have a boyfriend like that!

"Hello, Bethany. Goodness, you must have exciting news, judging by your sister's reaction."

"Well, it is very special, but I hate to think how she will react if I get engaged someday." Mrs. Prescott and Bethany shared a laugh. I gave her all the details of how he made me run around to all my friends getting clues as to where he had hidden a jewelry box containing a silver pendant of a knight on a horse. It doesn't sound romantic, but it is special to us. I had slipped one day and called him that when he had helped me with my guilt feelings over Scott. He has teased me about it, but then he thought about it picturing how he wanted to treat me—you know, protective and stuff like that. So he says it will be a symbol for our relationship."

"That sounds very nice. I am sure Betsy will fill me in on all the other details. I will share it with your father."

Just then Bethany could hear a voice in the background. "Is that my girl on the phone? Let me talk to her."

"Here's your dad, Bethany. He wants to talk to you."

"Okay. Bye for now, Mom."

"Hello, Bethany. What's new with you? Betsy is certainly wound up over something!"

"Oh, I was telling her all about how John presented me with a pendant to wear to show we are dating each other. I am sure she will love filling you in on all the details. You will appreciate what he said, I think. He gave me a pendant of a knight—it is a special symbol to us, but that is a long story. Anyway, he said it represents how he feels a man should be toward a woman he cares about—protective, helpful, watchful, and respectful."

"Hmm, I am anxious to meet this young man. I must say I am already quite impressed with him."

"I am glad you share my feelings on that subject, Daddy."

Mr. Prescott laughed. "I'm sure you are. Well, I'll let you go now. It was wonderful hearing your voice again. Your ol' dad misses you."

"I miss you too, Daddy. Goodnight. I love you. Give my love to Brian, please."

"Will do. Goodbye."

Friday night of that week, Bethany and John had dinner together and then found chairs in a lounge where they could visit. "I was going to tell you why I chose you for my girlfriend."

"I have been waiting eagerly to hear it."

"Well, like I have told you before, you are not stuck on yourself, even though you are extremely good-looking. You are mature and serious-minded, but also a lot of fun. We enjoy many of the same things. You are kind and gentle with hurting people, the elderly, and children; you are also very patient with the latter. I have Michael in mind."

She laughed.

John continued, "You are a soul winner; and you have high standards—both in your clothing and your conduct. I like it that you took a vow of purity and kept it even when Scott pressured and ridiculed you. You stood the test."

"Thank you, kind Sir. You had better be careful. You will give me a big head."

"I am not worried. I forgot to mention your modesty."

Bethany laughed. "Enough already!"

"Do you want to go see if the Ping-Pong table is free?"

"Okay. If it is, let's just play one game and then visit some more."

"That's fine with me. We don't have to even play one game, if you really would rather not."

Bethany stood up. "One game sounds good to me."

As they walked, John asked, "Anything in particular you want to visit about?"

"I am wondering exactly what you have in mind after you graduate? Also, are you going to go on for any graduate work? I am just wondering about your plans."

"I am still somewhat uncertain. I don't know what the Lord wants. I know I want to preach and use my singing somehow. I am praying He will show me His will more specifically. In the meantime I am taking pastoral courses, as you know, and private singing lessons."

They found the Ping-Pong table available, played a fast-paced game, and then walked back toward the dorm, visiting as they walked. "Have you heard anything from or about Carrie yet?" John asked her.

"No, but I have caught a glimpse of her across the auditorium at church services several times. She was with a redheaded woman whom I assume is her mentor, Miss Jordan. I just keep writing her short letters. It is hard when I don't get a response. Do you think I should tell her about us? I don't want her to be jealous or think I am bragging, but I don't want her to find out later and think I kept it from her either."

"I see what you mean. I would mention it, but not make a big deal about it. Anyway, Miss McGuire will let you know if she thinks it is acceptable."

"That's true. It sure would be nice to hear back from her."

"Well, I am proud of you for persevering in spite of that."

"I feel so sorry for her. I was blessed with a wonderful family. She has so much to overcome."

"Yes, but nothing is impossible with God. I can…"

Bethany joined in, "…*do all things through Christ which strengtheneth me.*"

"That reminds me," went on John. "How about we work on memorizing verses together? We will challenge each other. How about I choose one on Sunday, we say it on Wednesday; and then you choose one for us to memorize for the next Sunday?"

"Oh, that is a good idea! It will make it more fun and give us an extra incentive, in case we are ever tempted to neglect it."

"Which happens sometimes when one is so busy."

"Do you struggle with it, too?"

"Oh, yes," admitted John.

They sat in the lounge area again until time for Bethany to go in. Bethany told John about Betsy's reaction to her phone call. John shared that he had talked to his mother and told her about giving Bethany the pendant. He had shown it to his parents at Christmastime and explained about its meaning to them. "They are anxious to meet you."

"I would love to meet your parents, and I wish you could meet mine."

"I'm sure we'll be able to work it out before too long."

"Goodnight, John."

"Goodnight, Bethany."

The next day Bethany wrote a short note to Carrie, telling her simply that she and John were now dating exclusively. Then she talked about the bus route and soul-winning experiences. Miss McGuire approved the note, saying, "We can't shield her forever from the realities of things in other people's lives. That is one of the things she must overcome—being envious of other people's good fortune. She must learn to accept herself and her circumstances and, with God's help, move on to a new life in the center of His will. According to Miss Jordan, Carrie is making progress. She is fairly optimistic that she should be ready to return to college in the fall."

"That's wonderful."

"Would you be willing to have her for a roommate again?"

"Yes."

"That is good. But we will have to be sure she doesn't get too dependent on you. She has to stand on her own two feet."

The following week, to Bethany's surprise and delight, she received a note from Carrie.

Dear Bethany,

I am happy for you. John seems like a great guy. He was always kind and patient with me. Please write and tell me more details. Is he the romantic type? What do you do on your dates?

I am looking forward to coming back to college, even though I am a little nervous about it. Miss Jordan says she thinks I will be ready next fall and that I can keep contacting her even after I am back on campus.

I have made progress in my struggles to forgive my parents and to believe that I am not a bad person—that I didn't cause all the bad stuff. I know I am a sinner like everyone else. I haven't cut myself for several months and rarely feel like doing it. I have been able to make myself stop and to call her whenever I feel tempted.

Thank you for all your help, Bethany. You were a true friend. I am sorry I got angry with you; I know you did what you had to do, and it was for my good. I am sorry I left without saying goodbye. Thanks for all your letters. I have read each one over and over, and it is great that you kept sending them even when I didn't answer. I just couldn't before. I hope you understand.

Love,

Carrie

After reading the letter, Bethany hurried to Miss McGuire to share it with her. She rejoiced with Bethany that Carrie was doing so well. She also showed it to John the next time she saw him. "Is it okay if I tell her about the Valentine banquet and a little about the knight?"

"Sure and tell her about the wild goose chase I sent you on," said John, laughing.

"Then she will know your bad side."

"I have a bad side?" asked John, pretending to be shocked and insulted.

"You have admitted that you are a terrible tease."

"Oh, that. I told you before, the Lord makes us like that to teach you ladies patience."

"Yes, but certain men are worse teases than others."

"Maybe because the Lord knows their...eh, the ladies they are around, need more of it than some others."

"Oh, so it is my fault?" asked Bethany, pretending she was insulted now.

"Oh, definitely, definitely," said John, laughing so hard by now he could hardly get the words out.

Bethany was trying to keep a straight face as she retorted, "Just like a man to put the blame on the woman." Finally she had to give up and join in the laughter.

As soon as possible, Bethany sat down and wrote back to Carrie, telling her about going with John to the banquet, explaining what the knight meant to them, and telling her how John had made her search for the pendant. From then on, she regularly received letters in return from Carrie, and Bethany could tell from the tone that Carrie was doing better. She was now facing up to her problems, admitting she needed help, and seeking and accepting help. Bethany was happy for her.

The time came for auditioning for the tour groups. Both Bethany and John tried out. Before the results were posted, John was contacted by a member of the music faculty and asked if he could possibly travel on tour in the upcoming summer, as well as the following year. One man who had been selected had not been able to return to school. John was happy to accept, knowing that his following year at the college would be tuition-free. Also, he was told that this year the men's group would be visiting the Pacific Northwest.

He was hesitant to tell Bethany, knowing the keen disappointment she had suffered when she had not been selected the previous year. But since she had also auditioned, she would be checking the results.

When the lists were posted, he immediately checked the women's list, praying, as he had for the last year, that this time her name would be there. He spotted her name, and a rush of joy filled him. At least she would get to travel next year.

As he was leaving, he met up with Bethany. "Have you seen the lists yet, John?"

"Yes. I'll walk back with you so you can see for yourself."

Bethany hurried on. To his surprise and joy, John saw Bethany go to the men's list first.

With great excitement she turned to John. "You made it!"

"Yes. Now go check out the women's list."

"I am almost afraid to."

"Come on, get it over with," said John, leading the way.

After seeing her name, she sighed with relief and then said, "Thank You, Lord."

John said, "I have more news for you. I am going with the men's group this summer too. Someone didn't come back to college."

"John, that is wonderful! Is the group going to the Pacific Northwest this year?"

"Yes."

"Yes! Yes! Yes! That means you will be at my home church for the youth conference. You can meet my family, and we can see each other. Oh, the Lord is so good!"

"Yes, praise His name. The savings on tuition will be a big help, and I told you the Lord would work it out for me to meet your parents."

"Praise God!" answered Bethany. "Oh, John, I am so excited. I know they are going to lo…like you as much as I do," stated Bethany, blushing scarlet at her obvious slip of the tongue.

For once, John left it alone and didn't tease her. But he was secretly overjoyed that she apparently was beginning to love him. How he had waited and prayed for this day!

∾

When she called her parents, they suggested that they might offer to house some of the men and ask specifically for John, in order to have time to get acquainted.

"That is a super idea."

234 | Love's Choice

"Of course, if we do that, we will ask Kathleen's family if you can spend the nights over there. It would look better," explained her mother.

"Oh, I see. I had not even thought about it," admitted Bethany.

"In fact, maybe it would be best if Betsy went with you. Then John could use your room since there is no extra bed in Brian's room or in the spare bedroom. Then we could have a second man from the group."

"I am sure Betsy would like that, if it is okay with the Durhams."

"I am sure it will be fine. I will work out the details. I am very happy for you that you got picked for next summer. Hopefully, the ladies' tour group will come this way that year."

"I think they trade off every other year. I hope so. It would be so cool to sing for my home church and the youth conference."

"How are things going with your relationship with John?"

"Just great, Mom. Since I had known him for a while as a friend, I am more relaxed and comfortable than with a guy I didn't know. He had not shown me his romantic side before. Aside from when he is teasing, which is quite often, he is very considerate, polite, and protective. It makes me feel…special."

"I am looking forward to meeting him and ready for your school year to be over so I can have you home for a few months. Betsy and I are also anxious to see your pendant."

"Before I hang up, Mom, there is one other bit of good news I want to share. Carrie has been answering my letters and seems to be doing lots better. It looks like she may be coming back to school next fall. Miss McGuire has already asked me to be her roommate again."

"I hope it isn't as stressful as last time."

"Me, too. But I don't think it will. She will still be in contact with her mentor, Miss Jordan. I guess she has been a real help to Carrie; and of course, the Lord has also. And I think Carrie sincerely wants to have victory."

"I am sure that is a very important ingredient."

"We need to keep praying for her. I better hang up now; I have studying to do."

"Goodbye, then. I love you."

"I love you, too. Please pass on my love to Daddy, Brian, and Betsy."

"I will."

For the rest of the school year, Bethany had mixed emotions. She was looking forward to being with her loved ones again and excited that John would be at her home and church and be meeting her family. But it would also mean that she would not see him on a daily basis as she now did. She hoped the old adage "Absence makes the heart grow fonder" was true. She thought back to last summer—he had called her several times, and they had not even started dating officially. She was sure he would phone often during this summer.

When school was ended and she had said a tearful goodbye to John, she boarded the bus that would take her to the airport. She and Kathleen Durham would be sitting together on the plane again. Bethany commented, "It is so sweet of our fathers to make sure we can be together when we travel home. It is much better than traveling alone, believe me. Did I ever tell you about my experience at an airport when I had to change planes?"

"My folks told me something about your missing your flight, which saved your life. That gives me shivers! But they didn't tell me details about why you missed it."

Bethany told Kathleen the story about "Big Daddy" bothering and following her several years before when she was heading for her nanny's job in Detroit. "He wanted to buy me a drink! He had already had a few too many. He really frightened me, but the Lord used him to keep me off the flight that crashed."

Kathleen shivered violently at the thought. "Let's talk about something else. I am not that excited about flying anyway."

"How about Bob as a subject?"

"That is much better!" exclaimed Kathleen and then laughed. "He has been calling me at school, but we keep the conversations casual. I am looking forward to seeing him this summer. He has a job in Tacoma already lined up. Wish I did."

"Me, too. It didn't work out for me like last year. I guess I will apply at day care centers. What are you going to look for?"

"Retail sales, if possible. I might end up with childcare, also. There aren't a whole lot of options. My dad doesn't want me to do fast food because you work in such close quarters with guys. I guess some of them take advantage of that fact and get a little too familiar."

"I know, my dad said the same thing. I'll pray for you to find something, and you pray for me."

"Okay. I bet you are excited about John's coming with the tour group for the youth conference."

"Yes, but it seems like a long way away."

"Time will go quickly, especially if you find a job."

"Is your family planning a vacation or anything?"

"Not this year. How about you?"

"Just a few days at the coast, just before I leave. I am going back early to be in Donna's wedding in Detroit in August."

"What will you do until school starts in September?"

"The Davenports have invited me to stay at their house. I will enjoy visiting with Elaine and Michael and my friend, Mrs. Carpenter. John will be around also, as he is a groomsman."

"Sounds like fun."

"Yes, but it will cut into my time to work. I don't have much left of what I saved while working for the Davenports."

"I am surprised you have any."

"I wouldn't have except I have worked during school and had that good job as a nanny last summer. I hope it doesn't take me long to find a job this year."

The girls' conversation was interrupted by snacks being served, and then they took naps. When Bethany awoke, she read her Bible, followed by a historical novel she had wanted to start. Finally they reached Sea-Tac Airport, and the two girls rushed to the baggage claim area where their families were waiting. After greeting family members, they located their luggage and headed for the cars. Bethany commented, "It is so good to be home."

Betsy said, "I wasn't sure you would be very excited about being here this year."

"Well, I have to admit I will miss John."

Their mother said, "I am sure he will keep the phone lines buzzing."

"As much as he can. He will be busy traveling with the tour group."

Betsy added, "He better be a really great guy. I am giving up my room for him during the youth conference."

"I can assure you, he is."

"Do you have a picture of him, Bethany?" asked Betsy.

"It just so happens I do," said Bethany with a grin.

"Wow!" was Betsy's response when she looked at John's picture.

"Some dude, all right," said Brian.

Both of Bethany's parents commented that he was nice-looking.

"I can hardly wait for you to meet him."

"We are looking forward to it, Bethany," assured her mother. Mr. Prescott nodded his head in agreement.

Soon they were home, and Bethany ran around the house looking for changes. She was full of questions when she saw something new. "Where did you get this?" or "Who gave this to you, Mom?"

Within a few days Bethany had settled back into the family routine. On the weekend she helped on the bus route with Betsy. She began right away calling and visiting day care centers to ask about a possible job. After two weeks she was getting discouraged, but then she found one with an opening. They were impressed with her references from the Davenports and Mrs. Porter and told her to report to work in two days. Bethany was both relieved and elated.

Bethany also joined the choir at church. All the activities and work helped make the time go by quickly. John tried to call several times a week, and Bethany eagerly looked forward to hearing from him.

Finally the day came for the tour group to arrive and the youth conference to begin. Bethany was sorry she could not be at church for the day sessions but went in the evening on Wednesday and Thursday. The family took two cars to church so that after the services Bethany and Betsy could drive to the Durhams' house.

All the Prescotts hit it off with John from the start. He did not have much time at their home, but they visited over breakfast Thursday and Friday mornings. Bethany and Betsy left Kathleen's home early enough to stop at home to eat before Bethany headed for her job. Mrs. Prescott drove Bethany to her job and then took Betsy, Brian, and the two college men to the church. Sixteen-year-old Betsy was on cloud nine being with two college men. Brian, who was 14, was suffering from hero worship. When John and William had arrived in the afternoon on Wednesday for dinner and the opportunity to change for the evening service, they had found time to shoot baskets with him.

During the service Thursday night, the speaker emphasized the need to make a vow to God if you felt you knew His will for your life. Making a vow and then making it publicly known would help a person keep the commitment. Bethany went forward with many other young people to pray at the altar. She told the Lord she felt His leading to be a preacher's wife and that she was willing. She shared this decision with the youth pastor, who wrote it down and later shared it with the congregation, along with many others' decisions. Brian had also gone forward to surrender his life for full-time service. After the service, the Prescotts, John, and William went out for dessert to celebrate these two momentous decisions.

Later that evening Mr. Prescott asked John to stay up for a short, private visit when the others went to bed. He asked John about the progress of the relationship with Bethany and what his future plans were. John declared his hope to marry Bethany eventually, with the Prescotts' blessings. Both men agreed that they wanted both John and Bethany to graduate before getting married. John explained that since he was a year ahead of Bethany, he had decided to go on to earn a master of pastoral theology degree from the Crossroads Baptist Seminary, located on the same campus.

The days flew by far too quickly, and it was time for the tour group to leave for the next church on their itinerary. Bethany had to say goodbye Friday morning and entered the day care with red eyes from crying.

Life settled back into the normal routine of busyness. Brian found odd jobs in the neighborhood, mowing grass and weeding. Betsy was helping a woman in the church who had horses. She helped clean the barn and then got to ride the horses. Mrs. Prescott had a sewing project.

Donna had selected a pattern and fabric and sent them so Mrs. Prescott could make a dress for Bethany to wear in Donna's wedding. The dress would be of green fabric with a yellow satin ribbon for a sash to match her color scheme. It would have short sleeves and a calf-length full skirt.

For Bethany the summer passed quickly in spite of her loneliness for John. He called often; she also exchanged many calls with Donna, discussing wedding plans. The time came for the trip to the coast. They went to the Washington coast this time, and Bethany enjoyed the break from a busy schedule. By the time she had to fly back for Donna's wedding, followed closely by the beginning of school, she felt ready to tackle another year. She was anxious to see if Carrie would be at college, and if so, how much she had changed. Most of all, she was excited to be with John again.

CHAPTER FOURTEEN

John Finds His Life's Path

"By faith Abraham, when he was called to go out...obeyed...."
(Hebrews 11:8)

Bethany flew to Detroit on the third Monday of August. Donna's wedding was scheduled for the following Saturday. Donna had asked that she and John sing a duet during the wedding. They would need several rehearsals before Saturday.

The women of the church had planned a shower for Tuesday night, so Bethany, who was to be the maid of honor, could attend. The Davenports had been happy to have her stay with them for two weeks. Michael and Elaine were going to stay there also so they could have a good visit. For the week after the wedding, Elaine, John, and Martha Davenport had gotten together to plan some activities that the adults and Michael could all enjoy. It was a perfect arrangement for the young dating couple; they could spend time together and have Mrs. Davenport for a chaperone.

Donna, her father, and Peter were waiting at the airport to meet Bethany.

Bethany and Donna hugged. Bethany said, "Donna, I am so excited for you and about being in the wedding. Thank you for asking me."

"It wouldn't be the same without you. I am so glad you could work it out to have a part in our big day."

Peter added, "Yes, Bethany, you had to be the maid of honor. Without your getting me to go to Faith Baptist Church, I might not have met Donna."

Donna asked, "Have you heard if Carrie is coming back to college?"

"Yes, I got a letter from her. She is so excited, and it sounds like she has gained confidence. I have high hopes things will work out for her this year. She will continue contact with her mentor, Miss Jordan, and I will be a big sister. We will be roommates again. But I think things will be a lot different from last year."

"I hope so for your sake as well as hers."

"I know what you mean. It did get pretty stressful for a few weeks last year. I am so happy for her."

"I am so glad she is getting victory over whatever caused her to drop out."

"Yes, but keep praying for her."

"We will," agreed Peter.

His answer made Bethany realize fully for the first time how different her relationship with Donna was going to be when she became a married woman. Peter would be first in her life—after the Lord, of course—and they would be a new, united entity. Bethany was glad that Peter was already taking the spiritual leadership. She silently thanked the Lord again for the spiritual growth she saw in Peter since the day she had led him to the Lord while he was driving her in the Davenport's limousine. For a few minutes she mused about all the changes in her life since then. She had broken up with Scott, started college, and was now dating John. She knew in her heart that she loved John and was quite sure he felt the same way. She understood the wisdom of not expressing it yet, but sometimes she wanted to tell him how she felt. She turned back into the others' conversation—dwelling on those thoughts only made her impatient and frustrated.

They took her to the Davenports' home. When they pulled up, Bethany was happy to see John's car. The Davenports had thoughtfully invited him over for dinner and the evening.

After dinner they visited nonstop, mostly about John's experiences with the tour group. Bethany told John she was anxious for the school year to be over so she could also travel from church to church, being a blessing and, in return, receiving even more. He laughed and said, "Whoa, the school year hasn't even started. You better live for today and enjoy it to the fullest."

"Don't worry, I will. How could I not with you there? I missed you. And actually, that is one negative about the tour—we won't see each other again for several months."

"We survived this year. Did you decide that it is true that absence makes the heart grow fonder?"

"You tell me what you think first."

"I think it is true," he said looking at her with tenderness.

She whispered, "Me too."

John ached to say, "I love you," but he knew they had a long wait before them, and saying it would only make it harder.

∽

The next evening Bethany enjoyed the shower almost as much as Donna. Her dear friend, Mrs. Carpenter, hosted it at her home and had beautifully decorated with Donna's wedding colors. Some of the other ladies had brought finger foods and a decorated sheet cake.

Donna's mother was in attendance also. Because of having attended church with Donna a few times, she was slightly acquainted with a few of the ladies. Everyone was warm and welcoming to her and also welcomed Bethany back.

Donna received many beautiful, as well as practical, gifts including a set of dishes and silverware from her parents. Bethany had bought a picture frame and had it engraved with the bride and groom's names and the wedding date.

When she opened it, Donna said, "Oh, Bethany, it is beautiful! I will put our wedding photo in it. Thank you so much."

Bethany was glad that Donna seemed to genuinely like her gift.

The pastor's wife gave a short devotional about the joy one can have in a Christian marriage. She pointed out that a couple needed to keep the Lord involved and also heed the teachings of Scripture about submission and loving one another. She reminded the ladies of the sacrifice Donna had made when she got saved and how her first fiancé had no interest in the Christian life. She had given him up, and now the Lord had blessed her with a fine, strong Christian man who wanted to serve the Lord full-time. Bethany noticed Donna's mother had tears running down her face and started praying silently and fervently for her.

When the shower was over, Bethany went back to Donna's house to help carry in the gifts. Donna would take her to the Davenports' home a little later. In the car Donna's mother said, "That little talk was so nice. It made me wish I had known all about this when I was young, and we could have had a better marriage—not that we aren't happy together or anything like that. But we weren't very kind to Donna when she got saved; we just made life harder for her when she was going through a hard time. I feel so bad about that. Please forgive me, Donna."

"I have, Mother, a long time ago—I knew you just didn't understand."

"Well, I think I do now, and it is time for me to do something about it. I know your dad is ready too."

"That is great, Mom. There is no time like the present."

"I know. If Bethany doesn't mind, as soon as we get home I want to see if your dad wants to join me. With or without him, I am going to accept Jesus tonight."

"Oh, that is wonderful. Of course I won't mind. I feel privileged to be able to witness it. I have been praying for this for a long time."

"You have? You have been praying for me?"

"Yes, Donna has asked several people to pray because she loves and cares about you and her dad so much."

This caused the older woman to cry again, and they rode the rest of the way in silence. Donna and Bethany both prayed that her dad would respond also. When they arrived at their home, Bethany quickly helped carry in some of the gifts. Peter had been there visiting with Donna's dad, and both men went out and brought in the rest.

Before Donna's mother could say anything, her husband spoke up. Dear, Peter and I have been talking, and I have decided not to put off salvation any longer. I want to receive Christ tonight—will you join me?"

All three ladies burst into joyous laughter, and then Donna's mother quickly explained about what they had discussed in the car.

"Praise the Lord!" exclaimed Peter. "Let's all go kneel in the living room right now and get this settled."

Afterward, Donna's mother made coffee and brought out some cookies. Her husband went to the refrigerator, pulled out some cans of beer, and poured them down the drain. He did the same with an expensive bottle of wine he had purchased to share with some of their friends at home after the reception at the church. "Some of our friends are going to think we have gone crazy—just like we thought about our little gal here. But she stayed sweet, patient, and respectful, and that helped bring us around. We will wait one week to get baptized so you can be there to see it. You be sure to get back from that honeymoon in time for church because we aren't going to wait longer than that. Right, Mom?"

"Sounds good to me."

"You have just given me the most wonderful wedding gift possible," said Donna with tears brimming in her eyes.

Later in the car, Bethany pulled out her cell phone to call John and share the good news. She usually did not call him but felt this was a time when it would be appropriate. He was glad to share in their rejoicing. "Tell Donna I am very happy for her," he told Bethany before they hung up.

Bethany and John sat together in church the following night, and the Davenports very kindly invited him over afterward for a snack and a visit. As Bethany and John had to practice for their duet, Martha and George stayed to ride with them in John's car. Elaine went home in the limousine to get Michael ready for bed and to start the coffee for the adults. Michael was in his pajamas when his grandparents, Bethany, and John arrived. Michael was always thrilled to have his hero visit in his grandparents' home. Michael was impatient for the wedding to be over so he could spend time with John and Bethany. His mother had told him about some of the things she and John had lined up for them to do together.

After a few minutes, Elaine said it was time for Michael to go up to bed. John asked if he could take him up and pray with him. Elaine was happy to agree, especially when she saw the hopeful look on Michael's face. John gave him a piggyback ride up the stairs and into his room. When Michael had crawled into bed, John prayed with him and then told him goodnight.

"Goodnight, Brother Holman," answered Michael. "Thanks a lot."

"You are welcome, little buddy."

The following two days Bethany was busy helping with last minute preparations and decorating. Friday John was also at the church helping with decorating the auditorium and fellowship hall. They took some time out to practice their duet again with the church pianist.

Donna had joyfully shared the news about her parents, and everyone was rejoicing with her. The pastor spent a few minutes talking with them in his office and was especially happy and moved to hear of the steps they were taking already to make changes in their lives. That evening her parents provided dinner for the bridal party in a banquet room of a nearby restaurant, before the rehearsal. During the dinner, the pastor announced that they had both made salvation decisions, in case anyone had not yet heard about it. It was a wonderfully happy occasion, and Donna's father commented on what a good time they all had without having liquor to buoy their spirits. "Now I see what Donna has been trying to tell us. You can be a Christian and still have fun and enjoy life."

The day of the wedding Bethany had some nervous butterflies in her stomach. Besides her maid of honor duties, there was the duet with John. They were to sing at the beginning of the ceremony right after the wedding party had all entered. All had gone well the night before at the rehearsal, so that thought had helped her confidence. She prayed that it would go as well today.

During the wedding ceremony that evening, Bethany was relieved when the duet was over and it had indeed gone smoothly. Later in the ceremony, she started thinking about her future. Would she and John stand together at a marriage altar some day? She stole a look at John and found his eyes on her. They smiled at each other, and Bethany blushed, thinking she was glad he could not read her thoughts! Then she turned her attention back to what the pastor was saying, and just in time! Donna was ready to pass her bouquet to Bethany to hold for her.

Later at the reception, several times Bethany saw men speak with Donna's father, then turn away shaking their heads or with looks of disgust on their faces. She surmised they were the friends to whom he had referred who had expected to go to the home for drinks after the church reception. They were just learning that their friend had followed in his daughter's footsteps. Bethany said a silent prayer of thanksgiving and asked the Lord to keep him strong in his resolve.

The next day Bethany, John, and Mr. and Mrs. Davenport went home with Mrs. Carpenter for dinner and fellowship. As usual, there was a puzzle for them to work on together. In the afternoon they went back to church for the evening service. That night in the guest room at the Davenports, Bethany fell asleep and had wonderful dreams of a wedding in which she was the bride and John was the groom.

The next week seemed like a taste of heaven—time to relax, enjoy friends, and have no responsibilities. Michael had become a well-adjusted, well-mannered, and obedient child. Elaine had grown in her Christian walk and had learned homemaking and parenting skills. She gave Mrs. Spencer, the Davenports' cook, the day off on Wednesday; and she prepared a delicious meal with Bethany's help. She even made a homemade pie. She had invited John and Mrs. Carpenter to join them for dinner before church. While the girls cooked, John and Michael played and planned sneak attacks on the kitchen to make what John called "taste tests." Shortly before dinner was to be ready, John took Michael with him to pick up Mrs. Carpenter.

Saturday the honeymooners returned, and John treated them and Bethany to dinner at an Italian restaurant. Mr. and Mrs. Davenport had accompanied Bethany again, but they sat together at another table for their own "date." Donna and Peter were radiant with love and their joy over her parents' decisions to accept Christ. All four young people were eager to see the two of them make their public profession and be baptized the next day.

After church Donna's parents insisted on taking the four young people, the pastor and his wife, and Mrs. Carpenter out for dinner. During the summer when they had visited the church with Donna, she had pointed out Mrs. Carpenter and told them about John's spending Sundays with her whenever he was in town. They did not want to take him away from her today and were glad to include her. She had been very kind to Donna many times, besides hosting the shower.

During dinner, Donna's mother told Pastor Butler's wife how her talk had influenced her to make her decision the night of the shower. Mrs. Butler's heart was encouraged to hear that.

Monday Donna and Peter picked up Bethany from the Davenports' home for the trip to the college. Bethany regretted that the beautiful time of togetherness had come to a close and the hectic pace of college life would begin again. But she knew she would enjoy it as she had the first two years.

∽

When they reached campus, she started watching for friends from the previous year. Cindy would be coming back; but Sarah was at home, working and planning her wedding, which was to be during the spring break in March. Cindy and Bethany were both going to be bridesmaids. Both of Bethany's roommates from last year, Amy and Allison, were continuing their schooling also.

When Bethany walked into her new dorm room, Carrie was already there. Bethany was amazed at the difference in her. Her black hair was long and had been straightened in an attempt to be in the current style. It looked clean and shiny. She wore makeup, which had been skillfully applied. Her outfit looked stylish but was very modest and becoming. She was busily arranging her things, humming a Christian tune. She turned to see who was entering and ran to greet Bethany warmly with a hug.

Bethany was pleasantly shocked and returned the hug with enthusiasm. Then she held Carrie at arms' length, looked at her closely, and said, "Who are you? I don't believe I know this girl."

"Oh, Bethany, have I really changed that much?"

"You look great. Not that you were bad looking before, but..."

"I know what you are trying to say. I feel like a different person, almost. Miss Jordan has been such a big help. I just love her. I wish I could have been brought up in a home with a mother like her. But you know what? I have gotten over my bitterness toward my mom and dad. I really have. I have been able to forgive them, with the Lord's help."

"Wow, Carrie. That must have been hard to do after all you went through as a child."

"It wasn't easy, but Miss Jordan showed me from the Bible that God expects His children to do that. She had me memorize Ephesians 4:31 and 32, which says, *"Let all bitterness, and wrath, and anger, and clamour, and evil speaking, be put away from you, with all malice: And be ye kind one to another, tenderhearted, forgiving one another, even as God for Christ's sake hath forgiven you."* If you don't get out the root of bitterness, it just destroys you. Now I am getting a fresh start, and I am enjoying having a friend like her to help me. And a friend like you. I was so happy to hear we were going to room together again. After all I put you through last year, I was surprised you would be willing. But I shouldn't have been surprised because you are just so sweet and caring."

"Quit, Carrie," said Bethany, laughing. "You are going to give me the big head."

"Bethany, may I see your knight pendant? That is so neat—you and John getting together. I hope the Lord will have someone for me someday."

Bethany said, "I am sure He will," as she took off her coat so Carrie could see the pendant.

"Oooh, that is so cool! Tell me more about how he gave it to you. It is hard to get all the details in a letter."

Bethany obliged while she set about getting her things unpacked. After that the girls finished their tasks without conversation. Bethany enjoyed hearing Carrie hum. She would have to encourage her to join the choir; she had a very pleasant voice.

Carrie's words about forgiveness and carrying bitterness stayed with

Bethany all day. When they went together to the dining hall for dinner, Bethany shared her heart with Carrie. "You have made me think about my own heart, Carrie. I realized today that I am carrying bitterness toward a guy I had broken up with just before I came to college. He caused me trouble and embarrassment by coming here to try to get me to leave and to marry him instead."

"Why didn't you want to marry him?"

"He wasn't right for me, Carrie. He didn't agree with the dating standards I grew up with. He made fun of me because I wouldn't hold hands or kiss. I got swept off my feet because he was so good-looking, and I let my heart rule instead of my head. I need to get right with God about it."

"Goodness, Bethany, I didn't think you had any problems like that."

"I'm not perfect, Carrie. You know none of us will be until we get to Heaven. You have helped me see an area I need to work on. I am going to pray and confess it tonight. Thanks."

"I can't believe this," said Carrie, shaking her head in disbelief.

Bethany laughed. "That will teach you not to put people on pedestals."

"I guess I needed to be reminded of that."

"See, we can be a help to each other."

"Thanks, Bethany. That makes me feel really good."

When the girls returned to their room, two other girls had arrived. They were both freshmen. Mary was from Idaho, and Grace was from Maine. After introductions, Bethany and Carrie helped them unpack and store their belongings. They got their beds made up just in time for lights out. Bethany promised to show the girls around and answer any of their questions in the morning. When all was quiet, Bethany silently did business with the Lord about her need to forgive Scott completely. When that was accomplished, she was able to enjoy a night of sweet, peaceful rest.

The next time Bethany and Carrie had time to visit, Carrie told Bethany more about Miss Jordan. "She is so kind, Bethany, but also stern when she needs to be. She doesn't let me get away with anything! She took me shopping several times and showed me how to find things that are in style but still modest. Sometimes that is really a challenge."

"I know. The world is getting less and less concerned about modesty!"

"Right. She showed me how to layer things with a high-necked top underneath, how to check a neckline with three fingers below my collarbone, and how to check that slits in skirts don't go above my knee. She taught me what styles look good with my figure and to watch out for sweaters, dresses, and skirts that are too clingy or tight. She even bought me a couple of brand new outfits from a department store. That was a really special treat for me! When we went to thrift stores, she had a knack for finding new things that had never been worn—they still had the price tags on them. So now I have a nice wardrobe. She also helped me with my hair and makeup. I guess she gave me a complete make-over, like you see on television." Carrie laughed delightedly.

"And Bethany, she is a great soul winner, too. She took me with her to Phoster Club, her ladies' soul-winning club, as her trainee. I learned so much. Oh! I forgot to tell you the best news. She witnessed to my foster parents, and they both got saved!"

"Carrie, that's great!"

A few days later the young man who had asked Bethany about Carrie the previous year approached Carrie and asked if he could sit next to her in chapel. Afterward he shyly said, "Maybe I'll see you around," and hurried off.

Bethany had observed this and told Carrie, "He is the one I told you about who asked me where you were last year."

"He is nice-looking, isn't he? I don't even know his name."

"I think you will before long."

"I hope you are right."

The young man sat next to Carrie several more times before he got up enough nerve to introduce himself. "Hello. My name is Doug Whittier. I know your first name is Carrie."

"Carrie Douglas."

"Glad to officially meet you. Could we meet after your last class today? I will buy you a Coke or something—whatever you like."

"Sure. I'd like that."

They made arrangements as to where to meet, and Carrie left, humming and smiling. She spotted Bethany and breathlessly told her about all that had transpired with Doug.

Bethany hugged her and said, "I told you so! I am so happy for you."

Carrie didn't learn much in her classes that day. She was eagerly anticipating this first college date, but tense with nervousness. She need not have worried—Doug was having the same problems.

During that first date conversation was difficult for both of them, but they both actually found it helpful to know that the other was just as nervous. After several casual lunch dates, it became easier for them to talk. Then Doug asked her for a Friday night date—they would bowl and then get a snack. Carrie was floating on clouds. Bethany had to bring her feet to earth and remind her to concentrate on her studies. Carrie had called Miss Jordan, told her all about it, and was cautioned to take things slowly.

Friday night over coffee and pie, Doug told her he had been disappointed the previous fall, as he had just gotten up his nerve to approach her when she had left.

"I am sorry. It's nice to know you had noticed me. I was a mixed-up, miserable mess. This last year has been a real blessing. I have changed a lot. A very kind lady took me under her wing and has helped me so much."

"In what way?"

"Oh, with my appearance, shopping for clothes, and working through some serious problems I had because of my childhood."

"Did you have a dysfunctional family too?"

"Yes!" she exclaimed with surprise. "Did you?"

"I am afraid so. Finally I started going to church on a bus, got saved, and my life really changed. I had started experimenting a little with marijuana, but my bus captain somehow figured that out and helped me quit. I haven't touched anything like that since."

Carrie was silent. She was thinking about her cutting problem. Even though he had made his admission about marijuana, she did not have the courage to tell him about her problem.

Her silence worried Doug. "Did I shock you?"

"Oh, no," she hastily reassured him. "I was just thinking about some things I have struggled with. To be honest, I tried marijuana once too, but I choked so much I wasn't tempted to try it again."

Relieved that she was not shocked, he laughed and said, "That was a good deterrent."

"I guess we have quite a bit in common," mused Carrie.

"It would seem so," agreed Doug.

"The Lord is good. He has given us both a second chance."

"Yes, He is the God of second chances. Praise His name!"

"Are you planning to be a preacher?"

"Yes. I don't know if I'll be a pastor or just what. I would like to work with inner-city kids, with problems like you and I had."

"That is so needed, but it won't be an easy life."

"God doesn't call us to be at ease."

"That is true."

"What about you?"

"I have no idea about my future right now. I just want to learn to be a good Christian and grow spiritually stronger for now."

"Those are good goals."

"Thanks."

"I guess it's about time for me to walk you back to the dorm. I have really enjoyed this, Carrie. I hope we can do it again."

"I would like that."

When she entered the room, Carrie twirled around and around and collapsed, giggling, on her bed.

"What's that all about?" asked Bethany, laughing with her friend.

"Oh, Doug and I had such a good time. We are finally able to be more comfortable, and we actually talked. We have a lot in common, and he wants to have more dates. Isn't that just cool?"

"Very cool. Now get ready for bed," said Bethany, playfully stern as she gave Carrie a hug.

The dates with Doug went on for several weeks. They were together so much that other young men did not approach Carrie to ask for dates. Finally one Sunday Miss Jordan discussed it with Carrie.

"Carrie, how many young men have you had dates with?"

"Just Doug. I really like him, and I feel comfortable with him because he has a similar background and has had to struggle to overcome some things in his life. Just like me."

"Have you been turning down other guys?"

"No. They don't ask me."

"Why do you suppose that is?"

Carrie tensed up and started to be on the defensive. "I don't know," she mumbled, wishing something would interrupt this conversation. She had a feeling she wasn't going to like the outcome.

"Is it possible he hangs around you so much that no one else feels they have a chance?"

"I don't know," insisted Carrie.

"Carrie, you know I only care about your good. You are becoming defensive. We have discussed that before. It doesn't help anything."

"I know," she mumbled miserably.

"I think you know what I am going to suggest?" she asked and waited. Carrie made no response. "You need to see less of Doug and give some of the other men an opportunity to ask you out."

"How can I do that?" wailed Carrie.

"It won't be hard. Just start turning him down sometimes."

"He'll think I don't like him. He'll stop asking me at all. I'll lose him," objected Carrie with tears streaming down her face.

"I can see I should have intervened a little sooner," answered Miss Jordan. "If you two have learned to be at ease and talk, then you should be able to explain to him that I feel both of you need to experience dating with others also. You don't have to stop dating each other completely, but cut back. I am afraid you two will lean and depend on each other too much and not learn to communicate with others. If he is going to work with troubled people and others in the inner city, he needs to be at ease with more people than just you. You can't prop each other up. You both need to get stronger. Do you understand what I mean?"

"Yes, but that doesn't mean I like it."

"I know, but will you do it?"

"Yes, Ma'am," Carrie said reluctantly.

"The sooner, the better. I will ask you about it next Sunday."

"Okay," Carrie said with a sigh.

"Good girl. I am proud of you," said Miss Jordan with a smile.

Carrie had learned to get hard things over with, so Monday when Doug sat down by her in the cafeteria, she told him they needed to have a talk as soon as possible.

"Oh, oh. I have a feeling I'm not going to like this."

"I don't either, but…"

"Okay, how about I meet you for dinner, and we can talk afterward."

"That will be fine."

Carrie told Bethany about it, and they prayed together. Then Bethany prayed throughout the rest of the day.

After dinner Carrie and Doug walked outside while they talked. Carrie had practiced what she would say and that helped. At first Doug was upset, told Carrie he did not agree, and walked her back to the dorm silently. But the next day, he sought her out to tell her that after calming down and praying, he had to admit Miss Jordan was right. "I will try to get up the nerve to get acquainted with some of the other young ladies, and I won't be angry if you date others. I don't like it, but it seems like most spiritual growth comes with a struggle or something that seems hard. I will stay away from you for a couple of weeks. I will miss our comfortable companionship. How many times have I heard that we must step out of the boat to increase our faith? We have to do this so we can grow to be useful to the Lord. Will you thank Miss Jordan for me?"

"Thank her? For what?"

"Seeing a potential problem and making both of us face up to it."

"Okay, Doug. You do know that I don't want this, right? But I, too, am convinced it is for the best."

"I'll see you around, Carrie."

A week later a young man asked Carrie if she would sit with him in chapel, and the next day another offered to buy her a Coke after the last class of the day. Carrie was amazed and thrilled. Doug also was dating others.

∾

The last week of October, Evangelist Ralph Gibson came to preach for the whole week in chapel. He usually played a trumpet special before preaching. Brother Gibson preached at many youth camps in the summers and at churches for revival meetings. One day he was speaking about the need for young people to heed the call of God and go into full-time Christian service. He preached from Ephesians 4:11, 12: *"And he gave some, apostles; and some, prophets; and some, evangelists; and some, pastors and teachers; For the perfecting of the saints, for the work of the ministry, for the edifying of the body of Christ."*

Brother Gibson talked about the need for workers in each of the positions mentioned in the verse. He pointed out that each one offered great rewards and blessings, but that each also had its own particular challenges. Evangelism had some unique difficulties in that there would be times when the evangelist would be separated from his family. On the other hand, evangelists would not have what missionaries and pastors had that Paul described in II Corinthians 11:28: *"...that which cometh upon me daily, the care of all the churches."* Brother Gibson told the young people that in spite of some hardships, he found evangelism an exciting ministry with many blessings. He encouraged the young men to consider it if they were not already committed to some other full-time ministry.

All at once John had a certainty in his heart that God had just revealed His will for his life—he would go into evangelism and use his singing as this man used his trumpet. He went to the altar to pray during the invitation. While on his knees, he thought about the difficulties he and his future family would face. He prayed that the Lord would also help Bethany be open to the idea.

Friday night he and Bethany had dinner and then found a place to sit and talk. John told her of his assurance that the Lord was directing him into evangelism. "Do you think you could live with that if we should decide to marry?"

"Wow, I had never thought about that! I had prepared myself to be a pastor's wife or a missionary's wife. This will take some getting used to. But if that is God's will for you and if we decide it is His will for us to marry, then I would consider it was God's will for me too. I have told Him I would do His will."

"Well, that's a load off my mind. Hallelujah! I have other news, too. My folks called, and they would like you to spend Thanksgiving with them— actually both of us. They already have your folks' phone number and called them to ask if that would be okay. They agreed. Would you like that?"

"Oh, yes! That would be great. I have been so anxious to meet them! I just received an invitation from the Davenports also. I will write to them and explain that I can't come this year."

"I almost forgot. My folks are sending you a ticket for the airplane."

"They don't have to do that."

"They want to."

"That is very kind. Oh, I can hardly wait for Thanksgiving to get here!"

CHAPTER FIFTEEN

Meeting John's Family

"...but I trust to tarry a while with you...."
(I Corinthians 16:7)

As the time for Thanksgiving break came nearer, Bethany's initial enthusiasm was partially replaced with feelings of nervousness. She had begun to dream and to hope that she would be John's wife someday; therefore, she really wanted to make a good impression on his family. She desperately wanted them to like her and approve of her. She called her mom to share her concerns. After listening to her daughter's fears, Margaret Prescott said, "You need to trust the Lord. He will be with you, and He will work everything out according to His will."

"Thanks for reminding me of that, Mom. That helps some." But Bethany found that knowing it and actually resting in that knowledge were two different things.

It did not help when she and John talked about the planned itinerary the Friday night before Thanksgiving week. They would fly to California Tuesday afternoon. That night and throughout their stay, John would go to his grandparents' home to sleep. Bethany would stay in John's parents' home in an extra room in their finished basement. There was a private bathroom with a shower for her to use. She would have privacy—that part sounded good.

His mother wanted to have time to get acquainted, so she had already baked pies for Thanksgiving and put them in the freezer. John and his mother were going to take her shopping and out to lunch on Wednesday. They would have dinner at home with the rest of the family and go to church. Thanksgiving Day would be mostly spent at his grandparents'. Also present would be his aunt and her family and an uncle's family. Between them they had five girls who were between the ages of eleven and fifteen. John told her, "I guess all five of those girls and my sisters are beside them-

selves with excitement about meeting my girlfriend. My uncle also has three very lively young sons, but after Michael, they will seem tame to you."

Bethany gave him a forced smile in response.

He asked, "Is something wrong, Bethany?"

"No, no," she hastily answered, but inwardly she was quaking at the thought of meeting so many and trying to remember names and sort out relationships.

"I figured you would want to shop Friday morning, so my sisters are taking you. Mom and I will meet you for lunch. Okay?"

"Sure, it all sounds fine."

"Friday night we will stay home. Some of my friends from the neighborhood and high school might drop in. Saturday my parents and I will drive you around to see the area. We will head for the airport Sunday when morning services are over. We should have time to stop and get something to eat. Does all that sound okay to you?"

"Of course. It sounds like you have really been thinking and planning." Actually her head was spinning trying to take it all in.

"My mom and I have. She wants to be sure you have a good time."

"That is very sweet of her."

Finally the day arrived. The flight was uneventful, and when they went to claim their baggage, they met John's parents. The Holmans were friendly and warm and helped her feel more at ease. Mrs. Holman said, "We have heard so much about you, Bethany. We are happy to finally meet you."

"I am excited to be here and meet all of you too."

"Well, let's get you home. Dinner should be ready when we get there. John's sisters are cooking tonight."

John playfully groaned. "Are you sure that was a good idea?"

His mother answered, "Now John, you just quit that. You will give Bethany the wrong impression. You know your sisters have been learning and practicing for several years."

"Don't worry, Mrs. Holman, I know what a tease he is."

"Oh, he has already shown you his bad side."

"Now Mom, that's a little strong, don't you think?"

"No!" She and Bethany laughed as he tried to look hurt. Aside to Bethany she added, "He really is a wonderful son and brother." Bethany smiled and nodded her head.

"Hey, whispering is not fair." Mrs. Holman just smiled at him in response.

In the car the Holmans asked Bethany about her courses, how she liked college, and her family. They also wondered how John felt about the Bible college. They were curious about the dating opportunities and the college rules. John's oldest sister would be graduating from high school in the upcoming spring, and they were hoping she would attend there the following year. Bethany was feeling more relaxed and calm by the time they reached the Holmans' home.

His sisters had the table set and decorated with a bouquet of flowers, and a delicious dinner was ready. After introductions they sat down to the meal, and Bethany sincerely complimented them on their cooking skills. John and his brother James had to admit it turned out well; but they also managed to find small things to tease their sisters about, like a few small lumps in the mashed potatoes and a slightly lopsided cake.

The two girls, Ruth and Naomi, took the teasing with good humor, looking at Bethany at times to see how she was reacting. When she gave them a conspiratorial wink and a grin, they knew she was acquainted with John's teasing. After dinner Bethany insisted on helping with the clean up. "Working together in the kitchen is the best way for us ladies to visit," she remarked.

When they were finished, the family and Bethany had about a half hour to freshen up before church. Bethany was shown to the guest room, which she found to be comfortable and attractively decorated. During the Wednesday night service, she was excited to see that John's church and pastor were very much like her own in Tacoma. She felt right at home.

John had driven separately, so after the service he said goodnight and headed for his grandparents' home. When the Holman family and Bethany reached their home, they offered Bethany a snack. She politely declined, saying she was still full from the delicious meal the girls had prepared. She retired to the guest room and prepared for bed. John's family had been so friendly that she felt at ease and had no problem sleeping.

In the morning, however, when she awoke and remembered there would be a big family gathering that day for the Thanksgiving celebration, she again felt some apprehension. She hurried through her shower and preparations for the day, while still making sure she looked her best. Then she settled with her Bible, followed by prayer time. That time with God helped some, and she drew a deep breath and then went upstairs. She had heard movement and knew at least some of the family was up. She found she was just in time for breakfast and silently thanked the Lord for the good timing. John arrived just as they were sitting down. They greeted each other with their eyes as he hurriedly sat down before his father prayed. Afterward, his mother asked how things were going at her parents'. He assured her his grandmother was already getting the turkey in the oven. Mrs. Holman commented she needed to get over there to help as soon as possible. The girls, including Bethany, offered to clean up after breakfast so she could leave. Mr. Holman said, "We will come as soon as the girls are done."

During the rest of the day, Bethany alternated between spending time with John and wandering out to the kitchen to lend a helping hand. The ladies always told her she didn't need to feel obligated; she could spend the day with John. Bethany would answer that he was engrossed in the football game anyway. She tried to show interest and follow the game, but after a while, she was glad for an excuse for a break.

When the other families arrived, John's cousins stared with obvious curiosity at Bethany. Soon the boys joined the men in the family room in front of the television. The girls were shy and giggly at first, but Bethany's outgoing personality soon won them over. Eventually, she found herself in the living room surrounded by girls asking her questions about her experiences as a nanny and college life.

Bethany kept busy, which helped her own unease as well as homesickness for her own family. She knew her dad and Brian would be in front of the television, and Betsy would be helping her mother in the kitchen. They had told her they had invited another family, new church members, a military family who were far from home and relatives.

She was happy to discover the hours passed quickly, and she was actually relaxed and enjoying herself. She had been delighted to discover John's grandmother reminded her of her own, as well as Mrs. Carpenter. She was a warm, godly lady. At the end of the day, Bethany reflected that she felt invited into the family. She breathed a sigh of relief when she slipped into the guest bed and enjoyed a restful sleep. She had set her alarm for 4:30 a.m. to be ready for the day of shopping. The three girls had an enjoyable morning, filled with laughter and companionship. They did not spend a lot of money, but they all found a few things at good prices. Bethany picked up a scented candle in a lovely holder for a hostess gift, and the girls shopped for a gift for their mother's upcoming birthday. They met with John and Mrs. Holman for a delicious lunch, then went home and had naps. After her nap, Bethany felt fortified for meeting more new people—John's friends who were going to stop in.

John had games planned, which helped. Bethany did not feel like she was on display or that she had to make brilliant conversation with strangers all night. She expressed her gratitude with smiles and later with words when the last guest had left.

∞

Bethany found the drive on Saturday to be very relaxing and interesting. Sunday she again enjoyed being at John's church for Sunday school and the morning service.

She was actually sorry to have the time with his family over when they had deposited them at the airport to return to college. Mrs. Holman, Ruth, and Naomi all gave her a warm embrace as they said goodbye. She definitely felt accepted by John's family!

When his family had left them and they were through security, John said, "My family really liked you. They were impressed by your good manners, your helpfulness, and your outgoing personality. I was so proud of you. Of course, I never was worried. I knew they couldn't help but like you."

"Thanks, John. I really like all of them too. You have a great family. That didn't surprise me either. Thanks for the way you made things easier for me."

"You are welcome. Were you nervous before we came?"

"A little," she admitted. "But your family made me feel so welcome and included that I just relaxed. I hit it off with your sisters pretty quickly; and I already love your mom and grandma. I was actually sorry that the break was over."

"Well, now we go back to our studies and busy schedules."

"You do enjoy Bible college, don't you?"

"Most definitely. And now that I know which direction the Lord is leading me, I can determine better what courses I need to take. Even though I am enjoying college, I am anxious to get finished and start doing what God has called me to do."

"John, what are your plans for living arrangements and getting started?"

"I am not sure yet, Bethany. I am going to try to get in contact with Brother Gibson for advice."

"That sounds like a good idea."

They discussed the things they had done over the break, and Bethany asked John about various members of his family whom she had just met. He asked her how their traditions differed from her own family's and what she missed the most when she wasn't home for the various holidays. The year she had worked for the Davenports, she had not even gone home for Christmas. They examined the possibility that as an evangelist, John and his future family would probably miss many special events and holidays with their families. "We will just have to make our own traditions and find ways to make things special, even if we live in a travel trailer," commented John.

"At least you won't be as far away as a missionary—maybe you will be able to work it out sometimes."

Later during the flight, Bethany thought about the things they had discussed and silently prayed for the Lord to give her grace for whatever lay ahead in her life. She asked him to lead her to the husband and/or area of service He willed for her. "Lord, You know how I am beginning to feel about John. If he isn't right for me, please let me know. If he is, then please bless our future life together and help us work together for Your kingdom."

John also spent some of the time in prayer. "Father, I feel you brought Bethany into my life, and I have for quite a while felt that You intended her to be my wife. Please work everything out according to Your will; and if she becomes my wife, give her the grace necessary to be the wife of an evangelist, with all that You know that entails."

∾

After the Thanksgiving break, John and Bethany returned to their usual activities in the weeks until Christmas break. Bethany continued working on the same bus route and was delighted with the spiritual growth in Billy Logan, his aunt Angie, and his friend Trevor. The boys rarely missed a Sunday. Angie had become a real asset as she joined in with the songs and games and encouraged the children to participate, sat with troublemakers or new children who were timid, and even went visiting with them on

Saturdays whenever she could get her sister to baby-sit little Annie for her. The last Saturday before Christmas break, Bethany managed to get Billy's mother to promise to come to church with Billy and Angie the Sunday before Christmas. Bethany increased her prayers for her in hopes she would get saved that day.

Carrie was doing well in her classes, singing in the choir, and dating several different young men. Doug had contacted Miss Jordan and received permission to sit with Carrie and her foster parents in church during the Christmas break. Since Carrie's foster parents had gotten saved, they came regularly for morning services and sometimes for the evening or midweek services. Most of the time Carrie sat with them, as Miss Jordan had begun dating a young man who usually sat with her in church. At first Carrie had struggled with accepting someone else in Miss Jordan's life, but with Bethany's help, she had worked through that to the point of being happy for Miss Jordan and discovering she actually liked the man.

Before leaving for their respective homes for Christmas, John and Bethany exchanged wrapped gifts. Bethany had purchased a set of cufflinks for John, who enjoyed wearing French cuff shirts. He had found a pair of silver earrings with little horses dangling that she could wear with the knight pendant and another more elegant set. They were both anxious to see what the other had gotten for them, but had agreed to wait until Christmas day to open the packages.

Bethany enjoyed her time home with her family but found separation from John was beginning to bother her more. It was apparent that he felt the same way because he called her every day. Sometimes they only had a few minutes to talk, but at other times they had no problem talking for a half hour or more.

The painfulness of the separation made Bethany think about her future if she married John. She struggled with the fact that there might be long periods of loneliness if she couldn't travel with him. The idea did not appeal to her. She did not feel as brave or as submissive to God's will as her brave words to John had sounded. One day she was reading Joshua 3 about the Lord's making a dry path through the Jordan for all of Israel to pass over to the other side.

Joshua 3:17 caught her attention. *"And the priests that bare the ark of the covenant of the Lord stood firm on dry ground in the midst of Jordan, and all the Israelites passed over on dry ground, until all the people were passed clean over Jordan."* Bethany thought about the priests standing firm on dry ground—the Lord kept them from sinking in muck and mire that would usually be left if suddenly the water were gone. It was like God was the firm foundation, like a bridge for them to reach the other side. He is the same for believers today, but they must be willing to step out. The waters of Jordan were not cut off until, *"...the feet of the priests that bare the ark were dipped in the brim of the water...."* (Joshua 3:15)

If it was God's will for them to marry (and she was feeling more and more sure of that), then He would be a firm foundation for her to make it through any trial or testing when she needed it. She just needed to trust and step out in faith. The thought was reassuring and inspiring. She remembered Philippians 4:13, *"I can do all things through Christ which strengtheneth me."* She would just rest in that precious promise.

This year Bethany received another beautiful Christmas card. This one read:

To My Sweetheart, Wishing You a Blessed Christmas.

When she read it, she gasped. Instantly, Betsy asked, "What is it? What does it say?" Speechless, Bethany handed it to her sister. "Wow! Sweetheart, huh? Does he call you that all the time now?"

"No. He never has said it to me."

"Oooh! Maybe he will from now on. How do you feel about that?"

"How do you think?" answered Bethany with a grin.

The next time he called, Bethany thanked John for the beautiful card. "Did you like it?"

"It's beautiful and very sentimental."

"Did you mind my calling you sweetheart?"

"No, not at all. It touched my heart in a very special way."

"Do you know that I have thought of you that way for a long time?"

"Really?"

"Yes. Once I almost slipped and said it."

"When was that? I seem to remember wondering if that was what I had heard."

"Let me think—oh, yes, it was when you felt like you had failed Carrie, and you were going to have to tell Miss McGuire about her problem."

"That's right. So you did almost say it. Why did you stop yourself?"

"I felt it was too soon."

"You already felt like that, but you didn't think I did?"

"Right."

"Has it been hard for you to wait, John?"

When he answered, "Sometimes," Bethany whispered, "I'm sorry."

"No need for you to feel sorry. It's not your fault. I'm just happy that I can start calling you my sweetheart now."

"I am, too, John."

When they ended the conversation, they both felt like they were soaring above the clouds.

∽

Kathleen's family invited the Prescotts over for dinner the evening of the Saturday after Christmas. Bob was also there—Kathleen had told Bethany he had been calling her at school. Their relationship was growing in spite of being separated most of the year. It made Bethany appreciative that she and John were at college together.

At the end of the Christmas break, Bethany and Kathleen flew back to college together. Bethany was happily anticipating seeing John, but Kathleen was fighting tears after a tearful goodbye to Bob who had accompanied her family to the airport. Over the Christmas break, Bob and Kathleen had both admitted their lack of interest in dating others and had agreed to a long distance boyfriend/girlfriend relationship. Bob had even casually spoken of the possibility of medical students being married, even though it would be difficult, especially for the woman who would not have much time with her husband. Kathleen was pursuing a degree in secondary education in the field of English, in hopes of getting a job in a Christian school.

Bethany pointed out that she could keep herself busy by teaching, and they would not have to wait so long to get married. Kathleen assured her that that idea was already in her mind.

John was again waiting at the airport for Bethany. He immediately whispered, "I missed you, Sweetheart."

"I missed you too, John. The break seemed so long. Even though you called so faithfully, it isn't the same as being with you. Thank you for the darling horse earrings and the beautiful ruby ones. One set would have been enough!"

"The horses were just kind of for fun; they are casual. I got the ruby ones to add to your '*multitude of rubies.*' When I decided to get them for you, I thought about Proverbs 20:15, the verse your folks gave you with your graduation ring. '*There is gold, and a multitude of rubies: but the lips of knowledge are a precious jewel.*' I also wanted to get you something dressy. Maybe you can wear them for the banquet, or do they not go with your dress?"

"I had the same idea after I opened them. So I went shopping—I wanted a new dress anyway. I found one that will be perfect for Valentine's and for the earrings. I think you will like it."

"I like anything you wear. You always look beautiful."

"Thanks, John."

"What color is the dress?"

"Red and white. The jacket is white."

"Shall I plan on wearing a red cummerbund this year, then?"

"That would be perfect."

John laughed. "Well, we have the Valentine banquet all planned; now all we have to do is get through the next six weeks."

Bethany laughed with him. "I guess we better be getting our feet back to earth and think of something else besides romance and dates."

John groaned. "Do we have to?"

Good News Brings Hope

"Charity...hopeth all things, endureth all things...."
(I Corinthians 13:4-7)

When Bethany reached her dorm room, she and Carrie both had a lot to share. Carrie was eager to tell Bethany about her foster parents' inviting Doug over for dinner on New Year's Day. Miss Jordan had approved of the idea. Carrie surmised that Miss Jordan was falling in love, and it was making her more softhearted toward Carrie and Doug and their desire to spend time together. Bethany laughed and cautioned her. "Don't be taking advantage of that!"

"Don't worry. She made me promise to keep on dating other guys too."

Bethany shared with Carrie about the card and John's use of the term "Sweetheart" to her in person for the first time. She also told her about her victory over her fears of being an evangelist's wife.

"Bethany, you are so lucky. John is so romantic. Traveling around with him could be really exciting. You will see lots of interesting places and meet lots of people. You will be a good evangelist's wife because you aren't shy. You are outgoing and can easily talk to people. It would be harder for me or someone like Sarah. By the way, when is her wedding?"

"During spring break. Cindy and I are both going to be bridesmaids, and Donna will be the matron of honor. I am so excited."

"It wasn't that long ago that you were in Donna's wedding. What are Sarah's colors?"

"She is using yellow and lavender because it is a springtime wedding."

"What are your dresses like?"

"She found one she liked in a catalog so we could order them and make sure they fit well. It is a beautiful lavender jacketed dress, trimmed with an embroidered design of yellow flowers and green vines on the scalloped edge of an overskirt, above a chiffon flounce. It has the same trim on the scalloped edge of the jacket and the sleeves. Sarah's father kindly paid for them because he knows how expensive college is. We sent the dresses to Sarah so they can be hanging up and we don't have to try to take them with us on the plane and then worry about wrinkles when we get there. We'll be arriving Friday afternoon in time for the rehearsal, and the wedding is the next day."

"The dresses sound beautiful. You are going to have so many gorgeous dresses! Are you wearing the one from Donna's wedding for the Valentine banquet?"

"No, not this year. I will wear one of the bridesmaid dresses next year. I bought a new one for this year to wear with the ruby earrings John gave me for Christmas. Here, I'll show you." Bethany went to her suitcase and took out the earrings to show to Carrie. Then she pulled out a beautiful red formal with a white overskirt trimmed with rhinestones and gathered up at the waist on one side. It had a straight neckline that was high enough, but it had spaghetti straps and a low back. The neckline was also trimmed with the sparkling stones. Bethany had found a white jacket with long sleeves, also trimmed with rhinestones, to wear over it.

"Oh, Bethany, it's beautiful! I love full-length formals, and all those layers of tulle really make the full skirt stand out. And the jacket is such a good match—it looks like it was made to go with it."

"I know, but actually I found it at a different store! The Lord is so good. I prayed before I went. And you know what else He did for me? The dress was marked down!"

"That is so neat! I have never had a formal or gone to a banquet."

"Maybe you will get asked for the Valentine banquet."

"Even if I did, I don't know what I'd wear," she said in a melancholy tone.

Bethany put the dress away in the closet and changed the subject. "Cindy stopped me today and asked me to meet her for dinner. She said she has good news, and she looked very happy and excited. Maybe it's about Randy."

"Who is Randy?"

"A guy she dated our freshman year. She really liked him, but then he backslid. We have been praying for him ever since."

"Does she still care for him?"

"She hasn't said so, but she hasn't found anyone else that she has felt serious about, and lots of guys ask her out. She is so cute and lively, she attracts people—both male and female."

"I have noticed that. She is always really friendly to me. I hope things work out for her with that guy."

"I hope he has gotten right with the Lord. That would have to happen first."

"Let me know, if she doesn't mind."

When they met, Cindy handed Bethany a letter. "Do you want me to read it?"

"Yes, go ahead."

Bethany read:

Dear Cindy,

I know you prayed for me—at least for a while— so I wanted to let you know how things are with me these days. I finally got right with God, once I realized what a fool I have been!

It happened after Thanksgiving. I spent the day with the guys I've been hanging around. At the end of the day, I thought about how it had been meaningless. Knowing it was a holiday most people spend with their families made me feel lonesome for my folks. Then I started thinking about Christmas coming up. I remembered how I had spent it last year—partying with my friends. I woke up the next day feeling lousy, mentally and physically. Actually my spirit was weary of it all and disgusted, but I wouldn't admit it even to myself.

I also thought about last Halloween when I really went overboard. I got so drunk I blacked out. The next day I could not remember what I had done the night before or how I got home.

I could not get away from all that you had said the last time I called you. It scared me. Your words and the verses from Proverbs kept going through my mind. I had memorized quite a few, and now they kept coming back to me. I tried to ignore them, but I could not forget some of them, like Proverbs 11:19, "As righteousness tendeth to life: so he that pursueth evil pursueth it to his own death." Proverbs 12:11, "...he that followeth vain persons is void of understanding." Proverbs 12:15, "The way of a fool is right in his own eyes: but he that hearkeneth unto counsel is wise." Proverbs 28:7, "Whoso keepeth the law is a wise son: but he that is a companion of riotous men shameth his father." Proverbs 20:1, "Wine is a mocker, strong drink is raging: and whosoever is deceived thereby is not wise."

After Thanksgiving I was so lonely—I knew my so-called friends did not really care about me. They had brought me home Halloween night and dumped me off. I had been sick, and I was a mess. They did not care. No one checked on me the next day to see if I was okay.

I thought about my parents and how they had loved me and how my mother took care of me with tender care whenever I was sick.

I remembered times I had gone fishing with my dad—not many, but the few times we had gone, he had made it special.

I also thought of you and how sweet and thoughtful and caring you were. I knew that was Christ shining through you.

I got to thinking about the guy at college who was bitter, and I had let him influence me. I was amazed at myself—why did I listen to his lies—Satan's lies? Even if those things were true in his family, they weren't in mine.

I wanted to go home so badly, but I was afraid. What if they did not forgive me and accept me back? I wouldn't really blame them. Then as I was praying, the Lord reminded me of the parable of the prodigal son. It seemed like he was assuring me that my folks would react like the father in the story.

I quit my job and went back to my hometown. I went to a motel and just read my Bible and prayed until I finally got up the nerve to call home. My mom was so happy to hear my voice she started crying and had to give the phone to Dad. He was on guard, but when I asked if I could come over on Christmas day, he said, "Yes!"

I got my hair cut, shaved off the beard I had grown, got some new clothes and some inexpensive gifts. I didn't have much left of my last paycheck. I hadn't saved anything. I have nothing good to show for those one and one-half years. Anyway, the reunion went well. I went back to the motel for a few days. Sunday I went to church; it was hard to face everyone, but I did it. I went forward to repent and rededicate myself, and then I had a talk with my dad in his office after services.

He said I could move back in, but I had to abide by the same rules as before. That didn't bother me. I was even surprised that I did not feel any resentment or rebellion when he said it. Praise God! I had made up my mind and heart that God's way was what I really wanted. The other lifestyle was just empty.

I am sorry this is so long. I just wanted you to know because you had so much to do with my finally getting right. Thank you for that. I don't know if I will see you again. I don't even know if you are still at the college or if this will get to you. I don't expect an answer. I know I hurt you and insulted you. I am glad you didn't let me influence you. Please forgive me.

I am looking and praying for a job here. I am not sure what the future holds for me.

Sincerely,

Randy

Half way through the letter Bethany had stopped eating. By the time she finished it, tears were running down her face. Cindy was also crying. They wiped their eyes, blew their noses, and grinned at each other. "What an answer to prayer," said Bethany.

"I know. Isn't it great?"

"Are you going to answer it?"

"Yes. I will express my joy and let him know we have been praying all this time. I hope he will come back to college or at least keep in touch with me. I still have a special place for him in here," pointing to her heart. "I have never been able to forget him. I think that is why I haven't been able to feel seriously about anyone else."

"I have wondered about that. But don't..." She did not know how to express her concern without sounding negative about Randy.

"I know, Bethany. Time will tell whether he is really sincere and whether he can break away from the things he has been doing. Even if he comes back, I will have to be very cautious. I better go do some studying. Since you have been so faithful to pray for Randy, I wanted to share this with you."

"I really appreciate it, and I do hope he stays on the narrow path now."

"Me too. I'll see you around."

Cindy found she could not settle down to studying until she had written a short reply back to Randy.

Dear Randy,

I was so glad to get your letter. I am praising the Lord! I never stopped praying that He would draw you back into fellowship and obedience to Him. I couldn't believe you would continue in the other lifestyle since I was so surprised that you backslid in the first place.

You have some great qualities—I pray you will let Him develop them further in you and use them for His kingdom.

Thank you so much for letting me know that you have "gone home."

Sincerely,

Cindy

The first Saturday back, Bethany was bursting with impatience to find out if Mrs. Logan had kept her promise to go to church with Billy on the bus. When she arrived at the bus meeting, she rushed to Donna to ask her about it. Donna and Peter had made a quick trip to visit his parents for Christmas and then returned to Indiana by the weekend to work on the bus route. They had gone to Detroit to see her parents for New Year's.

"Donna, did Mrs. Logan come to church like she promised?"

"Yes! I was so excited. She said something about Angie and the boys changing so much that she was curious."

"Did she get saved?"

"No, but I think she is under a lot of conviction. We really need to keep her in our prayers."

Bethany was disappointed, but said, "Well, at least it is a start. We'll keep praying and working on her."

In early February Carrie entered the dorm room, rushed to Bethany, and threw her arms around her. "Guess what? Guess what?"

"What's happened?"

"Doug just told me he got permission from Miss Jordan for us to go to the Valentine banquet. Oh, I am so excited. I told him I don't have a formal, and he said he didn't care because he couldn't afford a tux either. I guess I'll just wear my prettiest dress."

"Carrie, I am so happy for you. How would you like to borrow a dress? You could wear the one from Donna's wedding. Even though you are a little taller than me, it should still be long enough. Let's see—try it on."

"Oh, Bethany, are you sure? What if I spill something on it or it gets torn or something?"

"It can be dry-cleaned. It could happen when I was wearing it, too. I'm not worried. Besides, I have other dresses. Come on, try it on."

"Okay, if you are sure. It is beautiful."

When Carrie had slipped on the dress and Bethany had zipped it up, Bethany stepped back to get a good look. "Oh, good. It is long enough. I am so glad. It looks wonderful on you. Won't Doug be surprised?"

"Do you think he will feel bad about not having a tux?"

"I don't think so. He doesn't need to worry. I hear that not all the guys rent tuxedos."

"Do you think I should tell him or just surprise him?"

"Whatever makes you feel most comfortable."

"I think I'll tell him you are loaning me a formal but not tell him what it looks like."

"Do you like it, Carrie? I won't be hurt if you don't want to use it."

"I love it, Bethany. I am excited about wearing it. It is so sweet of you!" She gave Bethany a big hug before taking off the dress and hanging it back up.

The next time Bethany had a chance to visit with Cindy, she asked her if she was going to the banquet this year.

"Yes, I did accept an invitation. But I just can't get excited about any of the guys I date. They are all really nice, but my heart isn't stirred. I don't know what's wrong. I even prayed that the Lord would take away my feelings for Randy, but it doesn't seem like He has."

"Have you heard anything more from him?"

"No," Cindy answered with a sigh.

Bethany had no idea how to comfort or advise her friend, so she said nothing. They sat in companionable silence for a while, sipping their Cokes, and then Bethany asked, "Would you like to share a table with us at the banquet?"

"I'd love to. That will make it easier. I hope Alex, the guy I'm going with, won't think I'm getting interested in him. I don't want him to be hurt. I really didn't know whether or not I should accept his invitation, but I know others who go with people who are just friends. I figure I have to try my best and leave the rest up to the Lord."

Bethany gave her friend's hand a squeeze. "I know He will work it all out, in His time."

Cindy pointed to her head and said, "I know it too, up here, but my heart is anxious because I really want to marry and have a family. Still, I know I have to be sincerely in love."

Bethany changed the subject. "Spring break and Sarah's wedding are only about a month away. I am so excited!"

"Me, too," Cindy agreed enthusiastically. Our dresses are so beautiful, and I love the colors she selected."

"Are you going home after the wedding?"

"Yes, what about you?"

"The Davenports are going to have to put up with me again. They have made a standing invitation for me to come whenever I'm not going home during a break. They have become like a second family to me. They are so generous.

"I better go now. I have studying to do. See you around. I'll make sure with John that it is okay for you and your date to sit with us."

"Thanks, Bethany."

∾

The day of the Valentine banquet, the usual excitement prevailed. Mary and Grace were also attending. Everyone needed help with zippers, pinning on corsages, and fixing their hair. Mary enjoyed "playing" with other people's hair, and she had a natural knack for fixing fancy styles. She curled Bethany's hair into ringlets, then pulled up the sides and fastened them with a rhinestone clip Bethany had bought to go with the dress. There were curls gathered at the top and also hanging long down her back. Mary also helped Carrie. She had Carrie leave her natural curls instead of straightening her hair and then piled the curls at her crown. She loaned her a tiara to wear, and it made a stunning affect.

Cindy came to the room just as everyone was finally ready. She, Bethany, and Carrie walked together to the reception area to meet John,

Doug, and Alex. Bethany's heart skipped a beat when she saw John—he looked so handsome in a white tuxedo with a red cummerbund and a red rose boutonniere. He had ordered a corsage of red roses for Bethany, which had been delivered to her that afternoon.

She went to him and whispered, "Wow, my awesome knight. You look great!"

"So do you. I like the dress and how it looks on you. Your hair looks great that way. If (I'd rather say when) we get married, you should wear it like that for the wedding."

Bethany's breath was taken away. When she recovered, she whispered back, "If that occurs, I will remember that and try to duplicate it."

"Would it help to have a picture?"

"Yes."

"I have a friend who is bringing his digital camera tonight. I have already asked him to find us and take our picture. I'll have him take one of the back of your hair, too. Okay?"

"Sure, Sir Knight. Then I could have a hairdresser copy it, for the…"

John whispered in her ear to complete her unfinished sentence, "…wedding." Bethany blushed, but John laughed.

When they finally looked at the others, they saw Doug was standing speechless, staring at Carrie. John laughed and went over and slapped Doug on the back. "Hey, old man, come out of it. Haven't you seen a pretty girl before?"

"Not like Carrie looks tonight."

Carrie blushed, but couldn't hide her pleasure.

John responded, "We have the pleasure of being in the company of three lovely ladies tonight."

Alex also looked pleased, but Cindy purposely did not look in his direction to observe his reaction.

John said, "Let's get going so we can all sit together, that is, if you would like to, Doug and Carrie. Alex and Cindy and Bethany and I had already planned to do so, if possible."

"How about it, Carrie?" asked Doug. "It's fine with me."

"I'd like that."

They were able to arrange that, and all three couples enjoyed the evening. For Bethany, with thinking about John's words all night, most of it was a blur. When people spoke to her, they would have to repeat what they said. Only John knew why she was so "spacy."

After the banquet, when John had walked her back to the dorm building, he said, "Thank you for a lovely evening, my little 'spacy' sweetheart."

"It's your fault."

With a twinkle in his eye and his dimple showing, he innocently asked, "What did I do?"

"Oh, nothing, nothing."

"Well, I want you to know, I love you even when you are 'spacy.'"

"Oh, John, I love you, too, Sir Knight."

He grinned. "I think it is time I told you the rest of the story."

"What do you mean?"

"Remember I told you there was more that I wasn't ready to tell you."

"Oh, yes."

"Bethany, I have loved you for three years—almost from the first time I saw you."

"Are you serious?"

"Perfectly serious, Sweetheart. I could not get you out of my mind after the dinner party. You looked so pretty that night, but you also looked uncomfortable. I watched you and saw that you didn't drink the wine. I could see Scott glaring at you. Then I saw the two of you leave early. Scott looked upset, and you looked almost ill. I found myself thinking about you when I tried to study. I kept apologizing to God for thinking about you so much when I didn't even know you. I prayed for you and about my feelings, a lot. I couldn't let myself get carried away because I did not know for sure if you were a believer. And then God worked it out for us to run into each other at the library, remember? And I found out you were a Christian. Then I relaxed my guard a little. I was so happy you went to the revival, and then you started going to the church all the time, and I got to sing with you. I was praying for you so much because of Scott. I knew he wasn't right for you, and to tell the truth, I soon started feeling like I was. I haven't been able to stop myself from caring a lot from the beginning."

"John, it's time for me to go in. You have surprised me and given me a lot to think about. We will have lots to talk about on our next date. Goodnight, Love."

John's heart quickened, and he whispered, "Goodnight, Sweetheart."

When they had enough time together to have a good talk, Bethany said, "John, I had no idea you had such strong feelings way back when we first met. I was still dating Scott and going to you for advice about whether to marry him or go to college; and I was treating you like a big brother. I am so sorry. It must have been hard for you, and I didn't mean to hurt you." There were tears in Bethany's eyes as she thought about that time in their lives.

"Please don't cry, Sweetheart. It isn't your fault; you did not know how I felt. I purposely made sure of that. I did not want you to turn to me on the rebound or enter another relationship before you were ready. I wanted your heart to be completely healed after breaking up with Scott."

Bethany swallowed hard, wiped away the tears, and when she had control, said, "John, I thought of something else I want to tell you."

"What's that?"

"You know what I said to you for the first time after the banquet? Those three little words?"

He grinned. "Yes."

"I am so glad I saved those words just for you. I had decided long ago that I would not say them until I knew for sure I loved a man."

John looked surprised.

Bethany asked, "What?"

"You never said it to Scott?"

"No, not even when he said it to me. Something stopped me, or probably Someone—the Lord. I just told him I cared for him."

"Why do you feel free to say it to me?"

"Because I don't have the doubts and questions that were bothering me about Scott. At the end I asked him some questions my father had suggested in a letter, and it confirmed that he wasn't right for me."

"His answers were wrong?"

"The few he gave. Mostly, he was evasive."

"So why didn't you ask me those questions?"

"Because I already know the answers—at least to most of them."

"Do you still have your dad's letter?"

"Yes."

"Will you bring it with you tomorrow? I would like to see it, and if there are any questions you aren't sure about, I could answer them for you."

"Okay, if it is important to you. I have not been concerned about it."

"It is important to me. I want to know if I measure up to your dad's expectations."

Bethany almost laughed, but stopped herself, seeing that he was very serious.

"Okay, when I get back to my room, I will dig it out and bring it tomorrow."

"Thank you."

Later Bethany looked in her special keepsake box where she kept letters, mementos, and her journal. She found her dad's letter and stuck it in her purse to be ready for the next day. Then she took out her books and attempted to study. Mixing romance with college sometimes made things difficult, but she would not give up the experience for anything!

The next day when she sat down across from John, Bethany handed him the letter. He unfolded it and read:

Dear Bethany,

Don't faint when you see it's your old dad writing for a change. I don't know much about Scott, but I wanted to remind you of some things you should consider before choosing a lifelong companion. It's so easy to get caught up in the romance and excitement of courtship and to forget the things that will affect you and your future children for a lifetime. As you make your decision regarding Scott's proposal, ask yourself these questions:

1. *Is he the man God has chosen for me?*
2. *Will he be a good spiritual leader for our home?*
3. *Does he pray with me now? If not, how can I expect him to later?*
4. *Does he love God and His Word? Is there evidence of this in his conversation?*
5. *Does he attend church faithfully?*
6. *How does he serve God in the church?*
7. *Is he a soul winner? A wife needs her husband to set the example.*
8. *Does he tithe?*

Please believe me—I am not trying to make things hard for my little girl. (I should say young woman, but you will always be Daddy's little girl to me.) I am just concerned and wanting the very best for you.

I love you,

Dad

"You have a wise, godly father, Bethany. If my hopes and dreams for us work out, I pray I can live up to his expectations as well as yours."

"I am not at all worried about that, Sir Knight."

"I guess the only question that you don't know about would be the tithe. I do tithe, faithfully, and give an offering above that. The others I try to do. I am sure I don't always live up to them as perfectly as I should."

"None of us perfectly live the Christian life, John. Do you have a list of expectations for your future wife?"

"Not written down."

"How about in your heart and mind?"

"Some would be the same as these," pointing to her dad's letter. "Let's see, I want her to be modest in her dress and actions, willing to be submissive (sorry, but that is what the Bible says)," he added with his grin that showed his dimple. "Not a gossip, cheerful and positive, caring, and gentle. You fit the bill."

"I hope I always will. I guess I won't really be tested in the submissiveness department until after I am married."

"I guess you are right. I will just have to hope for the best," he said, smiling warmly.

～

When spring break arrived, Bethany said a tearful goodbye to John. Being away from him was beginning to be very hard for her. She was glad to have the excitement of the wedding to fill a few days, and she always enjoyed staying with the Davenports and seeing Michael. But being in Detroit was not going to be as much fun this time because John could not get away from his job to go away during the break. "A whole week apart..." Bethany tried to push away the thought that if they married, she would probably have longer separations—not to mention the upcoming summer when they would both be on tour.

The plane ride was fun with Cindy, Peter, and Donna also going on the same flight. Bethany missed having Donna in the dormitory, and the three young women had lots of catching up to do. Peter had been wise enough to bring a book to read!

Sarah and her dad, Mr. Weeks, met them at the airport. The girls had a joyous, but tearful, reunion as Peter and Sarah's father patiently looked on. Then they piled into a van and went to Sarah's home. Mrs. Weeks greeted the girls quietly and then began performing her hostess duties. She was shy, like Sarah, and felt more comfortable doing things than trying to talk to strangers. She had only briefly met Donna and Bethany when dropping off Sarah at college when the girls were all freshmen. Sarah had told her about Cindy, but they had never met.

Donna and Peter were shown to the guest room, and Cindy and Bethany were given Sarah's brother's room. One would use his bed, and one would use a rollaway twin-sized bed the Weeks had rented. Sarah's brother Keith would sleep in the family room on a hideaway bed.

The girls did not have very much time to freshen up and change for the rehearsal and dinner that night. Bethany was wishing it could have been like Donna's wedding where she had had the chance to go to a wedding shower and help decorate.

Paul's parents had arranged for a dinner in a banquet room at a local restaurant. They all enjoyed the meal, except for Sarah who was too nervous to eat. She did not like being the center of attention. Even though she wanted a church wedding and knew it was important for a good start to a marriage, she was dreading having all those eyes on her the next evening.

Bethany knew her friend well enough to recognize what she was feeling. She told Cindy they would have to work on helping Sarah to relax and enjoy the experience. They did not have much chance for that until they were back at the house after the rehearsal.

Sarah's brother Keith went to the family room to play a video game, and Mr. and Mrs. Weeks retired for the night. Donna and Peter also went to the room they were using. The three young women drifted into the kitchen. When Sarah asked if the other two wanted anything, Cindy suggested hot chocolate. Sarah told Cindy to look in the pantry for marshmallows while she made the cocoa. Instead of marshmallows, Cindy found a can of instant whipped cream. Hiding it behind her back, she went over to Sarah and said,

"You better let me look at your throat. I remember reading that when people get nervous sometimes they get throat infections."

Sarah said, "Oh, come on, Cindy. You are just making that up."

"Oh, no, honey," she drawled, "I am serious. Just let me look, okay?"

"Oh, okay, if you will leave me alone afterward."

"Of course, sweetie, now open wide." When Sarah opened her mouth, Cindy whipped the can of whipped cream from behind her back and filled Sarah's mouth with the foam. Of course some of it missed her mouth and got on her face and her clothes. Sarah sputtered and made the situation even worse. Bethany broke out laughing at how Sarah looked.

When she could talk again, Sarah said, "I should have known better than to trust you!" She laughed and went back to stirring the cocoa. But she was watching, and when Cindy put the can down, Sarah quietly grabbed it. She sauntered over to the pantry. "Can't you find the marshmallows?"

When Cindy turned to answer her, Sarah squirted her with a generous spurt of whipped cream.

Now Cindy was the one spitting and sputtering. "I can't believe you did that. I would never have guessed you would retaliate. I thought you were too much of a lady."

All three of the young women were laughing hysterically, and Sarah managed to gasp out, "Shush, we're going to wake up my parents. We'll be in big trouble if Mom sees this. We've got to clean this up."

"I know. Get me a rag or a mop or something, and I'll clean it up while you serve up the cocoa. Are you sure there are marshmallows in that pantry?"

Bethany said, "I'll look while you two get yourselves and the floor cleaned up." She gave a conspiratorial wink at Cindy; they had finally gotten Sarah to relax.

When everything was cleaned up and they sat down at the table to drink their cocoa, Cindy and Bethany thought up things to talk about to keep Sarah from dwelling on the wedding.

Finally they said goodnight. When she awoke in the morning, Sarah was amazed that she had slept soundly. She thanked the Lord for the help of her good friends.

After breakfast, the four young women and Mrs. Weeks went to a beauty salon. Bethany had brought the pictures from the Valentine banquet and asked the hairdresser to copy the style. Sarah had her long brown hair braided and twisted up. Cindy's naturally curly hair was coaxed into ringlets hanging down her back, and Donna's strawberry blonde hair was pulled back and fastened with a fancy clip. Then Mrs. Weeks treated all the girls to a manicure. On the way home, they stopped at a tearoom for lunch. Mrs. Weeks insisted on treating them again, telling the girls she had saved up and planned for it for months. She wanted one last special day for Sarah to remember.

In the afternoon they had a light dinner before going to the church. After the wedding they would have a simple reception with just cake and punch. Cindy and Bethany kept up a lively banter and joked so much that Sarah forgot to be nervous and was able to eat.

The three attendants had not yet seen the decorations, so when they arrived at the church, they checked out the auditorium and fellowship hall before changing. They complimented Mrs. Weeks and Sarah on the beautiful job they had done. Bethany was storing away ideas for her own wedding. Cindy was not as hopeful about her own future but could not help hoping she would be a bride someday. She also got ideas she might use.

Both tall and slender, Sarah and Paul made a handsome couple. When instructed to kiss the bride, Paul gently took her face in his hands and gave her a sweet, tender kiss—the first that they had shared. He did not prolong it, knowing Sarah would be embarrassed. After the pastor introduced them as Mr. and Mrs. Paul Norberg, the wedding party followed them out as the recessional was played. Before lining up for the receiving line, her three attendants hugged Sarah, giving her and Paul their best wishes for a happy life together. She thanked them for helping her be able to really enjoy her wedding day.

Sunday they attended church with the Weeks and then were taken to the airport. Bethany, Donna, and Peter were all flying to Detroit. Donna and Peter were going to spend the rest of the break with her parents. Bethany was excited about seeing Michael, Elaine, and the Davenports.

This visit was a little shorter, but crammed with visiting and playing with Michael. Elaine wanted to hear all the details of the two weddings. One of the many things she regretted about her life before she got saved was not having a church wedding. She and Michael's dad, Mark Briscoe, had gotten married in a private ceremony in the Davenports' garden, as she was far enough along with her pregnancy to show. That was one of the many things she regretted about her life before she got saved.

Bethany enjoyed being at Faith Baptist Church for the Wednesday night service. She saw many friends, including Mrs. Carpenter. That dear lady wanted to hear how John was doing. She was delighted when Bethany showed her the knight pendant and told her the story behind it.

Thursday Donna's parents came by and picked up Bethany to take her to the railway station along with Peter and Donna. During the train ride, they shared about the last three days. Donna was so happy that now she could come home to visit and have a truly relaxing, refreshing time that included Christian fellowship. Her parents had grown very fond of Peter and treated him as part of the family.

Donna was excited that her parents were experiencing steady growth in their Christian lives. She told Bethany, "My mom has stopped wearing pants. She is helping in the nursery, and my dad is ushering. They both go soul winning every week. For the spring promotion, they invited some friends to church, and two of them got saved. My folks got the prize for bringing the most visitors."

"That's wonderful, Donna! I am so happy for you. What a difference the Lord makes in people's lives!"

"Isn't that the truth!" exclaimed Donna.

When she got back to campus, Bethany and John had a happy reunion. John said, "It is getting painful to be separated from you!"

"I know. I feel the same way."

"I am just going to have to do something about that," he said with his dimpled grin. "I wish it could be sooner, but your dad and I agreed you should finish college and get your degree first."

"You did? When did you discuss these plans?"

"When I was at your house during the singing tour last summer."

"Really? What else have you and my dad talked about?"

"I don't know. Let me think. The first time I called to ask permission to date you, I told him about seeing you at the dinner with Scott and how we met at the library. I also told him I couldn't get you out of my mind after I saw you at the party. I shared that I already loved you and that I thought the Lord had brought us together."

"Wow! My dad knew how you felt before I did."

"I'm sorry. I hope that doesn't bother you?"

"No. I understand about your not wanting to rush me. I admire your patience and that you were honest with my dad about your intentions."

"I am glad you understand, Sweetheart." He switched to a different subject. "The end of the year is not so very far away. Are you getting excited about going on tour?"

"Very much so! You know how much I have wanted and waited for this opportunity. All your descriptions from last year just fueled that. Besides, I figure we will both be so busy that it will really help the loneliness for each other."

"That is true, although I never got you out of my mind last summer. You will have so many wonderful soul-winning opportunities, and it is so exciting to see so many people get saved. They definitely make that a big priority. I couldn't believe all the places we went to find people—in the laundromats we did more than wash our clothes, and we went to malls and factory outlet stores. We witnessed in restaurants and to people in their cars waiting in fast food drive-up lines."

"I guess from now on we will be even busier with extra rehearsals and fittings for our outfits."

"Yes, Love, but busyness helps the time go by faster, and right now that is what I want!"

"Me, too," she softly answered, looking at him with eyes that said "I love you."

～

The next two months flew by for both Bethany and John, just as they had predicted. They did not have as many opportunities to be together but usually managed to eat some of their meals together and fit in a date on Friday night. John was also preparing for graduation with a bachelor's degree in pastoral theology. His family was coming, so he was making arrangements for hotel accommodations for them. Bethany was looking forward to seeing them again.

Finally the day for commencement exercises arrived. Bethany arranged to meet John's family so she could sit with them. She was as proud as his parents and siblings when he received his diploma.

John had received permission for Bethany to join his family afterward at a restaurant for a celebration. Bethany pushed all thoughts of the upcoming separation to the back of her mind and just enjoyed the evening. There would be time for tears later.

That time came when she said goodbye as their tour groups prepared to leave, going to different parts of the country. Knowing she would be at her home church for the youth conference took some of the edge off the three-month absence from John's company. She also knew this would be a growing time and a fruitful season in her Christian walk. It would be good preparation for being an evangelist's wife, and she would get to use her talents, which had been developed more from lessons and practice.

She and another girl were sharing the piano playing so they could both sing part of the time also. Bethany was happy with that arrangement as she enjoyed both playing and singing.

She enjoyed the tour even though at times they had long, exhausting days. They saw people saved almost every day, visited churches of every size, sang informally in several interesting settings, and took turns sharing their testimonies during the services. They were ambassadors for the Crossroads Baptist College and tried to get names and addresses of potential students to take back with them. The college would contact those young people with more information about the school. Bethany had no problem promoting the college because she was very enthusiastic about the three years she had spent there so far.

The highlight of the summer tour for her was, of course, being in her home church. The people in the church who had been her teachers, either in the school or Sunday school, were proud to have had some small part in the development of this lovely young woman. It was a special blessing to see one of their own young people traveling for the college and using her talents for the Lord. The members of her family were all proud of her and very happy to have her home for a few days.

Her sister Betsy was frustrated that they didn't have more time together. She was bursting with excitement and questions about Bethany's romance with John and their future plans. The first night Bethany was back in their room for the night, Betsy asked, "Has John proposed yet? Are you going to get married?"

Bethany laughed. "It's late; I have to get some sleep, little sister. No, he hasn't proposed yet, but he has hinted about marriage. Okay?"

"But do you want to marry him? Do you think you will?"

"Yes."

"Oooh!" squealed Betsy. "That is so cool! I like John. He seems like a nice guy, and he is so cute!"

"I agree. Now can we please go to sleep?"

"Sorry, Sis."

"It's okay. I totally understand. Goodnight, Betsy. I love you."

"I love you too, Bethany, and I am so happy for you."

The next night Betsy had more questions. "How soon are you getting married?"

"Betsy, I can't answer that. I don't know. Remember, he hasn't even asked me yet. He did say he and Dad agreed they wanted me to finish college."

"Oh," said Betsy in a disappointed tone, "that means at least a year. How can you stand it?"

"To be honest with you, sometimes I wonder the same thing, but at college I am so busy, the time goes by fast. And we get to see each other quite a bit, so we are getting to know each other better. In spite of our busy schedules, we manage to have lots of fun together."

"What do you do?"

"During nice weather we go out and toss plastic discs or play ball. When it is cooler, we bowl, play table tennis or board games, or just talk. We will have lots to share with each other after these summer tours."

Betsy sighed. "Dating sounds like so much fun."

"It is, but sometimes it's stressful."

"What do you mean?"

"Oh, if you have to turn someone down because you realize you don't want to encourage him when you know he isn't right for you. Or, most first-time dates with any guy, I was a little nervous. I was even a little nervous with John for a short time when he first let it be known he was interested in me as more than a friend."

"But you aren't nervous with him now, right?"

"No, I am relaxed and comfortable, but I don't take him for granted. I still consider my words and actions carefully so as not to offend or hurt him or make him think badly of me. I have learned from some of my classes that when you get married, you should just keep on doing those same things to have a happy marriage."

"That makes sense."

"I have got to get to sleep now, Betsy. Sorry we don't have more time to talk."

"That's all right. I sure do miss you, but I better get used to that, huh? The youth conference has been great so far, and your group is doing a really neat job! Good night, Bethany."

"Thanks, Sis. Good night."

Since the tour group did not have to travel far to their next destination, they did not plan to leave until Saturday. Therefore, the Prescotts had made plans ahead with the tour group leader to have them all over for a barbecue Friday evening. They had also invited their pastor and his family. The unpredictable Washington weather cooperated, and everyone enjoyed the relaxing time outdoors and the good food. James grilled hamburgers and hot dogs on the barbecue, and Margaret fixed several salads, baked beans, and a dessert with help from Betsy and Bethany. The three of them enjoyed the opportunity to work together in the kitchen again.

Saturday morning Bethany said goodbye to her family without a single tear. She would be home for part of the summer when the singing tour was over. She might be able to pick up a few babysitting jobs during that time. She was not concerned about money since she would keep her work scholarship campus job and get free tuition for her senior year.

CHAPTER SEVENTEEN

Happy Beginnings

"Whoso findeth a wife findeth a good thing...."
(Proverbs 18:22)

Bethany and John had both enjoyed their time on tour, but they were glad to be together again at college. They had many interesting experiences to share with one another. They talked about how the incidents they had encountered were preparing them for the evangelistic life.

Bethany was excited about doing her student teaching during the fall semester. She was also continuing private piano lessons. Bethany looked forward to taking some interesting required courses in the spring semester, and she was preparing for a recital. Her music education major had proven interesting and challenging for her and would be a help to her all her life, even if she never formally taught.

Because of the special problems Carrie was attempting to overcome and the help Bethany had been to her, she was again assigned to the same dorm room as Bethany. There were two other girls that they both knew slightly.

Carrie had much to share with Bethany. She and Doug had been allowed to see each other during the summer, either under the supervision of Mr. and Mrs. Briggs, her foster parents, or Miss Jordan. Even though they were continuing to grow closer to each other, they were also both going to continue dating others now that the school year had resumed. So far neither one had found someone else that they felt especially drawn to for a special relationship.

Carrie was excited that Miss Jordan had become engaged during the summer and was planning a wedding during the college's spring break. The best part, as far as Carrie was concerned, was that she was going to be a bridesmaid!

Cindy had also returned for her senior year. To her joy and everyone's surprise, Randy was back on campus, starting over as a freshman. He was quiet and withdrawn, staying mostly to himself. As time went on, those who had known him before noted that he did not hang around a group of friends as before. He appeared much more serious-minded. Cindy and Bethany discussed it and saw it as a good sign, to a certain point. But they were concerned because he seemed joyless. They increased their prayers for him.

Bethany was happy to resume her friendship with Donna, also. She and Peter had stayed in their apartment and continued in their jobs. Now Donna was cutting back her hours at work so she could take more courses in the homemaking department.

Bethany called her the first day she was back, and they agreed to meet for dinner on campus and include Peter and John. The men talked about the tour and Peter's bus route, while Donna and Bethany visited. Donna reported that Mrs. Logan had been coming to church fairly regularly and that she had gotten saved at church in August. Bethany was so glad to hear that, she could hardly wait until Saturday to visit her and Billy. Angie was continuing to do well and was dating a young man from the church. Though he was also a fairly new Christian, he had heard about the suggested dating standards, and they were adhering to them—dating only with chaperones. Bethany was thrilled with that news.

Now that they did not have practices for tour groups, Bethany and John's schedules were a little more relaxed. However, they were still occupied enough with studies, jobs, and dating to make the time fly by. They also continued challenging each other to learn memory verses.

∽

John's sister Ruth was starting her college career this semester. Bethany tried to spend some time with her, getting to know her better and building a relationship. She and John often included her with them for a meal. Ruth looked up to Bethany and often asked her for advice. She was already thinking of Bethany as her big sister.

Cindy and Bethany were still very close and often confided in one another. Cindy told Bethany that her heart still reacted whenever she saw Randy. He only politely acknowledged her with a nod when they passed each other. She was frustrated! He seemed to honestly have changed; he was attending classes faithfully and working on a church bus route. She had asked John about how he acted in the men's dorm, and he had assured her Randy seemed very serious-minded and stayed in his dorm room, apparently studying. He attended all the required dorm meetings and was always very respectful. Cindy wanted to convey to him that he was forgiven, and she wanted to be his friend (if not more).

Finally she and Bethany hatched a plan and recruited John to help them. One day they sat together in chapel, close to the exit door. As soon as the service was over, they hurried to the door and stayed close by. When Randy came out, Bethany acted like she happened to see him and greeted him. "Hi, Randy. I have wanted a chance to talk to you. I am so happy to see you back at college. Cindy told me about your letter, and I rejoiced with her that our prayers had been answered. Here is my boyfriend and Cindy. John, I want you to meet Randy Connor. Randy, this is John Holman."

"I'm glad to meet you, John." Hesitantly he added, "Hello, Cindy. Thanks for answering my letter."

Cindy answered, "I was so excited, Randy. The Lord answered our prayers, and now here you are back in college."

John said, "It was nice meeting you, Randy. I need to get to work. Walk with me, Bethany?"

"Sure. See you guys later."

When they had left, Randy looked flustered. Cindy pretended not to notice and asked, "How do you like being back in college?"

"It's great, but it's hard to get back into the studying."

"I hadn't thought about that. I guess it would be hard when you've been out of school for a while."

People were streaming by, chattering loudly as they left chapel. Swallowing hard to get rid of the lump in his throat, Randy hesitantly asked, "Do you want to go somewhere quieter? Maybe get a Coke? Or do you have something you have to do?"

"I have enough time for a Coke. Thanks."

When they reached the snack bar, he ordered two Cokes, and they found a table. Cindy asked, "How are things going for you, Randy?"

"Good. I am trying to take extra hours to make up for lost time. I pretty much study, work, and do my ministry."

Not wanting him to know she had been "watching" him, she asked, "What are you participating in for a ministry?"

"Right now I am working on a bus route. I am thinking about changing to something different—just to get more experience to help in my future ministry."

"Oh! Are you planning on being a pastor?"

"That's my hope."

"Do you like the bus route?"

"Very much. I have been working on one at my dad's church since I got right. God used me there, and I feel He is using me here. That continues to amaze me."

"Why?"

"I just feel so guilty and dirty. I was afraid He would never use me."

"But think about some of the men in the Bible, especially David. You didn't commit murder, did you?" He finally loosened up a little, enough to laugh in response. "No time for a social life?"

"I haven't been having one. I imagine yours is as busy as ever."

Her voice softened as she answered, "No, I turned guys down so much, they've quit asking me."

"You? The social butterfly of our class back then?"

"I have changed—I have settled down a lot and take things more seriously. Besides, I didn't really enjoy myself when I dated all the time."

"I can't believe my ears. You seemed to enjoy dating so much back then."

"I know. I think I probably still could with the right person." Cindy said this with her eyes down, concentrating on her drink. She felt a little too bold and a little embarrassed, but she wanted to give him a hint of how she felt.

There was silence. She finished her drink and rose to her feet as she finally glanced at his face, and said, "I've got to run. See you around," and hurried off.

❧

The next day Randy sought out Bethany. "Did I imagine it and it's just wishful thinking, or was Cindy trying to let me know she still cares, or at least would date me to see if there's still anything between us?"

"You didn't imagine it. What are you waiting for?"

"I just can't believe she would want anything to do with me."

"She has forgiven you. God has forgiven you. Have you forgiven yourself, Randy?"

"You are pretty discerning, Bethany. No, I guess I haven't. I feel like a lousy, dirty, sinful jerk."

"Maybe that was exactly what you were for a while, but you got right. It appears you really meant it. With God's help, you can keep going in the right direction. Did your dad accept you back and trust you with a ministry at his church? Or did he keep reminding you of your sin?"

"He accepted me—he reminds me of the father of the prodigal."

"That's great; now accept yourself. Forget the past and move on, like Moses, David, and Paul."

"Thanks, Bethany, for everything—for your prayers, your friendship, and your support for Cindy, and your faith in me. I still need a lot of prayer, that I can regain my confidence and sense of self-worth."

"None of us has worth in ourselves; we are all sinners. But as God's child we can have confidence in Him, be a branch that clings to the vine, and be used. Make friends with my boyfriend John. I am sure he would be a help to you. Now go find Cindy and talk things out."

Randy grinned a sheepish grin and said, "Okay. I don't need any more urging. She still has a special place in my heart. I never thought I would have another chance with her. God is so good!" He hurried away.

Bethany grinned with satisfaction and breathed a huge sigh of relief.

It seemed her "counseling" duties were not over. A few days later Carrie asked if they could go somewhere private and talk. She confided, "Doug and I have tried dating others, but we can't seem to stop our feelings for each other from growing. He asked me if I would agree to being his girlfriend if we can get permission. I told him I would discuss it with him Friday night when we have more time. He looked disappointed and confused, and I feel bad, but…"

Bethany broke in, "What makes you hesitant, Carrie? You just said you feel the same way."

"I do. There is nothing I would like more. But I feel like I have to tell him about…" Carrie hesitated. She found it hard to even talk about her cutting problem with anyone these days. It was behind her. She rarely had even a slight urge to do it, and she did not want to dwell on it.

"Your cutting problem?" Bethany asked to make things easier for Carrie.

"Yes. I am so ashamed about it, and I hate the scars; but it is only fair that he should know before he gets any more serious about me."

"I agree, but I really don't think it is going to make any difference to Doug. He has things in his past, too. If he really cares for you, and if he is the one the Lord has for you, it will all be okay."

"You really think so, Bethany?"

"Yes. We will pray about it and then go get it over with Friday night. Just tell him honestly. I am sure it won't matter to him. Think about Angie on my bus route, I told you about her. She had a baby when she was still quite young, but now she has a really nice guy dating her."

"Okay. Pray with me now and then keep praying until Friday, okay?"

"Sure."

Friday night when Carrie and Doug met, they ate dinner together and then found a place to talk. He had looked unhappy and uncertain all night. Carrie said, "Doug, I have to tell you something about myself. When you find out, you may want to reconsider being my boyfriend."

"This sounds really serious. Did you murder someone?" He asked with a little, tentative smile.

"No, nothing like that." She managed to smile back, and it helped her relax a little. "Remember I had to leave college and Miss Jordan was helping me overcome something in my life? Well, I had a problem with self-mutilation. I was punishing myself because I felt like I was a bad person."

"Cutting?"

"Yes. I cut myself quite a bit. I have scars," she confessed.

"Tell me about why you did it, Carrie."

"My stepfather Jim used to punish me pretty severely. He would use his belt, sometimes the buckle part, and burn me with his cigarette." She stopped when she saw Doug cringe in sympathy. She went on, "Things like that, and my mom never stopped him. She would say it was because I was so bad. When the authorities finally found out and I had to testify against him in court, she got mad and yelled at me because he got in trouble. That's when I was taken away from her."

"You must have scars from what he did, too?"

Carrie started crying. "Yes. I look pretty bad, under…" She was too embarrassed to finish her sentence.

"Carrie, please don't cry. It doesn't matter to me—honestly."

"But what if...?" Again she was unable to finish her sentence, feeling it would be too presumptuous of his feelings and too bold.

"If we love each other enough to eventually get married, I won't care. I really won't, Carrie. I will just ignore them. Do you think I don't have some scars on my body from all the crazy things I did when I was a kid?"

"But I probably have lots more."

"Please just forget about it, Carrie. I beg of you, don't let it worry you. I am very serious about this, Carrie. I don't want you to get yourself upset over it. I still plan to talk to Miss Jordan and your folks about our being girl-friend and boyfriend. I am tired of dating other people and trying to act interested."

"Me, too."

"So just concentrate on praying that they will agree. Okay?"

"Okay, Doug. Thanks. It is a relief to finally tell you."

"I am sorry you were worried about it."

Later, when both girls were back in the dorm room, Carrie motioned to Bethany to step out with her. They still had time for a short talk before lights out. "You were right, Bethany. I am so happy! Doug is going to talk to Miss Jordan and the Briggs on Sunday."

"I told you! I knew he cared enough about you that it wouldn't matter to him. I am really happy for you, Carrie," said Bethany, giving her a big hug.

∽

Sunday Miss Jordan asked Doug and Carrie to give her a week to think and pray about their request. She commended them for seeking guidance and advice before allowing their relationship to escalate, and she commended Carrie for continuing to allow her to have veto power for her decisions. Doug and Carrie assured her they appreciated her concern and realized what a blessing she had been to both of them.

The following Sunday they again met with Miss Jordan, her fiancé, and Mr. and Mrs. Briggs. Miss Jordan admitted to the young couple that she had asked her fiancé for his input. They all agreed that they could give their approval to the young people's request. This was because the young couple had complied with their advice that they each date others and had known each other long enough to be ready for this new stage of courtship.

Carrie was so happy and relieved that she cried. Miss Jordan understood and just hugged her. Doug was still learning about female emotions and asked, "What's the matter, Carrie? I thought you wanted this."

Joseph Harris, Miss Jordan's fiancé, laughed, slapped Doug on the back, and said, "Get used to tears. They use them when they are happy as much as when they are sad."

Doug sighed with relief and grinned at Carrie as she wiped away her tears and gave him a happy smile. He asked, "Is it okay if I get her something to seal it?"

"What did you have in mind," asked Linda Jordan.

"I'm not sure—some piece of jewelry."

"That's fine, but nothing too expensive."

"You don't have to worry about that. I don't have the funds, anyway."

In the meantime, Randy was going slowly, but he did ask Cindy for dates. On one occasion she told him, "Randy, if you want to ask other girls out also, I will understand."

"I don't have time for a lot of dating, Cindy, so why should I waste my time being with someone else?"

She had no answer for that admission, but hugged his words to her heart and secretly rejoiced.

In early November John called the Prescott home. Margaret answered. John spoke warmly but respectfully. "Mrs. Prescott?"

"Yes."

"This is John Holman."

"Oh, yes, Mr. Holman. It is nice to hear from you. How are you?"

"Just fine, thank you. And yourself?"

"We are all fine here."

"Is your husband at home?"

"Yes. Did you wish to speak to him?"

"Actually, I would like to speak to both of you. Could you ask him to get on another phone? Or is this not a good time?"

"We are not busy. That will be fine. Let me go tell him."

"Thank you."

Soon James Prescott said, "Hello, John. What can we do for you?"

"Well, sir, and Mrs. Prescott, are you there?"

"Yes."

"I want to ask your permission to marry your daughter. I would like to propose to her and get engaged during the Christmas break."

"We must admit we have been expecting this, especially since years ago you told me you already loved Bethany. That was before you started dating there at the college."

"Yes, sir. I assume you shared everything with your wife about how we first met and got acquainted?"

"Yes, he did, and I heard it from Bethany. I appreciate the fact you have given Bethany time to mature and finish college. That shows a lot of character and self-denial."

"Thank you, Mrs. Prescott. I have learned much in the process and grown close to the Lord. Has Bethany shared with you that I feel called into evangelism?"

"She has. When do you plan to begin?" asked James.

"I will need one more year at the seminary to complete my master of pastoral theology degree. I want to finish that, even though I may never actually pastor a church. One never knows what the future may hold.

"Having free tuition for two years really helped me save money, so we should be able to get by just fine with my continuing to work part-time. After that, I plan for us to travel with Evangelist Ralph Gibson to get some training and ideas from him—probably for about six months before Bethany and I strike out on our own. We will rent an apartment here until I graduate, and then I will get a truck and a travel trailer which will become our home for a while."

"That sounds like an excellent plan. When do you want to get married?"

"I was thinking about August, but we will see what Bethany wants assuming she says yes," he said, laughing. "Of course, it also depends on what is convenient for you folks."

"That is very considerate of you. I think August would be a good time," Margaret assured him. "What are your plans for the engagement? Did you want to come for a visit?"

"I have something special planned, if you agree. I would like Bethany to fly to California after Christmas. That part I would tell her about. The surprise is a banquet that depicts medieval times, complete with actors playing the parts of royalty and knights engaged in jousts. It will be a perfect setting for us. I'm sure she has explained our knight symbol to you?"

"Yes, she has."

"I have found a figurine in which to hide the ring. I will present it sometime after the banquet.

"If you give your permission, I will invite her to visit my family from December 26 to December 30. I will buy a round-trip plane ticket. That way she can have a few more days with you, and you can see the ring and start discussing the wedding plans."

James asked his wife, "What do you think?"

"It sounds like a workable idea to me. I appreciate your waiting till after Christmas, John, so she will be here with us for that. I think Bethany will be thrilled. It is a romantic idea. What will she need to wear for this banquet?"

"People come in very casual clothes."

"All right. When are you going to tell her about your invitation?"

"I think I will wait until after Thanksgiving. I have to be sure I can get plane reservations and tickets for the banquet. Well, I guess that is all for now. I will keep in touch. Goodbye."

"Goodbye," answered the Prescotts together.

$$\sim$$

Time for the Thanksgiving break arrived. Bethany knew this would be the last Thanksgiving spent at the Davenports' home. She would be graduating with her bachelor's degree in May. If John did not ask her to marry him, she would probably be back at her parents' home next year.

She enjoyed the time with the whole family, but especially Michael. He liked having her attention, but he did not "need" her like he once did, now that he had a good relationship with his mother.

John spent the break in Detroit also. He had some business he intended to care for on Saturday at a jewelry store he knew of where they would help him design a ring. He knew exactly what he wanted for Bethany's engagement ring.

Bethany and John sat together in church Wednesday night, and the Davenports kindly asked him over for dessert after church. He gratefully thanked them and accepted their invitation. He was happy to have extra time to spend with Bethany and also enjoyed visiting with Elaine and the

Davenports. Michael was excited about seeing his hero again, and John made some time for the little boy.

Elaine and Bethany got up early on Friday morning for the big shopping day, and they all went over to Mrs. Carpenter's for the traditional Friday night dinner and game night. This time, to his delight, Michael was included. Mrs. Carpenter had purchased a special puzzle just for him and also had crayons and a coloring book to keep him occupied. As usual, she also had a puzzle for the adults to work on.

John was again staying with Pastor Butler and his wife, so they invited Mrs. Carpenter and Bethany over for dinner Saturday night. John picked up Mrs. Carpenter and then drove to the Davenports for Bethany. She had not heard from him all day and wondered what he had been doing. But she did not ask, and John offered no information. Secretly, he was very pleased with the ring set he had been able to design and order for Bethany. He would drive to Detroit at the beginning of Christmas break, pick up the rings, and fly to California. His sister Ruth would be with him then. For Thanksgiving, she had flown home.

Bethany and John had been asked to sing for the Sunday service, so they practiced a little at Pastor Butler's home after dinner. Bethany had learned to play and sing her part at the same time, so John stood by the piano that night for the practice and again on Sunday morning. The pastor knew John's future plans and felt this would give them some experience. The congregation, including Peter, Donna and her parents, enjoyed hearing them sing again.

They had spent the Thanksgiving break in Detroit. Bethany had been invited to ride with them both ways, and that gave them a lot of time to visit.

Back at college after the break, John continued to express his love to Bethany whenever he could without being overheard. Bethany began to wonder if he was going to formally propose to her and when. However, she kept these thoughts to herself. She reasoned that perhaps he felt they should wait to get married until he had finished his master's degree, and he had told her he did not believe in long engagements.

Cindy and Randy were still dating, but cautiously, feeling their way and not rushing into a serious relationship. Randy was still doing well; he felt no desire to go back to partying or drinking.

Doug had also done some shopping over the Thanksgiving break. He had found a heart-shaped pendant and had his name engraved on one side, Carrie's on the other. Carrie was thrilled with it.

When John had received confirmation for Bethany's flight to California in December and the tickets for the banquet (his whole family would accompany them), he told Bethany of the plan. "I called your parents a few weeks ago, Bethany. I wanted to ask them if it would be okay for you to visit my family during the Christmas break. I asked them if you could come from December 26 to December 30. That way you would be with your parents for Christmas and New Years. I did not want to say anything to you until I knew I could get the airplane tickets. That is all confirmed—would you like to do that?"

"That sounds fabulous, John. I enjoyed your family so much on my other visit. We can save our gifts to each other and open them together, too. I love the idea. You are so sweet to think of it."

"I am glad you like the idea. I can hardly wait!"

"When you say things like that and get that cute grin and your dimple shows, you look like a little boy on Christmas morning."

"Hey! Don't be insulting—a little boy?"

"That's not an insult. All men are just little boys in a man's body, didn't you know?"

"Now wait a minute."

"How about when you are watching a game and you get so excited? Or when you are tinkering with a car, or you are served your favorite dessert and want seconds?" asked Bethany with a twinkle in her eye and her feminine, tinkling laugh that John loved to hear.

"How about you women—aren't you still little girls when you get up at the crack of dawn to go shopping and you cry over sentimental books or videos and even when you are happy? Does that make sense?"

"It makes perfect sense to me, but I will admit, we keep the little girl part of us, too. That's what lets us really enjoy life and have fun."

"As long as you admit it, I guess what you said about guys might be okay."

Bethany laughed. She loved teasing him when she had the chance—usually it was the other way around! Then she got serious. "Your parents know about this, don't they?"

"Of course. I thought you knew me better than to think I would invite you to their home without asking them first." His voice betrayed that he was a little hurt by her question.

"I'm sorry, John. I do know you wouldn't do that. I should not have asked you that. Please forgive me."

"You are forgiven." A mischievous grin broke across his face.

"What?"

"If we were married, we would have to kiss to make up," he whispered.

Bethany just grinned back but could not say anything in reply. Whenever he said things like that, it took her breath away; and it always made her hope he would go on and propose. But he did not do that, and she tried to stifle the disappointment and impatience she felt.

John was impatient to make their marriage plans official too. It felt like time was dragging between Thanksgiving break and Christmas.

John had called the Prescotts again to confirm the plans. When they shared the information with Betsy and Brian, Betsy immediately asked, "Is he going to propose to her?"

Margaret Prescott knew it would be hard for her to keep it a secret—even if she did not say anything to Bethany in so many words, her excited behavior would make Bethany suspicious. So she answered, "Now Betsy, don't jump to conclusions and don't suggest that to Bethany. If it doesn't happen, she would be really disappointed. We don't want to get her hopes up. I'd rather you didn't say anything or ask her anything about John proposing."

"Well, he should! Don't you think so? What is John waiting for, anyway? He better, is all I can say, if he's going to take her away from us for part of her Christmas break. This might be her last Christmas home, if he does ever marry her, that is," she said in a somewhat petulant tone.

Her father answered, "It is not any of our business. Let's just drop the subject."

Betsy's loud sigh spoke volumes.

When the time for Christmas break did arrive, Bethany was surprised to find out John and Ruth were not flying out from one of the Chicago airports. John just said that this time they were flying out of Detroit, and he was leaving his car at Pastor Butler's home. Bethany thought he was being a little mysterious, and she could see that Ruth was having a hard time keeping a straight face. But she couldn't figure out how it could have anything to do with her.

She had another joyous reunion with her family at Sea-Tac Airport, secretly wondering how many more there would be. She had lots to share with them during the ride home and in the days to follow—her experiences with student teaching, her anticipation (mixed with dread) of her senior recital, and details about Carrie and Cindy and their love lives. The latter was, of course, the most interesting to Betsy. She was also, as usual, full of questions for Bethany about her romance. Bethany could only say that things really had not changed much since they talked last summer. Remembering her mother's request, Betsy had to let the subject drop; but she did not want to!

Bethany enjoyed Christmas day with her family, and then she happily boarded the plane for the flight to California. She refused to get her hopes up that John had anything "special" planned and kept telling herself he just wanted her to get to know his family more.

When they were in his family's van driving home from the airport, he told her he had a special surprise for her. Her heart lurched with hope until he said, "Tomorrow we are going to a special event, but I'm not telling what it is. You will just have to wait and see."

So that was it; he wanted to take her someplace special. Well, that was nice. She was sure it would be fun, but… "Quit thinking about a ring," she admonished herself.

The next day they stayed at the house all day. They visited, played Ping-Pong on a table in the basement, and gathered around the piano as Bethany and John's sisters took turns playing while everyone sang hymns. John's mother had been a teacher for a few years and was interested in Bethany's experiences with student teaching. Naomi had lots of questions for Ruth about how she liked college life. Naomi had one more year of high school, and James would graduate one year after Naomi.

The family watched as John and Bethany opened gifts from each other. She had gotten him some cologne and Christian music CDs. John had gotten her a ruby pendant that matched the earrings he had given her last Christmas. Bethany exclaimed, "John, it's beautiful! It matches the earrings, doesn't it? You added some more to my 'multitude.'" John quoted Proverbs 20:15 so the family would know what she was talking about.

John had kept everyone busy so the time would not drag as they waited for the special surprise. John's siblings had also been kept in the dark about the evening's event. They left in the afternoon as they had about an hour's drive to reach their destination.

When they pulled up in front of a "castle," there were many questions and exclamations of surprise. "We'll just let you see what all transpires when we get in there," John said, not giving away anything, except that they would be having dinner there. Before leaving the car, John got the keys from his father, opened the trunk, and pulled out a plain paper bag. Bethany could tell there was a rather large box inside—but not a ring-sized box, unfortunately. John made no explanation, just carried it in with them.

They had arrived early enough to walk around and see beautiful horses in their stalls and displays of medieval weapons and items used for torture hanging on the walls. The females of the party shivered and quickly turned away while the men took a closer look. The ladies found displays of clothing from that time period that interested them more.

When it was time for the meal to be served, they were led to their table by a "wench" who would be serving them all night. There was no silverware; everyone had to use his hands to pick up his food. The ladies were happy they had worn casual clothes!

After they were seated and before the food came, John pulled a beautifully wrapped gift out of the bag and presented it to Bethany. The attached card read:

> "To My Sweetheart, Bethany
> With All My Love, John."

"Oh, how beautiful! But you already gave me a wonderful Christmas present, John."

"This is just a little something extra. Go ahead and open it."

"The package is so beautiful; I hate to spoil it. Did you wrap it?"

"No, my mother is the talented one."

Bethany turned to Mrs. Holman. "It is just gorgeous, but I have to know what's inside." Usually Bethany tore open a package without any concern for the wrap. But she felt certain that this was a special gift and possibly a momentous occasion. So she carefully loosened the tape, trying not to tear the paper. She might want to save it! She got it off with the top intact and only a small rip on the bottom.

Knowing all the Holmans were watching with great interest and patience, she set the paper aside to be folded neatly later and tackled the box. John pulled out his pocketknife to help cut the tape holding it closed. When Bethany had it open and pushed the tissue paper aside, she saw a knight in armor sitting on a horse. The metal figurine was about eight inches tall. Bethany exclaimed, "Oh, how appropriate! Thank you, John."

John smiled, enjoying her enthusiastic response. Then he gently took it from her and said, "We'll let it decorate the table, okay?" (He did not want her to handle the knight too much for fear she would discover that the face shield could be flipped up, disclosing a hollow space inside the knight's head. He planned to officially propose and let her find the ring inside the knight, after they returned home.)

"Sure, but I do get to keep him, don't I?"

John bent down and whispered in her ear, "You can keep your knight for life if you are sure you want him."

Bethany drew back so she could look into his face. His grin told her he indeed meant himself. "Why did he keep saying these things to her, making her heart pound until she was breathless, and then pretend nothing had happened?" she wondered.

John winked at her and said in a normal tone, "Do you have a place to keep him in your dorm room?"

"I'll make room to display him prominently."

Their wench was bringing their dinners—a whole chicken hindquarter for everyone, a baked potato, and pork ribs. They certainly would not go away hungry!

While they were eating the delicious food, the actors began the program. The contests were exciting, and they were encouraged to cheer on a particular knight, representing the section where their table was located.

When their knight won one of the competitions, the princess who stood on a raised platform with the king tossed him a flower. He galloped over to his section of tables, looking for a woman among the guests to give it to. Quickly John stood and in a booming voice called out, "Sir knight, my sweetheart would like your flower."

This caught the actor's attention, and he stopped in front of their table. "And which of these fair damsels is your sweetheart?"

John pointed out Bethany, and the knight handed her a long-stemmed carnation. Then he asked John, "Are you going to let this fair damsel slip away from you?"

Almost as a reflex action, John slipped to his knees and said, "Oh, no. I plan to make her my own." Then it struck him that he was getting ready to propose in public, in front of many people. Quickly he thought about what he should do and realized he had pretty much committed himself to going through with it. He thought about Bethany's personality—she was outgoing, fun-loving, did not get embarrassed easily, and could even laugh at herself, like when she did not bowl very well. He thought she could rise to the occasion. So he went on, "I love you, Bethany. Will you let me be your knight forever?"

Bethany answered, "Oh yes, my knight." She was both pleased and embarrassed.

The actor then asked, "Aren't you going to seal it with a kiss?"

Without taking his eyes from Bethany's, John answered boldly, "No, we are saving our first kiss for the altar. But I do have something with me to seal it." He pointed to the figurine.

Bethany looked in the direction that he was pointing. "The knight?"

"Something in the knight. Lift up the face shield." John rose to his feet and handed her the figurine.

Bethany took it and carefully lifted it up and saw the ring inside. She gasped.

John quickly grabbed the figurine, afraid she was going to lose her hold because of the surprise, and turned it so the ring fell in his palm. "Hold out your finger, my love."

Bethany obeyed and watched in wonder as he slipped a beautiful diamond and ruby ring on her finger. "More for your 'multitude,' " John whispered.

"John, it is so beautiful!"

"Later I will show you the wedding band so you can get the full effect."

By now, everyone at their table and the nearby tables were applauding. Smiling happily, Bethany held up her hand for them to see. The lights caught the jewels, and they sparkled, flashed, and glinted off the metal tableware.

Although Bethany enjoyed finishing her dinner and watching the rest of the program, it was all definitely anti-climatic.

In the van later while driving back to the Holmans' home, John told her and his family about his discussion with her parents. "How does August sound for a wedding?"

"It sounds perfect to me. Did my parents think it was okay?"

"Yes."

Bethany turned to Mrs. Holman. "Would that work out for your family?"

"Yes, that would be fine."

"Then August it will be."

"You don't mind being the wife of a student for a year?"

"Not at all. Maybe I can take some more of the homemaking courses."

"I think it will work out well," said John's father. "You will have a year to get used to married life and adjust to each other before you start traveling for your ministry."

When they reached the house, John got the ring box and showed Bethany and his family how the set would look after the wedding. The engagement ring had a nice-sized diamond with three rubies in a semicircle on one side. The wedding band had three rubies to complete the circle. Together they would look like a flower with the diamond encircled by rubies.

Bethany asked, "Where did you find the set? I have never seen one just like this."

"That is because I had it designed especially for you."

"That is so special, John. Thank you."

"I am amazed," Ruth added. "I never knew you had that much romance in you, John!"

~

It was getting late. Bethany hated for this special evening to end, but the long day and all the excitement were starting to have their effect. She was having trouble keeping her eyes open. John could see she was tired. "I better head for Grandma's. It has been an eventful day. I think we all need to get some rest."

John left. Bethany said goodnight to his family and went downstairs to the guest room. She quickly got ready for bed, slipped between the sheets, whispered "Thank You, Lord," and instantly went to sleep. Waking refreshed in the morning, she was surprised she had slept at all after such an eventful night. Dreamily, she rehearsed everything that had happened, as well as every word she and John had spoken to each other.

All of his teasing remarks had finally led up to a very dramatic proposal—one she could never have dreamed up. Now only eight months remained to wait for their first kiss, their first embrace, and the beginning of a lifetime of love.